Glass
Mountain

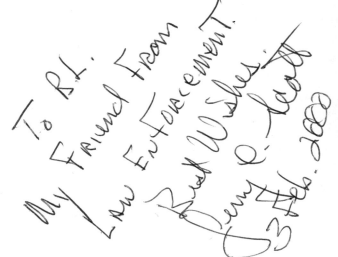

To R.L.
My Friend From
Law Enforcement.
Best Wishes.
Jerry R. Scott
3 Feb. 2000

Glass
Mountain

Jerry C. Scott

ISBN: 1-55517-436-1
v.2

Published by: **Bonneville Books**

Distributed by:
925 North Main, Springville, UT 84663 • 801/489-4084

CFI | Publishing and
Distribution Since 1986
Cedar Fort, Incorporated
CFI Distribution • CFI Books • Council Press • Bonneville Books

Cover design and page layout by Corinne A. Bischoff
Printed in the United States of America

Table of Contents

To Shelley, my darling wife.
She is my strength and my happiness.

Acknowledgment

I wish to thank Sgt. Cordell Jones of the Los Angeles Sheriff's Department, Detective Bill Eagleson of the Hollenbeck Division of the Los Angeles Police Department, and Sgt. Marc Johnson of the Utah County Sheriff's Department for their contributions to this novel.

I wish to express special thanks to Verdon Ballantyne for his literary contribution to this novel.

Preface

The police events in this story happened to real policemen in real places. This book is written by a police officer who tells it the way it actually was—his profession, his colleagues and friends, the challenges he and other police officers dealt with in the line of duty. Partially to relieve the inevitable tension of intense police actions involving actual events and real people, the story itself is fictionalized to tie individual episodes together.

The settings for these experiences are real; they can be documented. They come from the Hollenbeck Division of the Los Angeles Police Department and the Glass Mountain area, from which the novel derives its title. I have tried to authenticate not only the police officers and their experiences, but also the setting and environment where those experiences took place.

Not all the experiences detailed in this story happened to the author himself, but they did happen to his fellow officers and close friends. Every location, street, bar, taco stand, mountain gully, and dirt road actually exists. You can visit any of these settings, should you take the time to locate them. The police officers in this story are based on real people—real cops. They laugh, they cry, they bleed, and they sometimes die. But they also live personal lives, feeling what all sensitive human beings feel as they struggle to weave their private, personal, and professional lives into some kind of meaning.

I hope readers will see things from the law enforcement perspective—the way we who have committed our lives to police work see them—the pain, the humor, the hope, the sense of being lost, and the joy of recovery. Some of the experiences are graphic. There is no way to soften the reality this story invites you to share. Nor can you smile or laugh at the incongruities that interrupt the more intense dramas of cops' lives unless you experience them yourself. I have written this story so that you can share the way it really was. Fiction should tell the truth. I have tried to do so.

As you read, perhaps you will feel and understand some of the things that really happen to the 'men in blue.' I have been there; I have done that. Police work has touched my life so deeply and so indelibly that I had to let it out. This book is my attempt to share some of the experiences, some of the feelings, some of the consequences of being a policeman. So this is an inside story—the way it really was. I invite you to be there also—through the eyes of a cop. Paraphrasing Huck Finn as he described Mark Twain's effort to tell it like it is, "Mainly, I tell the truth."

Note: The Mexican Mafia does exist, but it was only used in this book as a vehicle to tie the story together and build toward the story's climax.

Chapter 1
May 1965

Simon Pavlo was enjoying the cool breeze off the Sea of Cortez as he sat on a veranda under a large umbrella protecting him from the hot morning sun. It was a clear day and he could see the mountains towering over the small town of San Felipe approximately 75 miles across the blue water from Puerto Peñasco, known as Rocky Point to gringos. He held his cold glass of beer to the side of his face as he collected his thoughts.

Simon had been a young boy when Al Capone and his friends often visited Puerto Peñasco to fish, drink, and gamble. That was before the U.S. Army Corps of Engineers paved the 55-mile dirt road from the little town that is now known as Lukeville, Arizona. After World War II, the new highway changed the quiet port forever. He learned a great deal from the fat Americans about living lavishly.

Approximately 600 miles to the south of Puerto Peñasco he had learned it was not enjoyable to work hard in the fields near the little village of Choix where he was born. His father and mentor taught him to forget the vegetable trade and to learn to grow marijuana and to deal in the lucrative drug business. He and his father, along with one younger brother, would float the Fuerte River with narcotics and make deliveries to Los Mochis. Drug shipments from Topolobampo to Guaymas would eventually be shipped in to Puerto Peñasco by the early morning shrimpers in the northern Gulf of California. He was now grateful his father had sent him to Nogales, Arizona, to live with his uncle, where he had the opportunity for three short years in the American school system to learn English.

Pavlo smiled when he heard Luis approaching his table. He wondered how his stupid son would digest his new plan to move the business to California where he would become a baron in the world of crime and deceit. He had a vision—to triple his fortune and power. The wine would flow, women would surround him, and the pure joy of living was going to be his repertoire for the remainder of his hard life.

"Bueno, Papa."

"Sit down, Luis, and speak English. We need to talk," Pavlo said, taking a cool drink as he gazed out to sea.

"This does not sound good, Papa. Have I done something wrong?"

"Shut up, pendejo; sit down and listen."

Luis pulled out a chair, glancing around at his father's entourage. Franco, No. 1 bodyguard, was in a far corner watching the stairway to the veranda. A uniformed policeman loyal to his father was standing at the bottom of the stairs observing his father's car parked by the entrance to Antonia's Seafood Bar and Grill. Two other men had been assigned to sit one table away with his charming young ladies. He did not recognize them and figured they were new imports.

A waiter came to the table, and Luis ordered a Margarita and a fresh shrimp cocktail in hot salsa. Pavlo peered at his only son. "I am not satisfied with our ventures here. We have lived here all our lives, and it is time for a change, at least for me. I'm leaving your mother for good this time. I hate her guts, and I am afraid I will kill her if I stay here."

"Forget Mama, what do you mean you are leaving? What are you going to do?"

"I have made preparations for moving to Los Angeles. There I will establish a branch of our services."

Luis couldn't hide his surprise and didn't try to. "What do you mean in L.A.? Where?"

"East L.A., the community of Boyle Heights is beckoning me."

"You have been talking with that cockroach cousin again. Papa, Carlos is all talk. He will get you killed and we will all sink. The Mexican Mafia has got control there. Hell, they took it away from the local Mexican gangs and the old Veteranos. Everyone knows they worked out agreements with the White Fence Gang, Dog Town, Avenues Gang, and even the Hazzards. What makes you think you can survive, and what is going to happen to our holdings here?"

"You question my abilities? Hell, I have been doing this all my life. You have seen my accomplishments. Besides, you little roach"—Pavlo felt his anger growing—"I am giving you the assignment of transporting our product to me in Boyle Heights. You will make more money by far than you are getting now."

Luis thought for a moment. More money was immediately

appealing. If his father was killed, he would have all the business in Sonora State to himself. He would instantly become wealthy. But killing his father would not be easy. Some had tried and all had disappeared with the mark of the Spiderman. No one here, to his knowledge, would mess with Simon Pavlo, and he was sure his reputation was well-known among the Mexicans in Los Angeles. "What about Mama?"

"I would have eliminated her long ago if it were not for her family ties and her being your mother. She is being taken care of handsomely. Good hell, she will be better off than she is now. She has her life; I have mine." Pavlo unbuttoned his shirt pocket, reached inside, and fondly pulled out a large tarantula and began stroking its stomach.

It was nothing new for Luis to see his father amorously fondling his spiders; it was what he was known for. He always had a spider with him. There was some unnatural bond between the old Mexican and the hairy-legged creatures. "How will you deal with the police? They may be difficult. The court system in the States is much easier than in Mexico, but they are very aggressive."

"The police are the least of my worries. I will deal with them when that time comes. I have no fear of them. I have my ways. They will be of no consequence. My first problem will be Joe Molino and Tommy Angelino, who are running the Mexican Mafia. They could be a serious problem; however, they do not expect to be challenged. After I establish myself, I will deal with them and then the police. In fact, I look forward to that challenge. The white police are puppy dogs. They bark and squeal but have only milk teeth with no real bite," Pavlo said, letting the words hiss from his lips.

"Then your No. 1 problem will be the Mexican Mafia. How will you deal with them?"

Pavlo jerked his head around and stared at his son. With one quick motion he put the tarantula to his mouth and bit off the front portion. Quickly he spit the head and front legs onto the table. Saliva hung from his lip, his eyes glossy. "That is how," he glared. "You remove the head of a mad dog and it cannot think or act. It is no longer a danger." He looked at the tarantula's legs on the table moving up and down and edging into a half circle. With his thumb he slowly smashed it flat and glanced at his son. "That is how I will take care of the Mafia and the police."

❀

Cy slowed down his horse, Cole, from a canter to a fast-moving gait. He pulled back on the reins a second time, slowing the animal to a walk as he approached Scotsman's Cove. He sat on his horse near the edge of the high cliff overlooking the Pacific Ocean. The bank was steep; only two trails led down to the beach below. Not many people knew about Scotsman's Cove. It had been carved out of a crusted cliff between Newport and Laguna Beach on the Southern California coast.

A dirt path from Highway 101 led from the road to the dead-end at the ocean overview. The beach was steep, and rocks jutted out of the water sporadically, interrupting the waves as they rumbled toward the shore.

Cole blew the warm air out his nostrils, anxious to be in motion. He especially wanted to feel the cool salt water on his legs. The descent down the switchbacks of the steep cliff always excited Cy, for it could be dangerous, but the quarter horse was sure-footed and was confident on mountains and rocky terrain. There was an outside chance the horse could stumble, but that only added to the thrill of the ride.

Two people sunned themselves on the beach. There were no bathers in the water. The rocks protruded out of the water like miniature islands, a beauty all their own. The rocks were home to barnacles, mussels, sea urchins, and other sea life, but dangerous to people not watching where they were snorkeling. Few people swam in these waters because of the strong waves over the rocks.

Cy was raised on a ranch in Alpine, a few miles northeast of San Diego. After high school he had gone to San Diego State College, graduating with a major in criminology. Six months ago he had hired on with the Los Angeles Police Department. Graduation from the L.A.P.D. Academy would be tomorrow at 11:00 A.M.

It was Sunday, and to keep his mind busy, he enjoyed his favorite pastime, riding his horse. It gave him time to himself, providing private moments to think of what he was doing with his life. It was difficult to suppress his excitement over entering the world of police work. He had always wanted to be a cop. Now the time was about to arrive.

With a light leg squeeze, Cy signaled Cole to begin the

descent. Taking his time, Cole carefully picked his way down the cliff. Cy caught his breath several times when Cole had to turn on the switchbacks and got too close to the edge of the steep cliff. Cy would take his downhill boot out of the stirrup so he could jump to the high ground side if Cole lost his footing and went over the edge.

Cy could feel the excitement as the horse reached the white sands and picked up his gait on the hard sand along the foaming surf. He pointed Cole south along the shore and let the horse have his head, maintaining an easy canter.

The water sprayed in the air beyond them and hit Cy in the face. He could taste the salty ocean and feel the sting in his eyes. It was wonderfully romantic to him. He loved his horse, the ocean, the thrill of his new job, and his life. Feeling the horse work under him and listening to his hooves hit the shallow water in rhythm were exhilarating. This was Cy's escape from the city and back into nature.

A trickle of doubt touched him as he pondered giving up the country lifestyle for the city. That emotion quickly gave way to the excitement of finally fulfilling a deep-seated desire to belong to the law enforcement community.

Now he would become part of a police team. The day after graduation he would be introduced to his new partner at Central Division in downtown Los Angeles. He looked forward to having a friend and mentor, solving complex criminal problems, and enforcing the laws of the city and state.

Cy never had a close friend other than his older brother, Richard. He experienced a tremendous feeling of guilt, thinking of this brother who had been recently killed in Viet Nam. According to the rules of war, because of his brother's death, Cy was not eligible for military duty in a combat area. His combat would be in the states, in law enforcement.

At 6' 1" and 180 pounds, Cy was athletic and in top physical condition. Under his cowboy hat, he had wavy brown hair. His beard was heavy, but he always kept his face cleanly shaven. His future was a bright star. All he had to do was reach out and take it.

He nudged the horse to a gallop. Cole was eager to move faster, and the cool salt water was refreshing. A couple of miles down the shoreline, the cliffs disappeared and Highway 101 came into view, paralleling the beach. The sun was warm, the water cool, and the arty town of Laguna Beach now appeared before him.

The waves slapped against the huge rocks, shooting sprays of foamy water into the air as if out of a fire hose. The tide was out, and Cy was just able to maneuver his horse into the water around the small rocky islands then back over to the cliffs, passing homes until he reached the smooth sandy beach of Laguna.

As the tide retreated, it made loud clapping sounds farther out in the water and then foamed smoothly to the beach. It was hypnotically stimulating. When he returned to Scotsman's Cove, he would have to ride along the highway for a distance because the water would be too deep for the horse. The rocks would be impossible to cross.

It was noon, and people were now populating the beach near the center of town. It was interesting for Cy to watch the families as he rode slowly by. He enjoyed people's expressions when they saw his horse on the beach. The children especially were excited to see a real horse.

Cy spotted a nice-looking girl standing hip deep in the water, her back to the sea. She jumped slightly each time a small wave hit her from behind. She splashed with her hands at the bubbles passing her by.

She turned and watched Cy as he came closer. "That's a pretty horse you have there," she gleamed.

Cy smiled broadly at the girl just as a larger wave hit her in the back and dumped her in the water. She came up spitting water and wiping her eyes, embarrassed at having failed to maintain her balance. Her hair was now wet, and she did look much different.

"Nice dive," Cy laughed, walking his horse past her. "I'm glad you came up. I was going to jump in and save you."

"If you come back, we could go for an encore," she laughed.

Cy turned in the saddle and stopped the horse. He gazed at the girl more carefully and enjoyed what he saw. He lifted the reins so they touched the left side of Cole's neck. Cole turned and walked out into the deeper water. Cy noticed her nervous giggle and her embarrassed silence.

When he reached the girl, the horse stopped and Cy smiled down at her. "My name is Cy, and I think I had better get you out of this water before another wave gets you."

"Oh, please do," she smiled.

"Here, take my hand and put your left foot in the stirrup," Cy said, taking her wet hand in his and moving his boot out of her way. He didn't like the thought of salt water getting on his leather, but sometimes one had to take a risk. He convinced himself that saddle soap would solve any leather problems.

He pulled her up and settled her on the horse behind him. She wrapped her wet arms around him and giggled, "Thanks a lot. You may have just saved my life. There's no telling what's out there in that water." She appeared quite happy and held on just a little tighter.

"What's your name?" Cy asked.

"Susan," she replied.

"Do you come here very often?" Cy asked, enjoying the moment.

"Every Sunday when I have the time, now that it's getting warmer. The water is still cold in May, but it'll start warming up now that summer is coming on. I go to Long Beach State and I needed a break. I'm sick of studying. My mind needs a vacation."

Cy didn't respond, but allowed Cole to maintain a slow walk out of the water and toward the city park that bordered the beach.

"I've lived here my whole life and I have never seen you before. Are you from around here?" Susan asked, trying not to display her enthusiasm.

"No, I live in Pasadena. I keep my two horses at Diamond Bar. It's not that bad of a drive, and I enjoy coming down to the beach." Cy pulled back on the reins when they reached the volleyball nets. He removed his foot from the stirrup.

Susan reluctantly placed her foot in the stirrup and let herself down, aided by Cy's hand. He released her and turned Cole back south.

Susan smoothed her sandy blonde hair back over her shoulders as she watched him. Her blood was pumping hard with disappointment. "Are you going to be here next Sunday?" she called, not wanting him to leave.

He looked back and grinned. After graduation tomorrow he didn't know what kind of schedule he would have. "I'll try," knowing he wouldn't see her again.

Traffic was at a medium flow going through the downtown section of Laguna Beach. Cy left the public beach area and crossed at the traffic light in the middle of town. A man standing on the corner in faded blue Levi's and a red plaid shirt, with long reddish brown hair and beard, waved at Cy as he crossed the street.

Cy returned the wave and said "Hi," but the man did not answer. He only shook his finger at Cy and returned his attention to the moving traffic. Cy had seen this man several times before, but he could not figure out his age or whether he was really friendly or mentally ill. The people in town didn't seem to mind. They honked their horns and waved back to him as they passed by.

Graduation was a special day for the cadets at the L.A.P.D. Academy in Chavez Ravine near Dodger Stadium. All the young officers were dressed in new navy blue tailored uniforms and spit-polished shoes.

The graduates had been issued Smith and Wesson 357 four-inch revolvers, along with new shiny black basket-woven Sam Brown leather equipment. A number of rookies assigned to the traffic division proudly wore their silver whistles and chains attached to the shoulder epaulet, hooked to their right front shirt pocket.

The officers assigned to parking, investigation control (P.I.C.), and accident investigation division (A.I.D.) already wore their shoulder patches and held their white traffic hats, in contrast to those cadets who would now be assigned to patrol enforcement. The patrol officers had dark hats and no shoulder patches but displayed a beautiful shiny silver badge above the left pocket, over the heart.

Excitement was in the air and the graduates appeared happy and eager to begin their new careers. It seemed to take forever for the last guest speaker to finish. Finally, the class president gave his graduation speech, and the awards were given to the officers who had distinguished themselves in their academy assignments.

Frank Golden wasn't surprised when his son won the firearms award. He knew Cy's shooting capability and felt justified pride in his son's top honors.

On the other hand, Cy's mother sat in a stupor. She could not comprehend her son going into police work. It was too dangerous. She had already lost one son, and now she was having difficulty accepting Cy's desire to be a police officer. Cy was her baby, and she was profoundly worried.

The final all-around academic award went to another cadet, and the graduation ceremony was over.

Cy found his parents standing behind the cadet seating area. June gave him a warm and loving hug. "I'm so proud of you, son." Her voice broke. "I have never been more pleased with you."

"Thanks, Mom. I know you really want me to take over the ranch, and I would if my heart wasn't into being a cop. I don't understand it. I've always wanted it." He gave his mother a tight hug.

"I know, son. You have to follow your heart."

Cy glanced at his father, who seemed displeased and stared down at the floor, shuffling one foot. Cy released his mother and stepped over to greet his father. Something was wrong. He had no idea what. He and his father had been exceptionally close when he was younger and worked on the ranch before his brother Richard joined the army. They had spent many hours working and talking. Cy used to listen to his father, and he was sure his father was the greatest man who had ever lived.

"Well, Dad, I made it. Bet you thought I couldn't do it."

Frank did not respond. Cy began to feel uncomfortable as he studied his father.

Frank continued his gaze downward. Finally his lower lip began the slightest quiver. His jaw knotted as he pressed his teeth tightly. He threw his arms around Cy, squeezing the breath out of him. Frank couldn't speak. The words were there, but his throat was swollen so tight he couldn't get his vocal cords to work.

June was moved. She stepped over to her son and Frank and hugged them both. Ever since Richard had been killed, Frank rarely expressed his emotions. This moment overwhelmed her.

It was an experience Cy would never forget. He knew his father felt desperately lonely for his older brother, and Cy often felt the pain of his father's grief. This closeness to his parents was special to him, and it touched him deeply.

Chapter 2
Assignment Central Division

Tuesday day shift, middle of July.

Behind the wheel of the black and white patrol unit, Cy worked the south central area of Los Angeles. His blood was on fire with enthusiasm for his new job. He had been assigned to Central Division, the first of eighteen divisions of the Los Angeles Police Department. The historic division was located at 231 E. 6th Street in downtown Los Angeles, right in the heart of the city.

After two months on the job, Cy was confident he fit into the groove with the patrol section. He enjoyed the excitement of working the busy streets and back alleys in the heavily populated downtown districts.

Central Division included business as well as residential areas. During the daytime it was chaos—people conducting their business, jamming the streets and freeways with traffic, commuting to and from work.

What amazed Cy most was the vast difference in the heavy crime activities during the night hours, compared to day-watch calls, which dealt mostly with the business world. After the sun went down, the street belonged to the people of the night.

Jacob Wilson, his partner and mentor, a black officer with six years experience, found Cy to be flexible, with a genuine desire to be a good public servant. It was a pleasure to introduce his new rookie partner to the real world of police work.

It was early afternoon and Jacob was riding shotgun with his new partner. He held a cold Pepsi in his hand while he listened to the police radio, which constantly squawked orders to the officers on patrol. He sipped the drink, enjoying the coolness as it slid down a throat as dry as a dusty road. It was a hot, smoggy day, and both men were uncomfortable in the afternoon heat.

Jacob pointed to the intersection ahead of them. "Turn left on 4th. Let's take a look along the Los Angeles River area. It's a place you're going to have to know like the back of your hand here in Central. We have a lot of police activity all along the frontage road to the river bed. Santa Fe Avenue will be like a second home to you."

"I've heard it's a hot place at night," Cy said, making a left turn.

Jacob studied Cy a moment before speaking. He appreciated Cy's attitude toward learning his new job. He had a lot of things going for him if he stuck it out in this career field. Cy had an advantage that many of the new officers in the field didn't—he had police sense, fortified by common sense. Studying a problem and using training and intelligent reasoning with common sense is what made a good officer. It was one of the most needed assets in field operation.

"So, Officer Golden, what is going on between you and my wife?"

Cy thought a moment and couldn't make up his mind how to respond. "I don't have a clue. Do you?"

"Don't give me that. You never answer a question with a question. Haven't I taught you better than that?"

"I thought you had. What do you think?"

"Gees, you white fool. You're doing it again. Don't you get it? I ask the questions, not you."

"Okay, shoot. What's your question?"

Jacob shook his head back and forth. "I just told you, I'm asking the questions. Now, what's the deal between you and my wife?"

"I don't follow you. Do you mind giving me a little more information so I can properly prepare an answer?"

Jacob took another sip. "Lila didn't like it when my old partner, Tony Valin, was transferred to the Hollenbeck Division. She insisted I put in for a colored partner. She went on and on, like a well prepared script, telling me all the reasons why I needed to stick with the race."

"Was Tony colored?"

"No. He was Portuguese."

"And so?"

"And so, now she gives me this big story of what a great person you are, and she thinks you're a pretty neat guy."

Cy was moved. "I suppose you want to know my feelings about her, right?"

"Okay, what do you have to say for yourself?"

"I love her. You have a wonderful wife, and I love your kids, too."

Jacob had to think a moment. "Okay, okay," he said grinning.

"I was hoping it was something simple like that."

Cy cruised slowly down a residential area, carefully observing the streets. "I can't stand you, Jacob, but your family is great. I'd keep you for a partner, just to have good colored folks as my friends."

Jacob didn't respond. The sun was bright. He put his sunglasses on to keep from squinting. He was thinking his new partner had turned out to be a good officer. He was dependable and got along well with the other officers on the patrol team.

It was his goal to teach Cy something new every day. He took the necessary time to explain the proper conduct a professional officer should maintain in dealing with and solving citizens' problems. He instructed Cy on the many dangers of cruising the back streets inhabited by the street people.

Cy was a natural when it came to law enforcement. Jacob decided he was born to be a cop. Jacob was amazed how quickly the young rookie had absorbed the tremendous volume of police skills during only two months on the road. Cy adapted to patrolling almost immediately. He could sniff out a suspect hidden in a building or dwelling, calling on his inner senses when danger was imminent.

Jacob glanced around at the people driving, walking, standing, sitting. Others appeared out of place with nowhere to go. Jacob took another drink. "The city is changing, Cy. People are changing. Even the tourists are drifting away from the obvious locations of high crime areas that were once a popular place to visit. After the sun drops behind the ocean, the local people avoid the areas they were accustomed to frequenting during the daylight hours."

"Living on a cattle ranch all my life was like a blanket that shielded me from what the world is really like. It's a different world from what I expected. I feel lucky to have you to show me the ropes."

"You want to know something funny?" Jacob grunted. "I didn't like you when I first met you."

"Serious?"

"Serious. I resented you taking Tony's place. You get used to a partner and it's hard to give him up. You learn to know what he's thinking and predict his actions. No, I didn't like you at all. I just didn't show it. You looked like one of those young starry-eyed boys that thought too much of himself."

"Are you saying you think I'm okay now?"

"Well, maybe."

"You're lucky, Jack."

"Why?"

"I was about ready to kick your skinny black butt out the door."

"In your dreams, fool."

Cy took a quick glimpse of Jacob. If he had been street trained by another officer, would he have been as effective in the field? Cy wondered. Jacob was a thoughtful officer who seemed to have genuine concern for the public.

After every traffic stop or interrogation of a person, he would not only advise Cy what to do, but why it had to be done in a certain way, including which laws supported that action. He constantly drilled Cy on policies and procedures, instructing him on pertinent police ethics. The California Penal Code became his constant companion.

Cy knew he was lucky to have Jacob for his partner. He also knew police work was going to be his life.

Same day, South Central L.A.

Gertrude Wallin stomped through the front door, slamming it shut with a bang. Walking to the front window, she jerked the curtain to one side. She couldn't believe her eyes as she looked out. "Henry! Get your silly face in here now!" She waited impatiently for a response. There was none.

"Henry! Get in here. I want to know why that ridiculous yellow truck is in my driveway." Her anger rose when her husband failed to give her an immediate response. Her husband had been gone for three hours. He said he was going to the liquor store for a paper. When he didn't show up, she went to the store and got the paper herself. Something was wrong. Whose truck was it and why was it on her property?

Henry jumped for the bathroom when his wife's voice erupted from the living room. He threw a handful of cool water on his face, raised his head up, and looked into the mirror. He shuddered at the sight of the face looking back at him. The skin on his bald head was blotchy with liver spots and lined with wrinkles. He felt old at 65.

He hated himself, as he had for most of his life. Why had he married her? He had asked himself that question thousands of times. He should never have gotten involved with the witch from hell and her two screaming brats. That was almost forty years ago, and his life had been a torment ever since.

The first year of their marriage was acceptable. She was pleasant the first twelve months, appreciative of a husband with a steady job. He figured her kindness was payment for having someone to pay the rent. She even cooked good meals and cleaned house. What happened after that, he didn't know. Their relationship changed. Gertrude's personality was different the second year. She complained constantly, always riding him. To shut her up, he cooked and did most of the house chores. Doing most of the work didn't really bother him a great deal. It kept him busy so he could ignore her.

"Henry! Get your lazy ass out here. I want to see your miserable face, now!"

Henry felt his hands shake. He was tired of her. He hated himself for heeling to her like a whipped dog. He was tired of her married children always coming to him for money he didn't have. They weren't his children, yet they expected him to provide for their needs. They used him as much as their mother did.

The bathroom door almost bounced off its hinges when Gertrude's fist banged on it. "Get your little scrawny butt out here now, or you'll never hear the end of it."

"I'll never hear the end of it anyway," he muttered under his breath.

Henry heard the nail slide into the hole of the door knob, releasing the lock. The door flew open. Gertrude filled the doorway with her ridged frame, her hands jammed into her waist. Her beady eyes bore down on him like a mad ferret.

"Don't think you have a safe haven in here, you stupid little man." She stood back and pointed toward the front room. "Out!"

Henry finished wiping his face with a towel, dropped it in the bathroom sink, and meekly walked out of the room. Gertrude stepped in behind him, pulled the towel out of the sink, wadded it up and threw it, hitting him in the back of the head. He stooped to pick it up. He returned to the bathroom, folded the towel, and placed it neatly on the towel rack.

Henry was tired. He was tired of being a punching bag for

his wife, a doormat for his stepchildren, and a sounding board for his boss at work. He only had two weeks left before he would begin his retirement. He had been a CPA for over thirty-five years. The thought of being free of responsibility gave him momentary relief from his present problems.

He walked to the front window and looked at his brand-new yellow truck, a 1965 Chevrolet half-ton. It was everything he ever wanted. He could use it for fishing. He could even sleep in it if he wanted. It would be a mechanism for escape. He couldn't hold back the smile breaking on his face.

Gertrude came up behind him. She rapped her knuckles on his shoulder. Henry wondered how she always knew exactly where to best inflict pain on him. She was an expert, and he hated her for that, too.

When Henry didn't turn to face his wife, she slapped him on the back of the head, knocking him forward. His scalp stung and he blinked out of reflex. Again, he did not respond, and she poked him with her finger in the middle of his back. "You'd better start talking, mister, before I really lose my temper."

Henry refused to change his posture. He maintained his stance, gazing out the window toward the Los Angeles River beyond Santa Fe Avenue. "Okay, okay. What do you want to know?" he asked quietly.

"You idiot. I said I wanted to know where that truck came from."

"I bought it this morning."

"What do you mean you bought it this morning? I didn't give you permission to buy anything but a newspaper, especially not that yellow bomb out there. Who in heaven's name would want a truck of all things?"

"Me, that's who."

"And just who the hell is you, Mr. Pimple Butt?"

"It was my money. I spent it the way I wanted." Henry gave a little laugh.

"And just where did that money come from?"

"I've been saving it over the years."

"You've what?" Gertrude spun Henry around and pushed him against the window. "You've been holding out on me?"

"I've been saving for years. In two weeks I'm taking my truck and leaving you for good."

"You what?"

"You heard me. I'm sick of you and those two leeches you have for children."

"And just how do you think you are going to afford leaving me, you little blockhead?"

Henry gave his wife his best smile. It was the best he could give without passing out from pure fright of the woman. She was crazy, and her temper frightened him. "I'm giving you all our property. Everything. I don't want nothing. We have no bills. With your social security, you'll do just fine without me. Probably better."

"You blundering idiot. Do you think for a moment I'd let you go with your retirement from the company? Half that retirement is mine, and half of your half will be mine after you're dead and gone. Now," Gertrude said, grabbing her husband by the lapels and pulling his face up to hers, "you listen to me, pimple butt. You get in that piece of junk and hightail it back to the dealer. You return your precious truck. That money you've been saving is half mine. I want it today and no later than today. You got that?"

Henry stared at his wife for a long moment. "You'd take my retirement and truck from me?"

"Did I stutter? You can bet your life on it, buster. I also expect interest on my share of the money you've been hoarding."

"Even though I went without lunches and personal items all these years, saving my money for something I wanted, you'd take it from me?"

"Do you see my lips moving? Am I standing here telling you something other than that?"

"No, no, you've made yourself clear." Henry pulled away and turned his back to her. He looked out the window. A police car was stopped in front of his driveway. Two police officers were looking at his truck. After a moment, they slowly drove away.

"Okay, Gertrude, I'll give you what you want. It's not worth arguing with you. You always win anyway." Henry went over to the TV, picked up his keys, and walked out the door. He went into the garage, picked up a couple of items, and drove away.

Pavlo did not like downtown Los Angeles but knew he had to get used to it. Too many people. Too many cars. Too much noise but lots of precious money circulating. He particularly did not like his cousin Carlos, who, it appeared, had turned into a junkie since he last talked with him in person. He had all the appearances of a user but knew Carlos would not admit it. He was a filthy, seedy character. He decided when his business with Carlos was finished, he would be eliminated.

"Are you sure Molino and Angelino do not suspect you doing business with anyone else other than their organization?" Pavlo asked Carlos as he puffed on a hand-rolled Havana.

"Are you kidding, man? They trust me like a brother. I supervise the West Coast transportation. There are so many people in between the mules and the distributors they could not begin to suspect me when business begins dropping off. Man, these gangs around here are difficult to control as it is. Once you understand their turf rules, the business flows okay. You just cannot do your own business in the wrong territory, that's all. I have the contacts to take care of that. You give me product at cheaper prices, we can buy into the gangs and let them do the selling. This is the wonderful thing about America—free enterprise, man. You can set up shop and keep losers between the Mafia and us."

"Are you sure no one knows we are related?"

"Hey, man, you know it, because I said it. I will never mention your name to no one—no one at all. You give me the greenbacks to cover cost, and I set you up in a solid business. I have my friends and I will work through my secret connections. No one will know nothing." Carlos put a cold bottle of beer to his lips and pulled a long drink, swallowing with a gurgle.

"If you are wrong, your cajones will be eaten by the dogs, my cousin." Pavlo frowned at his driver with distaste as they traveled along Santa Fe toward Boyle Heights.

Carlos looked around their environment as they proceeded down the street. "Now you know the boundaries, do you know where for sure you are going to set up shop?"

Pavlo grabbed the beer between his legs and took a quick drink. "Downtown on First Street a few blocks from the police station."

"You talking about the Hollenbeck police station? Are you crazy, man? Why would you do something like that? You do not want those pigs to even notice you."

"That is right, you pendejo. I set up an import/export business of my Mexican wares and do it downtown. I am invisible.

Tomorrow I will close the deal on office space on the main floor of a nice building in a respectable commercial area for the people on the street. It will be easy access for my legitimate export business and all drugs are done on the side and away from me."

"You can count on me for the best contacts. We have good people here wanting good work, good money."

"What I need from you is people who can be trusted and who are hungry for lots of money. That is the way we will be successful, the only way—money and loyal people to work the streets. Of course there is my favorite way—pain and the bite of fear."

Pavlo focused on a black and white police cruiser slowly coming toward them. As it passed he noticed a white officer chauffeuring a Negro officer. "These police are soft pigs. I look forward to having them on my payroll once I am established."

Carlos choked on his beer. "Hey, man, you cannot go buying them off that easy. These cops are bad news. You do not know L.A.P.D. boys. Very bad news. We stay clear of them; they will never know we exist."

"All the same, I take care of them if it becomes necessary. Money or blood, it makes no difference to me."

Cy watched the dark sedan going in the opposite direction with the two Mexicans but did not give them a second thought.

Jacob removed his duty hat and wiped the sweat off his forehead. "Mercy me, it's a hot one. I need to have that new yellow Chevy pickup and take off for Crystal Lake where it's cool."

"It had a sticker on the window. I'll bet the owner doesn't even have a hundred miles on her yet," Cy said, with a twinge of jealousy. "I've never owned a new vehicle in my life. But someday, I'd like to have one like that pickup."

"In your dreams, buddy. It'll be years before you could afford a new vehicle."

Cy drove south along Santa Fe Avenue checking out the area. The river was mostly dry, and heat waves hovered over the round rocks and concrete. "Speaking of being hot and miserable, are we going to work out tonight after shift?"

"We can. Better than mowing the lawn," Jacob said. "I'm not in the mood for any physical stuff. No jogging or practicing takedowns for me. After shift, let's head for Gabriel Canyon and do a little firearms practice. I don't want to get up a big sweat."

After shift, Cy picked up Jacob at his home in Glendora. They drove to the San Gabriel Riverbed east of Azusa near the mouth of the canyon. They spent an hour practicing their shooting skills in the dry riverbed, their favorite place to shoot, because people in town who heard the shots would think it was coming from the Fish Canyon Gun Club across the river. The only weapons they ever shot were their department-issued handguns. They wanted to be fully familiar with the revolvers they would have to rely on in a deadly situation.

Practice over, Jacob sat on a large boulder and studied his partner as Cy opened a gun box and took out a cleaning rod and other materials. He reached into his pants pocket, took out some gum, and slipped a stick into his mouth. "Want some?"

"No thanks," Cy smiled. "That stuff will rot your teeth out. I want to die with a full head of teeth," he said, laughing. Cy hesitated a moment, "I'll be honest with you on something, Jake."

"Yeah, what's that?"

"It really gets me how you people have the most beautiful, hard white teeth."

"Do I detect a slight jealousy?"

"Yes, sir. Yes, sir, you surely do," Cy answered, throwing an empty shell at Jacob. "I really care about you, buddy. You've made a difference in my life."

Jacob swallowed hard and forced a grin, looking at Cy out of the corner of his eye. "For a honkie, you're okay, too."

Jacob watched Cy clean his gun. After a few moments he folded his arms and looked across the riverbed towards Duarte. "Cy, I hate to say this, but you are the best shooter I've ever seen. No one shoots like you. I don't know how you do it. I can't hit those cans consistently like you do. How did you learn to shoot like that?"

"On the ranch when I was a kid I used to shoot a lot at ground squirrels. It was only a twenty-two revolver and I shot thousands of rounds. It's an advantage most people don't get, I guess." Cy wiped the weapon in his hand with a clean cloth.

"My dad told me I had a special gift—one that only comes rarely to a person." Cy didn't want to sound like he was bragging. "I knew as a kid I had a gift because I could outshoot everyone. My dad told me I couldn't have learned it; he said I was born with it. He said I had tunnel vision and could focus on the object I was shooting at, whereas other people can only

view the whole picture, and the target is only a small part of it."
Cy hesitated, looking over at Jacob on the boulder. "I only see
the target and the gun sights. I don't understand it. I focus on
the object and that's all I see. It's strange, but it is so easy to
me." Cy took out his pocketknife and began cutting his nails as
he continued, "I believe it was a gift that Annie Oakley and
some of the old wild west folks had. People didn't know what
it was. I really think the old gunslingers had a gift, coupled
with a talent. The two together were probably unbeatable."

Cy stood and turned to face Jacob. He gazed steadily. It
was quiet except for a bluejay in a nearby tree. "I'm going to
tell you something true, Jacob, but you won't believe it."

"Probably not, but go ahead." Jacob said.

Cy smiled back at Jacob, knowing he would not believe
what he was about to tell him. This was good, because it would
get him a free cold one on the way home. "You could stand in
front of me, Jacob, your gun drawn and pointed at me. With
my gun in the holster but with my hand on the handle, I can
draw and fire faster than you can pull the trigger."

Jacob spit on the ground and shook his head. "You sure are
one crazy cowboy. No way, man. No way, fool. You say I point
my gun at your ugly face and your gun is in the holster?"

"That's right."

"No way, fool," Jacob spit again. "That's impossible."

"Jacob, have you ever seen or heard of those quick-draw artists
that have competitions across the U.S.? They are so fast, you can't
see them draw, let alone shoot. The draw is faster than the eye."

"Yeah, yeah, I've seen it on TV, but that's trick photog-
raphy, my man. There's no way a white boy, like yourself, can
draw his weapon and shoot before me if I already have my gun
out and ready to fire." Jacob shook his head back and forth.
"Uh, uh. No way, my white cowboy. No suh," he shook his
head, "can't be done and that's a fact, Jack. Uh uh, no way."

"You want to put a drink on it?" Cy challenged.

"You got that right," Jacob said, standing up. He took his
weapon out of his holster and emptied the cylinder of its six
rounds. Cy did the same, and each exchanged weapons to
check the empty cylinders. Both satisfied, they exchanged
weapons again and both checked the cylinder again. When the
safety ritual was finished, Cy holstered his gun and backed a
few feet away from his friend.

"You point your gun right at me," Cy instructed Jacob. After Jacob pointed his gun at his partner, Cy smiled saying, "Now, I am telling you I will draw my weapon and fire before you can pull the trigger, right?"

"Right," Jacob replied happily. "I think I'll have a cold beer. I suppose you'll want a warm glass of milk or something tender for the tummy."

"You know, I might just have what I want," Cy replied, drawing his weapon with a blur and releasing the hammer with a loud click. Jacob stood, his legs spread apart, frozen in the draw position.

"Hey, that was no fair, I wasn't ready, man. You were talking. That's no fair. I cry foul, fool," Jacob whined, squinting in disbelief.

"Okay, okay. Double or nothing and we'll do it again," Cy said, putting his weapon back in the holster and leaving his hand on the handle of his weapon.

"Okay," Jacob said tight-lipped. He pointed his gun at Cy. "I'm ready and don't be no talking."

"Do you agree to double or nothing?"

"Of course I do, you—" Cy drew and dry fired his gun again. This time Jacob pulled the trigger, but clearly after Cy.

"Hey, hey, hey. Now hold on just one minute, I wasn't ready."

"Let's quit. You owe me two drinks. Let's head for home."

Jacob did not move, staring at Cy. "Don't even try it, man. You ain't going nowheres. We is going to do this again. My English is going to hell in a hand basket and I don't give a dog's balls. Now holster your weapon. We going double or nothing." Jacob spread his feet and pointed his gun at Cy.

Cy holstered his weapon and stared at Jacob, giving him a big smile. "This time I want you to..." He drew his weapon and fired again, beating Jacob to the trigger pull.

"That's it, you lousy cheat. You can't do that to me, you bucket of green-running puke," Jacob snarled. "You stay right there and we are going to do this again."

"You owe me four drinks. Double or nothing?"

"Yeah," Jacob said, and Cy drew and fired again, beating him.

Jacob just stood and stared at Cy in disbelief. "I don't believe this. That's humanly impossible."

"You owe me eight drinks, my friend," Cy laughed and holstered his gun. "Let's go," Cy said, turning to pick up his equipment.

"This ain't funny no more, sonny," Jacob sneered angrily. He wasn't going to be bested by a rookie cop. "You set your white ass in front of me and we are doing this again."

Now uncomfortable, Cy wanted to quit. "Let's go home, Jacob. You can have the drinks back. I don't want them. It was just a game."

"It was just a game," Jacob mimicked Cy in a baby's voice. "You little honkie. You go for your gun and it's double or nothing." Spit was coming from Jacob's lips when he screamed at Cy.

Cy turned, dropping his equipment to the ground. "Go for your gun, you black snake in the grass, and it's double or nothing." Immediately Cy drew and pulled the trigger before Jacob could squeeze the trigger, allowing the hammer to fall.

Jacob's face twisted grotesquely and his eyes glared with hatred. "You cheated again. I wasn't ready you...white trash."

Cy turned in an angry huff. He holstered his gun and faced Jacob not more than a foot away. They glared at each other, tempers flaring. Finally Jacob's face broke into a smile and he started laughing. "Man, I am one glad guy you are my partner. I never—" he shook his head.

Picking up their equipment, they headed down Azusa Avenue to the city center. Cy stopped at Lewis's Liquor Store on Foothill Boulevard and made Jacob buy him a six-pack of beer. He gave one to Jacob and headed for home.

Cy pulled up in front of Jacob's house, a half block south of Sierra Madre. He turned the engine off and faced Jacob. "My dad told me it wasn't a talent. He said it was something in you that just happens. He explained it to me this way. He said some people, like baseball players, have an extra hard or fast reflex. He said only a small percentage of people in this world could be a professional catcher. They have a rare reflex ability that enables them to respond quickly to catch the ball, whereas the average person is unable to even see the ball let alone catch it. A catcher doesn't think to catch the ball; it just happens on reflex."

Cy looked at Jacob, who was sipping on his beer. "That applies to the quick-draw artist. It just happens, that's all."

Jacob got out of the pickup and leaned back into the window. "You know, good buddy, we could sure win a lot of free drinks and a few bucks off you." He turned and walked to the house. "See you later, pard."

❧

Three days later, Friday day watch.

Cy and Jacob turned north from Pico Boulevard and traveled at normal speed on Broadway, taking their time and enjoying the late afternoon.

A compact vehicle made a right turn in front of them, not making a full stop at the red light, and then sped up. Jacob tightened his seat belt, anticipating a chase. Cy pushed the patrol car faster and tightened his own seat belt. Jacob called in the license number and looked back at Cy. "Do you know what you are going to do when you stop this car?"

"Yeah, I do."

"Give it to me," Jacob demanded.

"Once we know of any 'wants' or if he's clear, you will give our pullover position to Central Dispatch. I'll pull up behind the car with my fender slightly exaggerated into traffic to give myself protection from oncoming cars. You will position yourself on the passenger side, watching the interior of the car while keeping one eye on the public. I will check the back seat for anything amiss," Cy nodded to Jacob. "How's that?"

"What are you going to write him for?"

"Right now we have two violations—failure to make a full stop at a red light and exceeding the speed limit." Cy checked his speedometer. "The guy is going 45 in a 25 zone."

"Okay," Jacob bobbed his head up and down. "That's okay. That's okay. Now, when are you going to get yourself in gear and stop this fool before he kills someone?"

"Overhead's on," Cy said. "He's pulling over."

The driver slowed and curbed his car. A white male jumped out and ran back to the patrol unit. Both officers were out of the patrol car before the man got to them.

"Officer, I need your help fast!" the young man exclaimed nervously.

"What's the problem?" Cy asked, stepping up to the man.

"My name is John Baker," the young man panted. "My wife is going to have a miscarriage if I don't get to our medical clinic and pick up a shot that she needs to take right away. It's our first child and she's had nothing but trouble."

"Where's your wife now?" Jacob asked.

"She's on the bathroom floor. She's sick and can't move," Baker gasped.

Jacob took hold of the man's arm. "How far along is she?"

"She's three months. Can you guys give me a lift to the Shelton Medical Center? The doctor has a syringe made up for me. I'll take a ticket or anything if you'll help me," Baker pleaded, twisting his face in supplication. "Please, we are wasting time."

Jacob pulled the man by the sleeve and pushed him in the back seat. "I almost lost my first one, too, son. Hop in. We'll give you a lift."

Cy got back into the patrol car and pulled the police car around Baker's car and went north. He drove code-2, lights only, stopping at all lighted intersections. In two minutes he pulled into the medical center parking lot. Baker ran inside and was out in a few seconds.

"The nurse said not to go back to my car. Can you give me a lift to my apartment? Time is everything." Baker was so nervous he had trouble getting his breath.

"We'll get you there. Strap on your seat belt." Jacob radioed to dispatch they were on a code-2 run.

"I really appreciate you, officers. God bless you guys."

"Well shucks, man, thanks," Jacob said, smiling at him.

A few minutes later Cy pulled up in front of Baker's apartment. They followed him inside to where his wife lay on the floor. The three men picked her up, carried her to the bedroom, and placed her on the bed.

Baker took the syringe, yanked her bermudas down partway, and jabbed her in the fleshy part of the hip. When he finished, he took a deep breath and gave a weak smile to his wife who stared at the wall. "Love you, honey. You'll be okay now. I promise."

With that, Baker escorted the two officers out to their car. He thanked them again and told them he would pick up his car later. He did not feel comfortable leaving his wife until she felt better.

Both officers shook his hand and left feeling good about their aid to the young couple. Cy and Jacob got in the car. Jacob picked up the mike and pressed the transmission button. "Dispatch, One Adam 44, finished with the public assist. Clear for details."

"Roger One Adam 44, proceed to Sacramento Street and

Santa Fe Avenue. Report of a possible abandoned vehicle by the Los Angeles River bottom under the overpass."

"One Adam 44, copy. Request description of vehicle."

"One Adam 44, abandoned vehicle is a 1965 yellow Chevrolet pickup truck. No license plates. Be advised, an ATL was issued for a vehicle fitting this description last Tuesday."

"One Adam 44, copy, en route," Jacob responded over the mike. To Cy he said, "Let's check it out."

"On our way." Cy turned on Olympic Boulevard and headed towards the river bottoms.

"Depending how long it has been there, it may be stripped by now," Jacob said, snapping his seat belt.

"Doesn't that truck fit the description of the one we saw Tuesday around noon off of Sante Fe Avenue somewhere around Jesse or Willow Street?"

"Yeah, it does, now that you mention it."

A few minutes later, Cy crossed the railroad tracks and parked the patrol unit next to the overpass near 8th and Santa Fe. Both officers exited the patrol unit after giving dispatch their location. Jacob led the way. "This is not the best place to leave a vehicle. Let's see what's down by the riverbed."

Cy walked next to Jacob, all the while looking over his shoulders to see if anyone was paying attention to them. He was finally satisfied no one was following them.

Jacob and Cy walked a short distance down a road. They came upon a chain-link gate providing access to the Los Angeles River. It had been busted open. It appeared someone had rammed the gate with a vehicle. Shiny pieces of a chrome headlamp lay in the middle of the road.

"Someone was determined to drive a vehicle in here. No way would it be that new Chevy you were talking about," Jacob said, inspecting the round chrome liner.

"You're wrong, Jake. Look," Cy pointed to the new Chevrolet pickup parked partially under the overpass facing the river bottom.

"This don't make sense," Jacob said skeptically. The windows were so dark, visibility into the cab was impossible at their distance. "I don't like the feel of this. No one in their right mind would leave a nice truck like that here. It should have been stripped. Keep your eyeballs open. We don't want to walk in on a setup."

"I've been watching our rear. We're clear," Cy said, looking around them as they approached the truck.

Jacob stopped approximately fifty feet from the truck. "The truck looks okay, but someone has spray painted the windows black. Look at that."

"Why would anyone do that to a new truck?"

"Don't know. Why would anybody in their right mind park down here?"

Both officers moved closer, surveying the area around them. No one else appeared in the foreground. Jacob didn't like the feeling coming on in his stomach. "Someone painted the window a solid black, so there must be something inside they don't want us to see."

"Do you hear a noise?" Cy responded, cocking his head at an angle.

"I hear something. I'm not sure what."

"It's kind of a humming sound, but I'm not sure where it's coming from."

Jacob moved forward. "Let's watch our step here. I really don't like this."

"Wait a minute," Cy demanded, taking hold of Jacob's arm. "Look," he pointed to the rear of the truck. "We got a hose coming out the exhaust pipe and disappearing around the other side of the truck."

"Yeah, I see it. Well, what we got here, my man, is a nonbreather. This ain't good. Some dude has done himself in, or we have a homicide. You hear that noise now?" Jacob stopped and listened. "That is the sound of ten hundred thousand billion flies having a feast on whoever is in there."

Cy contemplated Jacob, a sick feeling in the pit of his stomach. "This isn't good here. It doesn't look good in there. Maybe we should call for backup?"

Jacob gave him a distasteful look. "We need to confirm what we have first. It could be a person or a dog in there. Then again it's probably a suicide. Come on, as first responders, we need to check it out before we call the plainclothes boys."

Jacob walked around the truck and found a garden hose leading from the tail pipe to the inside of the truck cab through the window wing. The open portion of the window had been jammed with a rag to block escaping air around the hose.

Jacob pounded on the window with his fist. The flies were so thick they did not respond to the vibrations and banging. He could not see inside. Cy tried his side and got the same response.

Jacob grasped the door handle of the passenger side. It was locked. "Try your side," Jacob ordered. "I don't want to stick my hand through the window wing and get those damn flies on me. Besides, I don't know what's in there."

As Cy pushed the release button, the door bolted open, and a body fell through the open door, slamming into Cy chest high. Automatically, Cy threw both arms forward, catching the corpse. The flies and the smell gagged him as he stepped backwards trying to remove his arms from under its armpits. He dropped the body to the ground and jumped away.

The lower back broke open, caused by the weakness in the skin tissue from the three days of decay and one-hundred-degree weather. The black fluid immediately soaked Cy's uniform—decomposing blood that turned into a foul liquid housing millions of squirming maggots. The main force hit Cy from his waist to his feet. His shoes filled up with the hideous dark juice, and maggots worked their way into his shoes.

Jacob ran around the truck to see Cy drenched in fluid and maggots. The corpse's torso had broken in half, allowing the millions of white squirming worms to gush onto the ground, followed by a slow stream of the blackening gore. "Oh hell," Jacob gasped, holding his hand over his mouth. The smell almost made him throw up. He backed away from Cy, trying to get up wind.

Cy was gagging. Without hesitation, he backed away from the truck, took off his shoes, and kicked them away. He removed his gun belt and dropped his trousers. He tore his socks off and was jumping up and down on the hot concrete. Flies followed his every move.

Cy gave Jacob a desperate look for help. Through the buzzing flies he saw his partner crying. Tears were coming down Jacob's face and a muffled sound came from his pressed lips as he held a white handkerchief over his mouth.

A closer look revealed a different story. Jacob was not crying. He was laughing so hard he lost control at the sight of Cy. His knees were weak, about to buckle.

Cy jumped around barefooted on the burning concrete until he got into the shade of the bridge. He swung at the flies in vain. He would have taken off his shorts, but that would have been too much. He couldn't stand the smell on him, and there was no water in the riverbed to wash himself off.

"Get over here, trooper," yelled Jacob through his handkerchief, after his laughing subsided.

"Over where?" Cy gasped.

Jacob walked over towards Cy but stayed back a safe distance. He didn't want the bloody flies on him. If he wasn't careful he was going to up-chuck everything in him for the last week. "Here," he said distastefully, laying his handkerchief on the ground and stepping back. "Take this, put it over your nose and mouth, and go over to the cab of the truck."

"What?" Cy said in disbelief.

"You heard me, rookie. This is the best OJT you'll ever get. And thanks to me, you're getting it," Jacob said, covering his lips from the flies. He continuously waved his hands trying to keep the pests from landing on him.

"What are you talking about? What is OJT?"

"On-the-job-training, fool. I could handle this thing, but you won't learn nothing by it. Now be thankful that I at least am giving you something to put over your ugly face. Check the inside of the truck. It looks like a note or something is taped to the rearview mirror."

"I can't do it, Jacob. I can't get near that filthy gut hole. I'll throw up." Cy shook his head disobediently.

"Listen to me, Cy. You will go over there and you'll do it now. If you're not cut out to be a cop, then haul ass out of here now! I never want to see you again." Jacob's eyes flared in anger at his partner.

Cy hesitated, furious at himself for being weak and sick to his stomach. He did want to be a cop and he knew it was his job. He stepped over to the white cloth on the ground, held it to his face, and hotfooted it to the cab of the truck and into the mass of angry flies. He tried not to look at the body but couldn't resist it. It was a ghastly sight. The white male's skin was black, deteriorated to a decayed mass of flesh. Maggots worked their way back inside his open cavity. Thousands of other maggots crawled on the ground. Cy realized he was stepping on the maggots with his bare feet. He almost screamed in horror. Taking a deep breath, he somewhere found the strength to reach up into the cab of the truck and remove the note attached to the rearview mirror by a piece of masking tape.

He took a quick glance around the inside of the cab. Single pages of fishing scenes were taped around the inside of the cab. A fishing box sat on the seat, open, exposing new fishing gear inside. He knew then the man had carefully planned his last fishing trip. He stepped back into a mass of maggots, screamed in anger, and hotfooted it back to the shade of the bridge, gagging.

Jacob had both hands over his mouth and was again laughing out of control. Wet trails ran down his cheeks to his neck. "Thank the Lord I have you for a partner. There isn't another man on this earth I could have gotten to go over to that truck and remove that paper." Jacob started howling. "I love you, man. You are my partner for sure."

Cy wasn't laughing. He called on every strength in his body to keep his nausea under control. Someday he would get even. He didn't know when or where. It wasn't over by a long shot.

Jacob held out his hand. "Here, give me the paper and let's see what it says. If it's evidence, we need to put it in an evidence bag and mark it." Cy handed him the paper. Jacob was careful to touch the filthy thing with only his thumb and fingertip on the very corner.

It read, "Gertrude, my sweet, you may have the truck. It's yours. Hah! I cleaned out our savings and checking accounts and donated the cash to a charity that you'll never be able to find. While you scratch out a living, I'll be on a permanent fishing trip. You got what you wanted, so did I."

Jacob handed the note to Cy. "Here, take this filthy thing. I really don't want to get my uniform dirty, so hang on to this suicide note. I'll go back to the car, call for backup, get an evidence bag, and I guess you need a blanket to cover those lily-white legs." Jacob burst out laughing. "You sure are a sight, my man. Yes sir," he shook his head happily. "Yes siree. You have made the cut. I accept you as my partner."

The flies continued to buzz around Cy. He watched Jacob walk toward the patrol car. "Someday, some way," he muttered under his breath.

Chapter 3
Watts 1965

The second Monday in August was hot and sultry from the smog hovering over the city caused by the high pressure system in the region. Jacob and Cy were on a swing shift in a black and white unit beating the streets in their assigned patrol sector when dispatch squawked on the monitor ordering them back to Central Division. Jacob was behind the wheel. He turned the unit around and drove to the police parking lot.

Both men reported to the shift sergeant as ordered. To their surprise there were over two hundred officers milling about excitedly, nervous with anticipation. Groups of officers were gathered together in cliques talking loudly, and there was a hum in the air, similar to that of a busy beehive. Captain Morris appeared at the briefing podium and spoke into a loudspeaker, ordering everyone to be seated. He proceeded to explain the dangerous and explosive situation that was quickly escalating in Watts.

Captain Morris was not his usual jovial self. He was serious and appeared deeply stressed. He related the story most of the officers had already heard on the news. Two California Highway Patrolmen had pulled over a Negro traffic violator in the Watts area. A small crowd of curious onlookers had become aggressive as more C.H.P. backup units arrived. The crowd grew and the officers attempted to take the prisoner away. The incident went from name calling to pushing and shoving and then to fighting. Then the situation again escalated into aggravated assaults and random shootings. A serious problem had developed for the city fire department. Fires were being set throughout the Watts area. The fire department was ineffective in controlling the blazes because sniper fire in the hot spots was rendering the firemen helpless in extinguishing the burning structures. The rioting and fires spread from Los Angeles to Long Beach and covered an area of approximately fifteen miles.

Everyone in the stuffy room knew that disturbances had been occurring for a couple of days prior to this date, but now city blocks were being set on fire. Stores were being looted and frequent shootings were occurring. White officers in the group nonchalantly glanced at the colored officers trying to determine if they were hostile or loyal to the police department. Some of the observations were just plain curiosity. The room had the aura of fear and mistrust.

As the captain spoke, Cy leaned over to Jacob, "How will the Negro officers hold up if and when they are confronted by their own?"

Jacob looked at Cy, scrutinizing his facial expressions. "The new and correct term is Afro-American, not colored, and they'll do just fine. I'm sure some may feel suppression or have families involved, but the job comes first." He glanced hard at Cy. "Are you worried about me?"

"Not on your life." Cy smiled, putting his arm across Jacob's back and hooking his fingers over his shoulder. Jacob smiled and looked away. He couldn't stop the pleasure showing in his eyes.

Captain Morris told the officers present in the room they would be going on eighteen-hour shifts but shortened to twelve hours whenever possible. The command post was being set up at the Coliseum on U.S.C. campus. The L.A. Sheriff's Department was providing twenty-five buses from the L.A. County main jail for transporting all sworn personnel to the north end of Watts because entry from the south was not possible. The L.A. sheriffs, C.H.P., city police, and National Guard would complement each other and provide support once the operation began.

The main body of law enforcement personnel was assigned to clear the streets of people causing disturbances and curious onlookers. The National Guard's responsibility would be to maintain secured intersections leading out of Watts to the north. Each section sergeant had been briefed by his division commander. The theory of operation was to start from approximately 106th North and proceed south until orders were given to set up the first outer perimeter. All people were to be ordered off the street, and if they refused to leave they would be arrested with no exceptions. This would be one of the more difficult tasks but necessary to maintain safety for the citizens, to restore peace, and especially to determine who was hostile. Transportation teams had been organized and would remove prisoners to a processing area. After shifts were finished and officers relieved from their post, those who made arrests would follow up with the proper arrest reports and documentation for prosecution.

After another half hour of briefing by the watch commander, each sergeant discussed duty assignments with his subordinates. Jacob and Cy were transported along with other officers to the Coliseum on the west side of Harbor Freeway at the Olympic offramp.

When they arrived, Cy and Jacob were amazed at the hundreds of uniformed officers from the different law enforcement agencies. Cy was nervous and Jacob told him to settle down. The problem they were facing now was the possibility of being separated when duty assignments were given out. Jacob didn't want to take that chance, so he left Cy at the rear of a column of officers and went over to one of the sergeants who was writing information down in his field notepad. They spoke a few minutes and Jacob returned, grinning at his partner.

"Come over here," Jacob said, keeping his voice low. He took hold of Cy's arm, leading him away from the other officers so they could talk privately. "Things aren't good, but you and I are staying together no matter what. You got that?" He looked squarely at Cy, making sure he had his attention. "If anyone gives you an order to follow him or wants to put you on another bus other than number 34, you act like you didn't hear them and keep walking."

Jacob and Cy were bumped forward and backward by other officers who were milling around, confused, and trying to find their assigned supervisors and buses. Others wanted to find buddy officers they knew and trusted if things in Watts went from bad to worse. Jacob spoke closely into Cy's ear. "If they stop you, you tell them you have been assigned to Sergeant Mecham's outer perimeter security team and keep heading to bus 34. I'll be right behind you. What you don't know is in situations like this, orders get mixed up. You could end up in the middle of a combat zone shooting it out with guys you know nothing about. We stay together. Right?"

Cy looked at Jacob, reflecting his nervousness. "I don't like this, Jacob. Racial rioting can be a bad deal for everyone."

"That's right, for everyone," Jacob said strongly. "There's a lot of innocent people caught up in this thing. That's going to be the tough part. We have to treat everyone the same. Watts is an older community of middle-class people and is normally a quiet residential area. Many people are going to be curious to see what is going on. We are going to have to treat them like they are the bad guys to get them back in their houses and to stay off the street. Most of the people haven't done anything wrong, and they are not going to like being told what to do." Jacob looked uneasy and was almost sorry that he was a police officer. "Cy, we ain't going to win with this one. We are going to be like the SS troops going down the streets arresting those people who won't cooperate. Many of those people are good folks. They're going to be victims of this thing."

Someone began yelling roll call on a hand-held loud-speaker. The police lined up at their assigned positions and sounded off when their names were called.

Sergeant Mecham came over to Jacob and Cy. Sweat made his face shiny, and he didn't have the normal controlled appearance that he usually displayed back at Central. "Okay, Jacob, you two get on bus 34. That bus will have twenty cadets from the L.A. County Sheriff's Academy. I've got to find someone else to fill the empty seats. You'll be getting off near 108th. At 108th you and four cadets with two other veteran officers will proceed south clearing the streets. Keep your portables on channel two and stay off channel one except for emergencies. Jackson and Riley's team will be transport vehi-cles for your assigned street to move prisoners. Their call signs will remain the same."

Sergeant Mecham handed white nylon flex cuffs to the men in his column. Jacob and Cy took the strips of nylon and tucked them inside their shirts. "The National Guard detach-ment will secure each intersection after you have cleared it. Here's the name of your contact guard supervisor."

The sergeant handed Jacob a piece of paper while he looked around at the other troops, letting his gaze come back to Jacob. "There's no telling what those National Guardsmen will do in a combat situation. You clear those intersections with a minimum of force. I don't want the Guard to start shooting up the city. We don't know what training they've had, and I don't want them losing control of their people. This is going to be hard on those boys because they have the fire-power and they most likely have not been trained for this type of detail. If any one Guard group has a loose cannon among them, they'll start a firefight for sure. So you got to keep control of the streets with no shooting unless you are fired on and with the least amount of force possible."

"Gees almighty, Sarge, those National Guard guys could send us to hell in a hand basket," Jacob sneered.

"Tell me about it. You boys just do your job and we'll get through this thing." Sergeant Mecham failed to sound convincing and knew it. "Go on," he said, shoving them toward the sheriff's bus. "Get going or you'll get a worse assignment."

Neither Jacob nor Cy felt like arguing. They turned toward the row of buses and the hundreds of law enforcement men queuing up in long lines and others walking in different directions in a confused state.

Buses were now starting up their engines and the diesel smell gave a noxious stench to the air. It was especially nauseating with the heat and the heavy concentration of smog.

Jacob and Cy hurried to their bus located near the end of the long line. "Come on," Jacob motioned to Cy. "We got to get on fast to get up front. We want a front seat in case we got to bail out in a hurry. We don't want to get boxed in at the back." He smiled sheepishly at Cy, "Besides, I don't...I do not...I hate the back of buses. You know what I mean?" Jacob gave Cy a big grin.

"Know what you mean," Cy said, grimly hurrying toward the bus. Visible exhaust fumes rose into the night air. The bus, the ground, and everything seemed to vibrate with the movement of the engines of the many buses in operation.

Sheriff's cadets were already finding seats on the bus, looking as if the world was about to end. They did have the "strack" or sharp look of rookies right out of the academy, but Cy imagined they could hold their own if necessary. The L.A. County Sheriff's Academy, along with the Los Angeles Police Academy, had the reputation across the United States as the most physically demanding training course of all the police courses available. Jacob found a seat on the fifth row, and Cy took a seat in front of him on the fourth. Most of the deputies sat alone next to a window, except for a few of the young deputies who wanted to stay with their friends.

Two smothering hours later the buses still hadn't moved and everyone was restless and tired. It was miserably hot and sticky on the bus, and all the windows had been pulled down to circulate the air. There were no portable toilets, so the men had to relieve themselves out on the pavement because they were not permitted to leave the immediate area. They were only allowed to leave the bus to urinate. The air held a strong sour stench that was not easy on the stomach.

Coming out of the night and sounding above the loud commotion outside was the sudden roar of motorcycles. They pulled off a few feet from the bus, approximately thirty motorcycle cops lined up with their black and white Harleys in a straight row.

"This is not good," Jacob exclaimed, his eyes wide. "This is bad. This is going to be hell, and we are going to get killed."

"What are you talking about? What's the matter?" Cy cocked his head inquisitively at his partner.

Jacob pointed to the line of Harleys. "That's T.E.D."

"Traffic Enforcement Division?" Cy asked. He was feeling a little more uncomfortable as he watched his partner begin to fall apart in front of him.

"Yeah, you fool! The Luftwaffe!" Jacob choked on the name.

Cy squinted and looked closer at the new arrivals. "What do you mean, the Loftwaffle or whatever?" He felt apprehension seeing the L.A. Motorcycle Patrol for the first time. He had heard about the motor cops but only had seen them from a distance. He had never spoken or dealt with an officer assigned to T.E.D.

"It's the gestapo of the L.A.P.D.! This ain't good at all. They're going to get on our bus. Gees almighty, we are going to get killed." Jacob usually displayed confidence as a police officer. Now he looked out of place and he wanted out of there. His eyes were opened wide as he searched the outside scene through the stained bus window.

Cy leaned out of the grimy window for a better look. Each Harley-Davidson was perfectly waxed and polished to a high sheen. Some of the men had even spit-shined their leather saddlebags. That was the first clue that just maybe some of these cops were fanatics.

They all wore black spit-shined leather leggings to the knee and baggy riding pants. Most outstanding were the shiny black and white helmets which reminded Cy of the Penn State football team. The six-inch .357 magnums attached to their gun belts really looked like nine-inch hog legs, giving the impression of miniature cannons. The majority of officers wore mustaches mainly of the handlebar style and waxed at the tip.

By now the cadets who had been seated on the far side of the bus were standing in the aisle and peering over the heads of their fellow deputies. It was now somber on the bus and no one was talking. They were only amazed at the intimidating sight before them. They were all policemen, yet this new group of officers seemed entirely different from them. They were the old salts and the other officers felt inferior. No one could claim police experiences like the motorcycle cops because they had been around for years and knew the street people like no other, except for beat cops.

Before anyone realized it, a tall motorcyclist jumped up the stairs in one leap and stared down the aisle. He hucked a large pool of tobacco juice on the floor hitting the shoe of one of the cadets. It made a spatting sound and everyone was quiet and glad they were not sitting in the first row. "Make a hole, you buttholes." Instantly everyone sat down and watched as a group of hardened and ill-tempered cops got on the bus. It appeared everyone was over six feet and, more likely than not, shaved with their boot knives.

Cy turned his attention to the front as each officer pounded his heavy boots on the floor of the bus as he walked toward the back. It was overwhelming to Cy, who was so new to the force. The Los Angeles City Police enjoyed being rated the No. 1 police department in the United States. Yet these men seemed anything but courteous and professional law enforcement officers. They resembled thugs and initiators of brute force. Cy tried to convince himself that they were fellow officers, but there was a definite separation of the motorcycle crew and any other division on the department, including other police agencies.

They were an enormous contrast to the deputies on the bus with their tailored shirts, well-groomed haircuts, aftershave cologne, and polished brass. The motorcycle officers had beer bellies and flat saggy butts and smelled strongly of sweat and tobacco. The glaring eyes and unfriendly stares convinced everyone that they were not a crew to be trifled with—no wonder they enjoyed the reputation for being the most desired division for police backup in hostile incidents.

A huge rough-looking sergeant planted himself next to Cy, sneering at him. He finally looked around to make sure everyone was seated. The bus started to move, eventually falling in with the column of buses.

The sergeant coughed and hacked a large wad of yellow bubbly spit on the floor. His cheeks bulged into small balloons, then he belched and grumbled his first words, glaring at the younger officers. "Nobody farts on this bus." He swung his attention back to Cy. "If anyone, I mean anyone, belches from his butt, his balls get cracked."

Out of nowhere a black leather sap appeared in his right hand and he slammed it down hard on the back of the seat in front of him, causing a loud cracking sound and barely missing the deputy next to the window. The deputy jerked his head around wide-eyed, not attempting to hide his fear.

Jacob frowned as he stood up. Turning his head slowly, he gave a sweeping glance at the others on the bus; however, he was careful to avoid eye contact with any of the motorcyclists. "Yeah, you got that, deputy dawgs?"

Sergeant Silva spun around, looking hard at Jacob. "Shut up, scrot." He slapped the baton in the palm of his left hand, threatening Jacob.

Jacob's eyes enlarged, displaying the white around his pupils. "Hey man, you got it." Jacob hated himself for opening his mouth. He had hoped because he was on the same department, leniency would be graciously extended. He knew without a doubt these maniacs were completely crazy and could be dangerous without cause.

Force and terrorizing is what the motorcycle crews lived by. They had to be mentally unstable to ride the motorcycles in and out of traffic and to conduct high-speed chases with them. Jacob had to admit to himself, though, that there was nothing prettier to watch than two motorcycle cops side by side traveling down a street swerving in sequence with perfect timing and motion in and out of traffic. Because of the expert cycle mobility of the two officers, they appeared to be as one traveling down the streets—their maneuvers were movements of rhythm and art.

One of the motorcycle officers near the rear of the bus turned on a small portable radio and tuned it to a country western station. He looked up waiting for a challenge. When he didn't receive one, he turned up the volume, sat back, and listened to Merle Haggard.

The seats were now filled and the aisles were loaded with standing motorcycle cops. The last officer getting on the bus appeared to have been in every bar fight in Highland Park. Underneath thick eyebrows his face was scarred, and his upper lip supported a large handlebar mustache. He lifted his head upward and sniffed the air. Officer Warenzki took two steps up the aisle. A long tangle of black bushy nostril hairs could be seen by the deputies who sat close enough to him. "If anything goes down while we are here on this bus, don't any of you scrotums get in our way. We'll take care of it." He hesitated and there was no response. "You got it?" He hesitated, glaring at the deputies. "I can't hear you!"

There were a few murmurs of understanding but no one dared to challenge him. Warenzki stomped over to a deputy who had failed to answer. The deputy stared at the motorcycle cop, bewildered by his rudeness. "Are you still in the academy, deputy?" he spit.

"No, I've been out for six months and assigned to the main jail," the deputy answered proudly.

"You're just a jailer then, huh?"

"That's right, I'm a jailer for now," the deputy looked at him defiantly.

"What you are, is a turd." Warenzki then poked the deputy hard on the chest with his forefinger, shoving him backward.

"I'm a cop just like you." The other officers on the bus were all quiet, carefully observing the interaction at the front.

Warenzki wrinkled his nose, sniffed the air, and squinted his eyes to confirm a bad odor. "You smell like a turd. You look like a turd." He pinched the deputy roughly on the side of his cheek. "You feel like a turd, so...you must be a turd." Warenzki and his comrades all laughed aloud, hacking and coughing and slapping each other jovially.

Cy decided he had had enough. He flexed his thigh muscles to stand and address Warenzki.

Sergeant Silva stood up and told everyone to quiet down. "Listen up, all you rookies. What my partner is telling you is, if and when it hits the fan, don't get in our way. We don't want any of you to get hurt. Inside this can, it's too close of quarters, and it's too dangerous if we all move in different directions. Once we are off the bus, you're on your own to get to your assigned areas, but on this bus we take the lead."

No one wanted to argue. If they could get to their assignment without incident, it might be a good day; Cy had to admit to himself that he would rather have the motorcycle cops on his side than against him.

❧

The convoy of buses left the Coliseum and headed south on Harbor Freeway. It was the first time Cy had observed the freeway without bumper to bumper vehicles, and it gave him an eerie feeling. The wait wasn't long before he could see flickering fires in the distance. Sporadic conversations between the men working on strategies and letting their imaginations loose filled the air with tension on the rocking bus as it traveled in line with the fleet.

Suddenly the real world engulfed them. Fires were on each side of the freeway and they appeared to extend all the way to Long Beach. It reminded Cy a little of the animated world of Disneyland. He thought of the miniature rockets that Disney portrayed with the fire blowing out and black smoke swirling in the air and disappearing into the darkness. At first it almost felt like his mind was playing tricks on him and his thoughts were out of control. Next the smoke and stench of the fires burned his nostrils, pulling him back to reality. This was no Disneyland.

"Hell, it looks like Viet Nam out there," someone yelled.

Jacob leaned forward on the edge of his bench seat and grabbed Cy by the shoulder. "When we get stopped, wait for me. It'll be real easy to get separated."

"I'll follow you out," Cy assured him. Cy let his gaze go back to the fire and destruction. He was astounded at the flashing blazes of fires and smoke. It was an enemy war zone. Disoriented people appeared to be running everywhere. People were hurrying in all directions without a purpose in mind except survival.

Cy could see Watts, south central of Los Angeles, on the east side of the freeway in the distance. It didn't look good; his stomach was unsettled. He would have preferred to be anywhere but here. The bus turned off the freeway and went left under the overpass. At the second major intersection the bus turned left again and headed north on Central Avenue.

For the first time he could observe what really was happening. Thousands of people were crisscrossing back and forth over Central Avenue carrying things in their arms and over their heads. Two black men had a couch balanced on their heads, supported with light pillows. Two giggly little girls were playing on the cushions as if this were all a new and wonderful game. The two men carried the couch across the street after they stopped for the buses passing by them. When Cy's bus passed, one of them laughed at Cy and yelled, "Hey, Bro." Cy could see his white teeth flashing a big smile.

Cy turned around in his seat and glanced at Jacob who was giving his full attention to the excitement on the streets. "Jacob, old buddy, if anything happens to you, can I have Elvira?"

Jacob looked at Cy, who displayed a weak grin. "You know my wife would never let her go to some white folk. We may be about to die. Now you tell me the truth. Do you really want my wife or just my daughter?"

Cy tried to laugh in the heat of fear. "Just wanted to give you something to think about." He swung back around in his seat and peered out the window. The drama was that of a futuristic other world. It was developing into a nightmare. Cy felt like he couldn't pull himself out of it. The hair stood up on his neck and his skin crawled down his back. A little black boy sat by an overturned trash can crying. Cy wished he could get off the bus and comfort him.

The bus bumped along and over debris scattered in the street. Outside the bus, direction unknown, was a sound like a pop. From inside the bus there was a panicked cry, "They're shooting at us!"

It never crossed Cy's mind to pull out his revolver. Immediately every one of the motorcycle cops had their guns out, and they began firing their weapons rapidly out the open windows.

Most of the seated deputies were neutralized. Before they had the chance to react, .357 muzzles blasted in their faces, blinding them and peppering their skin with powder burns. That was minor compared to the explosion in their eardrums. Some of the deputies were pinned down and couldn't move except to shut their eyes and try to cover their ears. There was absolute chaos throughout the bus. A few panic-stricken deputies managed to slide down under the seats. They hovered their heads just above the spit and grime on the floor and were grateful to be there.

Gun smoke filled the bus. Cy looked like a cartoon character with his fingers hooked tightly over the window rim of the bus, his mouth pressed to the edge with his nose poking over the top, and his eyes wide and dazed as he peered into the chaotic sight.

What Cy saw amazed him. At first he thought firecrackers were exploding on the curb and street. Then he determined it was bullet rounds hitting the asphalt and concrete, ricocheting like uncontrolled fireworks. People were running in different directions. All of a sudden one man did a back flip as if his legs were cut out from under him. A number of people who were racing across the street and down sidewalks actually had their feet knocked out in front of them and they fell on their backs or heads. Two teenagers jumped through a storefront window. Only one of the panes of glass was intact, and the youth hit it face first, stopping him like an invisible wall.

Cy figured at least thirty officers were rapid firing and reloading with their speed-loaders all at the same time. Within five seconds from the first barrage of shots, a person could not see across the bus because of the gunpowder smoke. His ears were ringing and he felt the saints were with him because he had the window to himself. It was a miracle for which he was grateful.

Shots came from each side of the bus as it sped up. Three people fell, and others were being dragged over bushes and broken-down fences by people who were complete strangers to them. Cy had no idea if the other buses were returning fire. He was experiencing tunnel vision and was only aware of the events in front of him. He was stunned and amazed that these policemen were shooting all these people in front of him. He did not see one person who looked threatening because everyone was running away and no one stood his ground in defiance. The firing lasted about twenty seconds.

The bus continued north on Central Avenue for several blocks then turned east. For the next few blocks the bus stopped at the intersections and several officers were ordered off the bus. National Guardsmen and other police were already at each intersection waiting for reinforcements and further police instructions.

At 108th Street, Cy, Jacob, and two other deputies scrambled off the bus into a crowd of National Guardsmen and other security personnel. Badly shaken, Cy turned to look at the bus expecting to see a perforation of bullet holes and extensive damage. Because his eyes burned from the gun smoke, the bus was a blur to him. When his vision cleared, he was stunned at what he didn't see. There was not one bullet hole in the side of the bus. People were wounded and for what reason? There was no evidence that the bus had been fired on. He felt sick to his stomach.

Other deputies were being removed from the bus to seek light medical aid. One deputy was taken away in a patrol unit because he suffered eye damage from a firearms blast inside the bus. Cy walked around the bus, inspecting it for any damage or dents. After circling the bus he stopped at a makeshift first aid station set up by a military team. Several deputies were receiving first aid to their faces. It was evident they had sustained powder tattooing of the cheeks and other facial areas. He knew he was lucky that he hadn't been injured in what appeared to be a misjudgment on returning fire by the motorcycle officers.

Jacob guided Cy over to a briefing in progress by the duty sergeant, Sgt. Kirkpatrick. The officers were ordered to proceed south on 108th, clearing the streets of everyone. Even homeowners in the residential areas were to be ordered inside until the curfew was lifted. There would be three teams, with two officers on each team. One team was to clear the streets on the left side and the other team on the right. The third team, two deputy sheriffs, were assigned to the center of the street. It was their responsibility to provide backup to either team that ran into trouble. A single patrol unit was assigned to follow from the rear for support and to provide transport of prisoners to a field holding area.

The National Guard would give support to the backup team and also leave detachments at each intersection once it had been cleared. If any officers encountered moving traffic, they were to turn the vehicles around and send them back south or allow the people to park their cars and walk back to their homes. No one was to be left to loiter on the streets. No vehicular traffic would be allowed to travel north into the outer perimeter in order to maintain safety to the officer's rear and to maintain a safe zone.

The basic plan was to develop a line north of the rioting and wedge violators into a centralized location for containment to the south, into the heart of the activity. Each clearance and containment team would be working from north to south and parallel to Central Avenue. This line of offensive action was several miles long, and each street team was to stop at each intersection until the other teams were cleared by radio traffic to proceed to the next crossing.

After another two hours of waiting, the final command was given for all lines of police to be in position for the push to begin. Cy and Jacob were assigned to the right side of the street on 108th. Since this was away from the main rioting, cooperation from the residents was received gratefully. The night was still warm, and off in the distance to the south Cy could see the flickering of fires and shadows of smoke billowing into the dark night. It was especially hot in riot helmets and flack vests. Each officer carried his nightstick and was armed with a Remington twelve-gauge pump shotgun.

After the first seven blocks were cleared by pushing people back into their houses, the next few residential people were more vocal in their disapproval of the police and of being told what to do on their own property. Most of the people were supportive of the police restoring peace to their streets; however, opposition grew as they proceeded closer to the rioting. On several occasions citizens who refused to clear the street were arrested and transported to the designated holding area for processing.

Jacob noticed a car ahead of their position as they cleared the street. Parked on the sidewalk facing toward them with the engine running was a beat-up white over yellow hardtop 1955 Chevy cut low to the ground. The window appeared dark inside as if something was obstructing the view. Jacob nudged Cy and continued to approach it cautiously.

When the two officers stepped closer to the vehicle, Jacob moved out further into the street while Cy walked along the sidewalk moving slowly to the car. Just as Cy turned on his flashlight, the passenger door flew open when the light hit the front windshield and a skinny black woman got out, screamed, and ran down the street away from them.

Cy tightened his grip on his shotgun with his right hand while holding the flashlight with his left. He expected someone else to jump from the car and start shooting. Jacob stepped further out into the street and squinted to clear his vision as he looked for the driver. He expected either an angry or frightened person to jump from the car who could be very dangerous.

"Hold it, Cy." Jacob stopped and listened carefully. He glanced over at Cy to make sure he wasn't moving forward. Cy had stepped further to the right and was near some bushes, partially concealing himself but still giving strict attention to the vehicle. The other people along the streets had backed into their homes and were now looking out the windows.

Jacob called over to the center team and the two deputies came over to him. After Jacob told them what he had, the two deputies spread out to cover the two city officers. Jacob moved left until he was standing about fifty feet from the passenger side of the suspect vehicle. Cy had moved forward and was nearing the front of the car on the right.

In the background and further south on 108th, the people anticipating the approaching police and National Guard troops could be heard yelling and shouting. Cy slipped the safety off his shotgun and stepped closer for a better view. Jacob was also proceeding forward in a crouch-like walk.

Cy moved up and Jacob continued forward slowly, careful not to take his eyes off the car while trying to distinguish its contents. The windows were blocked with some kind of material. Suddenly Cy stepped forward and thrust his flashlight into the car. The driver had disappeared, and the floorboard was full of empty beer cans, cigarette butts, and a bundle of rags.

The other two deputies came forward, and one of them stood watching the street and housing area while Cy and Jacob looked inside the car. They checked the back seat and were amazed at the amount of packaged food. The rear seat was stacked to the ceiling with deli foods—large chunks of turkey, ham, pastrami, and other meats wrapped in paper and cheeses of all sorts.

The assisting deputy reached in from the driver's side, turned the key to off, and removed it. He walked around to the rear of the car and opened the trunk, finding it filled with fresh and frozen steaks, roasts, hams, and hot dogs.

From nowhere a small, thin black girl about ten years old pushed by Jacob. She reached in and pulled a bundle of rags off the floor and was out of the car before anyone could blink. Jacob was amazed the little girl could move so fast and wondered where she had been hiding. Jacob reached forward and caught her by the dress, stopping her. She didn't scream or complain but continuously fought for release. Cy came around and held her arm while Jacob looked inside the bundle. To their surprise, inside the wrinkled rags was a sleeping baby, about two months old, wrapped in a dirty pink baby blanket.

"Let her go," Jacob said, sadly shaking his head. "That solves the problem of what to do with a baby, which we don't need right now. We'll find the owner of the vehicle by the registration." Jacob took his portable radio off his left hip and called for a wrecker.

Cy released the fighting girl. "The owner will only say the car was stolen," he said, watching her disappear up the street and around the corner.

Looking inside the car with his back to Cy, Jacob continued talking. "True, but who cares. We just solved this baby problem and the parents can at least be questioned later. I'm just wondering how much meat will spoil and how much will be stolen before inventory." He shook his head. "Doesn't matter either. We got other problems to worry about now. It just amazes me how a mother could abandon her child for fear of being arrested, and then that little girl coming after her sister the way she had." Jacob smiled and they made a few notes of the incident and started forward again.

The next encounter was one and a half blocks south. A middle-aged black man was standing on his porch watching the police advance down the street in front of his residence. He moved slowly from the porch to the front lawn and sat on a metal bucket turned upside down. He lit a cigarette and blew out the smoke in a long release of air, appearing completely relaxed. Cy watched him as they approached his home. Cy could see no weapons, and it puzzled him that this man watched them so quietly.

Cy cleared his throat and said, "Sir, would you please go back inside?" The black man did not respond, nor did he look at the officer addressing him. Instead he took another long draw of his smoke and exhaled slowly, watching it disappear into the grass. He now had his head bent downward.

Cy spoke louder and more sternly. "Sir, would you please go back inside? No one is allowed outside his home after dark until this is over."

Again there was no response.

Jacob could see trouble and stepped in front of Cy, hoping he could get the man to obey him. "Sir, would you please go back inside your home. We cannot go forward until all people are inside and do not pose a threat to the officers on the street." Jacob observed the man carefully, wondering what his problem was.

The man did not look up at the officers and continued smoking his cigarette, studying it all the more carefully. Finally he removed it from his lips. He spit a piece of tobacco on the ground and stared at the grass while he spoke to the black officer. "This is my house. This is my land. I'll sit where I want to sit. I'll stand where I want to stand."

Even as the man spoke, deeply and slowly, Cy had a feeling there was going to be trouble. It was not the kind of trouble he felt he could handle. The man was right. This was his home and now the police were telling him what to do within the confines of his own property. It was not a comfortable position.

Cy swallowed hard, opened the gate to the white picket fence, and stepped over to the sitting man who still had not looked at the officers. The two deputies at the center of the street also walked over and stood next to Jacob who was carefully analyzing the subject.

"This is the last time I'm asking you, sir. I want you to get up, turn around, and go inside your house." Cy was frustrated but knew he had to make a stand. He stared down at the man as he took another long draw on the cigarette.

Cy was angry at the man—angry at the rioters, angry at being a police officer; knowing time was of the essence, he had no choice. Cy turned around and handed Jacob his shotgun, removed his baton, and with both hands thrust the point into the pit of the man's stomach just below his sternum. The man fell backwards but immediately got back up and sat on the bucket without making eye contact. He did not hold his stomach and did not react to the pain.

"I am fifty years old. I work. I am on my property. I will not be told what to do on my land. I am not on the street. There I am fair game. Here is where I sit, and I will sit as long as I want."

Cy looked up at the tiny ghetto house. It was neat and clean, and the man's wife was staring out the window holding the lace curtain back with one hand, which even at a distance he could see was shaking.

Jacob stepped over to the man's left side and hit him on the shoulder with the butt of the shotgun. "Lordy sakes, man, get back in your house."

The man sat there, not saying anything. One of the deputies moved around to the side of the sitting man and hit him twice on the knees with his nightstick. Each time the man fell he would get back up and sit on the bucket. It was hot and beads of sweat ran down his forehead and his face now showed pain. It was peculiar that he did not respond physically. He was giving a message to these policemen, and it especially hurt Jacob, who respected him but couldn't condone his response.

The police had to show who was in control or everyone would defy them and more backup would be needed. A small incident like this could escalate into another full-blown riot if the neighborhood interfered, and that is what Jacob now anticipated. The black man was a very proud fellow. There was no way they could force him into his house and make him stay put.

Jacob arrested the man and had a transport unit pick him up in a matter of minutes; the march south then resumed. It was an unfortunate incident but nothing could be done, and Jacob and Cy both felt depressed. For the first time Cy was discouraged with his job in law enforcement.

Several more blocks south, the National Guard set up a break station on the southeast corner of the intersection. It was 0300 hours and everyone was tired. Cy sat on a curb and Jacob was over talking to some other officers that he knew. A tall National Guardsman came over to Cy and stood there a moment in front of him, just looking down at Cy. Cy looked up at him and wrinkled his forehead. "What?"

"I'm more scared here than I was in Viet Nam," the guardsman said as a matter of fact. He looked around at the milling police and then pointed toward the fires that by now had moved closer. "I feel more vulnerable here than I did over there. I was stationed with Negroes and they were part of us. Here, these are our people, but now they are the enemy, and I'm not sure who is friendly and who isn't. I know that all the colored folks don't participate in the riot and law violations, but when they're close by and just standing around, you don't know if they are friends or enemies with a gun under their shirts, ready to blow your guts out."

The guardsman twisted his head around, cracking his neck and looking uncomfortable in the steel helmet. He had not worn one, especially for long periods, since his tour of duty in Viet Nam. He pointed to the fires that were behind him, thumbing toward them over his shoulder as he looked down at the police officer. "That's a damn hot zone down there. Who the hell wants to shoot Americans? Good Lord, I would have never made it in the Civil War, brother against brother, and I can't stand it here. I've never been scared so much in my life."

"You're not alone, buddy. We're all scared." Cy grunted tiredly.

"What I don't get is how you guys do this every night. I don't know how you can be a cop every day by choice. You drive around in one of those black and white patrol cars with a bubble gum light on top. You're just a sitting target at a shooting gallery." The guardsman wrinkled his forehead, shaking his head negatively. He lit a cigarette and took a deep breath.

The sound of a racing engine from a speeding car could be heard coming from the south out of the riot area. It drew everyone's attention to the intersection. Cy stood up and looked down the street. He could see a dark colored vehicle about three blocks away, traveling north on their street, headed directly toward their intersection.

Instantly the city police, deputies, and guardsmen scrambled for cover behind parked cars. Cy crouched down and then stood to look over the top of a 1954 Ford hardtop at the men who readied themselves for a firefight. He estimated a minimum of forty shotguns and M-1 carbines trained at the oncoming vehicle as it sped toward them. Cy felt apprehensive at the thought of firing his weapon for the first time at a human being. He only knew the car posed a threat. Deadly force was the positive action to neutralize imminent danger.

Sergeant Kirkpatrick came up from the rear. He had been following the officers, overseeing their actions, and assisting them in making decisions. He was across the street from Cy and Jacob and yelled loudly for everyone to wait for his command to fire. Everyone was tensely ready. The car was gaining speed and racing with a bounce as it traveled on the rough surface. Officers were releasing the safeties on their weapons and training their sights on the approaching car.

The four black men in the speeding car were laughing carelessly. They had busted through a small blockade that residents had erected for their own protection. The three passengers had rifles and were positioning themselves for action as they approached an intersection which appeared to have more blockades. The stolen liquor in the trunk and on the floorboards was worth at least two thousand dollars.

The driver, Tim Wilson, was a meter reader in San Pedro who hated his job and his nagging wife. This was the most exciting adventure he had ever experienced. He was with his best friends and the city was theirs.

As he bounced across the last intersection, he focused on numerous shiny spots around the cars and in the street ahead. His eyes widened and his chest constricted with uncontrollable fear. He screamed and jammed his foot on the brake. He saw hundreds of cops in rank and file and in shiny helmets, and they all had guns pointed right at him. "Holy sweet mama! We're gonna die!" he screamed.

The car came to a screeching halt with all four wheels locked, smoking and laying burned rubber on the street. One of the passengers sitting behind Wilson slapped him alongside the head with the back of his left hand. "Get us out of here, fool!"

Cy lightened the pressure of his trigger finger as he watched the car spin its tires and turn right and disappear around the corner as it headed east with the four screaming passengers. Cy smiled, thinking about the terrified people in the car. He never saw the car again.

The next two weeks Cy and Jacob were assigned to Watts. Over 220 people were killed and in the morgue; however, not that many persons were reported dead. Many of them were people who had been wounded but did not receive medical treatment. Some had crawled off into alleyways and under bushes where they died from their injuries. Other seriously injured people died because friends and relatives were afraid to ask for help for fear of being prosecuted for being involved in the riots. Some families went to the extreme and removed all identification from dead family members and dumped them on a lawn or in an alley where they would be found, buried by the city or county, and hopefully never identified.

When the Watts riot was over, Cy was relieved and felt a closeness to his partner.

Chapter 4
Central Division, Area 1, 1968

Jacob walked out of the station after roll call. It was a pleasant March morning, and he took his time going over to the fleet of patrol cars to wait for Cy. He was excited, knowing he had made sergeant after nine years of testing and retesting for the competitive supervisory position on the department. Sergeant—what a beautiful word. It was the most coveted rank among P2 officers. It meant years of hard work, and now he had the new responsibility of a watch of his own—and not just being a corporal in charge of a shift when the sergeant was off duty.

The downside to his promotion was losing his partner. He cared for Cy like a brother. He knew Cy loved him and his family, especially his children. Cy spent a lot of time with the kids, and they all enjoyed family outings together.

There was no question in Jacob's mind that Cy was the best partner he had ever had. He was an intelligent person who cared for the people, especially his fellow officers. Most of all, Jacob was proud of Cy because he could see through a person's color. He never showed bias in making arrests or in his interrogations of possible suspects in criminal activities. It was hard to keep his emotions reined when he thought about Cy as his backup in dangerous situations. There was no doubt in his mind that his partner would give his life for him in a heartbeat.

He thought of the time when his wife was having their fourth child—Cy waited with him at the hospital. Cy showed his concern when the children were sick, and he helped out by babysitting.

A glassy film of emotion showed in his eyes, as he felt the joy in making the rank he always wanted. The bad part was losing his dearest friend and partner. They would not be able to ride together except on special occasions. Worse, the sergeant he was replacing had been his and Cy's duty sergeant and Cy may resent him now being his supervisor. If he ever had to discipline Cy, what would happen to their friendship? He knew their closeness would change. It surprised him when he felt a jealousy, thinking of Cy being assigned a new partner.

What concerned him now was wondering how Cy was

going to take the news. Cy was a level-headed officer who made wise decisions. A slamming door brought Jacob out of his reverie. He looked up to see Cy swinging his baton in one hand and carrying his shotgun in the other.

Cy smiled momentarily as he approached Jacob. Then he grew placid. He walked over to the police car, fixed the shotgun in the electra-lock and dropped his baton on the front seat. Then he backed out and shut the car door. He didn't like the look on Jacob's face. Jacob was not an artist when it came to hiding his feelings, especially the bad ones. "So what's wrong with you?" Cy tried smiling.

Jacob didn't answer. He attempted to speak but his mouth couldn't form the words. His throat tightened and he hated himself for it. He could feel tears coming to his eyes and he felt embarrassed.

"Good grief, Jacob, is Lila okay?" Cy asked, touching Jacob's shoulder.

Jacob was moved by Cy's genuine concern and took strength from it. "I'm sorry, Cy. No, it's not Lila."

"Oh, Jacob, is it one of the kids?"

"No..." Jacob was too slow in answering.

"Has something happened to one of the kids?"

"No."

"Oh no, your father died, didn't he?"

"Will you shut up and let me talk," Jacob gasped. "I've got something serious here and I'm trying to tell you."

"Am I being transferred?"

"No, I..."

"Jake, you can talk to me," Cy said, seriously taking hold of Jacob by the shoulders with both hands.

"If you don't be quiet I'm going to knock your fool head off."

"Okay. Okay, spit it out. Talk to me."

Jacob raised his index finger in Cy's face. Tears were readily filling Jacob's eyes and spilling over on his cheek. Cy thought he was going to be sick with grief.

"I made sergeant," Jacob finally spit out.

"What?"

"I made sergeant," Jacob said again.

"No one died?" Cy smiled.

"No, no one died."

"You made sergeant!"

"That's what I'm trying to tell you," Jacob said, wiping his face.

"That's wonderful. You waited so long for this," Cy laughed, giving Jacob a bear hug and enjoying a moment of relief. "Oh man, this is fantastic."

"You really mean it, pard?"

"You bet I mean it," Cy laughed, now wiping tears away from his own cheeks. "I love you, buddy. You'll make a great sergeant."

"You don't mind me making sergeant?"

"No, that's good."

"Then you don't mind me being your supervisor and performing your evaluation reports?"

"That's bad," Cy said, releasing Jacob.

"Then you don't want me as your watch sergeant?" Jacob frowned.

"No, no. That's great."

"Then you don't mind getting a new partner?"

"That's bad," Cy said, realizing now they would have to split up. "This is awful, Jake, you snake. I can't have another partner. You're it. There is no one else."

Jacob was glad to hear this. He grabbed Cy and gave him a hard hug. Four other officers walking out the station door saw Jacob and Cy. No one said a word. Everyone knew how close they were, as it was with most teams. The officers continued on, not looking at the two men. It was an awful and wonderful moment and the beginning of a good day.

"I hope I'm not interfering in something private here, boys," Michael Fin said, as he came up on the two men, drawing hard on a cigarette. He wasn't smiling and he wasn't sure if he should have said anything at that particular moment after he realized he broke up a serious conversation. Then again he didn't really care what they thought.

"So what do you want?" Jacob said, perturbed. He didn't like it when officers talked with a smoke in their mouth.

"So one of you guys is my partner and I'm not sure which one," Michael said, grooming the side of his head with his hand. He was tall and fair looking with a thick head of wavy brown hair. It was apparent he thought a lot of himself. "The captain said the ugly one standing next to this unit was my new partner. Both of you are standing next to this unit, and you are both ugly. So, I'm not sure which one of you I'll be riding with."

Cy had heard about Michael Fin. It was said he was arrogant and self-centered. Now he was sure of it and was disappointed. He wondered what kind of field officer Fin would make. He was told Fin came from the Hollywood Division. He transferred because he did not like working with the rich and famous. He also received several complaints from the citizens in the Hollywood area for being too hard of a cop. He obviously wasn't lenient enough for their taste in the rich community where some felt "artists" should have special privileges.

"Which one do you want to ride with, Officer Fin?" Jacob responded.

"It's your choice. I couldn't care less," Fin answered. "I see no color here, if that's what you're talking about. Blue is blue."

"This is Cy Golden. He's your new partner," Jacob said. "I'm your new sergeant starting tomorrow. Today you'll be riding with the best man in Central. If you can't cut it with him, you won't cut the division."

Fin reached out to shake Cy's hand. "I'm pleased to meet you, Cy. I've heard about you and I'm pleased to be your partner." He turned to Jacob. "Sergeant Wilson, I really didn't know which one of you was who. You both are still ugly. Nothing can be done about that, but I'm happy to have you for a sergeant and to be on your watch."

Jacob shook hands with Fin, perking up a little. "Cy will take you on patrol and show you all the reporting districts and then the ones in which you'll be working this week. I don't know anything about you, Michael, but you'll like working Central and the men on your watch. They're all good, solid men and stand their own ground."

"Sarge, I'm here by request. I'm not being shuttled around for disciplinary reasons. I didn't like some of the stiff-necked rich people in the Hollywood area. It was really hard to deal with people that wealthy because they thought we were their servants."

"We are their servants," Jacob said.

"There's a difference when they think they own you, Sarge. Because the wealthy pay more taxes, some feel that law enforcement should provide them with special treatment. I'm not into special treatment. There are a lot of good people there. I just needed a transfer. That's all."

"Good enough," Jacob smiled. "Cy, show him the ropes."

With the exception of Fin's chain smoking, Cy had a good shift showing his new partner around Central. They were assigned floater position for the watch, which gave them the opportunity to spend most of the shift going over reporting districts, cruising trouble areas, and giving backup to the patrol units. By the end of the shift, Cy decided he would hold back his first impression of Fin and give him a second look. He resented his new partner for replacing Jacob but knew it wasn't his fault.

Mid-day watch began at 1000 hours and finished at 1845. Many of the problems during this watch were traffic-related problems downtown. Thefts, burglaries, and assaults could happen anywhere in Central.

Officer Fin liked his new partner and felt refreshed with his new assignment in Central.

Cy lived in a rented apartment in north Pasadena on Glen Canyon Road near East Canyon Park. He liked this area because it was easy to catch the freeway to work. The heavy traffic into L.A. was mostly over by 0900 hours and he could be at work in thirty minutes easy.

The department did not expect the men to live in their assigned divisions, and Cy was happy with that decision. He needed his space. Being near the San Gabriel Mountains, he could enjoy jogging early in the morning after a rigorous physical workout. Three days a week he went to Azusa where he boarded his two horses and spent time grooming and exercising Cole and Colorado.

Michael Fin lived in Duarte behind the Log Inn Tavern off of Foothill Boulevard. With Jacob living in Glendora, all three men lived within a few miles of each other. They decided they would take turns commuting to work to save time and money. Each day Jacob would drive to Duarte and alternate with Fin in picking up Cy. The three would take turns driving to Los Angeles Central.

Both Cy and Jacob complained about Michael's smoking. He never had a cigarette out of his mouth except when talking to a citizen or other persons during police business. He had enough other good points, though, so Cy decided to try to tolerate his habit.

After the duty watch on Thursday, Cy went home, showered, changed clothes, and drove to Jacob's home. Lila stepped out the front door when she saw Cy drive up in his Ford pickup. She gave her little daughter a hug, "Now you be a good girl, Little Dickens, or Cy might stop taking you with him."

"Oh, Mama," Elvira said disgustedly. "I'll be good. I always am when I'm with Uncle Cy." She giggled and jumped off the top of the stairs in one leap and ran down the sidewalk to Cy's truck.

"Hi, Lila," Cy waved, standing on his side step looking over the top of his pickup. "We'll be back before dark."

"Okay," Lila waved back. It made her happy to see Elvira take up with Cy. It also made her wish Cy would meet someone and fall in love so he could start his own family and find real happiness in life. "You have fun, and Elvira, you watch those horses' hooves. One kick and you're in another state and we won't be able to find you."

"Okay, Mama!" Elvira waved cheerfully.

"I love you, hon, bye bye." Lila waved them off and went back into the house. Jacob came in the back door. He had been mowing the back lawn.

Lila went to him and put her arms around his sweaty neck. "I love that guy. I miss Tony, but Cy is a real trip. He's so down to earth. I just love him."

"I kind of like him, too," Jacob said, kissing Lila lightly on the lips. "So Elvira is gone, huh? And the boys are still playing at the neighbors', huh?"

"Good heavens, man, you can read my mind," Lila laughed. Then she kissed him hard on the lips.

Cy took Elvira to the stables and brushed the horses down and cleaned the stalls out. After he put fresh straw in the stalls he led Cole out to the arena. With only a halter and lead rope, Cy reached down and put Elvira on the horse and then jumped up behind her. Elvira giggled when Cy guided the horse around the arena in circles and figure eights at a fast walk. Her laugh reached the bottom of Cy's heart. He wished he had his own daughter.

"Now, honey, grab a tight hold of Cole's mane. He can't feel it so it won't hurt him. You pull back tight and squeeze your legs around his belly and we'll take him up to a canter."

"Okay, Uncle Cy. Make him go faster now."

"Okay, here we go." Cy gave the horse a slight nudge with the heel of his boot and clicked his lips. Immediately Cole went into a lope. Cy floated naturally on the horse's back with his long legs gripping the sides. Elvira laughed and sang "Get along little dogies" as they worked the horse. Elvira's little voice, her smiles, and shiny eyes gripped Cy. He was completely captivated by the little angel in his arms. He gave her a quick kiss on the side of her forehead. He didn't notice the blonde at the end of the arena next to the horse stalls.

The woman had come out of the tack shed when she noticed the cowboy on the horse in the arena. Her first thought was that he sat a horse well. Second, she liked the way he looked. He was tall, slim, and handsome. Thirdly, and most important, the real attraction came when she noticed the young girl sitting in front of him. The closeness of the two and their laughter touched her.

Guy Cook, the stable owner, stopped beside Mary Ann as he was passing by. He noticed she was eyeing Cy Golden in the arena. "Wondering who he is?"

"Hi, Guy," Mary Ann glanced at the old man. Guy was a widower and like a second father to her. "Well, kinda. It's kind of unusual to see a white man with a little black girl. I was thinking they look cute together."

"Were you now," Guy smirked, spitting off to the side. "So are you wondering if the little girl is his daughter?"

"No, not really," Mary Ann replied. "But now that you have my curiosity up, is she?"

"Well, if you don't care, I shouldn't have brought it up." Guy spit again and started to walk away.

Mary Ann took him by the shirt collar and the old man wasn't going anywhere. "Is she or is she not?"

"Not."

"What is the relationship?"

"The little girl is his best friend's daughter. The daughter happens to love him and horses some, too."

"He certainly knows his horses."

"That he does."

"I also like the way he takes time with the little girl. Children need time with older people."

"That they do," Guy said. He turned and walked towards the feed shed. Mary Ann walked to her car and drove away.

❧

Friday was Cy's day off. In the morning he drove to the stables in Azusa. Cy often rode along Sierra Madre Avenue toward Glendora. The orange groves would soon be gone. A large nursery and numerous homes were being built in the area and would soon take away some of his favorite riding locations.

Bud, a local homeowner, lived along Sierra Madre Avenue across from the Azusa Police pistol range. Bud had horses and liked talking to Cy when he rode by. Cy enjoyed the orange groves and some of the undeveloped country to the west of Glendora. He would often see cross country runners from Citrus College and cantered his horse with them for short distances.

Cy strolled over to Cole's stall and gave him a good brushing, cleaned his feet, and checked his shoes. He threw a blanket and saddle on his back, tightened the cinches, and led him to a hitching rack. Off to the far end of the riding arena, Cy noticed a pretty sorrel quarter horse doing figure eights being ridden by a young blonde woman. It was the rider that really caught his attention. She appeared to be in her late twenties and her blonde hair was tied in a ponytail. It bobbed up and down on her shoulders as she worked her horse.

Cy looked closer, liking the way she handled her horse. She was a good rider besides having a pretty, slim figure with an exceptionally small waist. He decided he had to find out who she was and whether she was married.

Guy scraped his boots walking out of the tack room carrying a saddle, blanket, and bridle. He was a homely old coot and all man. Cy was close friends with him and often the two had long talks and would even ride together when he had extra help at the stables.

"Howdy, old poke," Cy smiled at the thin wrinkled man walking toward him.

"Howdy yourself, boy," Guy replied, dropping the saddle and gear at Cy's feet.

"It looks like business is picking up, Guy. There seems to be more people around than normal."

Guy looked around, ignoring the blonde in the arena. "Looks normal to me."

"It doesn't look normal to me," Cy said, trying to act nonchalant. "There are several people I haven't seen here before."

"Oh, yeah, is that right now? You have anyone on your

mind in particular?" Guy spit on the ground and wiped his mouth with the back of his hand.

"Well, no. I just see some people I haven't noticed before."

"Take it from me, son, there's no one new here." Guy started to pick up his gear.

"Now hold on there. Why are you in a big hurry?" Cy said, blocking Guy's path. "I've been trying to think if I've seen that rider before. She doesn't look familiar."

"Is that right," Guy said quickly. "Hey, Mary Ann, Mary Ann. Over here," Guy whistled and motioned to the blonde, getting her attention.

The girl reined in her horse and walked him over to the two men at the south end of the corral. As she got closer, Cy could feel his face redden and his body turn hot.

"Hi, Guy, you need the arena?" she asked with a wide smile revealing a pretty set of teeth.

"Oh, heck no. My good friend here was asking me questions about you. I decided he could talk to you directly." He grinned and pointed to Cy. "This here is Cy Golden. Cy, this here is Mary Ann Seltzer. Now I haven't time for palaver. You two can talk yourselves out." With that, Guy picked up his gear and walked toward the stables, chuckling to himself.

Mary Ann liked what she saw in the bashful man standing before her. Cy was tall, lean, and good looking. He had a rough exterior but she thought he would be warm inside. She remembered him from yesterday when she saw him with the little girl and felt excitement in their introduction. "Cy, I'm pleased to meet you," she smiled broadly, showing him a genuine friendliness.

Mary Ann was so pretty. Embarrassed by Guy's humor, he could hardly look at her. "Miss, I'm sorry, I..."

"You're sorry to make my acquaintance?" she asked.

"Oh no, ma'am," Cy quickly responded. He hated himself.

"Then what are you sorry about?"

"Well, I'm not sure," Cy stammered. He noticed she did not have a wedding ring on her finger. "I'm having trouble thinking on my feet here. I've been kind of caught short-handed." He quickly glanced at her and gave a weak grin. "Would you care to go for a ride? I was going to ride up to the old Henry Dalton Mine a little ways up the canyon. I'd enjoy your company if you'd care to ride up with me."

"Sure, I'd like that." She watched Cy tighten his cinch and easily swing up into his saddle. "You have a pretty horse. What's his name?" Mary Ann asked as she pulled back on her reins, giving Cy ample room to turn his horse.

"This is my buddy, Cole," Cy replied, nosing him around to head north along Azusa Avenue on the horse trail.

It turned out to be a good ride and Cy enjoyed Mary Ann's company. She had graduated from Citrus High before it became a junior college. She went to San Jose State for two years and did part-time modeling. She didn't finish college because she married a businessman and had two children. The marriage busted up after five years. She moved back to Azusa to be near her parents.

Mary Ann worked at the large department store in Covina as a window designer and modeled clothing on the side. She was making it on her own along with the child support from her ex-husband. She was an outdoors person and enjoyed exercising horses for Guy at the stables from time to time. She was not involved in a serious relationship and hadn't been since her divorce.

She was witty, laughed a lot, and Cy found he was very comfortable in her presence. In return, Mary Ann was impressed with Cy. He was good looking, had a good job, and he appeared very capable of taking care of himself. She also liked his rugged cowboy appearance. Subconsciously she hoped their new friendship might develop into a good relationship and perhaps something more serious as time passed. Even though she was a cautious person, she felt an eagerness to be closer to a man. That particular desire had been missing for a long time.

Four weeks had passed since Jacob made sergeant. Cy was beginning to feel comfortable with his new partner. Because of Michael's arrogance, the other men on the shift had not accepted him as one of the team members. But Cy knew the man under his mask.

Michael Fin was a capable officer. He was twenty-seven years old and divorced with one six-year-old daughter named Tiffany. She lived with Jill, his ex-wife. With the exception of Tiffany, it was an unfortunate event that the two had married.

They barely knew one another, and it was only after they had lived together that they realized they were so different. Michael still liked Jill, and they were able to maintain a friendly relationship.

Fin was a solid cop, knowing his abilities and limitations. Just what those limitations were Cy was not sure. He appeared to be able to handle every situation and was thorough.

Cy respected men who were brave and did not shy from danger. It didn't mean a person couldn't be afraid or experience fear. Everyone had fear. Facing fear and doing what had to be done in the face of it is what made the difference. Firemen and cops have to face their fears or leave their career fields for something else; otherwise, they become a danger to themselves, co-workers, and the public.

Each morning, Jacob, Michael, and Cy rode to work together. They laughed and talked about work and the future. All three men became close friends. Jacob invited Fin and Cy over for dinner often, and they developed a strong bond during their time together.

Most of the men on the watch gradually warmed up to Michael Fin. They didn't know him as well as Cy did but liked the way he worked. They didn't like his arrogance and his superior attitude, and they thought he was conceited. Every time Fin passed a window or mirror, he groomed himself and smiled at his reflection. He seemed to be oblivious to their perceptions of him, but Cy wasn't and it bothered him. Cy was reluctant to discuss it with Fin because he did not want to be judgmental of his new partner. He decided in time they would accept him and let it go. He really wished his partner would tone it down.

The biggest drawback to having Fin for a partner was his smoking. He was a chain smoker and Cy hated the smell. The smog was bad enough. After numerous complaints from Cy, Michael agreed to keep his habit outside the car but didn't like it.

It was a hot day for patrolling. Cy heard a rumor that the department had made bids for patrol cars with air conditioners. Conditioners for automobiles was a luxury the police were not accustomed to. He hoped it was true. He went through a uniform per watch, and it was expensive keeping clean and looking sharp.

Cy was behind the wheel heading west on 5th by Pershing Square. Squawking "One Adam 22," dispatch broke the silence.

Fin answered on the passenger side of the patrol car. "One Adam 22, go ahead."

"Injury accident involving a single car rollover at 9th and Broadway. Provide backup for the traffic unit en route."

"Ten-four, we are four blocks away. Check us en route," Fin responded and hung up the mike on the side of the radio.

Cy turned on his overheads, switched on his siren and responded code three. He turned left on Grand and headed south.

"Fin, find out if they called for an ambulance," Cy said, turning left on Ninth to travel eastbound.

"Where's your mind been? They just acknowledged to the traffic car one is on its way."

"Good," Cy said, feeling anxious. He felt a little hot wondering how serious the accident would be and if he could provide the proper amount of first aid to sustain the injured parties until the ambulance crew got there. If he arrived on the scene first, Cy's job was to immobilize the injured, conduct a patient assessment, provide first aid and protect the injured in preparation for transportation. Once the ambulance crew and other backup arrived, he would have to deal with traffic control while the traffic officer investigated the accident. He was glad Fin was with him, but he still missed Jacob.

The siren screamed in their ears, drowning out the usual traffic sound. Dispatch messages were barely audible. Cy felt a little anxious, wondering if it was a possible fatality or people badly hurt. What plagued his mind the most were the "what ifs." He was good at basic first aid, but he always wanted to do more.

It seemed forever before they reached Broadway. In reality they were there in less than two minutes.

"One Adam 22 arrived at scene," Fin said over the police radio. Cy quickly surveyed the immediate area. It was a single-car accident. A 1965 Chevrolet station wagon was upside down. A woman was stooped over a little girl who was lying on her back and not moving. Another woman was crying by the curb, obviously badly hurt. Audible sounds from an injured person was usually a good sign—the quiet ones were normally much more seriously injured. "Dispatch, One Adam 22, we need backup now! Confirm ambulance en route!"

"Confirm ambulance en route. Will expedite! How many injured?" dispatch blared back.

"One Adam 22 unable to confirm now; it appears we have

two injuries." Fin put the mike back in its holder. "They're on the way," he said to Cy.

Cy got out of his car, ran around to his trunk, and pulled out a handful of flares. Fin quickly went over to the injured woman. Cy ordered a bystander to assist him, and two men immediately came to his aid. He showed them how to light the flares and instructed them to separate and stop traffic at both ends of the accident. They moved to their assignments and he ran over to the woman.

An older man and his wife were holding her on the ground firmly. She was in shock. Her collarbone was sticking through her bloody blouse and both legs were askew, indicating they were badly broken. Her right leg had a compound fracture. Fin applied gauze to her wounds.

"Don't let her move," Cy ordered the couple firmly. "Block her view from the little girl," he whispered in the man's ear. He nodded in agreement.

As Cy moved away from them, the mother yelled for her daughter. "Please...my Amy. Help my baby!"

The woman kneeling next to the little girl looked up at the officer and shook her head to indicate she wasn't doing well. "Ma'am, in the back of the police car is a blanket. Please get it for me."

The little girl was approximately five years old. Her blonde hair was matted with blood and saliva ran from her mouth. Her eyes were closed. There was no movement. He felt for a pulse but couldn't find one. He listened at her chest and he barely heard a noise. He couldn't tell if it was her breath or his heart. The asphalt was hot, so he slipped his hand under the little girl's head, protecting her.

"Amy! Amy, can you hear me, honey? I'm a policeman. I'm going to help you. Amy!" There was no response. Cy wiped her lips with his hand and forced her mouth open with his thumb. Her throat was clear. He desperately covered her lips with his and blew one short breath into her mouth. To his horror, blood immediately ran from both ears. "Oh, Amy baby, I'm sorry, honey." His throat constricted and his eyes moistened. He lay down on the street next to Amy and covered her with his arm. The woman returned and spread the blanket over the little girl.

Sirens were approaching from two directions. The mother was still crying for her daughter but was soon drowned out by the arriving ambulance. Two attendants ran over to the mother, not seeing Cy and the child.

Cy stared down at the little girl. "Amy, I'm sorry, honey." Her little body gave a big heave and he knew it was her death breath, a deep bubbly sound expelling from her lungs. He felt her life—her spirit—leave her little body. Cy hung to her tighter, not able to let go.

He didn't know how long it was before someone grabbed his shoulder and shook him hard. "Cy, it's okay. Let her go." He looked up into Jacob's eyes. He was surprised to see his sergeant.

"Let her go, son. She's gone." Jacob squeezed Cy's shoulder.

Cy went limp and released the little girl, and the second ambulance crew carefully removed her from his arms and left the accident scene. He sat a few moments on the street with his head on his knees and began to cry. His mind raced, trying to figure out what this life was all about. He wondered how God handled all the grief and unhappiness in his world. There must be days that he cried, too.

Cy assisted with traffic control while traffic officers finished with the accident investigation. After a tow truck cleared the wrecked vehicle, Fin drove Cy to the L.A. General Hospital to check on the mother. It was not going to be a pleasant experience. Cy had asked dispatch to contact the father and have him meet him at the hospital.

After leaving the hospital, Cy felt lost and confused, trying to focus on his self worth and the meaning of his existence. He found great difficulty in accepting the pain. When he was trained at the police academy and was hired on at the department, he never once thought about the misery in life. He never thought about dealing with tragedies and the emotional drain experienced in human tragedies.

As the two officers drove back to Central Station, Cy looked over at Fin, who also wasn't doing well. His eyes were red, agonizing over the thoughts of his own daughter. It could have been her in the accident. He was tormented. Cy remained silent. Their friendship advanced.

After the reports at the station were finished, Cy checked again at the hospital on the mother's condition. The woman's husband spoke with Cy about his wife. His wife was still in surgery but the prognosis was good.

Two hours before the watch was over, Cy and Fin were headed for a drive-in restaurant for a cold drink. They were driving north on San Pedro Street near 7th when a driver turned in front of them, almost causing a collision. Cy slammed on his breaks to avoid a sideswiping. The patrol unit locked all four wheels, laying black rubber in the street. The driver was in a new 1968 blue Ford and now was traveling north in the same direction on San Pedro.

"What the hell, over!" Fin yelled. "That was a close one."

"Yeah, I think we've got a live one. Look at him weave back and forth on the road," Cy said, hitting his overheads. He flashed his bright lights several times but couldn't get the driver to respond.

"I think we got us a drunk driver, Mr. Fin," Cy said. "I'll try burping the siren. Maybe I can get his attention with that."

After hitting his siren several times for two blocks further north, the car finally pulled over. Fin called in their position and got out of the patrol car as soon as they came to a full stop. Fin stepped out to the right side and stood in a defensive position as Cy approached the driver from the left.

Cy was approaching the car when it suddenly went into reverse and began heading for his patrol car.

"Hey, hey! Hold it right there, you're going to hit my car!" Cy yelled, waving his arms at the driver. Fin stepped back from his open door as the car backed into the patrol unit with a loud crash.

Cy ran over to the driver and pounded on his window. "Hey, what do you think you're doing?"

The driver slowly rolled his window down and looked up at Cy. "Just what do you think you're doing hitting my car like that?" the man asked.

The man was a blue hair, about sixty-five. His speech was slurred and he smelled strongly of alcohol. He opened his car door and stepped out of his vehicle. He was apparently a businessman, dressed in an expensive dark suit. He fell against the doorjamb and grabbed hold of the side of the car for support.

"You ran into me, buddy. I wasn't even in my car," Cy said angrily. The written report on this one would be terrible.

"Don't try and turn the tables around here, Mr. Cop. You're worse than a hit and run driver. I caught you before you could get away and you're a city servant." The man poked Cy in the chest with his finger to make his point. The strong, sour odor of the man's breath sent Cy backward a step.

"Mister, you're under arrest for drunk driving. Please step to the rear of your vehicle where I can talk to you away from moving traffic," Cy demanded, taking hold of the man's coat sleeve.

"Now hold on just one minute there, young fella. I'm arresting you. It's not the other way around. I'm an attorney at law and you are my prisoner." The driver turned and saw several people gathering around his car. He noticed a uniformed officer talking with some of the people and taking notes. "Officer! Hey, officer. Over here," the man called.

The officer excused himself and walked over to the man. "Yes, sir, may I help you?" Fin asked, holding back a smile.

"You most certainly can. Arrest this man. He struck my car and I believe he has been drinking. At least that's the way it appears to me, the way he is swaying around on his feet. He won't hold still for a moment. Look at him, officer."

Another unit pulled up. Cy went over to the traffic officer and asked him to call for a wrecker to hook the DUI's car for storage.

Fin removed his sunglasses and looked closely at the man. "What is your complaint, sir? What did this man do?"

"He hit me with his car. That's what he did," the man stammered. "He even got out of his car with the motor running and it got away from him."

The man turned to Cy. "That is why there are laws forbidding an operator from leaving a vehicle unattended with the motor running. It's to prevent foolishness like this, my dear fellow."

"What is your name, sir?" Fin asked, motioning for Cy to let him do the talking.

"I am Mr. James Davenport, attorney at law. That's who I am."

"Sir, we are placing you under arrest for driving under the influence of alcohol. May I see your identification, please?" Fin asked politely.

"Me under arrest? What about him? He's the one that drove into me."

"Sir, your identification, please."

"This is ridiculous," the man said, reaching into his coat pocket. He couldn't find his wallet and looked at his car. "It's on the front seat in the car. I'll get it."

The attorney turned around and walked back to his car. He

opened the door and sat down with his feet out in the street. Cy walked up behind the man and watched him push a bottle of Seagram's Seven under the passenger seat. He motioned to Fin to go around to the other side of the car. Fin opened the passenger door and reached under the seat and removed the bottle of whisky.

"Hey, hey, hey. You can't do that. That's improper search and seizure. That is fruit of the poisonous tree. Now put it back. It's not even mine. I'm protecting it for a friend." The attorney grabbed for the bottle but Fin pulled it away from him.

"I've got it, Mr. Davenport. I'll put this away for safe keeping." Fin reached over and took the keys out of the ignition and started to back out of the car.

"You can't do that!" the old man screamed. "You can't take my whisky. Now give it back!" He reached for it again but couldn't manipulate it from the officer. Cy reached down to pull the man back by his coat collar. Before he could, the man swung, catching Fin off guard and hitting him in the temple, pushing his fist upward toward the top of his head, knocking off the officer's full toupee.

Shocked into immobility, Cy looked at it on the floorboard while Fin wrestled with the old man. During the altercation, Fin grabbed his toupee and quickly tried to set it back in place. It went on crooked and Cy couldn't help laughing quietly to himself.

Fin now had the toupee on sideways, allowing it to lap over into his eyes. He finally grabbed the man in a headlock and straightened the toupee the best he could while struggling with the prisoner. Cy wasn't any help, rooted to the ground. He stood there as if dazed.

Fin pulled the man out of the car and dragged him around to the hood of his car. He put the man in a bear hug and bent him over the front fender. He quickly applied the handcuffs and led the man back over to the patrol unit. "I'm not reading you your rights because we're not going to ask you any questions."

Cy opened the rear door for Fin to place the prisoner in the back seat. He was careful to avoid eye contact with his partner, afraid he might laugh out loud. He really didn't want that. It was one of the most embarrassing things he had ever witnessed. He wanted to savor the moment in silence.

Fin slammed the door shut and checked his reflection in the side window. "You ever tell anyone about this, I'll tear your tongue out. I'm not kidding, partner. You'll wish you were dead."

Fin's threat amused Cy but he didn't respond. They took the prisoner to the station in silence. After they processed the drunk driver at division, he was booked at Central Jail.

After the shift, Cy picked Mary Ann up at her apartment. It was their fourth date and he was looking forward to being with her. The babysitter told them to have fun and shut the door. Cy figured the young girl made a beeline for the telephone to talk with a girlfriend. He drove Mary Ann to Duarte and stopped at the Sunset Inn on Foothill Boulevard.

"Have you ever eaten here?" queried Cy quietly. He was in a solemn mood and was having a difficult time shaking it.

"No, I haven't. How did you know about this place?" Mary Ann asked as Cy got out his side of the car. She waited for Cy to walk around and open her door.

"Sam Kellogg is the owner here. He's a close friend of my sergeant. They have a special dish called the Sunset Size. It is so good you'll die," Cy laughed.

They walked to the entrance of the restaurant. "It's two hamburgers on half buns covered by the best chili in the world and smothered in onions." Cy opened the door and they both walked in.

The hostess greeted them at the front and led them to a table in the back dining room next to a window with a spectacular view of the San Gabriel Mountains. It had rained that morning and the sky was clear, revealing a blue background to the green mountain terrain. It was romantic and Cy felt good, looking into Mary Ann's beautiful light blue eyes.

They talked but the conversation slid off every now and then. Finally Mary Ann stopped eating and asked Cy if something was bothering him.

He apologized. No, nothing was wrong.

"Cy, when you're asked if something is wrong, you should be honest and answer if you trust the person who is asking." Mary Ann's voice was soft and her words bothered him. "That is, of course, if it isn't too personal to relate to a dinner partner."

"I'm sorry, Mary Ann. It has been a rough day." Cy paused,

feeling regret because he was wearing his heart on his sleeve for the little girl who died in his arms. Cy thought about the incident and told Mary Ann in great detail what had occurred. She was so touched she reached out and put her hand over his and smiled warmly at him. It was the first time she touched him affectionately.

Mary Ann was relieved when Cy began talking about his new partner, Michael Fin. He told her how he lost his toupee wrestling with the attorney in the front seat of the car with people looking on. Cy started laughing and Mary Ann laughed with him. She felt relief that Cy had loosened up and began to enjoy the evening.

She watched Cy, thinking how handsome he was. Her two children, Millie and Donny, thought he was great. He was especially gentle with them and sensitive to their feelings. She enjoyed watching him play with her children and sincerely thought he could learn to love them as his own children.

As Cy was saying goodbye to Mary Ann at the front doorstep, he smiled easily in his country boy fashion, looking at her longingly. Cy was not aggressive physically and she smiled to herself, thinking she would have to be the one to make advances. She hesitated only for a moment then reached up and kissed him lightly on the lips as they said good night.

His warm and passionate lips were a wonder to her. She realized she was falling in love and wondered how Cy felt about her. Falling in love scared her. She was still in the mending process from her broken marriage. She felt a nagging pain that constantly fogged her mind when it came to exposing her heart again. Her children were the most important thing in her life.

Mary Ann looked at Cy carefully, feeling his strength. She felt secure and safe in his presence. She knew he could protect her from almost anything. She searched his face. He was a closed-lipped person who didn't express his feelings easily. She decided in time he would loosen up and become more free with himself. Mary Ann watched Cy walk from her porch to his pickup, thinking he was certainly worth waiting for.

Chapter 5
Patrolling Central

Pavlo stepped out onto the sidewalk facing First Street. He rechecked his wooden sign with the deeply carved letters spelling out "Mercado Latino." He nodded his head in approval. The sign gave a nice touch to his store. He walked to the corner, stepped a few paces to his left on State Street, and checked the sides of the building two doors down from his store. The Mexican graffiti was there as promised. The painted face of a clown was frowning while the second face was smiling. The many colors surrounding the scene gave status to the building. It also reflected life's story—the face of drama depicting life with its bad moments, and the comedy clown showing that life went on and one must enjoy the moment and live it to the fullest. This was Hollenbeck. This was now his home, and even the noise of many people was a pleasant sound.

Pavlo turned around and saw Franco standing at the corner smoking a cigarette and paying no attention in particular to anything. They both walked back to the store. Inside, Franco said, "Your son called. He says he worked out the miscommunication with the Mexican Border Patrol. All is well."

"Sometimes Luis pleases me. His greed for money and lust for women is a good incentive in our behalf," Pavlo smiled.

"After all, Spider, he is your son."

"Cayate! Don't call me that here. No one is to know who I am. I trust no one," Pavlo growled.

"No one is around to hear my words," Franco said evenly, looking at his boss.

Pavlo brushed it off. "So the border is clear again? We can resume our air drops?"

"Tomorrow, operations resume. Our new location is the Salton Sea on the Torres Martinez Indian Reservation at the north end of the lake. The transportation crew will use Highway 86 to Interstate 10 and head west to L.A. Very neat, eh?"

"Perfect. My son's government connections are working better than I expected. Our outlets here are waiting hungrily for our shipments at cheaper prices. Come on," Pavlo said, taking hold of Franco's arm. "Let's review our local contacts and our agreements. I do not want any more, shall I say, elim-inations that are not necessary. These Hollenbeck cops are difficult to penetrate, if not impossible. I did not expect them to be untouchable—much different than our boys in Mexico."

"It is taking too much time. I do not like these police in Boyle Heights," Franco said distastefully. "They are too serious and need to relax. They need to enjoy what pleasures life has to offer them."

"I am working on it. I have never seen a cop problem that could not be handled. If one cannot bite into the pleasures before him, he can vanish into the night."

"It is safer to silence one if he does not cooperate, but it is better to buy our way into the pockets of a greedy officer. Much cleaner and no heat from the locals."

"You are right, of course, but I too prefer death. I hate these pompous authorities. I myself prefer the taste of their blood. We will see who gets his way. Money or blood."

Fall didn't arrive fast enough for Cy. It was his favorite season. The weather was cooling off, and the division had sent written orders to change the uniforms back to long sleeves. Michael, Jacob, and Cy had developed a close friendship, Michael often showing up at Jacob's house uninvited for dinner. He would even bring his daughter with him. He played with the children and sang songs with them. Lila thought he was funny and got a kick out of him. Jacob was amazed his two best friends were white. He took a lot of ribbing from his black buddies, but he didn't care. A friend was a friend.

The three officers spent many hours at the Fish Canyon Gun Range in Duarte practicing shooting their revolvers and hunting rifles. Afterwards they would stop at the Log Inn on Foothill Boulevard for a beer. None of the men were heavy drinkers, except Michael. He often tried to outdrink his companions. It was usually their responsibility to curtail his beer consumption before he got too soused.

It was Friday evening and the sky was dimming quickly with the absence of the sun, which had dipped down over the Pacific Ocean. Dispatch was running at full strength. It seemed the radio never stopped. All reporting districts were busy and the paperwork would be horrendous toward the end of the watch.

Cy turned left onto Los Angeles Street from Boyd. Immediately a small Honda whizzed by, heading toward a busy residential district. Michael got busy on the radio with dispatch, asking for a registration check on the license plate.

The car appeared to be driven by a large woman. Her hair was rolled up into a bun. Cy turned his headlights off and on several times attempting to get the driver's attention; and each time, the driver touched her brakes, illuminating her red rear lights, acknowledging his presence and his silent order, but failing to comply.

"What do you make of that?" Michael asked. "She knows you're behind her, but she's not even slowing down."

"Doesn't make sense, does it," Cy said, watching the car ahead of him. He honked his horn. In the distance they could hear a return honk. "This is crazy. She blinks her lights and honks her horn letting me know she knows we're behind her. But she won't pull over."

"It can't be an emergency—all the medical centers are in different directions," Michael answered.

"I hope we aren't being taken for a ride," Cy finally said. "I don't like this. Something has got to be wrong." He hit the toggle switch for the siren, but the car continued to the next corner and turned left onto 6th Street. The driver drove right past the police substation on the corner and headed west several blocks to Gladys Avenue. The driver made a right turn, went two blocks, stopped and parked the car, then jumped out of her vehicle. She ran across the sidewalk to some outside stairs leading to a second floor apartment. Though a hefty woman, she bounced along the sidewalk at a surprising pace.

Cy was right behind her giving chase while Michael gave their position to dispatch requesting backup. He dropped the mike and followed in the foot pursuit. Cy stayed behind the woman as she flew up the stairs.

"Lady! Hold it right there! You're under arrest," Cy barked, coming up to the woman as she nervously tried to fit the key into the lock. She was a woman of about fifty-five years of age; her hands shook and she refused to look at Cy. The expression on her face indicated pain and torment.

Cy couldn't figure out her problem. He was extremely irritated with her for not obeying his commands. The woman was jumping up and down as the key finally went into the door lock and turned. She was crying and moaning as Cy reached out and grabbed hold of her sleeve. The lady hauled back and hit him with her purse, pushing him backward into Michael who was just appearing at the top of the stairs.

She glared at Cy, and her eyes were now frantic as she pushed her way into the apartment and crossed the living room at a gallop.

Cy reached out for her again just in time to catch her purse square in the mouth. "I said stop, or I'll shoot your guts out."

"Go ahead and shoot," she screamed, running into the bathroom next to the kitchen. "You can arrest me in a minute."

The woman did not bother to shut the bathroom door. Cy was right behind her. He did not notice the brown liquid trail on the linoleum floor just outside the bathroom door. "You're under arrest, lady, now!" He hesitated, "Good heavens. What are you doing?"

The woman pulled up her dress, slipped down her boxer underwear, and plopped herself on the toilet. "You can't arrest me now, you blundering idiot. I've got diarrhea and I'm leaking in my pants. Now get out of here."

Cy stopped in his tracks only a few feet from where the woman was squatting. Michael, bursting into the bathroom, bumped him in the middle of his back. Cy fell on top of the lady just as she released her bowels. Gastronomical hell broke loose, and it wasn't pretty, as if someone had taken a gallon bucketful of sludge and thrown it at the toilet and missed. Human waste went everywhere but in the toilet and it didn't stop coming. Horrible grotesque sounds echoed in the toilet bowl, and Cy and Michael fought to get out of the room, needing fresh air.

The rotten smell had already escaped from the bathroom as they stopped for air in the kitchen. In the bathroom it sounded as if a dog fight were in progress. "Ma'am? Forget it. You get a free one today. Forget we were ever here." Cy gasped, turning to the exit while touching his cut lip gingerly with his fingertips.

Cy and Michael made a quick exit down the stairs. Both were now worried the woman would file a complaint against them for improper intrusion, trespass, or invasion of privacy or whatever. Life was not good at the moment.

Finding a hose nearby, they washed themselves off the best they could without actually touching their soiled shoes with their bare hands. As nauseating as the situation was, what Cy feared most was the other men on the shift finding out about the disgusting ordeal. Neither Cy nor Michael would ever live it down if it got out.

Cy went back to the car and Michael canceled the cars that would be responding for backup. They soon discovered why the backup unit did not respond to their call when dispatch immediately came back on the air. "One Adam 22, provide backup to other officers answering a disturbance complaint at 6th and Gladys Park. Loud party with alcohol involved."

"One Adam 22, copy. We're sixty seconds away," Michael answered.

Cy drove two blocks and pulled into the park at the north end, noting the numerous police units. Several officers were gathering in the parking lot. Jacob was pulling everyone together for a briefing.

Jacob gave the men his last instructions before they went to the party. "The last thing we need here is a riot. You all know how booze can do that. Isolate any troublemakers and let's break the party up before it gets out of hand. We don't necessarily need to make arrests. Let's get them to leave and it will be sweet and easy."

Jacob turned around looking across the grass toward the beer party when some of the group started making more noise and whooping it up. It was obvious some of the people at the party were too loud and getting disorderly. "Let's break it up and send them home," Jacob said, looking at the group of either teenagers or young college-age kids.

The group was gathered around a fire built inside a 55-gallon barrel. The firelight illuminated a beer keg off to one side. The officers paired off and spread out to circle the party with the intention of getting the people to pick up their belongings and vacate the premises. If it worked, there would be no arrests unless participants were obviously underage.

As the party goers were milling around, some of the officers began interacting with the group. Most of the people were college age and did not want any trouble with the police. They cooperated by gathering their stuff and moving to their cars in the adjacent parking lot.

One group of young adults near the beer keg was more vocal. Michael headed straight for that area, not wanting to miss any of the action in case something broke loose. Cy could hardly keep up with him. He had observed Michael Fin in action many times. He was most capable of handling himself and was fearless in a fight. Watching his partner head into the thick of things made Cy like him even more.

Matt Riggs, a tall longhair with holes in his Levi's and a sleeveless grey sweatshirt, pointed his finger at two of the officers standing before him. "It's our American right to have a party in this park. Our taxes paid for this park. We are taxpayers, so this is our park. No one here is underage, so you fascist pigs back out of here before you get hurt."

The officer pushed Riggs' hand away from his face. "You do as you're told. This park is regulated by city ordinances and everyone has to comply."

"Everyone does not have to comply, Mr. Police Officer. You work for us, and I expect you to do as you are ordered by a taxpaying citizen."

"That's enough, now roll it up," the officer ordered.

"This is our park; now you roll it up." Riggs pushed the officer backwards.

Michael Fin reached out and dropped Riggs to the ground with a fast takedown. The rowdy man never saw it coming. His face was in the grass and both hands were being pulled behind his back. A painful pressure was pushing in the small of his back. He quickly decided not to resist when the pain was too great.

Another party goer, Rich Baricol, was arguing with an officer when he saw his drinking buddy taken down. He spun around and took off running. He dove over the backs of the two officers standing next to Matt, who was being handcuffed on the ground. With a "Sunday round-house" swing he hit Michael, who was bent over working on his friend. The blow hit Michael on the left side of his face, tipping him and his prisoner over on the lawn. Michael refused to let go of his prisoner and continued cuffing him. His face was smarting but he couldn't release his prisoner until he had both hands secured behind his back.

Baricol got behind the officer, wrapped his forearm around Michael's neck, and choked him. Michael strained getting the last cuff locked into place. He released Riggs and grabbed Baricol's little finger and twisted it until it snapped with a pop. Baricol gasped, releasing the officer from his choke hold. Officer Jeremy came up behind Baricol and slammed him on the head with his flashlight, cutting his forehead. At first it was a clean open wound and then it began to fill with blood. Baricol groaned, falling sideways to his knees and grabbing his head. Blood ran down into his eyes. Officer Jeremy and another officer cuffed Baricol and two others. Six people were arrested and placed in a small gathering near a police prisoner van for transport. Cy pushed his prisoner into the group and looked for his partner. He had lost Michael from the very beginning of the ruckus when he was busy making his own arrest.

Smiling, Michael walked over to the officers near the van, obviously happy. He couldn't hold back his pleasure thinking how much he loved this work. It was a high for him and he was pleased with his team members because they held their ground. Michael noticed the other officers smiling and making muffled sounds as he approached them. He decided they were just excited from busting up the beer party. The excess of the adrenaline flow often affected officers after a decent brawl. Cy had just pushed a prisoner into the prisoner van and turned to Michael, who was grinning from ear to ear. Yeah, Michael loved this work and got paid for it, too. He rationalized that it was only natural for the others to enjoy themselves also. Why not? If one didn't like arresting people, what was the sense of being a cop?

Sergeant Jacob Wilson appeared around the front fender of the Ford van, looking disgusted but definitely satisfied the altercation was over and the crowd contained. "You men have the names of your witnesses, I presume? I want us to pull out of here as soon as..." Jacob paused as he noticed the grins on his men's faces.

Jeremy was winking at his sergeant, raising his eyebrow and motioning over the back of his shoulder to Michael who was behind him. Michael was brushing himself off and moving to readjust his Sam Brown. His head was completely bald with the exception of a little hair around each ear. A pair of two-sided adhesive strips were dangling limply off the top of his head. One strip was hanging off the back of his head onto his shirt collar, the other was hanging over the side of his head so far it appeared it was sticking in his ear. He looked like Dagwood.

Behind Michael, Cy was holding both hands over his mouth, unable to stop the tears running down his cheeks. His shoulders were shaking and he went to his knees trying to get his breath, afraid of making any noise that would alert his arrogant partner.

Michael noticed a strange look on his sergeant's face but ignored it. "Sarge, we didn't want this dispute to escalate into a brawl. I think booze is the culprit here. These wimps didn't cause us that much of a problem." His facial expressions displayed his usual confidence. The men around him started giggling openly.

"Are you okay, Officer Fin? You seem a little lightheaded," Jacob asked seriously.

The other officers smirked but were careful to avoid eye contact with Michael in fear of losing it.

"No, Sarge, I feel great," Michael laughed confidently.

Jacob looked at the other men circled around him. "I want a report of injuries. Jeremy, you said someone had a broken finger. What's the story there?" The sergeant sounded angry.

"Yes, sir, that's right, Sarge." Jeremy moved a little closer, afraid to look at Michael.

"Well, what happened?"

"Well, Sarge, I was helping the other guys separate a cluster of drunken fools and I saw something shiny in the night off to my left where two other men struggled nearby. I fought my way through the crowd toward the brightness. I didn't know what it was at first, but I maintained a steady course. The shiny globe was like a guiding light, Sarge, assisting me across a sea of grass."

"Cut the crap and tell me what happened," Jacob snapped.

"Well, Sarge, I will if you'll let me finish." Jeremy loved the moment awarded him. A moment like this would only come once in his career.

"I cautiously moved to the shiny light. It was like a bubble or a crystal ball...that's it, Sarge, it was like a shiny crystal ball glowing in the dark."

"What on earth are you talking about, you dufas?" Michael cut in.

"I know it sounds crazy, but I'm telling you this drunk was trying to lift a crystal ball off the top of some shoulders of one of our officers." Jeremy pointed to the van holding the prisoners. "It was one of those ruffians in there, Sarge."

"You're joshing me, right?" the sergeant frowned, worried he was going to laugh.

"No, sir. As I got closer, I realized the shiny thing had been covered by a beaverlike rug that somehow got removed in the heat of the battle."

"What in Sam's name are you talking about, twit?" Michael said, stepping closer. The adhesive tape jiggled up and down as he moved. The others were losing it and so far Michael hadn't a clue. "Jeremy came over to assist me with this punk who was trying to choke me out. What are you talking about—a beaver tail or whatever?"

Officer Tom Franklin pushed his way through the officers. "I believe this is what Jeremy is talking about, Sarge." He lifted his hand forward holding out a limp toupee between his fingertip and thumbnail ever so delicately. It had been trampled in the mud and dirt and now it resembled a miniature beaver skin.

Jacob didn't want to touch the dirty thing with his bare hands. He withdrew his nightstick from his baton ring and held it out for Franklin to place the hairpiece on the end. Jacob made a scowling face at the other men. "What in heaven's name is this nasty thing?"

All eyes went immediately to Michael Fin. He quickly reached his hand to the top of his head. He felt the bare skin with the two adhesive strips. The one over his ear he tore off. The expression on his face was too much for the other men.

"Officer Skin...I mean Fin. Is this disgusting varmint yours?" Jacob asked, losing himself. He threw his head back laughing and everyone openly joined in.

At first Michael was furious. He pulled out his nightstick and made a circling motion. After the shock of the incident, even he joined in. As he laughed, the more he thought about it, the louder he bellowed.

After a long moment the men began to gather themselves. Sergeant Wilson called the men to order. He looked at Michael and called him over to where he was standing. "On your knees, officer."

"What?" Michael looked puzzled, losing the smile from his face.

"On your knees," Jacob ordered, pointing to the ground with his baton. The toupee was gone and he had no idea where it was in the dark.

Officer Fin did as he was told. The rest of the men grew quiet, not knowing what was going to happen next. The sergeant stepped up to Michael and placed the tip of his baton to the left shoulder and then to the right. Then he tapped him lightly on the top of his bald head. "I now dub thee Officer Skin, by which ye shall now be known by the rest of the officers in this division and for the remainder of thy law enforcement career."

A loud cheering erupted and Skin was warmed by the hearty welcome into the group of officers for the first time. All hostilities held by the other men because of his overbearing attitude vanished. Michael was humbled and he felt accepted by his co-workers for the first time.

The next day at roll call, Michael Fin showed up without his hairpiece. He had completely shaven his head bald and the other officers approved. The officers chanted "Skin" three times, and Michael mentally confirmed that he had finally become accepted as a team member. The watch commander stood up after his sergeant gave him the floor. He gave the general orders for the day and other items of business. Finally he picked up a letter on the podium and opened it removing a single-page letter.

"Listen up, men. I have something special here. I want you to think about this letter when you're on patrol today."

The commander looked at the letter a moment, wrinkled his forehead, and cleared his throat. It was tight and he had to clear it again. "In the spring of 1965, Sergeant Wilson, then a patrol officer, and Cy Golden had the opportunity to assist a desperate man seeking assistance for his sick wife in her early pregnancy. The two officers stopped a speeding car and ended up giving the driver a ride to and from the doctor's clinic with a critical serum for the man's wife. Otherwise the expectant mother would have lost the baby. That's the story in short; here is the letter in reference to that incident:"

Dear Officers Wilson and Golden,

I didn't write for the last three years because I had to make sure the news was good in its entirety. The serum you helped us get saved our baby. It was a boy.

There have been many health problems with my wife and especially our son. I did not want to write until I knew his prognosis was good. When he was born he had a hole in his heart and when he was a year-and-a-half old, he required open heart surgery.

Today the doctor gave our son a clean bill of health and he has a bright future. Our family physician has assured us our son will be in good enough health to play baseball.

Because of the circumstances and because you so graciously gave that precious time we needed to save our son, we have named him CeeJay. Cee is for Cy, and Jay is for Jacob—the best two police officers of L.A. Central. Here is a picture of CeeJay. We sincerely thank you with love and appreciation. You will always have a special place in our hearts.

Sincerely, John, Mary, and CeeJay Baker

The commander folded the letter slowly and put it back in the envelope. He took a deep breath and looked out across his men seated behind their desks. "Okay, men, go out there and do a good job," he said softly. "And remember CeeJay. It's what we're all about."

Cy walked up to the captain, who gave him the letter. He removed the picture from the folded letter and turned around to walk out of the room with Jacob reading over his shoulder. It was a great moment. Both men were taken back because they had completely forgotten about the incident with the desperate husband.

Cy had a lump in his throat and Jacob wasn't any better off. "Can you believe this little guy here?"

"Well, he's white, but he is kinda cute."

Cy looked at Jacob. "You're so funny. You love this guy, don't you. It's like you helped father a white boy."

"Let's not get carried away here, cowboy honkie."

"Well, we did a good thing here. I'm glad it was you and me on this one."

❧

Cy opened the door for Mary Ann to step out onto the soft dirt. The wind caught her hair blowing back and forth over her shoulder. The warm, refreshing breeze seemed to rejuvenate him with a pleasant sensation.

Mary Ann wore a white short-sleeved blouse and bright yellow shorts that enhanced her dark tan. Cy was always stealing quick glances at her. Her good looks attracted him, and the pleasure of looking at her when she didn't notice rewarded his secret feelings for her. Cy thought she was totally lovely but did not want her to think he was only interested in her because of her beauty. He wanted to express his feelings to her but was not quite sure if he would lose ground with her if he did. He often noticed other men turning their heads to take a second look at Mary Ann, and it made him feel a little taller to be in her presence.

Sometimes he wondered if it bothered Mary Ann because he was several years younger than her. She was twenty-eight and he had just turned twenty-five. But that was only part of the problem. He also thought Mary Ann was too good for him. She was a sweet, loving lady and a particularly wonderful mother. It almost intimidated Cy at times because she always thought of her children before herself and for that matter anyone else. Cy decided she was right, and he needed to think things out as a parent would and not selfishly as a single person. He excused himself because he had never been in love or around small children other than Jacob's family and Mary Ann's. He was not sure of their needs, but he had a strong desire to learn. He did enjoy their company and loved playing with them. It brought a wonderful joy to him, being around Millie and Donny. It gave him a deep feeling of anxiousness, thinking someday he would perhaps himself be a father. He wondered when that would occur and what his future held for him.

Mary Ann noticed Cy was quiet and decided to bring him out of his thoughts. "What a beautiful view, Cy. I always love it when you bring me to Scotsman's Cove," Mary Ann laughed with her hair tossing in the breeze.

"It won't be long before it isn't our private beach anymore," Cy said dishearteningly. "The state is going to close all this off. We'll have to pay to get in here. I'll bet there won't be any parking near the cliff like there is now. With land improvements, people will flock here like flies on a dead cat."

"Like what?" Mary Ann laughed, hitting Cy on the arm with her fist. "Ouch," she said rubbing her hand. "It's no fun hitting you. You're as hard as a rock."

Cy laughed, taking her hand in his and walking to the edge of the cliff overlooking the vast Pacific Ocean. The sky was mostly clear blue with scattered puffs of soft billowy white clouds. Seagulls squawked, flying back and forth in search of food on the sandy beach. A warm sensation spread in Cy's chest looking out over the beautiful ocean, especially the feeling he experienced by holding on to Mary Ann's hand. He felt he was going to do something foolish and had to regroup his thoughts. His throat was a little strained and his mind was swimming like a whirlpool. A seagull flew close to them and they could see its eyes blink as it passed by. The feathers were clean, white, and smooth.

"I love this place, Cy. I'm so glad you love the outdoors."

"I do that," he smiled warmly. "Let's walk down to the sand."

Cy led Mary Ann down the dirt trail to the beach and they took off their shoes. Cy had his trunks on but he did not plan on going swimming. It was only 70 degrees and the water was too cold for swimming. They strolled south on the beach floor with the waves sidling up around their feet and back to sea, disappearing in the mass of salt water. For several minutes Cy did not speak. He was deep in thought. Mary Ann wanted to ask him if something was wrong but decided he needed his thoughts to himself. His silence was heavy but if he was to talk, it would have to be on his terms.

After a distance down the beach they turned around and came back along the white sandy beach, watching the waves slap into the rocks offshore as the tide pushed toward the cliffs. Dried seaweed was broken and scattered across the uneven surface with thousands of tiny flies busily feeding off the drying plants as the two walked nearby and interrupted their feeding frenzy.

Cy's thoughts were of his life and of his brother, Richard, buried in the small cemetery in Alpine. He wondered if Richard had suffered before dying. He thought of his father who had quickly gone into a slump, slowly letting the ranch run down. The new freeway cutting into the ranch was not helping matters. His thoughts started going sour. There were many good memories in his life and he didn't want to let the bad thoughts crowd them out. He felt a warm sensation in his heart as he visualized a reflection of his smiling mother who always comforted him. She was such a strong pillar of strength in his life. She was a religious woman but did not attend church out of deference to his father who was against her faith. She never pushed her spiritual thoughts on him. Instead she was an example of a person with high standards and good moral strength. Her wisdom had always impressed Cy. He felt an inner strength because of her determination to give him love and guidance. She willingly received his arms around her whenever he had the desire to be near her for comfort and love.

The cold water brought Cy out of his thoughts. It almost shocked him when a small wave swept around his bare feet. He had not realized they had stopped walking and were facing the sea. Each time the water came around his feet he sank deeper into the sand. He thought about that, and thought about Jacob and his wife, and about his new partner, Skin. He wondered what life had in store for him, whether he was going to reach out and make decisions or just let things happen naturally. His father always told him if he wasn't aggressive someone else would get the apple pie. He said to reach out for life and not to let it pass him by.

"I have a problem, Mary Ann," Cy finally said, staring out to sea.

"What kind of problem?" she said quietly, afraid of what he might say. She didn't want to lose Cy. He had never really been romantic with her and she wondered if he secretly cared for someone else, though he never mentioned dating or interest in other women. He was not committed to her nor had he made any promises, although she had hoped that would change in time.

He hesitated and his voice was hardly audible. "I'm sinking."

She waited a moment when he did not go on. "Sinking? Do you want to move up higher on the beach?"

"I'm sinking fast. Faster than I can deal with."

"Let's move then," she said, squeezing his hand and starting to move to higher ground.

Cy didn't move and continued to stare at the ocean. "I'm sinking into despair."

Mary Ann turned back toward Cy, letting herself touch his side. Her face was close to his, but his mind was so distant. "I don't understand. Is your job getting to you? I can't imagine how hard it would be to be a cop. It's a scary job and dangerous. I don't know how you do it."

"I'm losing myself, Mary Ann," Cy said to the gentle, warm woman next to him. He glanced down into her light blue eyes. "I see the sky in your eyes. The sun follows your every movement. My heart stays with you every time I leave your presence."

Mary Ann's heart was suddenly pounding like a wild drum.

Her mind was racing and she felt her eyes burning as she listened for words she had wanted desperately to hear for so long. "What are you saying, Cy?" she whispered, pressing her breast to the side of his chest.

"I have never cared for anyone before. These past few months I have cared for you as a close loving friend. I have been seeking myself out to know the difference between loving someone and being in love."

"And?"

"Well, I know I love you," he hesitated. He looked directly into her eyes. "My heart soars every time I hold you in my arms or when I kiss you. Or even when I leave you. I miss you when I'm at work. Even when I've gone off with the guys fishing or I'm doing other things, I'm thinking of you."

"And?"

"Well, I'm a slow mover when it comes to feelings for a woman. Now I'm having trouble keeping my thoughts in check."

"In check? You think of me as a check?" Outwardly Mary Ann sounded confused and irritable. Inside she felt herself bursting open. This was the first time this man of her dreams was showing his emotions to her. These were not surface emotions. They were from deep inside of Cy and she was moved by his sincerity.

"No, not you as a check. I mean I'm having trouble controlling my thoughts."

"You mean you have nasty thoughts of me?"

"No, no. Not those kinds of thoughts, honest."

"You mean you don't desire me as a woman?"

"No, no, I don't mean I'm not thinking of wanting to be close to you."

"Well, what are you saying then? Are you lusting after me?"

"No, no, I'm not lusting after you," he said frowning. Everything was coming out wrong. He wished he had never brought up the subject. He wanted to kick himself and would if he could.

"Cy, you better lust after me," Mary Ann said, bringing herself around to face him. "You had better want me. That doesn't mean you can stop respecting me or treating me improperly. It means it's okay to love and want me. We just have to take it slow." She bit her lip and wished she hadn't made that last remark.

"I'm sorry, Mary Ann. I never in my life told a girl I loved her. It's because I haven't. And it's not because I haven't wanted to. I have to think about commitment and keeping proper perspective."

"Oh, Cy, just shut up and kiss me. You're going to say something that's going to hurt my feelings, and I don't want to lose this wonderful feeling I have." Mary Ann slipped her hand up behind Cy's neck and pulled his head down to hers. His warm moist lips captured hers and they held on to each other as if they would never separate.

The breeze had picked up and the seagulls didn't seem to notice the couple on the beach.

Chapter 6
Hollenbeck 1971

The last three years had introduced many changes in Cy's life. His relationship with Mary Ann had grown considerably, but not without domestic and personal problems. Her ex-husband wanted the children and made an appeal to the court for custody. That became a serious battle. It meant she had to spend a lot of time in the Oregon courts.

Fortunately, Mary Ann was a fighter, someone not to be threatened. She also decided to give up her time at the stables and went to night classes at Citrus College. She became eager to secure her future with a bachelor's degree in business. She was deeply involved with Cy emotionally but domestic problems had an impact on their relationship.

In June, Mary Ann had developed some health problems and was seeing a physician on a regular basis. When Cy questioned her, she would shrug it off and say it was nothing serious to worry about. He did worry but also respected her privacy.

Cy found himself deeply involved with Mary Ann, but the night he started to bring up his feelings concerning their future and began discussing their lives on a long-term basis, she became evasive, begging him to enjoy the moment. She told him serious commitments could come later. He was confused but let it go for the time being. He loved her and her children. That is what seemed important. They enjoyed their time together and it brought them both happiness.

Jacob had been promoted to lieutenant after completing three years as a sergeant in Central. He recently had been transferred to the Hollenbeck Division, also known as the Mexican District, in East Los Angeles. The Hollenbeck station was located at 2111 East 1st Street and had been there for as long as anyone could remember. The division had a reputation for being one of the toughest divisions to work. An officer either liked it or hated it. There was no in-between. Most officers liked Hollenbeck and would not put in for a transfer if they had been assigned to this location for at least a year. The officers who were happy to get out of Hollenbeck were on short-term assignment or on loan from other divisions. When an officer was not familiar with the Boyle Heights people, it could be a frightening place to work.

Cy had been called back to the police academy for a year as an academy instructor, teaching firearms and physical training/control holds. After leaving the academy he was assigned to Hollenbeck and eventually promoted to sergeant. He now had his own patrol team. His men thought highly of him and respected his commitment to the department and the support he gave to them. He was always concerned about their personal lives besides their work productivity. He set high standards and assisted his subordinates in achieving maximum professionalism in their job task.

Cy had learned the commonly used California codes by memory and knew the more important policies and procedures so well that other sergeants would often counsel with him. He was always eager to assist his co-workers. It was rumored within the department that it would not be long before Cy made lieutenant. At least everyone but Cy expected it.

The down side of the last few years was that he was emotionally drained. He often went on lonely rides on his horse trying to reason with himself. Three years ago his mother and father had been killed in an auto accident on Highway 80 between Alpine and El Cajon. They were on their way to dinner at Anthony's on the San Diego boat harbor when another vehicle swerved over the center line at the big dip approximately three miles west of Alpine, causing a head-on collision with no survivors.

Being the sole surviving heir, after two years of serious consideration, Cy sold the ranch. He placed the windfall in bonds and safe stock market ventures. He had recently audited his account, and his net worth was over a million dollars. After serious study and consideration, he decided to invest most of it in Hewlett Packard and IBM stock. He was confident interest in computer and office wares was going to take off and that now was a good time to invest.

Cy began to hate the city but was totally engrossed in his profession. It amazed him how he wanted the best out of both worlds. In times of frustration and when things were not going well with Mary Ann, he contemplated quitting the force and buying a ranch in mideastern California near Bridgeport and living the life of a recluse.

The smog in Los Angeles was getting unbearable. With the heat of July, coupled with the environmental deterioration of the air, it was not pleasant working in a hot uniform, even in a short-sleeved shirt. The patrol cars were finally equipped with air conditioning. The disadvantage of air in the units was having to keep the windows rolled up and not being able to hear the outdoor sounds of the streets.

Cy walked over to the black and white unit, opened the door, and eased himself in behind the steering wheel. He could hear the squeak of leather as he leaned across to unlock the door for his ride-along and new transfer to the division, Bobby Blanca, recently transferred to the Hollenbeck Division from the Harbor Division. He was assigned to Cy's team. Lieutenant Jacob Wilson was their watch commander.

Everyone who knew Bobby liked him. He was Hispanic and small in stature with black hair and mustache, but his heart made up for his size. He was born and raised in San Diego. The department preferred job applicants who were bilingual, and being Mexican-American would enable him to neatly fit into the division. He was a sharp-looking officer with four years experience.

Bobby was a heavy beer drinker off duty and loved to party. On the job he was completely loyal to his work and everyone at his former division liked him. Bobby never started a fight but never walked away from one either. Cy wasn't sure whether Bobby just liked to fight or was exceptionally good at it. Regardless, he was a good officer to rely on when the going got tough. One quirk in the officer's otherwise realistic nature puzzled Cy. Bobby was superstitious. He didn't like black cats or cracked mirrors, and he wouldn't walk under a ladder. An entry in his portfolio by his previous sergeant said he avoided calls and police services that dealt with the mentally ill. Bobby felt it may be "catching" to handle people considered insane. He wanted nothing to do with them and only questioned those types of people when no one else was available.

Bobby opened the passenger side of the patrol unit and leaned down to look at his new watch sergeant. "Sarge, I forgot the shotgun. I'll go to the kitroom and check one out. Be back in a moment," he said, as he turned and re-entered Hollenbeck Station.

Sergeants normally do not ride with subordinates unless the shift is short. Usually when a man is newly assigned to the area, a supervisor will double with an officer in order to check him out, defining his police attitude and familiarizing him with the patrol area. When the sergeant is finished with his orientation, the new man is assigned to ride with an experienced officer to enhance his learning of the Hollenbeck procedures.

Hollenbeck had over 150,000 population in 15.1 square miles and was divided into approximately fifty reporting districts or RDs. Most patrol units were double manned and given several RDs depending on the size of the district. Trouble areas might require more patrol units than business districts with lesser criminal activity. There were four overlapping watches plus a graveyard shift to cover in a 24-hour period. Day watch began at 0700 and ended at 1545, midday watch ran from 1000 to 1845, and mid-PM watch went from 1800 to 0245. The watch commander held the rank of lieutenant and under him was a desk sergeant to handle problems and questions at the station plus a watch sergeant for each tour of duty.

Officers fresh out of the police academy were P1 officers, which meant they were still on probation. Officers off probation and full-time certified peace officers held the rank of P2. Only P2 officers were eligible to take the exam for promotion.

When Bobby returned to the car with the shotgun, Cy began his orientation of Hollenbeck, describing the people and current and past police problems. Bobby only asked questions when necessary. Cy decided he had a good attitude and was willing to accept new ideas even though he was an experienced officer.

Cy told Bobby his greatest fear was getting a new man who was badge-heavy. He wanted to know how a new man handled anger. Did he only use what force was necessary to effect an arrest or control police situations? He also wanted to know whether the new man was prejudiced against any race. Hollenbeck was predominately Mexican. A few Asians populated Hollenbeck, and in some areas the African-Americans dominated small pockets in the division perimeters. Cy did not like officers who distinguished people by their race, so there was no room for prejudiced officers on his team.

Bobby laughed at his new sergeant. "I understand what you are saying, Sarge. You won't have any problem with me. I like everyone."

"One other thing, Bobby. Don't ever make the mistake of asking a gang member if he belongs to a certain gang. If you give the wrong gang name, you go on a hate list. In other words, don't ask a ganger suspect if he is a Clover, because he may be a Hazard. He will never forgive or forget you. Dishonoring a gang member is the very worst of insults, okay?"

"Okay," Bobby answered. "So I ask what gang he belongs to, and he can tell me on his own if he belongs to the V & E gang, Brown Berets or the White Fence gang, or whatever. I just don't assume he belongs to any certain gang until he identifies it first. I learned that as a kid. It's amazing I never had nothing to do with them when I was growing up. Why I didn't, I don't know. Maybe I was too scared of them."

"Being Hispanic you'll do better than most whites. It doesn't hurt to make a few friends out here when you can. But even if you make friends, you may still have to arrest one. If you don't make the arrest because he is a friend, that's a sign of weakness and you lose face. When you make an arrest of a gang member who you know, you have to do it professionally and with dignity. That gang member and his friends will respect you for it because they know you have to do your job and they expect it from you.

"One of the toughest RDs to work is 448. It's the Hazard district. It's a gang like no other. It's a tightly-knit family and they are about as dangerous as you can get. Pride and honor are everything to them. No one messes with a Hazard member and especially with the older parents and old-time gangers or 'verteranos.' They are very protective of their own.

"Even though this area is controlled by the gangs, the Mexican Mafia or Mafiosos, and sometimes the Italian Mafia, have their territorial struggles for control. They may not live in this area but they want the drug business and it is a very deadly game. When control is established, the Mafia have a man called the Mark. He is the same as a lieutenant. He gives orders to a mouthpiece from the residential areas he represents. The mouthpiece is also known as an associate. It is his responsibility to collect taxes. Taxes are dues that must be paid for selling drugs in a Mafia-controlled area. It does not matter how much money is made in selling drugs, as long as the taxes are paid."

Cy took his time driving along the streets discussing Hollenbeck. Every now and then he glanced at Bobby to make sure he had his attention. "It will take a little time to remember everything. What I do expect is for you to be honest and neat in your report writing. I expect you to finish your reports before you leave your watch." Cy looked at Bobby. "Don't lie and color your reports in favor of prosecuting your suspect. If you always write down the truth, you won't need to remember what you did or said. The truth always comes back to you clean. A lie is dirty and it demands more lies and you'll drown in it. Okay?"

"You got it, Sarge. I'll do a good job for you. You won't have to worry about me," Bobby smiled back at his sergeant.

After three hours on the road Cy took Bobby back to the station. He instructed him to study division procedures and learn the reporting districts including the boundary streets.

Skin came into the station and saw Cy working with Bobby. "Hey, guys," Skin smiled at the two men standing over some charts. "So you're my new partner." Skin had a big grin on his face. He walked over and took Bobby's hand in his and shook it hard.

"Boy, am I glad you're dark-skinned. I need a Mexican partner. I need a friend out there, my man," Skin laughed.

Bobby didn't smile. "What makes you think I'm a Mexican? Maybe I'm Italian."

"No way," Skin's face lit up. "You're too ugly to be a spaghetti eater."

"Speaking of spaghetti, let's grab some lunch," Cy cut in.

"Let's do. My stomach is gnawing on my backbone," Skin said.

"If you guys don't mind, I'd like to study these RDs so I can get my bearings straight," Bobby said to his sergeant. "And I'm not really all that hungry right now. I guess I'm a little nervous."

"We'll let it go this time. You're after my heart. I like it when an officer wants to study." Cy looked at Skin, "Some of my men have a hard time hitting the books."

"Being new, I want to get more familiar with the stuff I'm going to be responsible for," Bobby said, raising his eyebrow. "I'm also looking forward to being your new partner, Skin. I've already heard some stories about you from some of the guys. I think we'll get along just fine."

Cy and Skin walked out the side door of the station. Cy steered Skin toward the parked cruisers. "Come on, I'll drive. We can ride around together for a little while. It'll be like old times."

Skin didn't protest. "I could use a chauffeur. I was out late last night. By the way, that reminds me. Last night at Jack's Bar, a couple of fellas from the S.O. came over looking for you. They want to challenge you in a quick draw. They said they worked out of the Firestone Station. The sheriff's office sure looks like they're hiring young deputies these days. They hardly looked over twenty-one."

The watch commander stuck his head out the front door of the station and whistled, "Cy, we have a domestic. I need you two to take it for me. I've got everyone tied up on calls," Jacob yelled.

"Okay, we'll take it. I'll start the car up, Skin. You get the address from the lieutenant and I'll pick you up around front."

Skin climbed into the patrol car, adjusted and locked the seat belt around his waist. He pushed his sunglasses back up higher on the bridge of his nose with his right forefinger. "I've been to this house before, Sarge. This is one mean lady we're going to visit."

"You've been there before?" Cy responded, tightening his seat belt. He pulled out onto the street when the lane was clear. Traffic was heavy on 1st Street. "What's the location?"

"Fresno and Garnet," Skin answered.

"RD 488," Cy mumbled out loud. "You still don't like family squabbles, do you?"

"I hate them. You never know where you stand with the members of the family. Usually the wife only wants to scare her husband and doesn't want the old man carted off because she'll lose his paycheck. He gets mad because we're on his property. Once we get him out of the house and arrest him for assault or destruction of property or whatever, the wife backs down and he spits in our faces, threatening to sue us for false arrest."

"True, but that's only a small percentage. There's a lot of spouse abuse, and I particularly don't like guys who beat up women." Cy stopped for a traffic light and adjusted the air conditioner to a higher speed. "It's a hot one today," he said, feeling the sweat run down his neck.

Approximately four minutes later, the patrol car pulled up in front of the complainant's residence. It was a middle-class neighborhood and all appeared quiet. There was no yelling or noise coming from the house as Cy and Skin exited the vehicle. Both officers placed their batons in the holders on their Sam

Browns and walked along the sidewalk to the house.

The sergeant reached his hand upward to ring the doorbell when the door opened. A large sour-faced woman in her forties stood before him. She was one of the heftiest women Cy had ever seen. She was at least six foot and weighed well over four hundred pounds. The floor squeaked as she stepped aside and ordered them to come inside. She was so large both officers had to brush against her belly to get through the threshold.

Cy removed his notepad from a clip on his belt. "Are you Mrs. Marshall, ma'am?"

"Of course. Who the hell else would I be?" she answered with a scowl. "He's the one you want over there." The woman pointed with an arm as big as a side of beef to a man quietly sitting on the living room couch. "Get his skinny ass out of my house. I want him out now!"

Cy didn't like Mrs. Marshall. He wondered what it would be like living with a woman so overbearing. "Mrs. Marshall, what is your first name?" Cy asked the question stiffly. Before she answered, he motioned for his partner to go talk with the husband to get his side of the story.

"Ginny."

"Your phone number, please."

"Look, I gave that information to the desk sergeant." The woman's face was wrinkled with hate and anger. Her hair was in disarray. Her left sleeve was ripped and her eyes showed only hostility. "That S.O.B. touched my daughter. His daughter. I want him out of here."

"Are you saying he has sexually abused your daughter, ma'am?" Cy glanced over at the husband sitting down on the couch with his arms folded carefully over his stomach. He appeared calm as he spoke in quiet tones to Skin.

"That's what I'm saying, you little nitwit."

"Where is your daughter now, Mrs. Marshall?"

Mrs. Marshall pointed to the hallway. "She's in her bedroom."

"May I speak with her, please?"

"Yes, you may, please," she mimicked a sweet sing-songy voice. "Come on, I'll show you, but you can't talk to her alone."

"I wouldn't expect to, ma'am."

Cy followed the mother to the girl's bedroom. He walked in behind the mother and found the girl sitting on the bed with her knees pulled up to her chest. Cy looked at the huge woman in front of him and decided her husband would get the worst end of the stick if he ever messed with her.

When Ginny sat on the edge of the bed, the mattress pushed downward and the young girl, atop the bedspread, involuntarily rolled over toward her mother. She was out of breath from the effort of sitting and was taking in short gasps of air. Her profile was shadowed by facial sideburns and sporadic hairs on her cheeks and chin. Cy wondered to himself why she didn't shave.

He scanned the girl quickly and did not observe the usual signs of crying, spaciness, or inadvertent eyes—no bruises or torn clothes. In fact, the girl was very tranquil, except she appeared to be afraid of her mother. Her eyes narrowed when her mother sat down next to her, and then she looked up at the ceiling.

Cy pulled a chair over to the bed, sat down, and spoke to the girl softly. "My name is Sergeant Golden, but you can call me Cy. I'm with the Los Angeles Police Department. My partner and I were called here because there is a problem. Would you mind talking to me about it?"

There was silence for a moment and the girl didn't break her concentration on the ceiling. It appeared she was afraid to look at her mother. After a quiet moment she spoke. "Is it all right, Mom?"

"It's all right, honey. You answer all his questions and don't leave nothing out," the mother answered softly. Cy was taken back by the woman's tender voice when she addressed her daughter.

"Yes, sir. What do you want to know?"

Cy leaned over and spoke in a soft tone. "What is your name, dear?"

"Nancy."

"How old are you, Nancy?"

"I'm twelve, sir." For the first time the girl looked over at Cy and felt considerably more comfortable. He had a handsome face and he smiled warmly at her. She noticed he was writing down information as she spoke. "I was born on June the second, 1959, at the Los Angeles General Hospital."

"Is the man in the other room your father?"

"Yes, sir."

"What is his name?"

"William J. Marshall. Most people call him Bill."

Cy looked at the mother, "Mrs. Marshall, could you tell me his date of birth and where he works, including the phone number and address?" When the mother gave him the information he turned his attention back to Nancy.

"Nancy, did your father hurt you?"

"No, sir."

"Did he do things to you or with you that he shouldn't have?"

"Yes, sir."

"Did he do something today that he shouldn't have?"

"He makes me do things every day." A single tear appeared at the corner of her eye and ran down her face dripping onto her forearm.

"What kind of things does he make you do, Nancy?"

Nancy didn't answer. Her throat muscles were working but her voice couldn't break through the strained muscles. Cy placed his hand on her arm and squeezed it softly. "It's okay, Nancy. No one is blaming you. You haven't done anything wrong, but I need to know what your father has done. Did he touch you where he shouldn't have?"

"Yes," she cried. She raised up and her mother put her arms around her daughter and warmly hugged the little girl. Cy looked at the woman's massive arms. He estimated they were bigger than his thighs.

"Sweetheart, Mommy isn't mad at you. You haven't done anything wrong. Now tell the cop what went on between you and your father. You have to tell him if you don't want Mommy to get into trouble."

Cy frowned, pondering her statement. He failed to understand her meaning. He looked back at Nancy. "Where did your father touch you today?"

"Where I go to the bathroom," Nancy whimpered. Tears were running down both cheeks. She continued hugging her mother searching for security and acceptance.

"Was it on top of your clothes or underneath?"

"Underneath."

"Did you touch him?"

"Yes, but I didn't want to. He always makes me. He said he'd leave us if I ever told anyone." Nancy sucked in a lungful of air and burst out crying.

"Has this been going on for a long time, Nancy?"

"Yes."

Cy patted the young girl on the head. He understood the mother's anger now and felt ashamed for judging her so sharply at the door. He stood up and addressed the mother. "Mrs. Marshall, we need to have Nancy talk with a juvenile officer to take a full statement. We have enough information to incarcerate your husband. Would you mind taking your daughter to the station or would you rather I have an officer come here? Which would you like?"

"Have an officer come here, please. I don't want her to be around anyone else right now—especially strangers." Mrs. Marshall looked bewildered by her daughter's violation. The mother relayed to Cy she had only found out today that things had been happening for some time and was having difficulty dealing with it. Cy felt sorry for them both.

He reached down and touched Nancy on the head again and assured her everything would be all right. He walked back into the living room. Mr. Marshall was still seated in the same position on the couch where he was when they first walked into the house. Skin was seated across the room talking to him about police work in general.

Cy walked over to Mr. Marshall and stood a few feet before him. He didn't like the man but knew better than to display his emotions. The father hadn't shaved for a couple of days and his body odor was rank. He sat on the sofa with his arms crossed as if nothing were wrong.

"Do you have anything you want to say to me, Mr. Marshall?" Cy asked, studying the man.

"What for?" he answered gruffly.

"Your daughter states you have sexually abused her. Do you want to talk about it?"

"You want my story? You already have an opinion, don't you?" The man crossed his legs and showed a slight grimace in his facial expression.

"Have you anything you want to say now, Mr. Marshall?"

"Am I under arrest?"

"Don't you think you ought to be?" Cy wanted the man to explain himself before arresting him. Once he was under arrest, he would have to advise him of his rights. In most cases suspects stopped talking until they had their attorney present and the attorneys never let their clients talk.

"I haven't done anything to be ashamed of," Mr. Marshall

answered. He looked over to the hallway to make sure his wife wasn't listening. "Nancy is my daughter. She's my flesh and blood. I can do anything I want."

"What do you mean by anything, Mr. Marshall?"

"When I tell her to do something, she better do it, or I'll beat her butt, that's what. If I want to fool around a little, I have that right. What's the difference in spanking her butt and just patting it slowly?"

Cy's anger rose. He quickly stepped forward. "I'm placing you under arrest, Mr. Marshall. You'll have to come down to the station for booking. You can talk to an attorney and get bail set there." Cy grabbed the man roughly by the arm and pulled him to his feet. That was a mistake. Skin who was now standing next to him gasped in horror.

When the man was jerked to his feet, without the protection of his arm supporting his stomach, his entrails fell out onto his knees. The stench cut the air. Cy was shocked to see the huge round light green stomach wall and knotted intestines dangle nearly to the floor.

"Gees almighty, man, sit back down!" Cy pushed the man back on the sofa and nervously grabbed a handful of entrails and pushed them back in his lap. "Skin, give me a hand!" Cy snapped at his partner.

"You got it, Sarge," Skin was getting sick and ran for the front door, holding his hand over his mouth and gagging. Bile was working its way up his throat. "I'll...I'll..." He belched a gurgling bubble and ran out the door to get some fresh air. "I'll call an ambulance." He left the door open and threw up onto the middle of the porch.

Cy was frowning heavily. He desperately attempted to push the man's stomach back in its cavity. He was losing ground fast. The human bile smell was too much to bear. He clenched his teeth together trying to hold down his own stomach.

Mr. Marshall had passed out on the sofa with his stomach lying in his lap. There was a fourteen-inch slash across his sagging stomach just below his naval. It amazed Cy that there was hardly any blood.

Mrs. Marshall stepped into the room with a large grin spread over her face. "It serves the bum right. I want him out of here now!"

"Did you do this?" Cy looked around at her. He thought she

was getting ready to jump on her husband, seeing a fiery glare in her eyes.

"You didn't think this coward would commit hari kari, did ya? He should be dead, that's what he ought to be," she answered.

Cy was desperate as he continued to shove the man's slick stomach back inside the dark gaping hole. The wet entrails were slipping between Cy's fingers hopelessly and the smell was getting worse. Sweat was running down his face and he could feel his back dripping wet. He leaned over to peer out the open door. He was immediately discouraged to see Skin on his hands and knees on the front lawn.

He yelled, "Skin, get out to the car and call dispatch!"

Mrs. Marshall moved over to her husband. For a moment Cy thought she was going to jump on him. "I hope you die, you miserable little worm!" She leaned over and slapped him hard across the face but he did not respond. He was unconscious and Cy knew he was dying from shock.

"Mrs. Marshall, get away from him! You'll kill him!"

"I could care less after what he did to my baby." She leaned over and clubbed her husband with a fist alongside his head.

"I said get away from him, you crazy..." Cy never got the words out. Mrs. Marshall slammed him with a left hook between the eyes, knocking him on his back.

Darkness momentarily overcame Cy. Spots were developing and fading away. He blinked his eyes and after a few seconds focused on Mrs. Marshall. To his horror she was bending over her husband, pulling out his stomach with both hands. She was screaming while she yanked at his entrails. "I'll kill you, you slimy gutless wonder!"

Cy pulled himself up and jumped on Mrs. Marshall's back. He slipped his left arm around her neck and applied extensive pressure, but he couldn't get her to release her husband's stomach. The man's intestines had not been severed and they stretched out like spaghetti under the woman's slithery grip.

Skin heard the commotion and came running back into the room to help. He saw his sergeant on top of the woman choking her out as she was yanking out a large armful of intestines, and he thought he was going to faint when the odor overwhelmed him. He grabbed his mouth with both hands, turned around, and went back out onto the lawn to give up the rest of his breakfast.

After Cy had applied the sleeper hold for a few moments, Mrs. Marshall released her husband's stomach and fell to the floor. In attempting to pull her backward to keep her off her husband, he slipped and fell under her.

That's where he was, under Mrs. Marshall on the floor, when backup arrived. Two officers ran inside and found the woman out cold on top of Cy who was almost unconscious from the woman's weight.

Officer Chuck Fulton bounced into the room with his partner, Officer Billy Garcia, prepared to assist their sergeant. When they found their supervisor squirming for freedom under Mrs. Marshall who was sprawled out like a huge walrus, they both looked at each other in unison. Chuck couldn't suppress a convulsive loud squeal. The woman's mouth was open wide. Her massive arms were raised above her head on the floor as if yielding in submission. Their dwarfed sergeant was mostly obscured beneath her, and it was apparent he was helpless under her massive weight. Sergeant Golden, looking horrified, pleaded speechlessly for help. He could not get the air he needed and was turning blue.

Officers Fulton and Garcia looked to their left when they got a whiff of a terrible smell. When they saw the man reclining on the couch with his stomach lying at his side, they both ran out of the house and retrieved Skin off the lawn to assist with the detail.

Tommy Angelino stepped from the shiny black Lincoln and carefully looked up and down the street for anything remotely suspicious or out of place. He was near the top of the most dangerous Mexican Mafia family in East L.A., and competition was growing and becoming difficult to control.

For many years, only the White Fence gang ran the streets. But Joe Molino, along with Angelino, had shown intelligence and wit to such a high degree that he had grown in strength and power—a status so powerful people died at his wish. Together the two men formed the Mexican Mafia. The existing gangs stayed to themselves and did not want to confront them.

The Mafia wanted to control all the territory and in order to expand, it required complete allegiance from its people. When a brother became part of the Mafia family, it was for life.

To barter or trade with any street gang or other organization was intolerable and almost always required elimination of the offending member. This was necessary to retain respect and for the people to understand the serious consequences.

The American people were not aware of the Hispanic strength in their own country. They feared gangs like the Hell's Angels, Black Panthers, and the S.L.A., or those who wanted to be known to the public. The Mexican underground gained strength because they were only known by their own people and did not and would not talk about their own. The price of a loose tongue was death. Cutting out the tongue was not enough; death was respected. The Mafia had to be feared.

Tommy Angelino was viewed as a man with class and expensive tastes. His suit was tailored by a private firm, and expense was of no consequence. His diamond and gold rings were impressive and his shoes were the best money could buy. A full-cut, two-carat diamond stickpin was set in the center of his imported silk tie. But most people admired Tommy Angelino from a distance. No one was allowed close to him except by permission. On the few occasions when strangers were near enough to see his eyes, they instinctively knew he was extremely dangerous. They could see death and it was frightening. Most people would not look him in the eye; instead they would look submissively down at the ground, and it pleased him to have such power.

Juan Mores was Angelino's right-hand man. He was a massive man who stood over six feet four and weighed over two hundred and fifty pounds. His cold black eyes swept back and forth beyond his boss to check the south streets and sidewalks for anyone giving them unwarranted attention. He didn't smile at his boss; he was strictly business and was prepared to die or kill for his patron. Juan quickly glanced at the front of the car. Herman Duran was in position a few feet away observing business to the north.

"Juan, you say Carlos is in his apartment?" Tommy Angelino spoke softly out of the corner of his mouth without looking at his bodyguard.

"Si."

"Are all the positions covered?"

"Si, Señor Angelino, everything is in place." Juan's deep voice convinced his boss that they were not wasting his time.

Ricardo Padilla, acting rear security, moved from the rear of the car and led the way up the concrete steps to the front door. He opened it, stepped inside, glanced around, and then held the door open for Angelino. Ricardo moved slowly up the stairs to apartment 201. He turned to check the hall and glanced back at the boss. Juan was standing impatiently behind Angelino near the top of the stairs.

Armando Sausedo quietly stepped outside apartment 202 with a Remington 12-gauge pump shotgun and took his position with his back to Carlos's room. He was prepared to stand guard while business was taking place inside.

Tommy Angelino looked hard at Ricardo and nodded his head once. Ricardo kicked the door in with his right foot. The door flew open so hard the door handle stuck through drywall on the inside wall. Ricardo flew inside with a sawed-off shotgun in his hands that he had been carrying under his light jacket. Juan was right behind him. Both men raced into the living room where Carlos had been asleep on the couch. He lurched to a sitting position and without looking at the intruders, grabbed for a .38 revolver on the coffee table. Juan kicked Carlos in the head, knocking him backward. Carlos cried out as his eyes searched the room to see who was after him.

"Alto, you stupid little pig," Juan cursed, as he grabbed Carlos by the hair and slammed his head face-first onto the coffee table, scattering beer bottles everywhere. Carlos made a grunting sound and slid to the floor. The sound of a dull thud filled the room as Juan kicked him between the eyes. The big Mexican bent over and pulled the dazed man to a sitting position. Angelino motioned for the others to sit down and the two men obeyed. Tommy Angelino carefully observed Carlos sitting with his head resting on his chest, his back to the couch. Both eyes were swelling and would be closed within minutes. Blood dripped onto his flowered shirt.

The room was filthy. One Mexican blanket hung on the wall and another lay across the back of the sofa. Mexican-themed pictures also hung from a cracked and dirty wall. Flies worked on a plate of refried beans and rice that was on the floor next to the kitchen table. The radio was turned down low to a Mexican station.

Angelino noticed a slight flicker of Carlos's eyelid. "Carlos, amigo, we must have a conversation." He spoke very quietly with only a slight accent. Carlos did not move or open his eyes.

"Hey, amigo mio, you must respond or you will feel a blade at the base of your testicles." Angelino's words were low, below a whisper.

Carlos's lower lip quivered and beads of moisture appeared on his forehead. His eyes were shut as he spoke. "Por favor, Señor Angelino, I have for nada. Por nada. I am loyal."

"Loyal to whom?"

"Loyal to you."

"Are you loyal to Pavlo, Carlos?"

Carlos twitched slightly. "Por favor, Señor, what does Pavlo have to do with me, with business?"

"You do not know, Carlos?"Angelino squinted, as he watched Carlos, who would not open his eyes out of fear.

"Por favor, no. No lo se, I swear. I know nothing. I only do what I am told to do. I swear it on my mother."

"A very interesting story has come to my attention, Carlos. The story does not make me happy. No, it does not even make me smile. Yes, it causes me great anger. Pavlo intercepted one of my mules on a run with a large quantity of goods." Angelino leaned over and nudged Carlos on the cheek with a ballpoint pen that he'd removed from his inside pocket.

"Pavlo is a dead man, Carlos. You must tell me now, who has betrayed me? Who gave your cousin confidential information?"

Carlos flinched and opened his eyes but only stared at the floor. "He may be my cousin, but I do not claim him. He is a dog of the streets. I have nothing to do with him. I swear on my mother. You must believe me."

"What I must believe is for me to decide." Angelino leaned a little closer to Carlos. "You must convey your thoughts to me now and be very careful not to deceive me. Do you understand, Carlos?"

"Si, I will speak the truth. I swear." Carlos's face and neck were completely wet with perspiration.

"Do you know where your cousin received information on my street business?"

"I swear I do not know. You must believe me." Carlos shook his head back and forth. He could not understand how he could have gotten himself into such a predicament. He had worked for the family for over five years and never once was dishonest. Why his filthy cousin would do this to him, he could not comprehend.

"Let me see your arm, Carlos," Angelino demanded.

Reluctantly Carlos showed both arms, each with needle tracks like little avenues up and down from elbow to wrist.

"Tsk, tsk...I am disappointed in you, Carlos. You have been warned about indulging. It is a death sentence and you know it. You are of no use to me when you are like this."

Angelino stood up and walked around the room knocking lamps and chairs over. He came back over to Carlos and motioned for his two men to pull Carlos up on the sofa. "This place is not fit for a dog to live in. You are a very poor representative of myself and the business."

"I can get off the stuff. It is only a momentary problem. Por favor, give me a chance and I will do it, I swear." Carlos was shaking and needed a fix quickly to help control himself.

"Do you prefer to live in this condition, or die? It is your choice, Carlos. What is it?"

Carlos stared at the coffee table, refusing to look up at Angelino. "I want to live. I will do what is necessary."

Angelino motioned for Juan and Ricardo to stand Carlos up on his feet. "There are two requirements for you to live, Carlos," Angelino whispered, leaning over to the shivering man. He slipped his right hand into his pocket and removed an object, keeping it concealed from Carlos.

"I will do what you order me to do. I will do anything. I know nothing, so I can say nothing."

"First you will go cold turkey and clean yourself out. You are no good to anyone the way you are. You only have one chance." Angelino hesitated, then spoke slowly and carefully. "You will find out from Pavlo where he got his information."

"I cannot get you that information. His people will kill me."

Angelino's right hand shot forward, the blade slitting Carlos's throat from two inches right of center to the base of his ear. Blood squirted into the air and Angelino jumped back to keep clear of the shooting stream of blood that came in pumping sprays.

At first Carlos had not realized what had happened. He felt something tug at his neck but there was no pain. It was the massive amount of blood that made him realize his throat had been cut. He panicked and covered the gaping cut with his hand to control the bleeding. Every time his heart beat, a surge of dark red blood squirted against his hand. The windpipe had been expertly missed, but the main artery had been severed.

Carlos felt his legs buckle underneath him and he crashed to the floor. He was dying. He focused on the carpet trying to comprehend what had happened. How did this all come about? After joining the organization he quickly gained power and money. Then he tried drugs only to see why so many people were selling their souls. At first he took occasional hits because it did relax his tension. When he got headaches or back spasms, the white powder always made him feel better. He never knew he was hooked, but he had broken the pusher's code of abstinence—never use the stuff, only sell.

Pain began to pulsate in Carlos's neck. He felt dizzy and the lights softened. A familiar voice echoed in his head. "¿Carlos, quieres vivir?" Carlos felt a hand slapping him on the face. His eyes opened and for the first time he had the courage to look at Señor Angelino. For the first time the fierce eyes of Angelino did not frighten him. He was already dead. Tommy Angelino was not a threat anymore.

"¿Carlos! Quieres vivir?"

Carlos was going to faint and then die. Perhaps Angelino could save him. He tried hard to speak but had little strength. "Si, Señor, I want to live. Help me. Por favor. On my mother, por favor." The air gurgled in his throat.

Angelino stepped back and looked at Juan. "Take care of him."

Without answering, Juan reached into his pocket and pulled out a packet of dental floss. He pulled out a large strand and cut it off. "Ricardo, pull the vein out and steady his head," ordered Juan.

Angelino walked over to the phone, picked it up, and called the police. He explained there had been an accident. A drunk Mexican had fallen on a broken beer bottle and cut his throat. He was bleeding to death and the situation required an ambulance. Without answering any questions he hung the receiver up after wiping his fingerprints from the hand grip.

Ricardo did as he was told. He reached into the deep cut and grabbed the end of the severed vein. It was slippery and he had difficulty keeping a grip as he pinched it between the tips of his thumb and forefinger. Lumps of coagulated blood pushed up out of the cut and slid down the wet skin onto Carlos' shoulder.

Armando had been standing guard in the hallway. There was no action outside the apartment. He was disturbed by the strange sounds coming from inside the room. He peered around the doorjamb and saw Juan tying off the main artery. Blood dripped from the ceiling and was everywhere in the apartment. He saw the big blood clot sliding down Carlos's front.

Armando closed his eyes and quickly turned back around to concentrate on the hallway. He had a sick pounding in his stomach. He wished he had listened to his mother and stayed off the streets. His mother was always right. She only had love. He could not understand why he had not paid attention to her counsel. He immediately made the decision he would never cross Tommy Angelino. A shiver of fear ran down his back, and he made a second promise to himself never to do anything that would cause suspicion of his loyalty to the organization. He made a third promise to himself. If it ever became possible, he would leave California and never be heard from again.

Juan appeared at the door. Armando looked into the eyes of the meanest and ugliest man he had ever seen. He always felt that way around Juan. A jagged scar ran from the center of Juan's right cheek over the nose and downward into the upper lip, leaving a large gash in the fleshy part just above his teeth. Armando had heard a story that Juan's nose was completely cut off in a knife fight. After Juan cut the man's tongue out, he found his nose on the floor, picked it up, took it to a doctor friend, and had it sewed back on.

Juan's big head turned to Armando. "Is it clear?"

"Si, it is clear."

"Vamanos," Juan said, stepping out the door and looking up and down the hallway.

The four men took their time walking out of the building. They entered the waiting car and the driver drove them away.

Chapter 7
Patrolling Hollenbeck Division

Thirty minutes later at the Hollenbeck Station, Cy leaned over the sink in the men's room to wash his face in the cool, clear water. He finally decided that just patting his face wasn't enough. He put his head under the faucet and turned on the water full force over his head. When he was thoroughly drenched, he turned the faucet off and leaned on the porcelain sink with both hands for support as he stared down at the washbasin. He studied the water dripping into the sink from his head. He closed his eyes and thought about Mrs. Marshall pulling her husband's stomach out with her bare hands. He fought back the nausea and shook his head. Cy took a deep breath, ignoring the pain in his chest from the bruised ribs he received when Mrs. Marshall fell on him. It had taken all four of the officers to remove her from the living room. She had to be restrained from her husband until the ambulance arrived and transported him to the hospital.

The locker room door swung open with a loud bang. Four officers walked into the latrine. One of the men stepped over to the side and leaned against the wall next to the sergeant while he studied the washroom sink.

"Hey, Sarge, how ya doing?" Detective Tony Valin grinned. The other three men went about their business but were being quiet so they could hear the conversation. "Lieutenant Wilson told us you have a gut-wrenching story to tell." All four officers laughed through closed lips, hissing in unison. "Is it true, Sarge? Did you assist in performing a tummy tuck on some poor fellow and then try to steal his wife, but you couldn't get her out the door?"

Cy didn't respond. He washed his face again. He noticed the sink was dirty and wondered why the trustees weren't more careful in their job assignment. Tony was his good friend but he wasn't funny today, and Cy wished everyone would leave him alone.

"Come on, Sarge. I gotta know. Is it true? Was this luscious lady really passed out in a romantic ecstasy after you both gutted her husband?" Tony was guffawing between breaths, holding his arms across his stomach. "Come on, Sarge. You're my main man here. Out with it. What's the story?"

At first Cy didn't think it was funny. He did not like his subordinates laughing at him either. Tony worked in drug enforcement and was Jacob's old partner. After a moment of thinking it through, it struck him he was taking the incident too seriously. It was over and no one had died. The more he considered it, the more he saw the humor. He first broke into a smile and then began laughing as the full memory hit him— Mrs. Marshall leaning over her husband on the couch, screaming wildly and pulling out her husband's stomach like old laundry out of a basket.

The men in the latrine wouldn't let Cy leave until he told the whole story. By the time he left the room, a crowd of over fifteen officers had gathered, including Chuck and Billy who showed up for backup. The story took a whole new avenue and got better.

Cy walked down the hall to the break room to get Skin. Jacob came out of his office and spotted Cy. "Hey, cowboy. Where you going?"

"Jake, you snake. You couldn't keep quiet on this one, could you?"

"No sir. This is one detail that is going to hang on for quite a while," Jacob laughed. "Let's get together after the shift is over and go to Jack's Piss Hole. Some new recruits who think they are real hotshots are going to be there tonight. They'll be guzzling beer like soda and bragging on themselves. It may be worth fifteen or twenty dollars to us. Wha' da ya say, my man?" Jacob was referring to the tavern across the street from the police station. Many of the law enforcement community frequented that particular bar and grill before going home after work. Cy had a reputation for his fast draw. The older officers knew better than to challenge Cy; however, everyone enjoyed the entertainment watching the new men take him on.

"Sure, why not. Skin and I will be off shift at 2000 hours. We'll meet you at Jack's about 2030. That okay?"

"That's fine, cowboy. Don't mess up your arm tonight, we're gonna need it later."

"See you later, Jake." Cy grinned and went down the hall to the break room where he could hear laughter from inside. Skin was in the corner telling the story to other officers who were on break, and Cy had to repeat his story before they would let him leave.

Outside they walked to their patrol unit. "Skin, you take the wheel. I'm tired and can't think. This has been one heck of a night. Can you keep us out of trouble?"

"You got it, Sarge," Skin said, catching the keys from Cy. "I won't get us into anything that we can't handle."

"You better not, I'm mentally shot," Cy groaned quietly. He was exhausted and needed a quiet watch.

They patrolled for thirty minutes, giving backup to two other units on suspicious persons. Skin finally stopped the patrol car at Orozco's Taco Stand at the corner of Pomeroy and Soto. Each ordered two hard-shell tacos and sat on the outside table close to the car so they could hear the police radio.

It was normal to check out the area for street people and possible perpetrators before sitting down at a table open to the street. Skin walked around the business to check on anyone who might come up on them while they were eating. When the tacos were ready they sat down facing each other so they could cover each other's back. The two officers opened their food wrappers and began eating, all the while keeping watch for each other.

"Mike, I need to talk to you about something. I want you to really think about it." Cy looked at Skin and studied his face then glanced behind him. Two men were across the street at a service station sitting on the ground next to a block wall drinking something out of a brown paper bag. It had to be booze, but they appeared harmless and they were more than seventy-five feet away.

"Are you getting ready to chew me out, Sarge?" Skin responded with a worried tone in his voice.

"No. Why?"

"The guys, my friends, always call me Skin. You must be heading for something important if you're calling me Mike."

Cy took another bite of his taco and shook is head. "I didn't realize I said Mike. Sorry. What I have to say is personal. No, it's not a chewing out. I'm going to take you into my confidence, so just hear me out. I need to know your feelings on something that may or may not put us at risk someday."

Skin looked at the sergeant and nodded his head while eating his taco.

"I had an understanding with Jacob, and I want one with

you. As long as we ride together or happen to answer the same police detail, someday this agreement may become important. The lieutenant and I made a pact that we would never give up our guns to a suspect even if he had the drop on us," Cy said dryly, staring at Skin and trying to read his face.

"What do ya mean, Sarge? If a person has a gun on you, or I'm a hostage, you won't give up your weapon?" Skin stopped chewing and put down his taco.

"That's right. You remember the two cops in *The Onion Field*—one was under the gun and the other officer gave his weapon up to save his buddy. One cop ended up dead and the other was ruined for life." Cy took a drink of his Coke. "I will not give up my weapon for anybody including you." Cy carefully studied Skin who sat dumb. "Do you realize what I am saying? I am not going to die without my gun in my hand. You give your gun up, you are at the mercy of the bad guy. I can't and I won't get caught in that predicament."

"I never figured you would, Sarge. I know how fast you are and I trust you. But that doesn't matter. I wouldn't give up my weapon either. I have always believed what we learned in the academy and more so after being on the street. Once you give up your gun, you put yourself and your partner's life in jeopardy. End of story."

Skin took a quick drink to wash down his food. "Jacob told me you both had an understanding. I had my mind made up a long time ago I'd rather die fighting than be on my knees crying for mercy and getting my brains blown out anyway." Skin looked at his sergeant with sudden affection. "I want you to know you can count on me one hundred percent. I wouldn't expect any less from you."

Cy glanced at Skin and looked away quickly. Skin had a light film over his eyes. He was emotionally moved, knowing he was totally in his sergeant's confidence. Cy gripped Skin's forearm and squeezed it briefly. "Your friendship means a lot to me, Skin."

Both finished their tacos in silence. Cy noticed before they resumed patrol that one of the two men across the street had passed out. He was thankful he did not have a drinking problem as so many cops do.

Back in the patrol unit the radio squawked continuously, barking out orders to the different cars. Skin made two traffic stops but yielded a dry run on each car. No stolen vehicles, and driver's licenses were in order. As both listened to the radio they observed the people on the streets and alleys.

"Sarge, have you heard about Chuck Fulton leaving?"

"Leaving for where? He's not quitting, is he?" Cy was genuinely surprised.

"Yeah, he is. He told me at the beginning of shift. He said he was going to talk to you about it tonight at Jack's. His wife is from Walla Walla, Washington, and she wants to move back to be near her parents," Skin said, shaking his head. "He is one good officer. I hate to see him leave—and whoever heard of Walla Walla?"

"I heard him mention it once or twice. I think Chuck is from that area, too. I know they have a prison there and there's supposed to be some good deer hunting in the Cascade and Blue Mountains. I hate to see Fulton go. He's a funny guy and I've enjoyed his humor."

"Well, I know Chuck. You watch, he'll make chief there someday and live the good life," Skin laughed.

"Let's hope so. We need another contact location for hunting and fishing," Cy said. "Which reminds me. We have to plan our fishing trip to Gold Beach and our deer hunt at Glass Mountain. We only have a couple of months before we leave."

"It's taken care of. The lieutenant told me he's got the time off. As soon as we're finished fishing for three days, deer season opens in Mono County. I'm looking forward to getting back to our camping spot. We've had some good meals on that old mountain."

Cy looked out the window and gave a friendly wave to a man standing on the corner. Nothing seemed out of order. People were quietly going about their business. "I think it's the most beautiful place I've ever seen. My dad loved it there. You have the Mammoth Ski Resort just a few miles away to the south, the Yosemite Mountains to the west, Mono Lake to the north, and the west Nevada desert to the east. Right in the middle of it all is Glass Mountain. A person wouldn't believe it until they saw it. The whole place is a geological wonder with the highest mountains in the state and those volcano craters, let alone the best ghost town in existence—Bodie."

"I can hardly wait," Skin said excitedly. "I can taste the steaks and potatoes now." He turned the corner as the radio blurted their number.

"Four Adam 55, answer a 415 family disturbance at 2885 Blanchard. Downstairs tenant stated they could hear screaming from the above apartment."

"Four Adam 55, copy en route," Cy answered.

The domestic disturbance was in the middle east side of L.A. and a heavily populated Hispanic neighborhood in the middle lower-class area. Skin was driving, and they found the location within three minutes of responding to the call.

Arriving at the address, Skin pulled the patrol unit to the curb and Cy reported their position and arrival time. "Request backup to stand by our unit. We'll be going in at this time."

"Copy, will send unit Four X-ray 68 for assist," the radio barked back.

Cy and Skin placed their batons in their belt rings as they stepped out of the car. Both men looked up and down the street. Several Mexican boys were standing together a half block away on the same side of the street. They stopped talking and stared at the two police officers. Cy turned to his partner. "Check ETA for the backup." The sergeant glanced back around to the boys and the four stood their ground, watching curiously to see what was going to occur. Even though it was September, Cy was getting warm. He could feel little beads of sweat slide down his neck and back.

"Chuck and his partner are three blocks away," Skin said, loud enough for the boys to hear. "He said they would sit on the car."

The sergeant and Skin checked the numbers out and confirmed it was an upstairs apartment to the four-plex. Skin noticed the downstairs apartment living room curtains move slightly as they approached the building.

"We're being watched," Skin said under his breath.

"I saw the curtain. Probably the complaining party," Cy murmured, as they climbed the stairs. He glanced out of the corner of his eye at the window again and thought he could see the silhouette of someone standing motionless behind the curtain.

Both officers cautiously ascended the stairs. A light at the top of the doorway revealed the correct number. There was no trash in the hallway and no graffiti on the walls. The apartment complex appeared cleaner than the average in the projects.

Cy motioned for his partner to step left so that when the door opened, he would be able to quickly assess any danger that might be present. Cy stepped to the right of the door. He made sure he was clear of the door in the event someone shot through it. Skin knocked and waited a few moments but nothing happened. Cy knocked harder and glanced at his partner. "Strange we're not getting an answer. It's too quiet in there." Skin looked back at him and raised his eyebrows.

Cy wondered whether it was a phony call so someone could vandalize their patrol car. "Let's get back downstairs," he said, moving away. He happened to look at the doorknob as he was turning. He quickly raised his hand and signaled Skin, pointing to the doorknob. It was turning very slowly. Cy studied the brass handle to make sure it was revolving. At first he thought his eyes were playing tricks on him. He glanced at Skin and frowned. "Something isn't right," he whispered, then gestured to Skin to unsnap his weapon. Cy's heart began to beat faster, wondering what it was all about.

The door opened very slowly and at first Cy could only see dark shadows as he quickly tried to peer inside. His right hand rested on the handle of his handgun and was tense, ready to draw. His eyes finally focused into the dark room and objects began to appear as he stared beyond the crack of the door. Cy could see a face just beyond the narrow opening. He frowned, drawing upon all his senses, when he thought he heard a whisper coming from the figure. Little splatters of blood materialized on the edge of the white door as the whispers gave way to soft puffing sounds. Cy's brain was numb. He attempted to decode what was happening. He leaned closer and saw large swollen lips dripping with bloody bubbles. Cy could see now it was a young woman trying to say something through her badly broken lips. As the door opened a little more, the two officers could see more of her face. The girl's nose was enormous and had dark blood running down both nostrils, over her lips, and off her chin onto her white blouse. She continued to move her lips in a whisper.

"What are you saying, ma'am?" Cy said, leaning a little closer.

Eventually he understood her to say her husband had beat her up but she did not want him to go to jail. She wanted the officers to tell her husband to quit beating on her. The girl stepped back and opened the door enough for the two officers to enter.

The Hispanic girl was in her early twenties. Cy first observed that her hair was matted against her head with wet and dried blood. Her white blouse was splattered with blood spots, and some were so large and wet that in some areas the blouse clung to her chest. It was apparent she was not wearing a bra.

Both officers determined she was not a national as she did not have a heavy Mexican accent. Her English was excellent and she appeared to be Mexican-American. Cy glanced around the room and did not see anyone else. The apartment was plain with only a few pictures on the walls, and the room was orderly, but the furniture arrangement was strange. The kitchen and other rooms were to the left of the living room. Oddly, the couch by the left wall was pulled out about four feet with the front side facing the wall. There were no doors to the right of the room. Cy reasoned it was the adjoining apartment.

"Where's your husband?" Cy asked, glancing around the room. The girl's eyes were filled with pain. She slowly lifted her hand and pointed to the couch. Cy walked over to the couch while Skin moved to the center of the room in order to observe the entryways.

Cy looked over the back of the couch and saw a medium-built Mexican stretched out in his boxer shorts. He was lying on his back with his eyes closed. He was not snoring but breathing deeply. Cy leaned over the back side of the sofa and shook him by the shoulder. "I want to talk to you."

The man didn't move; however, Cy knew he was not really asleep. Cy took the man's right thumb and pressed his thumbnail into the base of the man's thumbnail. There was no reaction. He pressed harder and again there was no reaction.

Cy was coming to the conclusion it was a lost cause because of the woman's first remarks at the door. She didn't want her husband taken to jail. It was something so hard for him to understand. Why any woman would accept physical abuse and allow her husband to escape answering for his cowardly actions was beyond his comprehension. It happened so many times in family beefs. It never made sense to him.

Cy pinched the man's earlobe and pulled upward in a fast movement. Still there was no reaction. Cy looked over at his partner and raised both eyebrows. He leaned over the couch and spoke very sternly. "I guess you don't have to get up, but if you hit this lady one more time, I'm going to come back and take you to jail."

While Cy was speaking, the girl stepped to the right of the couch and carefully sat on the edge of the sofa at her husband's feet. The husband abruptly sat up and smashed his fist into his wife's swollen nose. Blood splattered her face and the wall after her head slammed against it. Cy thought her neck snapped because there was a definite popping sound as she flew backward. For only a brief moment he saw this action in slow motion and felt sick because he couldn't react quickly enough to prevent it.

The sergeant grabbed the man by the hair with his left hand and held him back. He glanced over at the girl's bloody face. Her head fell backward, her eyes rolling to the back of her head. Cy turned back to the man and swung a right hook and caught the Mexican square on the jaw with his gloved hand. The man was hit so hard he crashed backward on the couch and ended upside down with his head on the carpet.

Cy lost his temper and dove over the couch. The Mexican's feet had been sticking straight into the air as the couch turned over because of Cy's weight as he went over it. He smashed his left forearm into the man's neck. Cy's feet were now sticking up in the air too as he lay over the couch with his head down and his back against the wall. He grabbed the man by the hair with his right hand and pulled his head forward until his head touched his chest over Cy's forearm.

The husband blacked out. Cy let go and turned over with his feet still in the air. He looked up and immediately saw Skin twisting the man's foot, gritting his teeth as he applied pressure. Cy rolled back to a standing position and told Skin not to break his leg. Skin let go of the man's leg, and they set the couch to its normal position and attempted to revive the husband. When one of his legs jerked and began shaking, they knew he would be all right. After a few minutes Cy pulled the man to his feet. He was shorter than Cy and in his early thirties.

Cy sneered at the man and demanded angrily, "What's your name?"

"Henry," he choked.

"Last name?" Cy glared at the man.

"Vasquez," shaking his head in confusion. "What's your problem, man?"

Cy glanced around at Mrs. Vasquez. She was sitting on the floor with her back to the wall. Both eyes were beginning to swell shut and saliva was hanging on her chin. She was trying to focus on the three men standing before her. She tried to get up but couldn't stand straight on her rubbery legs. Instead, she turned over on all fours and slowly climbed to her feet with the help of the couch.

Skin was standing behind Mr. Vasquez, holding both his arms. He stepped to one side, released the man and told him to get his clothes on because he was going to jail. He began reading him his rights. Mr. Vasquez reached down to the side of the couch, grabbed his pants, and pulled them on.

Mrs. Vasquez maneuvered her way toward the three men. It was obvious she was in a lot of pain, and it appeared she was going to faint any moment. She moved up to the sergeant and peered through the tiny slits of her eyes.

"Please, sir," she pleaded, "don't arrest my husband."

"What!" Cy exclaimed. "What do you mean, don't arrest him!"

"Please, sir, don't take him to jail," the woman whispered and there was gurgling deep in her throat.

The sergeant lost his temper. "You stupid fool. You're more pathetic than he is." He almost felt he understood her husband. He was so angry he lost what pity he had felt. He even thought he understood why the husband beat her. Red flashes blocked his vision and a ball of anger swelled his stomach. Cy pointed his index finger at her large bloody nose when she opened her mouth to speak. "Don't say another word." He stared at her in complete anger. "Not a word!"

Skin patted Vasquez's pants, hesitated, then stuck his hand inside the right pocket. He removed eight yellow capsules. He gave a stiff smile to Cy and then told Vasquez he was under arrest for possession of a controlled substance. Skin immediately handcuffed Vasquez with his hands to the back and led him barefoot from the apartment, guiding the man by gripping a handful of his hair.

Down at the patrol car Cy gave a thumbs up to the backup unit stationed a couple of car lengths behind his vehicle. He put Mr. Vasquez in the back seat and pulled the seat belt around him. A protective prisoner screen separated the front seat from the back. Cy went to the passenger side, opened the door, slid inside, and shut his door. Skin had gone back to speak with Chuck and Billy.

Cy closed his eyes and shook his head, dots of sweat patterned his face. He was bewildered by people and their sick lives. He wondered if he understood anything. Perhaps he was the oddball.

Skin returned to the car and sat a moment before starting the engine. He pulled out a cigarette and put it between his lips. After it was lit he rolled down the window and exhaled. "Sarge, don't let this get to you. It's been a hard day. Let's book this guy, finish our reports, and head to Jack's for a cold one. I need a steak sandwich bad."

Cy nodded his head but didn't respond. He reminded himself not to get personally involved in domestic complaints. He thought to himself if he ever married, he would give of himself totally and seek that special deep commitment between a man and woman.

Mary Ann was a beautiful, kind, and loving woman. He knew she loved him and she would be a wonderful partner. He loved her and at the same time felt desperately lonely because he was not "in love" with her. He enjoyed her company, her personality, and beauty. So why couldn't he be in love with her? He became depressed and remained quiet on the way to the station.

After a few blocks en route to the Hollenbeck division, Cy thought of their prisoner. A small grin began to cross his lips thinking of the booking officers at the Glass House where Henry Vasquez would be incarcerated. The Glass House, also known as Central Jail or the Parker Building, was located at Central and San Pedro. It was approximately a mile west of the Hollenbeck Station. Patrolmen who brought prisoners to Central Jail for booking often felt their lives were endangered or at least felt highly intimidated by just being in the booking room at the jail during the booking process. The booking officers in Central had reputations for being the meanest, most foul-tempered cops anywhere. The jail officers had overbearing personalities and were rightfully compared to the older motorcycle cops for aggressiveness. If the jailers at Central were not harsh and assertive, they would not last long in an environment that only understood strength and dominant power. If jails were not authoritative and controlled by strict rules and regulations, the employees and prisoners would be in constant danger of their lives, health, and welfare.

Most people did not understand the life behind the chainlink fence that stood as the first perimeter line of barricades between the public and the building that housed some of the most vicious criminals in California. Jailers had to be tough. They had to be strict or they themselves were at risk. Criminals didn't respect weak jailers. It was important to a career criminal to be able to maintain an admiration among his peers as a respected person. Status as a prisoner set him apart from the weaker ones or the snitches. The true con was a person to be feared if improperly treated by other inmates or even guards. A bad ass reputation was quickly established when a prisoner put an officer to the floor. Though to his peers he was a person to respect, to the courts he was just another number who assaulted an officer. To some of the minority groups and organizations like the A.C.L.U., the prisoner is only protecting himself and his rights when he is being unlawfully abused. Cy's thinking along this line was interrupted when the car came to a jolting stop.

Skin parked the patrol car in the station's east lot, and the two officers and prisoner entered the building. Inside, three things had to be accomplished before Vasquez could be taken to Central Jail. First it was necessary to process him by taking identification pictures and prints. The field interrogation (FI) card had to be filled out. Second, a check for wants in the warrants section would be conducted. Third, the watch commander had to give his permission for the prisoner to be booked.

Lieutenant Jacob Wilson did not hesitate giving his consent for Sergeant Golden and Officer Michael Fin to book Henry Vasquez. He took Cy aside before they turned to leave the process room, leading Cy out into the hall away from their prisoner. "Listen, brother," Jacob whispered. "You best put a move on it. We have a little business to take care of tonight across the street. Jack's is going to be busy and I'm getting a might thirsty. Do you see any problems tonight?"

"We've got an hour and a half before the end of the watch," Cy answered. "We'll be there when our paperwork is finished."

Jacob wrinkled his forehead, squinting his eyes at Cy. "You don't look so good. Is anything wrong?"

"Nah, I'm okay. It's been a hard shift. See you in about an hour." With that, Cy followed Skin and their prisoner out the door to the police car.

Skin opened the door and pushed Vasquez in the back seat.

Vasquez sneered at Skin through piercing eyes. "You bald-headed freak. I'll be out of there before you get back to your black hole, pig." Vasquez's voice hissed his words between tight lips, leaving a light film of spray on Skin's face.

"That right?" Skin said, licking his lips in defiance. He leaned back out of the car, dropping the seat belt he was about to buckle around Vasquez. "You little puke tough guy."

Skin came around to the driver's side of the car and got behind the steering wheel. He pulled out onto 1st Street, turned right, and headed west to the Glass House. After several blocks en route, Skin took his foot off the accelerator, intentionally slowing down to miss the green light. When the light turned yellow at State Street, he accelerated as if making an attempt to make the intersection before it turned red. At the last moment he slammed on the brakes and skidded to a stop at the crosswalk.

Vasquez flew forward, smashing his face into the mesh prisoner screen. His head then slammed backward into the seat. "You pig!" Vasquez hissed. "You did that on purpose!"

Skin looked innocently at his sergeant. "Sorry, Sarge. He must have got his seat belt loose. I'm sure I secured him in."

Cy glanced at Vasquez. Blood appeared on the bridge of his nose. The screen left its impression deep on his forehead. Cy thought how the prisoner beat his wife senseless. "I don't like it, Skin," Cy snapped angrily, looking away so Skin could not see his face. "Don't let it happen again." The words were hard, but his face cracked a smile as he stared out the car window. He almost allowed a chuckle to escape through his clenched teeth.

Skin thought Cy was mad at him for the minor mishap. "I'll be more careful, Sarge. Promise." Skin drove to Central Jail without further incident.

Vasquez was visibly angry when he was removed from the back seat of the cruiser. Blood trickled down his forehead and was turning dark as it dried in place. Skin gave his prisoner a warm smile and jerked him to his feet.

Cy picked up the paperwork and walked up the cement walk and through a chainlink gate that led to the jail entrance. Both officers placed their weapons in separate gun boxes. Cy pressed a button to gain entry. After a moment the door buzzed and the three went through the steel door.

Inside, Skin moved to the right with his prisoner and unhandcuffed him. They stood next to the wall and waited quietly for a booking officer to approach them. Cy went over to the booking counter and gave the admitting papers to the officer behind the desk.

The man behind the counter was in his forties and wore gold-rimmed glasses. He looked up at Cy when he finished reading the watch commander's permission to book. "Okay, Sarge, we'll be with you whenever," he sighed, looking overworked.

A few feet away in front of the long booking counter, three booking officers were swearing at two other prisoners, giving them orders and shaking them down for contraband. Next to the wall stood the two arresting officers carefully observing the jailers in action. It was obvious the policemen did not want to get in the jailers' way and stimulate an unwarranted confrontation.

In the Glass House, a street officer was in the jailer's domain. It was sacred territory that all peace officers respected. It was a place where one did not violate jail rules, especially those having to do with safety. Every rule dealt with safety, so one did not break jail rules. All outsiders were at the jailer's mercy, either for protection or for quick and efficient service. Breaking a rule could cause an injury to someone or cause long periods of waiting with red tape as a work slow-down would most likely occur.

After Cy and Skin waited for approximately ten minutes, a mean-looking, tall black jailer walked over to Skin. "What in the hell are you doing here again? You were here yesterday with a DUI. You think we got nothing else to do around here?"

"Well, hello to you, too, Mr. Groucho," Skin cordially answered. "We thought you could use the business. We heard your jail population was down and you needed to justify the latest request for more personnel. So, here we are, sir. We wanted to do our part by upping your head count with a dirty wife beater."

"Funny man," the jailer bellowed. "What do they call you, Bubbles?" He reached up and put his large hand on top of Skin's head and squeezed it like a basketball. "You are one ugly dude. Did you know that?"

"Yes, sir. Yes, sir, I sure did...sir."

"That right, now," the big black man replied coolly. "How did you know that?"

"My mama told me," Skin answered, wondering where this was going.

"Right answer, Bubbles," as the jailer looked over at Vasquez with his best frown.

"Okay little wife beater with a waffle iron print on his face, turn around and face the wall and assume the position. Move!"

Skin moved away and stepped alongside Cy, praying Vasquez would maintain his sarcastic profile.

"You know the position. Expedite!" The jailer snapped his crisp words directly into Vasquez's face.

Vasquez took his time turning around, showing his defiance. He put his hands on the wall and spread his legs.

"Further apart, little hombre!"

"Yeah, yeah," Vasquez responded.

Cy and Skin moved back. They could see it coming. Cy felt a chill of exhilaration within. He knew what would eventually happen with the Mexican's poor attitude. He thought about the way Vasquez beat his wife into a bloody mess. She had been beaten into complete submission. Cy was starting to feel good. Things were looking up.

"In here you move when I say move. You say 'sir' when you speak. You got that?" the jailer yelled at the prisoner.

Vasquez maintained a strained stance, staring at the wall. He failed to show the slightest fear of the big jailer. Tattoos covered his arms and back indicating his gang relations. "You do not know who you are messing with, Mr. Big Deal. You ain't so tough. On the street, you are nothing but a black toad, Mr. Big Deal," replied Vasquez.

The jailer slammed a hand in the middle of Vasquez's back. "That's it. Keep your mouth shut and spread your legs."

Cy and Skin were both surprised the jailer was maintaining his cool. It was unanimous—Vasquez was nuts.

Vasquez looked around at the jailer. "Oh yeah, you inbred monkey! Now you want to have some fun?" He moved his hips back and forth. "Check it out, man. It's your dime."

The jailer was so quick it amazed Cy as he watched the Mexican go to the mat before the smile left Vasquez's face. The big arm of the black officer slipped around Vasquez's neck and applied pressure for the sleeper hold. From nowhere two other jailers were on Vasquez pulling his legs apart. A third jumped in the middle and hit Vasquez hard in the testicles searching for drugs and weapons. Vasquez would have screamed but his vocal cords had no air to allow them to vibrate. In less than six seconds he was unconscious. He lay limply on the light green floor mat. In fifteen seconds the prisoner was completely undressed to his shorts and thoroughly searched.

The black jailer was alone again and standing at the foot of Vasquez with his bulging arms folded, looking down at his prey. Vasquez shook his head, grabbed his throat, and focused on the jailer.

"Battered, bruised, and bewildered?" the jailer sneered with a wiry grin. "Get on your feet, scumbag, now!"

Vasquez genuinely tried to get his feet under him. Dazed, he did not move fast enough for the adversary. The jailer leaned down, grabbed a handful of hair, and jerked him to a standing position.

Skin elbowed Cy in the side and nodded his head approvingly. "Don't you just love these guys? They're great. They really know what they're doing here, don't they, Sarge?" Skin put a cigarette between his lips and lit it up, taking a long drag.

"Be quiet, you fool. Don't get this guy looking at us," Cy whispered, moving away from Skin.

Vasquez gathered his strength, hacked up a big louie, and spit in the jailer's face. "You cockroach. You're dead on the street, scab."

The jailer didn't bother wiping his face. He kicked Vasquez's feet out from underneath him in a sweeping move with his right foot. With his left he stepped hard on his neck. "You little greaseball. That's it." He looked around at his assistants. "We have a violent fighter here."

There was no mistaking the error Vasquez made. He fought desperately to get out from underneath the jailer's foot. His arms and legs swung ineffectively like a bug stuck to the mat. Three other jailers jumped on top of him.

Skin laughed, moving over to Cy and elbowing him in the ribs. "Like I said, Sarge, we're talking doom and gloom here."

Cy shook his head. "This guy is dying on the vine and doesn't know it. If he keeps resisting, they'll knock the daylights out of him."

Cy realized his headache was gone. He rolled his head around in a circle feeling pretty good about the whole thing. It amazed him how he was depressed earlier and felt so good now.

Chapter 8
Cigarettes Could Kill

Skin thought it was the street light that woke him up. It didn't matter. He had been tossing and turning for the last forty-five minutes. He couldn't get Mrs. Marshall out of his mind. After shift he had three beers, trying to wash the thoughts of her out of his mind. It didn't work. Enough was enough. His throat burned for a cigarette. He reached for the crumpled pack of Marlboroughs and fumbled hungrily for a smoke. It was empty and he got worried.

He crawled out of bed and stumbled into the kitchen. All his smokes were gone. He reached into the trash can and rustled through garbage. He pulled out six used cigarettes. After stripping them and finding some zigs in the drawer, he rolled a smoke. The taste wasn't great but it helped.

He opened his living room window and felt a cool breeze tickle his hairy chest. He rubbed his bald head and sat in a soft chair and looked out into the night. Skin's chest heaved when he coughed hard, almost going into a fit. He knew it was from smoking, but that was something he could never give up. There was too much pleasure in it, and it calmed his nerves. After dinner, having a drink or sitting on the throne with a smoke was life itself. A smoke was a smoke and nothing could replace it. He tried too many times. He wished he could get Cy to start so he would get off his case. He was tired of Cy's complaining every time he lit up in the squad car or in a closed room.

It made him angry because now he needed another smoke and he was out. It was three in the morning and he was disgusted with himself. He was getting desperate, so he went back into the bedroom and slipped on some pants and a T-shirt. He stepped into some shower thongs, grabbed some change, went out the door, and crossed the street to Ken's Liquor Store.

Skin accepted he was a chain smoker. He blew away an average of three packs a day. Lately it had gotten worse.

Every time he woke up during the night or had to use the bathroom or for whatever reason, he had to have a cigarette. He wouldn't admit it to his sergeant but he was badly addicted. It had gone beyond enjoyment. It had become a necessity.

Skin did not take a weapon to the store. He had forgotten it. It was a quiet neighborhood, a nice residential location dominated by working families. There were very few criminal problems in this particular area. He felt uncomfortable without his gun but decided against the odds of his needing it.

Skin walked into the store. Marilyn, the graveyard employee, was at the counter facing the door. She was a thin lady, about forty-five, with gray showing in her hair. She was a hard-looking woman but smiled easily at the few people she liked, and Skin was one of the few people she liked. Since she was a divorcee with four kids, this was the best shift for her to work, so she could be home with her children during the daytime when they returned from school.

A large glass donut case in the front of the store faced the customers. To the right was a long aisle that contained liquors and food items. Along the right wall was a wall-to-wall refrigerator with cold items. The cashier's counter was situated to the left of the door. Behind the cashier's counter was a large shelf with numerous tobacco products for sale. Marilyn was aware Skin was a cop. She often allowed him behind the counter when she was busy with customers. It had become a habit for him to serve himself.

No one else was in the store. Skin decided to go behind the counter anyway and picked up three packs of smokes. "Morning, Marilyn," he growled under his breath. "Got a burning in my throat. I gotta lubricate it with nicotine."

"Must be hurtin' to be in here this late, or this early," she giggled in a hoarse voice. "I know how it is, though. When you need it, you need it. No 'ands' or 'buts' about it. I just can't stand coughing up the green slime every morning when I get out of bed. One of these days I'm going to try to quit."

"That sounds real good," Skin smiled, shaking his head. He stayed behind the counter, not making an effort to leave.

"You ever get the coughs? I hate it," Marilyn frowned, shaking her head. "It's that green stuff that gives me the willies."

"Gees almighty, woman, you're making me sick."

"You've got to call it as you see it, friend."

While Skin was talking with Marilyn, the front door opened and two black men walked in. Skin didn't think anything about it. He was standing only a few feet away from her behind the counter. Suddenly both men pulled guns and pointed them at both Skin and Marilyn. The larger and meaner-looking black had a semiautomatic .45 Colt. The other man, who was short and thin, wore a black ballcap. He held a .22 semiautomatic pistol. Both men appeared high and a little fuzzy. The smaller one held his gun on Skin. "Don't you move, boy, or you're dead!" Both men were weaving on their feet and waving their guns back and forth. They appeared nervous but in sync.

Skin held his hands part way up, so the robber could see they were empty. "I'm not moving, man. You can have the store for all we care."

"He's right," Marilyn said, surprisingly calm. "Take what you want. We won't get in your way. This ain't my store. It's yours as a gift."

"Shut up, you ugly thing," the bigger man snapped. "We don't want conversation. You hear what I'm saying? Just give me the money. Now!" He held out his left hand to Marilyn. She was frozen directly behind the cash register.

"Move, you ugly witch, or I'll blow your sucking head off," the man yelled. Both men started screaming at the top of their lungs.

Marilyn froze, then panicked. "Don't shoot, please! I've got kids at home. Please, you can have anything you want. Don't shoot!" She dropped behind the counter to the floor, covering her head with her arms for protection.

The bigger man came around the counter. Skin moved back and to his left, giving the man plenty of room. Marilyn saw the robber's feet near her. She started crying and scooted towards Skin for protection. Skin couldn't move and didn't want to be near her in case he needed room for a defensive move.

The bigger black grabbed Marilyn by the hair and jerked her to her feet. He screamed in her face to open the cash register. She started screaming and the man hit her square in the nose, smashing in her face. She wet her pants and passed out cold on the floor. He kicked Marilyn in the side and spit in her face. He jumped over her to the cash register and began banging on it. He swung around to Skin, screaming "Can you open this?"

Skin knew he was going to die. His mother always told him cigarettes were going to kill him. He didn't know it was going to be this way. "Hell, I don't know, but I'll try." Skin had worked in a service station when he was younger and thought he could manage it. He moved to the register and worked on it until it opened.

The man gave Skin a rough push backward and grabbed the money. He turned, scowling at Skin, and left. It surprised Skin when the man shoved past him. He felt relief because he thought the guy was going to kill him. When the man got to his partner, who was covering Skin, he shoved past him with a big grin.

Skin was thinking if he had his weapon, he could take them both. He cursed himself for being lazy and not going back for it.

The man with the .45 hit the door with the gun and walked out onto the street. The smaller man followed him to the door, then hesitated. He turned around, now about seven feet away from the counter, pointed his gun at Skin, and started shooting.

As he fired the gun, he kept lifting his aim after each shot, mimicking the gunfighters in the old Western movies. He let the light recoil of the weapon pull his arm up and back. After each recoil he would throw his arm forward and shoot off a round. When he emptied his gun, he quickly turned around and skipped out onto the street, joining his companion and laughing wildly. They ran to a waiting car, jumped in, and sped down the street, turning left at the first corner.

Skin stood wide-eyed and looked down at his T-shirt for holes. He had always heard if the bullet doesn't hit bone, you won't feel the penetration. There was no blood. He jumped to the phone and called the police station.

After he hung up the receiver his hand started shaking and he felt nauseous. He grabbed the cigarettes from the counter, wrinkled them up, and threw them against the wall. "You almost got me killed!"

The police arrived about three minutes later. When Skin related the story of the holdup, the officer smiled at him. The incident officer didn't believe Skin's account, accused him of exaggerating. "No way, buddy. There's no way he could make that many shots and miss you every time," he said. "I've heard of people being missed at close range but not seven or eight times."

"I have to admit the robber was disappointed also, but it's the truth," Skin said, still shaken. "He couldn't hold a steady aim and follow his target laterally. He kept pointing the gun and firing it, then lifting it up with the kick and pointing it again with jerking movements and firing." Skin demonstrated the action.

"Come around here and look." Skin pointed to the freezer behind the counter. Paper signs were taped all over the front, but eight holes could be seen with a closer look.

The officer looked amazed. "I don't believe it, partner. You weren't kidding. You are one lucky person. You know that?"

"Yeah, I know that." Skin looked around when the other officer got Marilyn to her feet. She got sick to her stomach and went into the bathroom.

Skin stood there a moment, thinking. "It's a funny thing. I don't remember the sound of the shots. I can't recall the sound of one shot."

"At that close range, our brains do funny things."

Skin shook his head, looking at the ground. "There are two important things I learned tonight, boys. I'm making a declaration here and now."

"What's that?" the interviewing officer asked.

"One, I'm never leaving my pad again without a weapon. Two, I'm swearing off cigarettes and switching to a pipe. Eventually, I'll give up smoking altogether."

"Talk's cheap," the officer laughed, motioning for Skin to come closer. "Come on, I need to have you sign your statement and we're out of here."

The next day at the Hollenbeck station, Skin told his story many times over in the locker room and during roll call. Most of the men didn't believe he would quit smoking; all told him it was stupid to walk out onto the streets without a weapon. Skin swore it would never happen again. He swore again when Tony Valin, from investigations, told him the two black suspects fit the description of two men who killed four people without provocation and fit the M.O. of two guys who had robbed over sixteen liquor stores.

The PM watch had begun and Skin was assigned to patrol as a single unit and had to be split up from his partner for the shift. His call sign was changed to Four Lincoln 55. The Lincoln sequence indicated he was a single man car. Skin was given RDs 467, 466, and 477. Bobby Blanca was assigned Four Lincoln 88 and given adjacent RDs to patrol—478, 487 and 488.

It was not uncommon to split up two-man teams when a shift experienced manpower shortages and more police units were needed to patrol the different reporting districts. The appearance of a fleet of police cars gave the public a greater sense of safety. Preventive patrol was a tool used to give possible suspects the idea that committing a crime and getting away with it would be too difficult when numerous police were patrolling in the area.

Skin was driving around his sector taking his time, looking for any type of disturbance or unusual activity. He was thinking about seeing his new girlfriend at the Rainbow Angling Club in Azusa when his partner, Bobby Blanca, only a few streets away, received a dispatch.

"Four Lincoln 88," Blanca's radio sounded. "We have a man on his front lawn acting strange in RD 478. Neighbors are concerned, requesting the subject be checked out. Address, 3005 Guirado Street. One white male, long brown hair, wearing only boxer shorts. Complainant states the man is acting weird on his front lawn and wants police assistance."

"Four Lincoln 88, copy. En route." Blanca responded, turning left at the next block to head toward the address given by dispatch. He did not like handling calls that involved mental people. It gave him the willies. Fact is, mentally ill people scared the holy hell out of him. Witch doctors, spooks, and witches all came from the same batch of voodoo. He didn't like dealing with them.

"Dispatch, this is Four Lincoln 55, I'll roll as backup," Skin said over his radio. He took his time driving up to Guirado. He was interested to see how Blanca was going to handle the call. If he got there first, Blanca would expect him to take charge. Skin knew his partner was uncomfortable around strange-acting people. He wanted to give Blanca the opportunity to deal with this situation on his own. Skin turned left on Guirado from Euclid Avenue and saw Blanca driving very slowly ahead of him. Finally he pulled into the man's driveway.

A few feet away the white male subject was sitting on the lawn in his dirty boxer underwear with no shoes or socks. He was acting strange and looked like a hippie, with long straggly hair matted to his head that looked as if he slept for weeks without combing it out. Skin thought of it as a rat's nest as he watched the man touching imaginary objects in the air around him.

Skin pulled alongside the curb, got out, walked around his patrol unit, and leaned against his fender waiting to see how

Blanca was going to handle the call. Skin was surprised that Blanca had driven up on the suspect's property. He decided not to say anything negative because it was Blanca's call.

Skin almost wanted to laugh out loud when the man on the lawn started bobbing his head in and out like a chicken. His eyes were wide and his Adam's apple made him look like a rooster. Skin involuntarily let out a giggle when the man turned and looked at Blanca who was sitting inside the patrol car watching him. The man began making a clucking sound from the back of his throat. Skin thought he did an excellent imitation of a chicken.

Blanca sat in his vehicle unable to make up his mind if he should get out or what method to use in communicating with the man. Then the man got up on all fours and did a dog crawl over to the patrol car. He leaped up on top of Blanca's fender.

Skin stayed in position waiting to see what action Blanca was going to take. The man leaned over Blanca's windshield, squinted his eyes, and peered inside. With his left hand, he reached up and started scratching the glass.

Skin walked back around to the driver's side, got in the car, and called over the air, "Four Lincoln 88, I think you're in trouble." Skin started laughing. Blanca did not answer and Skin decided his partner was frozen in position.

After a few minutes the man jumped off the hood and was looking around the sky at imaginary flying objects. It was apparent he was loaded on drugs, probably LSD. He staggered around to the right front tire and stooped down. This gave Blanca an opportunity to exit his vehicle and take charge.

Skin was surprised when Blanca didn't budge, so he stayed in his vehicle waiting for Blanca to make his move. He was parked in a position where he could see the subject sitting on his haunches and studying Blanca's right front wheel. With his bare fingernails, he popped the police car's hubcap off and stood up. He flipped the chrome hubcap in a circle, making it spin like a top on the surface of the hood of the police car. This gave Skin a start, because it would have taken super strength to complete such an act. He now was concerned and stepped out of his patrol car, motioning for Blanca to join him.

It was apparent to Skin they had a drug-related problem because the strength to do what he just did was superhuman. The man was about twenty-four, small in stature, weighed roughly

160 pounds and was about 5'10". The man began spinning in circles, holding his arms out and laying his head back, emitting strange sounds from his throat. Blanca grabbed his nightstick and walked around the car. Skin had his stick in his baton ring which was hanging on the left side of his black leather gun belt.

Blanca approached the man cautiously. Skin stepped forward, wanting to take charge but knowing better. He walked around the back of Blanca's car to the passenger side. The man moved to the front of the car, acting as if he was not aware of the police officer's presence. Blanca stayed close to his door, for what reason Skin didn't know.

Finally the man looked at Skin, continuing with strange noises as he walked toward the officer with his arms outstretched. Skin knew he had a problem. He glanced around, seeing people in the distance, watching quietly. He tried to assess the danger factor of the man moving toward him. At the last possible second, Skin removed his baton, grabbing the end of the stick and exposing only two inches around his grasp at the end. He held the baton as if in a crowd control stance, stepped forward, and gave a forward thrust into the man's solar plexus, lifting him to his tiptoes. The suspect fell on his back, instantly neutralized. The wind was knocked out of him. Skin replaced his baton in his holding ring and advanced forward. He grabbed the man's arms and pulled him to his knees. The action enabled the subject to suck enough air into his lungs to get him on his feet.

Skin nodded to Blanca to take over the arrest. Skin did not speak to his partner while he observed him cuffing the prisoner and placing him in the back of Blanca's patrol unit.

The next day at roll call, most of the officers were at their desks early, before Skin and Bobby entered the room for pre-shift briefings. Skin came around the corner with a smile on his face and winked at the other men. Blanca came into the room, walked over to an empty chair, and placed his notepad on the table top. Lieutenant Jacob Wilson walked over to the podium, placed his hands on each side and took a firm hold. "Okay, listen up, men. We have some important things to discuss before you hit the road. Today, I need three single units to float eight reporting districts. Skin, I'm splitting you and your partner..." the lieutenant hesitated, forgetting Blanca's name. In unison, all the officers in the room, including Cy, began scratching the table in front of them. "...Scratch...that's it. Officer Scratch, will you please take a few moments and discuss with the men why you stayed in your vehicle and let that poor white fool jump on your police unit and scratch your window, and you failed to respond in the proper manner?"

Bobby Blanca gave Skin a dirty look. "I had it under control, then my so-called partner took over," he accused. "I had an excellent plan of action, Lieutenant."

"Yeah, let's hear it, Scratch," Fulton laughed. "We want a full report of what you were thinking yesterday with that goofball."

"Hey, look you guys. Don't call me Scratch," Blanca looked hurt. He didn't want a new nickname. "It is a tradition in my Hispanic family. This thing goes back a long ways. When you deal with a crazy, it's best to do nothing sometimes. You know, that stuff can rub off on you."

"So you let this long-hair nut on your patrol unit and you just sat there while he scratched on your windshield?" Billy Garcia questioned. "Where is your pride, man? People were looking at you, wondering what you were going to do. You hurt all the Hollenbeck Division when you didn't jump out and thump the guy, man. I mean, arrest him."

"Come on. Give me a break here. That guy was nuts. Don't you know, sometimes a mental case has special and secret powers and they can cast a spell on you," Blanca was dead serious.

"That did it," the lieutenant slapped his hand on the podium. "You are hereby known as Scratch. All those in favor," Jacob looked around the room, "say, aye."

Everyone said "aye" in unison while Blanca shook his head back and forth. "My mother will not like this, you guys. The name Bobby goes back long into my family history of Robertos. They will turn in their graves."

"Signed, sealed, and delivered," Jacob said. "Now, we have another problem. For the last six months we have had a health concern that is originating in the men's bathroom." Jacob walked away from the podium, gesturing with his hands as he spoke. "One of our own has a serious flushing phobia. One of our own seems to forget to flush the toilet when he has finished eliminating his filthy grotesque bowels. By failing to flush the toilet properly and allowing the disgusting contents to surge into the lower depths of the sewer system where it belongs, it floats around the surface of the toilet, causing a horrible smell and contaminating this whole damn building." The lieutenant slapped his fist into his open left hand in an angry exclamation.

"Lieutenant, if you know who it is, tell us right now. We'll take the sucker and throw him in the shower," Chuck said seriously. "I personally have been wondering who the pisser is because I have to flush the toilet before I can use it. It's disgusting and deplorable and I am sick of looking at and smelling someone else's mess."

The other men chimed in. "Hear, hear."

"Very well," the lieutenant said. "We all agree this has to stop. The only way it is going to stop is to identify the varmint and brand him." Jacob removed his baton and walked around the tables looking into the eyes of each of his men.

"We have suffered and suffered with this lowlife who thinks his crap doesn't stink—a man who feels it's necessary to share those natural private matters of the elimination process with his colleagues." Jacob walked over to Chuck Fulton and glared into his eyes.

Chuck immediately pushed his glasses back up on his nose and looked wild-eyed at the lieutenant. "It wasn't me, boss, honest. I admit my stuff smells pretty bad, but I wouldn't share that with anyone. I swear."

"It might as well have been you, Chucky, because you did not keep tabs on your partner," Jacob said with force.

"What!" Chuck said aghast. He swung around, glaring at Billy.

Billy Garcia shook his head from side to side. "It wasn't me, Chuck. Don't look at me that way, man."

"It was you, you lousy, dirty toilet monger." Chuck got out of his chair and stuck his finger in Billy's face. "You lying sack of crap. Now I know why you are always disappearing. I thought it was to get out of work. You've been running to the latrine, leaving your slimy, green, yellow, and brown presence for the rest of us to suffer with. You miserable little bag of scum."

The lieutenant walked over to Garcia, hitting the palm of his hand with his baton. "On your knees, Garcia, now!"

"Oh please, Lieutenant, I can't help it. I hate to touch the dirty handle on the toilets. I have to put paper down before I can even sit on the filthy thing. It's all I can do to go in there and do a number. Usually I go in the bushes or out in the park or anywhere but a toilet. I can't use toilet seats that everyone else has used. I have a phobia about this thing. I can't help it, honest."

Chuck stared at his partner. "You mean to say all these times I thought you were taking a leak, you were really taking a dump in the night?"

"Well," Garcia put his hands up, "I can't help it. I'm neurotic when it comes to public toilets."

"We have smelled your messes for the last time, Garcia," Jacob said. "On your knees." He pulled the officer from his seat and pushed him to the floor.

Garcia reluctantly got on his knees before his watch commander. Jacob took his baton and touched the tip to each shoulder and Garcia's head. "I now dub thee 'Flush,' for which you will be known for the remainder of your assignment at Hollenbeck. So be it. Let me give you a word of warning here. If we catch you not flushing the toilet one more time, I give permission to the men to jump on you, take your car keys, and throw them in the toilet."

"No, you wouldn't," Garcia's eyes grew large. "Not that, man. I could never get them out."

"I mean it, Flush, one more time and we'll do it. Understood?"

"Understood," Garcia said, looking around at the other officers in shame. "And don't any of you guys call me Flush. It ain't right, man."

"Okay, Flush," the men chimed in together, laughing.

Jacob turned and walked around to Bobby Blanca. "On your knees, Slick." Jacob gave him the name of "Scratch" as all the men cheered.

The following three days at the division were hectic. It was busier than usual and Cy was glad his days off would start tomorrow. He planned on taking Mary Ann to dinner and a movie. For the first time in months the men's locker room at the station smelled cleaner. It was determined Garcia, now dubbed, refused to use the men's room after the roll call incident. The name stuck with him and everyone, including the captain, used his new name. The story about Bobby Blanca made the circle and everyone called him Scratch.

Cy was patrolling in downtown Hollenbeck, RD 466 east of Soto, when his thoughts were interrupted. The emergency chimes sounded on the radio, hitting a chord in his brain. All went quiet as he listened for an emergency message. The chimes sounded like the ding-dong of an old clock. When the chimes went off, all officers stopped talking and listened to the message.

The call went to Four Adam 55, Skin and Blanca, in RD 469 which borders the Los Angeles Sheriff's Department jurisdiction.

"Four Adam 55, go to 3408 East Lafranco Avenue. Report of a suicidal off-duty deputy with a gun."

Blanca picked up the mike while Skin turned right on 6th Street. "Four Adam 55, ten-four on the location."

"Additional information, Four Adam 55. An off-duty deputy is with the suicidal suspect and has been taken as a hostage. Information was submitted by the wife of the suspect."

"Four Adam 55, copy that. Request backup."

"Four Lincoln 22 and Four X-ray 68 will provide backup," Cy said, breaking into the radio traffic. "Do you copy, Four Adam 55?"

"Four Adam 55, copy," Scratch answered in Skin's unit.

In a few short minutes Skin pulled up a few houses short of the suspect's house. Four X-ray 68 also skidded to a stop two houses down from the opposite direction. Fulton and Flush jumped out of the car and went over to Skin and Scratch.

"Four Lincoln 22, arriving at the scene," Cy hung up his radio mike and exited his vehicle. He made his way over to Skin while he looked at the house in question. "I don't like this kind of call, boys. Going against one of our own is not good. If we have to shoot a fellow officer, the shooter will never get over it. I got a hold of the lieutenant and he's sending the SWAT boys in. We are to hold the inner perimeter. Four X-ray 40 and 45 have taken the outer perimeter in preparation of evacuating the residents once we determine our course of action."

It was evening and the house was dark. Several other police units arrived and Lieutenant Wilson walked hurriedly over to his sergeant.

"Cy, here's what we got. The deputy inside has been experiencing marital problems. He's got a gun, according to his wife. She says his best friend went into the house, thinking he could reason with him and give him some comfort. Now the deputy is refusing to let his friend leave the house." Jacob looked around at two other units pulling up. The officers got out of their cars and stood by for further orders.

The lieutenant answered radio traffic. "The outer perimeter is set up. I want your men to contain the inner perimeter. I want you to be prepared to go in if something goes down before the SWAT team gets here. Take the front of the house, and I'll send Barber and Mitchell around to the other side. I'm going to set up a line of communication next door."

"Okay, Lieutenant, you've got it." Cy replied, watching Jacob walk quickly to the house next door. "Chuck, you and Flush take the two corners of the house next to the sidewalk. Skin, you take the right side of the front door. Scratch, you take the left side of the door, and I'll keep communications open with the lieutenant on a hand-held radio." Cy pointed to the locations he wanted his men to go. "If we go in, I'll follow you two and give you rear security. If the SWAT team gets here, we'll provide outside backup."

The officers took their positions, and the watch commander set up communications from next door on a land line, permitting conversation back and forth. Jacob was able to make contact with the off-duty deputy inside his home. At one point the suspect declared he was going to kill himself. He also refused to release his deputy friend, though he did not threaten his life. The deputy's name was Jim Blanchard. He said things had gone too far and he couldn't back out at this point. He told the police lieutenant if anyone came into the bedroom he would kill himself.

Cy was told the deputy and his hostage were located in the far bedroom down the hall to the left after entering the house from the front door.

They were anxious taking a call against a brother officer. The last thing they wanted to do was get involved in a shootout situation. Whoever shot the deputy, no matter how justified it was, would never live it down among his fellow officers; his career would be ruined.

Cy waited nervously for the SWAT team to arrive and take over. As time went by, the negotiations—if they could be called that—deteriorated drastically. The lieutenant got antsy. He was trying to decide if the men could make a quiet entry. The wife told Jacob the end bedroom where her husband was held up was at the other end of the house and the men could get inside without being heard if they were quiet.

The officers were getting more nervous, as only bits and pieces of information were getting through to them. The tension was heavy, and the anticipation of a possible shooting did not sit well with anyone; all felt sick with fear of shooting one of their own.

Suddenly, Jacob came running from next door. "Green light, he's going to kill his partner! Get in there, now! Go! Go! Go!" A gunshot was heard inside the house. No one knew who shot who or why the weapon was discharged.

Skin was waiting on the doorstep with Scratch. Without hesitation, Skin stepped back and kicked the front door in with a loud crash. He ran inside, keeping to the right, and disappeared. Scratch was on his heels keeping to the left and stopping at the hall entrance going to the left.

Skin thought perhaps the cop had killed himself, but then he wondered if he shot his friend and was trying to get up enough nerve to shoot himself. If the guy did shoot his friend and there was a lot of blood, he may have gotten scared and decided he wanted the police to shoot him.

Cy followed Skin and Blanca into the house while Jacob secured the front door, crouching down low to the right of the opening. Chuck and Flush maintained their positions outside, not knowing what was going on inside the house except that a shot had been fired and the front door was obviously broken down by a forced entry.

This complicated things, having friendly officers inside. To identify a good officer in the dark was not an easy thing to accomplish. Accidental shootings occurred frequently, and both men grew more nervous as they gripped their weapons in preparation of firing them.

The momentum of Skin kicking the door in carried him through the entry, past the hallway entry, and into the living room, crashing his knee into a coffee table. He fell into it, shattering it to pieces. He did a right roll and came to his feet. His knee felt like it had been hit with a hammer. He could not take the time to inspect his injuries.

Cy hovered against the right wall, now all the more worried because Skin was missing somewhere in the dark house. He couldn't imagine where he had disappeared to. He wasn't in the hallway at his intended destination. Now he was concerned because they had failed to conduct a safe entry.

Finally, he heard Skin groan in the next room. A moment later he limped up to the opposite side of the hallway from Cy. He gave an okay sign to Cy and Scratch. His face was barely visible and it was covered with perspiration.

"You okay?" Cy whispered harshly.

"My kneecap is in the other room. Otherwise I'm okay," he said, crawling up to the corner of the hallway. He leaned over peering down to the other end of the dark hall towards the bedrooms.

Jacob moved up a few feet behind them with his weapon out, securing the rear. Scratch was on the left wall in a crouched position ready for action. He tried not to concentrate heavily on the detail. If he thought too much about it, he would begin to worry. If a cop wanted to kill himself, was he mentally ill? If he was, was it catching?

Down the hall, yelling came from the last bedroom on the left. The four quickly cleared the bedrooms, moving down the hall to make sure they were not being sucked into the open. They made it to the last bedroom.

Skin and Cy were breathing heavily. Cy motioned to Skin that he was going into the room and move left. He motioned for Skin to go right. Just then a muffled sound came from inside and another round discharged. Cy kicked the door in and immediately moved to the left side of the room. Skin dove for the right bringing his shotgun up to the front position ready to fire. The window crashed and someone—maybe suspect, maybe hostage—dove through it.

Skin heard a sound in front of him. He also saw a man lying belly down. His hands were not tied, so Skin didn't know which of the two he was. Regardless, he jumped onto the man knowing Cy and Scratch would be covering him.

Not wanting to get hurt, the man knew better than to resist. "Jim is the guy you want. He went out the window. He popped a couple of rounds into the ceiling before jumping out the window, hoping to stall you before you broke in."

Jacob yelled, "How many breathers do you have in there?"

"One," Cy answered back. "One good guy in here and one bad guy is sucking air outside somewhere."

Outside, more yelling could be heard. Cy went to the window and could see three officers doing a foot chase heading west toward 6th Street. The pursuing officers could have shot the deputy but didn't. Jacob and Cy left Skin and Scratch with the man in the bedroom. They ran from the house and down the sidewalk one block where they saw the three officers crouched around a man in a prone position in the middle of the street. All the men were taking in big gulps of air.

One of the officers turned as Cy and Jacob approached them. He explained that they had accidentally broken the suspect's leg when they tackled him. An ambulance had been on standby, around a designated corner. The suspect moaned loudly. He whined and said he was sorry as he waited for the paramedics to pick him up.

When Cy and Jacob got back to their cars the hostage was talking to Skin, explaining that his partner, Jim Blanchard, was being investigated for fitness for duty as a result of work burnout. He said Blanchard had heavy duty-related stress plus marital problems because his wife was stepping out on him. The department had not helped him and he continued to be a disciplinary employee. His supervisors were unable to assist him in dealing with his problems and suspended him until counseling gave him a clean bill of health.

When Cy heard enough he walked away with Jacob toward their two cars. "I don't need this kind of stress," Cy said, pushing in on his temples. "This has been too much."

"My guts ache something awful, Cy. I thought for sure we were going to be in a combat situation," Jacob said, taking off his duty hat and wiping his forehead with the palm of his hand.

Cy put his arm around Jacob as they walked along. "Me too, boss. Me too."

Skin came up and put his arms around both men. "Hey, I want you both to know something. I love you guys and I will never do that to you."

For a moment the three stopped and stared at one another and then looked at the ground without talking. They thought about the incident and how easily it could have gone bad. Finally Cy broke the silence.

"The worst part of it is," Cy said quietly, "I would have capped the guy. Officer or not. That's the worst of it. I would have shot him dead."

The three men were talking in low tones when Scratch came over to join them. "Hey, guys, whatever happened here tonight was too much. I almost cut one in my shorts." Blanca hesitated and smiled warmly at his companions. "Let's go get a taco, man. This Mexican is hungry. Orozco's is waiting for us, man."

"You need a taco, Scratch. I need a beer, bad," Jacob said to no one in particular. "Let's say we meet at Jack's for a quick one after we finish our shift?"

"How about if we get a taco now, as in right now. We can meet at Jack's later." Scratch said, looking for support.

"You guys go ahead," Jacob said turning away. "I've got to finish my paperwork. I'll see you fellows after work."

"How can you do work on an empty stomach?" Skin asked, taking out his new pipe and stuffing tobacco in it. "A real man would eat tacos now with his comrades, then do his paperwork, then go have a beer after our duty watch."

Jacob continued walking away. "Catch you later."

Cy was standing with his two men watching Jacob walk away. "I think he needs to be alone. Do you realize the pressure there would be on him if one of us killed that deputy cop?" Cy thought for a moment and backed away from the other two. "I think I want to be alone. I'll tie up with you later."

Skin understood what was bothering his sergeant. He turned to Scratch. "Come on, Scratch. Let's go eat. I'm starved."

"You got that right, partner," Scratch said happily. "I guess you know it was not good for me in that house. A suicidal is temporarily mentally deranged. I hope the bad spirits went out the window with that crazy guy when he dove through it. I don't want anything strange entering my brain."

"Have no fear there, Scratch. A voodoo wouldn't be able to find your tiny little mind."

Chapter 9

Police Calls

Cy finished his written report on the suicidal deputy and was back patrolling the streets. He was mentally exhausted. He didn't know if he could make it until the end of the shift. Going in on the suicidal deputy was enough stress for a month. His stomach was still upset thinking about the incident.

As he patrolled through the inner business districts, he thought about his mother and father. He missed them greatly. He longed for his brother's company. Now there was no one left but him. It was a lonely feeling. He thought about Mary Ann and how much he cared for her. He had to force himself not to call her at that moment. She had not been feeling well for the last week. Pains were strong in her lower back, and they both thought she must have strained her back muscles. He decided he would go back to the station and give her a call anyway. He needed the reassurance of her voice.

The shift was only half over. Cy felt as if he had already worked a straight twelve-hour watch. Making a U-turn at the next intersection, he headed toward the station. The communications division sounded the bell chimes, the ding-dong sound jolting Cy. His heart thudded as he waited for the message. He hoped the call would not be in his area.

A male dispatcher came over the air. "Any police unit in the vicinity of RD 466, 2-11 in progress at a gas station at 1st and Mott Street, single white man with handgun."

Skin's voice immediately could be heard over the radio monitor. "Four Adam 55 responding. ETA one minute."

"Copy, Four Adam 55. Requesting other backup units," dispatch sounded.

Cy grabbed his mike, "This is Four Lincoln 22 rolling on that 2-11. Request Four X-ray 68 and Four Lincoln 37 to assist." With Skin and Scratch riding double and Fulton and Flush in Four X-ray 68 he could use Jim Stilson riding single in Four Lincoln 37 as a chase vehicle if necessary.

"Four X-ray 68, copy and en route," Flush responded on the radio. Chuck turned right at the next corner proceeding to Mott.

"Four Lincoln 37 en route," Jim Stilson answered, swinging his vehicle around to head east on 4th.

The first car on the scene was Four X-ray 68. Chuck and Flush positioned themselves across the street at an angle in full view of the gas station. Chuck could see Four Adam 55 approaching from the south on Mott. The police unit stopped short of the gas station. Coming east on 1st, Chuck could see red lights blinking in the distance and figured it was the sergeant. Traffic was fairly slow and there were only a few pedestrians in the area.

It was the intention of the police not to startle the robbery suspect. If possible, Skin wanted to apprehend the man or men when they cleared the front door of the gas station.

Cy pulled around the far corner from behind the gas station positioning his unit near the front of the station with his headlights out.

Skin moved his squad car toward the front of the station, being careful not to hit any bumps that would make a sound. There were several parked cars on the lot. He did not want to give his position away while he and Scratch visually searched the property. Neither officer could see a suspect car or suspicious person.

As Skin was pulling into the front of the gas station, dispatch relayed information that the victim had called to report the robber had left the building and a robbery had occurred with a weapon involved.

As Skin backed up and drove around to the rear of the station, the attendant ran out the back door pointing to the alley, motioning for the officers to hurry. Skin could see the person was wearing a uniform shirt and Texaco ball cap. He drove further ahead and looked down the alley to his left. Halfway down, he spotted the taillights of a car speeding away.

"Four Adam 55, the suspect's going down the alley behind the station. Four Lincoln 22, make a U-turn and head back around to cut him off at the other end of the alley. We can box him in."

"Four Lincoln 22, copy. Swinging around code-2," Cy responded on the radio, making a 180-degree turn, accelerating, turning on his headlights, and hitting his overheads.

The armed robber made a right turn onto the first street and drove head to head with the sergeant coming around the same corner in the opposite direction. Cy slammed on his brakes and skidded to a slanted stop in the street. The suspect vehicle came to a screeching halt, causing it to sway back and forth after it stopped.

Cy turned his stationary spotlight onto the suspect vehicle and jumped out of his car. He bore down on the driver with his revolver, cursing himself for not having his shotgun out of the electro-lock.

"Get out of the car, now!" Cy yelled, standing behind his car door for protection. "Move it now or you're going down!" He could only see one person in the vehicle.

The subject did not move. Cy decided the man was preparing for a shootout. Cy took one step to the side of his cruiser, maintaining his coverage.

"You're dead in the car if you don't get out," Cy yelled, taking a tight aim on the suspect.

Four Adam 55 quietly rolled up behind the suspect vehicle and instantly realized he was in a crossfire position. Skin got out of his car, stepping to his left behind the suspect vehicle, and observed that the suspect was watching the officer in front of him.

Scratch took the shotgun and positioned himself at the right front fender of the police car. Skin decided it was best to let the sergeant maintain control from the front of the suspect's view while he and his partner provided backup from the side and to the rear. Skin motioned for Scratch to move off to the right, out of the line of fire. Skin stepped quietly to the left of the suspect and out of direct fire of his sergeant.

Taking his time and not in the least intimidated, a large youth got out of the dark blue El Camino which was well lit by the sergeant's headlights. Two red rotating lights from the police unit circled the area, giving a red glow and illuminating buildings, cars, and trees.

When the suspect exited the car, a can of glue fell onto the street, making a metallic sound in the tense night. He was approximately 6' 3" and looked to be about eighteen. His hair was long and straggly, and it appeared he had not shaved nor bathed for several days. His clothes were dirty and wrinkled and his whole appearance was unkempt. He had a strange glare in his eyes. He slowly leaned back into the car and pulled out a handgun.

Skin figured the suspect did not see him because the spotlight from Cy's unit blocked his vision. The kid might have been thinking he was alone and did not realize two officers were behind him. The taste of danger hung heavy as the suspect started moving away from his vehicle.

Skin decided things were going down fast and deliberately jacked a shell into the shotgun with a power action, breaking the youth's concentration.

Shock was the expression on the youth's face as he stared at the police lights in front of him. It was as if he was afraid to look behind him. Skin was only approximately fifteen feet to his rear. Completely surprised, the suspect never heard the car pull up behind him with the lights out nor did he hear the opening car doors. Neither one had been shut.

"Freeze right there or I'll take you down!" Skin growled. "It's your choice."

The suspect's hand slowly came down and dropped the gun onto the street. Cy ordered the suspect, "Interlace your fingers on top of your head."

The kid didn't put his hands up as ordered. He stood there with his head down, staring at the pavement and shaking his head back and forth.

"It's your game, Slick. Do what you're told or take a hit," Skin snapped at the suspect.

Cy moved around to the side of the suspect to keep out of a crossfire between Scratch and Skin. As he got closer to the youth he kicked the gun away, quickly holstered his weapon, and grabbed a handful of the suspect's hair, pulling him down to the ground. The kid hit the asphalt with a slam. Cy placed his knee in his back, twisting his left arm behind him.

"Don't hurt me. Please don't hurt me," he yelled, with his face smashed against the ground.

"Don't move," Cy yelled. He could hear Skin and Scratch running around the car to his position.

Blood was spilling out onto the ground where the kid's mouth was pressing hard onto the pavement.

Skin whispered with a short laugh of relief as he stepped closer, "Easy, Sarge. You're going to knock his teeth out if you apply any more pressure."

Scratch busily cuffed him while speaking to the kid in his best Mexican accent. "Say, you big puke of a snot-nose kid.

Why'd you go pulling a gun on one of my sergeants like that? We almost shot your guts out."

"I can't breathe," he sneered. "I can't breathe." Red foamy bubbles came from his mouth as he tried to speak. Cy had moved forward to place his knee at the back of the suspect's neck, pushing his face into the street while Scratch worked on securing him.

Two other police cars rolled up, giving additional swirling lights and dotting the landscape with their red overheads, rotating silently.

Chuck and Flush walked around the suspect's car and double checked it for another suspect, but it was clean except for a wad of bills on the front seat.

Skin went over to Cy. "You may want to take your knee off his neck now, Sarge. You're going to kill him if he can't get any air."

Cy didn't realize he was applying that much pressure. He was surprised to see the foamy blood leaking into the street. The sucking sounds made by his prisoner brought him to his senses and he immediately released a small amount of pressure. "He's okay."

The sergeant turned to the other officers while he held the prisoner down. "Chuck, you and Flush go check with the attendant at the gas station. Get a written statement and see if there were any other witnesses."

For the first time, Cy noticed Four Lincoln 37 a few feet away. "Jim, I want you to stand by the suspect's vehicle and wait until the detectives get here for the crime scene processing."

"You got it, Sarge," Jim Stilson said, grabbing his flashlight and moving toward the kid's car.

The sergeant stood up, washed his hands in the air, and shook them. He put his foot on the prisoner's neck and applied pressure. He looked at the two officers who assisted in the arrest. "You two," he nodded to Skin and Scratch, "take junior here back to the division and start processing him. If he doesn't cooperate, I'll take care of him personally when I get back to the station. I want a full statement in detail."

He motioned for Skin to step closer to him and pressed his lips to Skin's ear. "This guy is ready to spill his guts. If he thinks I'm going to be alone with him, he might give you his mother on a platter."

Skin looked down at the prisoner. The kid was staring at Cy out of the corner of his eye, scared to death of the sergeant. "I'm the good guy on this one. We'll take care of it, Sarge," Skin whispered back.

"I know you will. Now do a good job. I want a confession and the works on this guy. Okay?"

Skin pulled back. "Okay, you got it." He was relieved when Cy lifted his foot and walked away. He thought about how much he cared for his sergeant. He loved this action. It was his life. There was nothing like being a cop.

Skin motioned for Cy to hold it. Before he moved, he leaned over and whispered to his prisoner. "If you move, sport, I'll kick your face in." Skin gave a small shove to his prisoner and walked over to his sergeant.

Cy smiled happily. "Yes?"

Skin grinned at him. "You like this, don't you?"

"This is what it's all about, isn't it?" Cy glanced briefly at him and then back to the prisoner on the ground.

"You got that right. This is the best part about being a cop. Getting the felon is a rush that you can't describe," Skin said softly. "You don't know if you're going to shoot someone or if they're going to shoot you. When you come out on top, it's a real high. I live for that high."

Cy nodded, understanding.

Skin took Cy by the arm and pulled him closer. "From this point on, you rattle this guy's cage. I'm going to enjoy being the good guy for a change." Skin pointed a finger at himself. "You got it? I'm good, you is bad, fool...I mean Sarge."

"Got it," Cy said, turning back to the prisoner. The kid blinked his eyes wildly.

"What are you looking at, you bucket of spit," Cy growled at him and got down on one knee. He leaned over, put his hand on the kid's neck, and pushed down on his face. "You don't look at me unless I tell you to look at me! I may think you're trying to escape!" Cy screamed into the young man's face, spitting saliva into his eyes. Cy grabbed him by the collar and pulled his face close to his own. "Are you trying to escape?"

"No, I swear I wasn't," the prisoner cried. He squinted his eyes, afraid Cy was going to hit him in the face.

"Did you swear at me, you piece of crap!" Cy acted as if he was going to lose it.

"No, no. I was agreeing with you," he stammered.

Cy grabbed the man by the hair and pulled back. "Oh, so you were trying to escape, huh!"

Skin had been observing this conversation from the suspect's vehicle and wondering how far Cy was going to go.

"No! I don't know what I'm saying," the suspect whimpered.

"What's going on here?" Skin said gruffly as he walked quickly back over to his sergeant.

Cy sneered at his prisoner, his tone changing. "This little worm was looking for a way to escape and I caught him just in time."

"I swear I wasn't. Get him away from me."

Skin kneeled down and pulled the man to a sitting position. The kid was big and stout. "Don't get this officer mad, boy. He'll pull your tongue out and stomp on it." Skin reached down and tenderly brushed dirt off the arrestee's shoulder and wiped his face with the back of his hand.

The prisoner seemed to relax as Skin comforted him. "I'm sorry about him, kid," Skin said, pointing to Cy who was standing back a few feet and scowling at him. Cy spit on the ground in disgust. He coughed deep in his chest and blew a wad of spit on the suspect's shoe.

"Good lordy, boy, don't rile him again," Skin warned the boy. "Now, has anyone advised you of your rights?"

"No."

Cy stepped forward as if to kick the prisoner. "No, *sir*! You little cling-on from a mangy dog's butt." Cy looked at Skin. "Let me have him, partner. He has no respect for the law," Cy snapped, kicking the ground.

Skin jumped up, grabbed his partner by the shoulders, and pushed him back. "What in the hell is the matter with you? This kid has his rights. He did nothing to you!" Skin angrily pushed Cy backwards. "Now knock it off or I'll be on your butt. You got that?"

Cy grabbed Skin by the shirt and almost ripped it. "Can't you see this little jerk is a killer and robs people for kicks?"

Skin's voice was almost shaking. His eyes widened and his nostrils flared, snorting for air. "What the hell is this? Can't you see the kid is scared? He's made a mistake. There's no sense in taking this personal." Skin wondered if Cy was still acting now or taking it too serious. "Now back off!"

"Back off yourself, you bald-headed freak."

"Who are you calling bald?" Skin said, grabbing Cy again by the collar. Both officers were in a tight grip. The other two backup officers watched from a distance, enjoying the moment.

"Give me two seconds with this crybaby and I'll show you what I'm talking about. He knows that I know what he's been up to."

Skin snapped a glance at the prisoner who was trying to hide his head in fear. "What's he talking about, kid?"

"I...I'm not sure," the suspect answered, sneaking a look at Cy.

"That lying piece of nothing. He knows exactly what I'm talking about. Some people have a sense, and he knows I have that sense," Cy growled angrily.

Skin turned, looking for his partner. "Hey, Scratch. Take the Sarge here with you for a couple of minutes, will ya."

"This is none of my business," Scratch said. "I'm here for backup only. If this officer is pissed at this bad bandit, it's not my business."

"Gees, all mighty, I've got no help here," Skin sighed, looking down at the kid.

The kid shook his head from side to side. "I'll talk to you, Mr. Skin. Just keep that other officer away from me."

Skin watched Cy walk over to Scratch. He glanced back at the prisoner. "Okay, bud, listen to me carefully. You have the right to remain silent. Anything you say can and will be used against you in a court of law. You have a right to an attorney. If you cannot afford an attorney, the court will appoint one to represent you. If you decide to answer my questions without an attorney present, you have the right to stop at anytime. Do you understand your rights?"

The kid didn't answer and stared at the ground. The crazy cop started walking back over to him. The kid answered. "Yes, yes. I understand my rights."

Skin took a small pocket notebook and pen out of his pocket. "Good. Now what's your name, sport?"

"Roger Hall."

"How old are you?"

"Eighteen, almost nineteen."

"Roger Hall, you are under arrest for armed robbery and assault with a deadly weapon on a police officer. You are in some deep cat poop, kid. We need to talk here. My sergeant thinks you got some other problems. So let's hear it."

Roger shook his head back and forth. "I needed a hit of glue."

"That's it?" Cy yelled. "I want his slimy butt and I want it now." He walked over to the prisoner but Skin stood up and pushed him back.

"You walk away from this, partner. This kid is my prisoner. He has had some bad problems and I'm going to give him all the help I can."

"No way." Cy pushed Skin away and grabbed Roger's leg and pulled hard.

Scratch quickly grabbed his sergeant's arm and pulled him over to the patrol car and out of sight of Skin and the prisoner.

Skin kneeled down next to Roger. He thought a moment and sat down on the asphalt next to him. Red flashes of light swam across his face with the rotation of the police lights. "Kid, you need to talk to me. Whatever you're hiding, we're going to find it out."

Skin touched the boy on his knee with his right hand. "You're about the age of my little brother. I would want someone to help him. So give me a chance to help you, kid. Okay?"

Tears swelled up and spilled over onto Roger's cheeks. He maintained silence for a brief moment then his voice broke. "I can't help myself. I need your help, sir." Roger looked at the officer sitting with him on the pavement. "I'm in big trouble," he said, staring into the street.

"Well, tell me about it, and we'll see what I can do." Skin spoke softly.

"I stole a gun from my dad. He brought it home from the war. It's a German Luger and it's frozen up and doesn't work. I couldn't have shot you if I wanted. At first I wanted you to shoot me. I chickened out."

Skin nudged him on the side of his leg. "Go ahead, kid, let's hear it all."

"I think I killed my friend."

"What friend?"

"Helen Morrison."

"Who is she, Roger?"

"She's been like a mother to me. She's my next-door neighbor."

"You mean *was*," Skin said, looking at Roger.

"Yeah, I guess, was."

"When do you think you killed her and how?"

"I think today. I was at her house. She found my stash of glue in her garage and threw it away. It pissed me off, so I busted her with a claw hammer."

"Where was this?"

"I live at 3015 Inez Street near Larena Park. She lives next door."

"Lives or lived?"

"I don't know for sure. I was out of it."

Skin motioned for Scratch to get on the radio and start checking out the kid's story.

In a few moments Cy came over to Skin and motioned him over to the patrol car as Scratch stood by the prisoner.

"Skin, this is the kid we've been looking for. On our hot sheet we had a description of a big kid who assaulted a woman earlier today on morning watch. This is the suspect of that assault. The watch commander just told me she died about an hour ago. We just arrested a murderer. I'd say this has been a good day after all."

"Hells bells and cockle shells, I never put the two together. I got so wrapped up in this armed robbery, I never thought about the hot sheet."

"Let's get him down to the station," Cy said in a low voice, moving away from the patrol unit. "We need to have him give us a full statement before the attorneys get to him."

"I'll say this, Cy. You were right on this one," Skin said, slapping his gloves on the sergeant's arm.

"I had a hunch. It was biting me on the butt and wouldn't let go," Cy said, walking toward the prisoner. "I feel good about this arrest. I almost shot the kid. My finger was pressing on the trigger and I almost couldn't release it. When he dropped the gun, I almost dumped him anyway."

A patrol car spun around the corner, slamming to a squealing stop a few feet away. Billy Garcia came out of the car on the run. "Hey, do you guys know what you have here?"

"Yeah, I think we do, Flush," said Cy. "Roger just confessed to whacking some gal with a hammer. The kid's been spilling his guts."

"Good job," Garcia said and leaned over to whisper in his sergeant's ear. "The problem is to get it to stick. Roger's dad claims his kid's brains are fried like eggs from using glue. I knew he was on something by the dumb look in his eyes."

The sergeant clapped his hands together. "Come on. Let's get him down to the station."

Chapter 10
Tensions of the Heart

Two weeks later on the first day of August it rained, leaving the skies cloudy. The air was hot and humid, establishing a moist film on Cy's skin. Cy stood impatiently at Mary Ann's door. He was excited to see her. When she opened the door he was shocked to see the miserable expression on her face. Her eyes were swollen from crying. There were no smiles in her greeting.

"Mary Ann, what's wrong?" Cy asked, touching her tenderly on her arm.

"We have to talk, Cy. Please come in." Mary Ann turned and moved back a step to let Cy inside. Normally she would have thrown her arms around Cy's neck, kissed him, and told him she loved him. This time she moved away from him. She was wearing a light green dress; no stockings or shoes. Her legs were losing their tan. Normally she would have been pretty. Not today.

"Has something happened to someone in the family?"

"No, no. Everyone is all right. I just got off the phone with Mom. Dad is all right too," Mary Ann declared in a hoarse voice, taking Cy by the hand. She led him to the couch in the living room and gestured with her hand for him to take a seat. She sat down first.

Cy sat back so he could have a full view of her. His heart was pounding hard and he felt a deep ache in his stomach. He could not take his eyes off her.

Mary Ann looked at Cy and tried to smile, but instead tears began rolling down her cheeks. Cy started to move closer, but Mary Ann held up her hand indicating she wanted him to stay where he was. She wiped the tears away and took a deep breath. She tried to speak but the words wouldn't come. She stared at Cy's knee resting on the cushion and then finally looked up at him. He was so gorgeous. She never had gotten over his good looks. She loved his wavy hair and shiny blue eyes, his lean and hard physique. Never had she seen or known a man who appealed to her like Cy.

"I'm going to tell you what love is, my darling. I'm going to give you a full understanding of what commitment is all about. The giving and the taking. The sharing and sacrifice." Tears began to show in her eyes again, and she continued talking.

"When I first met my husband, Donald, he was a charming, happy-go-lucky type of guy. I was young, in college, and I fell madly in love with him." Mary Ann blew her nose in a handkerchief and rubbed her eyes.

Cy didn't attempt to speak. He knew his place. He waited for the revelation to come. "He had a good job, I graduated from college, and we got married and had two beautiful children. Life becomes much more challenging when you marry someone, Cy. The thrills of love and the excitement of getting someone to fall in love with you, or you may call it the thrill of the hunt, is over once you are married. Maybe not for everyone. It was for Donald. It seems when a man has the same woman over and over again, sometimes he loses something in his heart for her. She has used and abused her body to have his children, and now she doesn't look quite so good to him.

"To make a long story short, Donald left me for another woman, whom he never married. But I must say he has been a good father. I've tried hating him, but as yet I haven't accomplished that. I could have, if he had neglected the children. If he hadn't helped financially or failed to give his time to them, or never called on special occasions like birthdays, I could have hated him. Donald does love his children. In fact, he has lived up to every commitment in the divorce.

"I have finally accepted that it is probably not his fault that he fell out of love with me or that he couldn't remain faithful to me. I have also decided that I am not a bad person. I'm not sure what it takes to hold a man, but I have felt a great love and devotion from you, Cy. You have been a gentleman in our relationship. You have liked me and you love me. You loved me for me, for what is in my heart, in my head—not for my looks, not my body.

"You have a strong moral character. It's so strong that at one point in our relationship I detested it. I thought perhaps, again, I was not desirable. Then I had to remind myself of all the other men who have tried dating me for reasons other than my personality and character. So maybe, just perhaps, I am desirable, and I finally met and fell in love with a real man who loved me for me—for what's in my heart, for what's in my head, how I think and for what I feel." Mary Ann hesitated, looking forlornly past Cy. "But now, that's not important anymore."

"Mary Ann," Cy said, quietly reaching out for her hand. "What are you leading up to? Have I done something wrong? What have I done?"

"Oh, Cy." Mary Ann began to cry again. "Oh no, my darling. You have been perfect. You were my dream come true." She hesitated, trying to compose herself. "At first I was drawn to you because you stood out as a handsome, rugged cowboy. You were kind to my children and better than that, they loved you. You were the answer to everything I have ever wanted in a man. Somewhere in your soul, honor is deeply rooted and that's what made me fall in love with you.

"But I've been brutally awakened and now I have to face reality." Mary Ann moved closer to Cy. She took both his hands in hers. "My problem, Cy, is...my problem is, I don't have the time to take you into my life. This is where my children come before you. They are the most important things in my life, including you or my parents."

Cy wrinkled his forehead and shook his head. "I don't understand, Mary Ann. Whatever it is, we can deal with it together."

"We could, yes. You and I could, yes. But that is why I say my children come first." Mary Ann took a deep breath, gathering her strength. "Cy, I'm going back to my husband."

Cy stared at Mary Ann in disbelief. He tried to release her hands, but she refused to loosen her grip. He couldn't believe what she was saying. "You're what?"

"It's not what you think. Please, hear me out." Mary Ann suddenly looked very different. Her eyes changed color and a deep anxiety came forth. "Something has happened to me unexpectedly. I have no control over it. I am going back to my husband because he is willing to take me and the children. He has always wanted the children and they belong with him. I have to give them that needed and precious time before I die. He wants us to be together as a family until the end."

"What? What do you mean, until you die? What are you saying? What's wrong, Mary Ann?" Cy felt his face turn red.

"All those backaches and stomach problems that I refused to go to the doctor about were progressively getting worse. I didn't want to be a complainer, and I thought they would go away. I thought if I didn't ride horses for a while I would get better. When I didn't, I finally went to my doctor and then to a specialist without telling you because I thought it would be nothing and I would get over it. That's not going to happen, and I'm not the brave little person I thought I was. Cy...I have pancreatic cancer in the advanced stages. All the tests are finished now, and there is nothing that can be done. Whatever treatment is available will not cure me. It's just a matter of time—a very short time.

"Donald is kind enough to give us a home. The kids need to be living with him so that the bonding process can begin again between them. They need to be with him so that there isn't a big change in their lives when I'm gone."

Cy slid to the floor and held his head in his hands. Tears came quickly to his eyes and he had no control. "Why can't I take care of you? I love you. I would be good to you."

"That's why I said I had to sacrifice, my loved one. The children are everything. Their recovery will be slow and difficult. You're a strong person, Cy. You'll be able to deal with it. They won't."

"Mary Ann, you don't understand. Everyone I have loved in my life is gone. My father and mother, my only brother, my grandparents. I have no one else. I don't want anyone else. I've never cared for anyone before. I really love you. Just you. Until I met you, I thought I was incapable of loving someone. I need you."

"Cy, I know you love me, but you are not 'in love' with me and that's a big difference. In time, I know you would have fallen in love with me, as I have you, but I have to give this time to my children. There is no other option. My parents agree. I love you with all my heart, but I have to let you go and provide my children with the love only their father can give. Donald has always loved his children. He's devoted to them, and they need him."

Mary Ann took a deep breath and slid off the couch onto the floor next to Cy. When she saw his tears, she lost control. She slipped her arms around him. The instant she touched him, Cy undammed his emotions. His shoulders shook and he cried deeply.

Mary Ann was his first love. He didn't want to be near anyone else. She was his life. He felt completely lost and regretted that he had not been more forward with his feelings. He loved her. Now he was losing her. He knew she was right.

The children needed to come first. That didn't lessen the pain in his heart.

He cried long and hard. He cried for the pain Mary Ann would have to endure. He cried for his loneliness at her loss. Where would he be without her? He had no clue.

It had been a busy night. The streets had been alive with people earlier in the evening.

Scratch, Skin, and Cy sat at Orozco's Taco Shop on a much-needed break. Cy wished he could double with Skin. He was not in the mood to be alone.

It had been three weeks since Mary Ann moved back with her ex-husband in Oregon. She called Cy several times in finalizing her farewell. Her health was failing fast now. She decided against chemotherapy because it would not cure her terminal cancer and she would rather die with her own hair than none at all. Being bald was the horrors of all horrors for her. Chemo, she said, would only give her more time to linger in misery. She told Cy her pain tolerance was very low. She made him promise to stay away in order to give her the time she needed with her children.

Skin was constantly worried over Cy's predicament. He had thought about the situation many times and they discussed the options over and over. There were no clear-cut answers.

"Sarge, you have so many things going for you. There are plenty of wonderful women out there just waiting for you to discover them." Skin felt a tremendous heartache for his sergeant. Cy was one of his closest friends and it bothered him to see him experience the pain he was enduring. "I'm not suggesting you forget Mary Ann, but you do have to move on. Life does go on and you need to let it go."

"That's easier said than done," Cy said, looking across the night lights toward General Hospital.

"Four Adam 55," dispatch scratched over the car speaker. The patrol car was parked next to the curb, and Skin walked over to it and picked up the mike through the door window.

"Four Adam 55, go ahead."

"Four Adam 55, received complaint of a suspicious vehicle in a residential area. Request made to have it checked out. Go to Forest Avenue and Cincinnati in RD 457. A black late model

Chevrolet two-door is parked at the corner away from the curb, creating a traffic hazard. Could possibly be a 23102-A."

"Ten-four, Four Adam 55 en route." Skin looked around at his partner. "Come on, Scratch, we better check it out. We might have a DUI dangling on the end of a hook. We won't even have to work at reeling him in. Catch you later, Sarge."

The two officers threw away their leftover food in the trash bin, got into their patrol car, and drove off. Cy continued to sit at the table staring off into the distance. He sipped on a Coke and wondered what he should do with his life. The loneliness was like a ghost haunting his spirit. Life was not good. Life was despair.

"The sergeant doesn't look too good, does he?" Skin said, driving down Mott Street.

"No man, he doesn't," Scratch replied. "I think it's a good thing you boys are going deer hunting in a few weeks. The change will do him good."

"I think you're right."

"Who's going with you?" Scratch asked with a twinge of jealousy.

"Well, there are four of us going—Jacob, Tony Valin, Cy, and myself."

"What a group, man. You guys are going to have a blast. I wish I could go. It's too bad we don't have more manpower on our watches so I could go, too."

"Hey, don't feel left out, compadre. I'll tell you all about it," Skin laughed, pulling his pipe from his mouth and setting it on the seat. "This damn thing is so hard to keep lit. It's almost not worth smoking it."

"Hey, man, I am so sick of your bitchin' and moanin'. Why don't you just start smoking again? At least I wouldn't have to listen to you complain all the time."

"Not on your life, partner. I'm never touching smokes again." Shivers ran down Skin's back thinking about the liquor store robbery. He turned left onto Cincinnati and drove east to Forest Avenue. Off to the far corner was a dark-colored, late model Chevrolet parked with the front tire up on the curb and the rear fender too far in the street, impeding traffic.

Scratch picked up the mike and called dispatch. "Four Adam 55, arrived at Cincinnati and Forest. Be out of the car on vehicle, California plates, Nora James Ida 475."

"Copy, Four Adam 55," dispatch squawked a response.

Skin put his nightstick in the baton ring as he exited the patrol unit. Scratch did the same as he walked behind the suspect vehicle and stood to the rear, looking the car over while Skin cautiously approached the driver's side. He could see a man passed out behind the driver's wheel. His flashlight did not reveal any weapons but there were two empty wine bottles on the floorboard.

"Scratch, the engine is running. I see a large bottle of Gallo wine and the driver is passed out behind the wheel. We at least have a 647 in or about a vehicle with alcohol." Skin moved his light over to the other side of the front seat. He recognized the passenger. His eyes were closed but did not appear passed out. Skin immediately knew the man as a wannabe Hell's Angel. His name was Marty Dominguez. He was an Indian/Mexican in his early twenties who was small, rode a Harley-Davidson, and thought he was real bad. He did not wear colors. He was in the Hell's Angels' periphery, but only as a gofer, flunky, and wannabe.

Marty was sarcastic, arrogant, and tough-acting, known to the department as a drinker and fighter who liked going around the streets making obscene gestures at citizens.

Skin leaned into the open car door window. "Excuse me, sir, are you okay?"

Marty opened his eyes, looked at Skin, and instantly became mouthy. "You know who I am, who I hang with." Marty threw his head back arrogantly. "You've seen me around a lot." He took the Gallo wine and took a long draw from it. "You mess with me, you're inviting a lot of trouble, man."

Scratch came around from the back of the suspect car to the passenger side. The half-breed in the car was a disgrace to his people. He detested this lowlife that reflected on the other Hispanics. "Hey, amigo, step out of the vehicle. Your mouth is running faster than your crap-for-brains can function."

Scratch reached down and opened the car door, and a hostile Marty emerged. Scratch ignored his antics, spinning him around. He was arrested on a penal code 647, public intoxication.

Skin pulled the unconscious driver out of the car and arrested him for intoxication in control of a vehicle. After cuffing the prisoner Skin placed him in the back seat of the patrol unit, while Scratch took care of Marty. Skin requested a wrecker to hook up the vehicle for impound. After Larry's Wrecker Service arrived and removed the suspect car, Skin headed back to Hollenbeck Station to process the prisoners.

About a mile from the station, Marty leaned forward, straining against the seat belts, and addressed Skin. "Hey, man, you are nothing. You are nothing but a bald-headed ugly cop."

Over the years both officers had had several run-ins with Marty. Skin hated the little mouth. He was like a bantam rooster, flapping his wings and making a lot of noise but with no substance to back it up. Skin enjoyed taking him in for booking.

Marty screamed and screeched in the back seat, spitting at Skin. "You are lower than a chicken, man. You are nothing but a coward, and you don't know what it's like to be a real man like me." The blood vessels on his neck popped out and his face was contorted. "You sucking cops are nothing but a bunch of punks. You bald-headed freak. You are scared of my shadow. You must wet the bed at night wondering what it's like to feel like a man."

Skin swallowed hard. Scratch turned his head and said patiently, "Don't you do it, partner. I don't like the look on your face." He pointed over his shoulder with his thumb at the mouthy prisoner. "He is nothing. Pay no attention to him."

"The little prick is asking for it," Skin protested.

Marty hissed and spit. "I could kick your ass up between your ears, you freaking pansy. You are worthless, man. Worthless."

Marty pushed the wrong button. Skin pulled over to the side of the street and stopped the vehicle. Never before in his career had Skin done anything like this.

Scratch gave Skin a worried look. "What are you doing?"

"I'm going to give this little rooster a chance to prove himself," Skin said, climbing out of the car.

"No, don't do this, man. It's not worth it."

"I don't care. I want to see what this bantam is made of."

"No, no, no. Let's go. He's not worth it. We can book these guys and take a break. I'll buy you a beer at Jack's after work. Come on, forget it," Scratch called to him, climbing out of his side of the car.

Skin went around, opened the door, and pulled Marty out of the car. He took his handcuff key and removed the cuffs. Scratch was afraid to say anything more in front of the prisoner for fear of promoting the idea of filing a complaint against

Skin. He remained quiet, trying to determine what he should do. He nervously looked up and down the street for any witnesses. Luckily there was no one out.

Scratch and Skin had equal rank; however, it was still illegal for one police officer to allow another officer to break the law. Scratch was trying to determine if a law was being broken. If Skin released the prisoner, it would be a fair fight, an agreement in common. This meant it was not an assault but an altercation of consent. At least he hoped this is what it was. He didn't know for sure. He did know Skin was breaking department policy, and that was a major disciplinary violation which could yield serious repercussions.

Skin didn't care about his job or the future. He didn't care about his partner getting into trouble. He did care about this little pup who thought he was so tough. When Skin threw the cuffs on the ground, he stared at Marty. "You little hemorrhoid. Let's see what you're made of. Take your best shot."

Marty stepped back and assumed a martial arts stance. Not knowing Skin was a part-time martial arts instructor at the division, Marty tried a kick, and Skin maneuvered a parry to the right. A self-defense movement, instead of using force it created a deflection, throwing the opposition off-guard harmlessly. Marty threw another kick and Skin parried him again to the left. Skin then moved in with a solar-plexus side slam with his wrist and forearm. Marty lost his breath, and Skin did an instant takedown and applied his thumb to a pressure point behind Marty's ear.

Skin released Marty and stepped back. "You need another chance here, you little rooster?" Skin's eyes reflected a mean glare. Marty knew he was in trouble. He wished he had not let the bottled courage from the wine get the best of him.

Marty threw a right swing. Skin stepped forward making a cross with his arm, catching the blow, and pulled Marty to the ground. This time Skin maintained a handhold, twisting Marty's arm by applying pressure to his bent hand. Skin then stepped on Marty's neck and held him to the ground.

Scratch took a deep breath, greatly relieved that Skin was not going to mark Marty up. It was still serious if a complaint was filed. Marty did not move on the ground nor did he say anything. He wouldn't show his pain but submission was evident.

Finally, Skin released Marty with a shrug, and he slowly

got to his feet. Skin stepped backward, maintaining silence.

Marty brushed his arms off, looking at the officer who had just taken him down twice. "I gave it my best shot. You took me fair."

Skin didn't respond. He put the cuffs back on Marty and shoved him in the back seat. Scratch remained mute, giving his partner a disapproving look. Skin got behind the wheel and headed to the station. On the way, Skin thought about what he did and could see his law enforcement career evaporating. The more he thought about it, the more he was ashamed. Skin looked in his rearview mirror trying to figure a way out of this. He knew he could be dismissed, and Scratch could be reprimanded for not interfering. He gained a new respect for his partner but now guilt took hold.

"Marty, there's not one person on this department you could take. I have personally trained them all in self-defense; I'm a member of the Police Self-Defense Instructors' Association."

"Hey, man, I really respect you. You know what I'm saying?" Marty stammered from the back seat. "You were man enough to give me a break and you took me. I gave it my best shot. I have no complaints, man."

Skin saw the light bulb switch on. To his right Scratch was pantomiming breaking a pencil. He knew what it meant. He had permission to break the prisoner loose.

"I really respect you too, Marty." Skin pulled the car over to the side at Chicago and Brooklyn, only four blocks from the station. He got out of the car and walked around to the right side of the unit and opened the prisoner's door.

"Marty, I'm going to give you a break. You don't need this on your record. I'm going to let you go, but I'm going to book your sidekick. You can bail him out tomorrow." Skin held his breath, hoping the little worm couldn't read him.

Marty put his hand out and shook Skin's hand. "I'm outta here, man."

Skin was so relieved he almost hugged the man. It was the last time Skin ever had any trouble with Marty Dominguez.

Skin walked over to Scratch and threw one arm around his neck and put his head on his shoulder. "Scratch, I'm sorry. I put you in a bad position. I could have ruined my career and hurt yours. I'm sorry, partner."

Scratch waited a moment, feeling the anger slowly subside.

"Don't ever do that to me again," he said as he shoved Skin away and started for the car.

"After work let's go to Jack's. I need a beer, bad," Skin said, feeling the guilt of his partner's tone. "I owe you one, pard."

"You owe me crap, Skin. Don't ever put me in that position again."

"I promise. And I mean it," Skin answered as he walked around to the driver's door. They both got in and drove to the station with the drunk driver.

The two officers booked the prisoner into the Glass House. Scratch was still sore and wouldn't speak to Skin unless it was necessary. He took the wheel. Being in control of the car made him feel better and perhaps aided him in cooling off. He did not like someone interfering with his future. Even though Skin was a great partner, he wouldn't allow him to jeopardize his career with the department.

Over the car radio they heard Four Lincoln 37, Officer Jim Stilson, advising Central Communications he was behind a stolen vehicle and was having trouble getting it stopped. Several civilian cars were run off the road, no one hurt.

Scratch headed back to Boyle Heights to RD 473. Stilson declared he was traveling east on 4th approaching State Street.

Skin did not like the sound of Jim's voice when giving his position to dispatch. He sounded overly excited, though perhaps that came with being a rookie. Jim was in his first year with the department. He appeared to be a good officer, taking advice and asking questions. Jim had told the other officers that his wife did not like his work and wanted him to quit the department. He said the arguments were long and exhausting to both of them. He always wanted to be a cop and he was sticking with it.

"Four Lincoln 37, the suspect vehicle just ran another car off the road at Chicago. I'm still heading east on 4th," Jim's voice broke frantically over the radio.

"Copy, Four Lincoln 37."

"Four Lincoln 37, this is Four Adam 55. We're two blocks behind you. If you get him stopped, try to maintain a secured position until our arrival," Skin said calmly over the police radio. He glanced at Scratch. "I don't like the sound of his voice.

He's breathing too hard into the mike. You better step on it."

Scratch didn't look as pleased as his words sounded. "Gotcha. He sounds like he's on his first lone felony stop," he said, accelerating.

Stilson yelled into his transmitter. "Four Adam 55, unable to copy. Sirens overriding transmission." There was a short hesitation and then he continued, "Subject turned right on Matthews. It appears he's pulling over on Matthews next to the middle school." Jim was now screaming into the mike.

Cy was traveling south on Soto feeling anxious as he listened to the radio communications. He went code-2, hitting his overheads to get through lighted intersections expediently and proceeded as fast as he safely could.

Scratch had his nose up against the windshield. "I see his lights," he said, partially relieved.

"Come on, get going," Skin cried.

After a few moments they pulled to a quick stop behind Jim Stilson's unit. His overheads were on and he was out of the car. He failed to make a standard felony stop by waiting for backup as most officers do if time permits. There was no reason why Jim could not have waited. He was told he had assistance.

Jim was standing a few feet back and to the side of the driver, yelling at him. The driver was still in the car behind the wheel. Jim had his revolver out and was holding it in an outreached position, pointing it at the suspect. His body language was not good. He was shaking and jerking instead of remaining calm and in control.

Sirens from other police units could be heard in the distance, closing in. The stop location was a residential and school area. Heads were popping up and down as people tried to see what was going on from their fences and lawns. People were gathering at the corner to watch the police in action. The high school was across the street from the Hollenbeck Middle School. Some kids who had been playing basketball now gathered at curbside.

Two patrol units were stopped and two others were approaching. When Jim stepped up to the driver's window, it put some of the officers at a disadvantage because they didn't have a clear line of fire. Other assisting officers arrived, blocked off the streets with their vehicles, and tried to provide coverage.

Jim's hands shook as he held the revolver on the suspect. He recognized the Hispanic male as a local hood who was always in trouble. The man was in his early twenties and had a police record of thefts and gang-related crimes.

The officer was acting irrationally. He pushed the barrel of his .357 magnum into the neck of the suspect, grabbed him by the hair, and started yelling profanities.

"What in the hell is the matter with him?" Skin muttered to Scratch.

"I don't know, man, but we got trouble," Scratch replied, looking to see what police car was rolling up. "Hey, it's the Sarge."

The sergeant parked his car next to the curb, exited, and joined his men.

"Sarge." Skin waved Cy over to his position. Cy surveyed the people and the area as he walked quickly over to Skin and his partner.

"What in hell's name is going on here?" Cy said breathlessly. "Has Jim gone nuts?"

"You got me, Sarge. He's as nervous as a cat having kittens in the middle of a dog fight," Skin said seriously. "It's not good. Not good at all. We have a major problem here."

"He's suffering from professional constipation...I think," Scratch said, not smiling.

"The dipstick—too much, too loud, too soon, Sarge," Skin said, glancing at Cy. "He's falling apart before our eyes."

"I don't like it," Cy said. "Scratch, walk behind me to my right for cover," Cy ordered sternly. "Skin, go to the other side of the suspect's car but stay back out of the line of fire. I'm going to approach Stilson. He may know something we don't. The driver may be a real piece of work. If I can, I'm going to talk him down. Okay?"

"Got it." Skin moved immediately toward the suspect's vehicle. He called out, warning Jim that he was approaching from the side.

The other officers were surprised at the unconventional behavior by an officer who normally was calm and courteous to violators. Jim was well liked by the other men on his shift. Now he put the other officers at the scene in a bad predicament because they could not assess the situation to determine what police action should be taken.

All they could do at this point was to provide a perimeter from the citizens and partial coverage if the suspect started shooting. The support officers felt some relief when they saw their sergeant carefully approaching the frantic officer.

Skin moved to the far side of the suspect's vehicle. Officer Stilson did not acknowledge Skin's presence. Scratch stayed behind the sergeant and carefully followed him over toward Jim. As they approached the suspect's vehicle, Scratch lifted his shotgun in a port-arms position—a position he could level down in one quick movement for firing if warranted.

Skin positioned himself into a crouched position behind the suspect vehicle looking for other occupants. When he determined the driver was alone in the car, he carefully walked over to and looked inside the passenger side of the suspect vehicle. The window was open and Stilson saw Skin for the first time.

"Jim, take it easy, my man," Cy said carefully, as he came up behind Jim. "We don't want any unnecessary shooting here."

"I got this faggot," Jim said, slurring his words and nervously maintaining his rigid stance.

"Jim, your hammer is cocked," Cy said. "Point it upward and uncock it now."

"I've got him, okay? I'm not going to shoot the scum if he doesn't try anything," Jim slurred. "You got that, puke face? You got that?" Jim stepped backward, maintaining his aim at the suspect and refusing to uncock the weapon. The officer was almost frozen from excitement.

It was obvious the suspect was streetwise and not scared of the cop. "You back off and I'll get out of the car, okay? You hear what I'm saying? You move back, I'll get out."

The Mexican had gang tattoos across his forehead and neck. He wore a black tank top, revealing his tattoo-covered arms. It was apparent he was a hardcore ganger. At the moment he was insulted by this officer acting like a fool and a coward. "I'll get out of the car. You," he pointed his finger at the cop, "get out of my face with that peashooter."

Officer Stilson withdrew his gun and opened the door. He grabbed the driver by the hair and pulled him around to the front of the car. As soon as the driver was out of the car, Skin ran around to the front of the car to give further assistance if needed.

Stilson slammed the suspect over the hood of the car and shoved the barrel of the gun in the suspect's neck.

Cy came up behind Stilson. "Come on, Jim, ease up. The threat's over. There's no need..." The police revolver discharged explosively, sending a .357 round into the suspect's neck, blowing blood and bone over the hood of the car and onto Skin.

Skin jumped to the side and dove for the ground, rolling to his right side. When he came to his feet he had dirt stuck to the blood on his shirt and face. Bits of bone and grass were sticking to his clothing. He brushed madly at the residue to get it off him.

Stilson stood motionless. He was dazed and obviously overwhelmed as he stared at the body sliding off the hood of the car, thudding to the asphalt. He shook his head slowly back and forth, unable to comprehend what had just happened.

The other officers were stunned and didn't move. Several women on the sidewalk screamed and the children were in total shock. Voices raised and people started moving around angrily at the policeman's action.

Cy grabbed Stilson's arm and pushed his gun hand in the air. Stilson released his hold on the weapon and gave it to Cy. "Take it easy, Jim," Cy spoke strongly to Stilson. He didn't like the look in Stilson's eyes. He handed the weapon to Skin. "Take care of this."

Stilson was glaring at the blood and gore on the hood of the stolen car. "Jim! Listen to me. Turn around and walk away," Cy commanded.

Stilson couldn't speak. Cy and Scratch took Stilson by the arms and led him to another patrol car parked nearby. Cy ordered two standby officers to take Stilson back to the station and call the department psychologists to check him out.

Skin checked the man on the ground. "He's dead," he said quietly, looking around at Scratch.

Cy walked back to the man lying in the street. "Scratch, get to your unit and call for detectives ASAP." The sergeant gave a hard look at Skin. "You stay here and protect the scene. I'll be back in a moment."

Cy walked over to four officers standing a few feet back. "You guys set up traffic cones and get some crime scene ribbon and tape this whole area off. I need two of you to get traffic diverted out of here." Cy noticed three other officers were already taking responsibility with crowd control and getting witness statements.

Cy's heart was on the verge of exploding. Perspiration ran down his neck and chest. Skin moved over to him and held out Stilson's gun in a plastic bag. The date, time, and location were written in the corner.

"Thanks," Cy said, taking it from him.

"You know what this means," Skin said in a tired voice.

"Yeah, I know what it means. We have a dead punk and an officer who just lost his career and a life, and we're facing a lawsuit against the department." Cy turned to look at the body. "Let's get a blanket over him."

Skin didn't move and looked around at the crowd of people being held back by other officers. A great sadness came over him. "Sometimes this job really sucks."

"You got that right," Cy responded.

"Stilson was young but he was a good officer. He made a mistake. A man is dead and an officer's life is over."

"It was an accident. I doubt that the prosecutors could go with anything criminal. What's for sure is, Jim's career is over." Cy looked sadly at the dead man.

Days later, rumors spread throughout the division and the community of the shooting. The people who had seen the incident voiced their opinions to the press. There was no reason for the shooting to occur. Claims were made that the involved officer was a liability to the community. Stilson was put on administrative leave until a shooting board could determine if the incident was lawful or warranted.

Stilson came to the office to fill out his paperwork concerning the incident. The other officers shied away from him. It was the natural thing to occur after an officer was involved in a bad shooting. No one wanted to work closely with him and he became a marked officer.

Two weeks later, Jim Stilson voluntarily resigned from the department. The press had turned against him. His wife and daughter left him and his life took a nosedive. The stress was too much for him. Eventually he got a job in another city as an animal control regulator.

Jacob walked out of his office when he saw Cy coming down the hall. "Cy," he motioned with his hand. Wrinkles were formed between his eyes. "You have a phone call. Why don't you take it in my office."

Cy felt Jacob's hand touch his back as he went to the messy desk. Jacob didn't have to tell him who it was. It was written all over his face like a road map. He took a deep breath and picked up the receiver. "Sergeant Golden."

"Is this Cy Golden?" the man's voice asked.

"Yes it is. Is this Donald?" Cy's voice began to falter. His chest tightened and he felt blackness all around him.

"I'm sorry, Cy. Mary Ann passed away a few moments ago." Donald's voice was raspy and it was evident he had gone through a hard time.

"Where are you, Donald?"

"We're at home. Mary Ann wanted to be at home with the children." Donald's voice broke and he momentarily lost control of his emotions.

Tears filled Cy's eyes. "Did she...did she say anything before she died?"

"Yes, Cy, she did. It was a peaceful death. The doctor had given her medicine for the pain and the children were with her, and also her parents, sister, and brother."

"Cy." Donald had trouble making his words work their way out through trembling lips. "Mary Ann asked me to tell you that you were in her last thoughts and that she loved you deeply. She wanted me to thank you for her, for giving her the time with the children. She wanted to thank you for the wonderful happiness that you had given her. She never stopped loving you for a moment, Cy. And she loved you to the end." Donald's voice broke off.

Cy wasn't doing any better. Tears streamed down his cheeks openly, and when he saw Skin come quietly into the room and felt his hand on his shoulder, he let the tears flow freely without control. "Donald, I know this is hard for you. Thank you for calling. It means a lot to me to know her feelings. I missed her greatly these past few weeks. I'll plan on being at the funeral if no one objects."

"No, no. We expect you. I'll be looking forward to meeting you. I feel like I know you already."

"When and where is the funeral going to be?" Cy asked.

"In Glendora at the Oakdale Cemetery on Grand Avenue, probably Friday. I'll have to call you after the arrangements are made."

Cy gritted his teeth. He felt great sorrow because he could

not take charge or at least be a part of the arrangements in taking care of Mary Ann. "Is there anything I can do to help?"

"Yes, there is. Mary Ann said she wanted you to pick the spot for her resting place. There are no other relatives buried there, so it's your choice. Would you mind doing that?"

"No, not at all. Thank you for letting me be part of it. Thank you, Donald. Will you call me on the specifics?"

"Certainly. I'll call by tomorrow. Goodbye, Cy." Donald hung up the phone..

"Thank you." Cy dropped the phone on the desk and threw his hands over his face. His whole body tightened as he felt a surge of heartbreaking trauma envelop him. It didn't help when he glanced at Skin who was never emotional. He had wet trails running down his cheeks.

Cy looked to Jacob for reassurance. It was a mistake. His lieutenant was weeping openly. The three men stood in a circle for a long moment. None of the other officers in the division approached them. Scratch saw them from down the hallway and hastily turned around. He knew he would lose it if he got close to them. He went out the front door onto 1st Street and leaned against the building.

Flush came walking around the corner from the police parking lot. When he saw Scratch, he walked over to him. "Hey, man, what's up?"

Scratch nodded his head to the inside. "Don't go in there, man. It don't look good."

"Why not? I got reports to do. What's up?"

"It's got to be bad news. The lieutenant, Sergeant Golden, and Skin are in a huddle and it don't look good, man. I wouldn't go in there if I was you. I think Mary Ann probably died."

"Oh no," Flush said, shaking his head. "Well, I ain't going in there. Let's go get a taco, man. My stomach is starting to act up and I need to feed it."

"Yeah, let's get out of here. It ain't a good place to be right now." Scratch turned and walked with Flush to the parked police cars. "I'll meet you at Orozco's, okay?"

"I'll follow you over there," Flush said. He felt guilty for not going inside to comfort Cy but he felt this was not the time to interfere. He knew the lieutenant and Skin were what his sergeant needed. No, there was no way he was going to make a fool of himself. Flush knew if he were having a bad time of it, he would want to be left alone. If his best friends were inside having a hard time trying to hold back their own emotions, it would not be good for him to witness such a thing. No, there was no way he was going to make a fool of himself. He needed a taco, the only thing that would take care of the deep growling pain in his stomach. He began thinking of a place where he could go afterward and sit on a toilet and think about things.

Chapter 11
Jack's

It was two weeks before the deer hunt. The more work and police problems for Cy, the more he relished in it. He hadn't even considered meeting other women and gave all his attention to the department and his horses.

Once the funeral was over Cy slowly began recovering from the loss of Mary Ann. People who spoke at the funeral opened Cy's eyes to things he did not know about her. She had been a songleader at her high school for three years. Even though she was one of the most popular girls in school, she was warm to everyone and treated everyone with respect. She smiled easily and was friendly to everyone. She had a genuine concern for her fellow schoolmates and they in return loved her for it.

During Mary Ann's junior year, she wore braces on her teeth. She tried desperately not to smile because of her embarrassment. Sometimes the rubber bands, applying tension on the braces, popped off during choir practice. She had a difficult time accepting her orthodontist's orders not to chew gum. She loved gum and she missed it terribly. It was always a problem getting the gum unstuck from her braces before going home. Her father was more lenient with her, but her mother enforced the rules.

Cy had not been surprised at how many people loved Mary Ann. She had volunteered her services and talents during high school and college by visiting the sick and elderly. She had touched many lives, especially his own. She had assured him of his own goodness and strong character. He privately thanked her for it. Warm thoughts of her comforted him, strengthening him when he felt depressed or lost.

After Cy and Skin finished filing their reports on Friday night, they changed clothes in the locker room, then they left the station and walked across 1st Street to Jack's. Inside, the smoke was heavy. The laughter was loud, and booze had slackened the behavior of almost everyone, releasing their inhibitions. A jukebox was playing Merle Haggard's "Okie from Muskogee."

Cy felt his spirits lift as he worked his way around the tables to Jacob and Tony Valin. Cy liked Tony. He was a good cop who knew his business. He was a twelve-year veteran and had been assigned to drug enforcement for the last few years. Tony knew everybody. Everyone who knew Tony liked him, especially the women. He was of Portuguese descent, about 5'10", and had a muscular build. He had thick dark eyebrows and his dense black hair was curly. With his charming smile and personality, Cy could see why the women were drawn to him.

Tony looked up from his conversation with Jacob and gave Cy an inviting smile. "Hey, buddy. Have a seat. We've been waiting for you. Where's that ugly bald-headed guy?"

Cy pulled a chair from the table and dropped his body into it. He pointed over his shoulder to Skin, who was slowly walking toward their table. His pipe was stuck in his mouth while he stopped at different tables conversing with friends. A good portion of the customers were law enforcement personnel, others the local people who stopped for a cool one before heading home after a night's work.

Cy felt a soft hand on his shoulder and then a woman's lips brushing his right ear. "You want the usual, hon?" Christy smiled, kissing Cy on the top of his ear.

"A cold brewski," Cy grinned at her. She turned on her heels and stepped over to an adjacent table with four loud customers and began talking with them.

Tony studied Cy and shook his head. "You're a fool, Cy. That woman wants you bad. Why not ask her out? You know she'd go with you. You have got to get out of this rut you're in and meet some new women."

"She's not my type," Cy shrugged, failing to show any interest.

"Well, I've been with her a couple of times, and she's a fine person," Tony said, looking over Cy's shoulder as Christy walked away.

"Someday your wife is going to catch you and you'll be out in the street," Jacob said as a matter of fact, taking a long drink from his foamy glass.

"No way, Jake," Tony laughed. "I'm very careful. Besides, I love my wife. It's just that I have this thing in me that won't let me rest. You guys know what I mean."

"I don't," Cy said. "You have two great kids, your wife is gorgeous, plus she loves you. What more could you want?"

"I know, I know. Susie is a great domestic engineer but..."

"A what?" Jacob frowned at Tony.

"A domestic engineer. You know, a working housewife," Tony laughed.

Cy looked at Tony and shook his head. "I love your guts, Tony, but I don't like the way you treat your wife. She's a marvel and it's not worth taking the chance of losing it all."

Skin came over and pulled a chair out and sat down. "Tony, I just heard you lost a C.I."

Tony frowned and glanced down at the table. "That I did. Someone did a double tap on my confidential informant with a twenty-two in his right temple and dumped him in a pond. He'd been gone for three days. I thought he had left town."

"That's what one of the guys was just telling me. He said your man floated to the surface, bloated like a balloon."

"I've seen floaters before, but this guy looked like a sea lion," Tony said. He looked at his three companions with a serious expression. "We've got something going down with the Mexican Mafia. I can't figure if it's a war brewing or gangs testing their strength and wanting in on the local drug action."

Christy returned with Cy's beer and a Budweiser for Skin. They both tipped her. She wiggled away with a tray of drinks for another table.

Jacob took a long drink of beer and swallowed slowly. He turned the bottle around and around in his hand. "Something's going on, Tony, and I don't like the smell of it. There's all kinds of talk going down about East L.A., Hollenbeck, Soto, St. Peco, and Ramo streets. You got your ear to the ground, so what is it?"

Tony stared at Jacob a moment before answering. "You know I can't talk a lot about my assignment. It's confidential. No offense. I will say, though, the old gangs are acting strange. White Fence is one of the oldest gangs since before the thirties. Rumors are floating that they don't want trouble, but they ain't walking either."

Tony moved his chair closer to the table and talked lower. "You guys know about the old Dog Town Gang that started way back at the old dog pound and the Frog Town Gang. These are gangs you just don't mess with. Well, the Cypress Park Boys and the Avenues Gang are sending messages through snitches—no more turf violations. They don't just talk about things like that. Turf is everything."

Jacob didn't like what he was hearing. He gave Skin a disturbed look, then returned his attention to Tony. "Don't tell me we are going to have a war out there. The gangs have been keeping to themselves, policing their own people. Are they spreading out?"

"The Mexican Mafia have the power and they are scared of no one. They're spreading their wings and violating space. The saying 'drive-by shooting' will be a phrase that everyone across the United States will know in a few years, and it will reach into everyone's city and town. No one will be safe and it's just the beginning."

"Aren't you overreacting just a little, Tony?" Skin smiled, showing doubt in his eyes.

"The problem is, I'm not telling you just how bad it is really going to get. You guys have no idea how bad things are under the carpet. You can't scare the Mexicans. They are the toughest, meanest people I know. You know why they are so tough?" Tony hesitated, looking at the others, then went on. "Pride, man. These guys have pride and nothing else matters. A Mexican doesn't care about the punishment. He will go to jail with honor and do a thirty-year hitch. A Mexican will kill a snitch in front of a guard for honor and could care less about the consequences."

Tony took a drink of beer; the others didn't respond. None of the men at the table took their eyes off him. Each man was thinking the streets were bad enough. This was not good news they were hearing. The work was hard enough without inter-gang fighting.

As Tony spoke, his Hispanic accent became heavier. "Have you guys ever heard of Tommy Angelino? Angelino and Joe Molino are headpins of the Mafia. Juan Mores is No. 1 body-guard to Angelino and Molino. He worked his way up from the street gangs and became the No. 1 hit man for the Mafia. He is a massively built giant, meaner than a pit bull on a raw cat hide. He is so sadistic that his own people are scared of him. He has a jagged scar from the center of his right cheek that goes over his nose and down to his upper lip. He wears a long black mustache and short goatee. It is unspeakable what he did to the guy that cut him.

"Pavlo is patron to an opposing underground. His cousin, Carlos Noriega, showed up in the hospital a while back with his throat slashed. The jugular was tied off with a string of green dental floss."

"Mint-flavored floss? What are you talking about?" Jacob asked.

"Hang on, I'll get to that in a minute." Tony didn't like being interrupted. "Prostitution and fencing stolen goods used to be the main financial source to the gangs. Now it's drugs; big drugs coming in from South America, especially Colombia and Peru. Pavlo is strictly into drugs and nothing else. He wants it all. Well, nobody, I mean nobody, messes with Juan Mores. He's been here longer than anyone, and he always fixes his own problems.

"Carlos was working for Angelino. Carlos was supposed to have been an outcast of the Pavlo family and a distant relative at that. Well, Carlos was so scared at the hospital that he wouldn't say a word about who cut him. Of course, he was half dead and weak from loss of blood.

"The police couldn't get him to talk, and my narc team couldn't get anywhere with him, either. He kept saying he was dead and it was all he could do to get air into his lungs. He really is a little coward."

"How did you tie this in with the underground?" Cy asked.

"That was easy. You see, they think we are oblivious to most everything they do. Not so. We have our sources, too. The bodyguard, Juan Mores, has a craving for anything mint flavored. He eats chocolate mints all day long. About two months ago we went through his garbage and found mint-flavored dental floss. So you see, it was easy to put this together."

Tony motioned for the guys to get closer and lowered his voice even more. "You guys have got to swear not to tell anyone what I am going to tell you. If you don't promise, I clam up. All of you swear silence." All agreed.

"We set up surveillance on Carlos' room at the hospital. We wanted to know who he was going to contact because we don't know for sure what side he is on. He works for Tommy Angelino, right? But he is a cousin to Pavlo.

"Anyway, at the hospital our surveillance guys heard this blood-curdling scream from Carlos' room. They were next door and didn't see anybody go in there. Well, when they get to his room five seconds after he starts blowing his lungs, Carlos is standing barefoot on the metal frame of his hospital bed screaming his guts out. On the bed is a huge live black tarantula with a long pin stuck through it's body, holding it to the bed; its legs were moving, trying to crawl away but couldn't.

"Carlos now has blood pouring from his neck wound because the stitches couldn't hold his rage and he goes into total hysterics."

Skin squinted at Tony, "Tell me you're putting us on. Everything was okay until you mentioned the spider." The skin on his back crawled and a heavy shiver shimmied through his whole body.

"What you fellows don't know is Pavlo's nickname is Spider. You see, back in the old days when he was young—he's sixty-three now—he used spiders of every kind to coerce his victims to talk. He even used black widows." Tony paused a moment, looking around making sure he had everyone's attention, then went on.

"Can you imagine being tied up and having a jar of black widows emptied down the inside of your shirt? You'd scream your bloody vocal cords through the roof. Any man in his right mind would." He raised both eyebrows searching for agreement from the others. "At least I would."

Jacob finished his beer and looked around the table. Everyone was staring at Tony. "So now Pavlo put the pinch on Carlos not to talk, which means he probably is working for Pavlo and now he has been warned."

"I'd call that a double warning, which makes me wonder who's working for who? Carlos could be working for either one," Jacob said gravely.

"Do you think Carlos could have been double dipping and working for both organizations?" Cy asked.

"That's a strong possibility. We don't know what to think," Tony answered.

The four friends sat around the table throwing around ideas but nothing and everything seemed plausible. The music seemed to grow louder. Johnny Cash sang "A Boy Called Sue" and the atmosphere livened up.

Two young men in their early twenties came over to the table and asked which one was Cowboy.

Cy turned to face them. "I'm Cy. What can I do for you?"

The shorter of the two men smiled out of the corner of his mouth. "We hear you think you're pretty fast on the draw. Is that right?"

"Don't know what you're talking about," Cy answered, looking back at his drink. He ignored the two men and glanced at his friends around the table. "When are we going to discuss the deer hunt, boys? We haven't got much time before we leave."

"Hey, I'm talking to you, buddy." The shorter one poked Cy on the shoulder with his forefinger.

Skin jumped up while pushing his chair back, and it crashed to the floor. "Back off, butt-face, or you'll find yourself on the floor shaking your head wondering how you got there."

"He's not talking to you, baldy," the taller man said sourly.

"Hey now, hold it right there, you guys," Cy said standing up. "We don't want any trouble. This place has enough problems without us creating more. We're here to have a few beers and enjoy ourselves. So just back off and give us some room, okay?"

"I asked you a question. I want an answer. Are you the one they call Cowboy?" the short man asked sarcastically.

"Are you a cop?" Cy asked. His tone held an odd mixture of disinterest and aroused interest.

"Yeah, what about it?"

"Well, pull up your chairs and let's have a friendly drink. We've had a bad day and we don't want any problems, okay?" Cy tried a weak smile on them.

Skin backed up a few feet and moved around to the side of the two strangers. The crowd noise faded out and attention was focused on their table. If there was going to be any action, the patrons didn't want to miss a beat.

"Where are you guys out of?" Jacob asked.

"L.A. County Sheriff's," the taller one answered.

"What's your names, boys?" Jacob asked in a friendly voice.

"Who you calling boys?" the taller one answered.

"No, no, don't take me wrong. I just want to know who I'm talking to." Jacob gave them his best smile.

The shorter one pointed to himself. "I'm Rick White and my friend is Ward Spencer."

Jacob arose, clenching his teeth. "Well, listen, Slick, and you, Wart, or whatever your name is, you don't know who you're talking to here. I suggest you back off and leave us alone." He hesitated and then went on. "Unless you've got some money you're aching to lose. Is that your problem? You got money to throw away? Because that's what's going to happen if you don't walk away now."

"I've got a hundred dollars, buddy. I want to see what the rumors are all about," Rick said, pulling five twenties out of his shirt pocket and dropping them on the table.

Cy downed the last of his beer and stood up. "Hey guys, that's too rich for my blood. Besides, I'm too tired. Come on, let's go home," he said to Skin.

"Are you afraid? What's a little bet?" Rick smiled.

Cy felt his anger rising. It bothered him to see young hot-shot cops. "You sound like a loose cannon that needs a rag jammed down your barrel. You want a bet? You got it." Cy pointed to Skin. "But my friend, Skin, is my part of the wager. You can bet your hundred bucks with the lieutenant here, but I want something different."

Rick's expression revealed his surprise and he looked at Jacob. "You a lieutenant?"

"That's right, boy, and I say that lightly."

"I'm sorry, sir, I didn't know you were a lieutenant."

"Doesn't matter. You made a challenge," Jacob said seriously. "You want to continue on or walk out of here with your tail between your legs?" People laughed but Rick ignored them.

"No, sir. I want to go through with it." Rick wanted to protest but changed his mind.

"Just a minute. I've got something to say here," Cy said. "I'm not betting any money. I do have a stipulation to the bet."

"What stipulation?" Rick asked.

"My friend here is follicly deprived and has been for years," Cy gestured to Skin. He reached up and placed the palm of his hand over the top of Skin's head. "He wears his feelings on his sleeve, and I feel compelled to relieve him of any emotional trauma he may have experienced by your heartless remarks about his baldness. So, if I win the contest, your buddy, Wart, has to kiss the top of his bald head."

Skin smiled, liking the idea. Other people listening laughed, giving their approval.

"No way," Rick said, shaking his head. "You can't expect something like that. That's no bet."

Ward was angry and didn't like the crowd laughing at him. "We bet money. Nothing else."

"It's my part of the bet or you walk away in shame," Cy said sternly. "You came in here strutting your stuff; you meet my demands or turn tail."

Tony took the last drink of his beer and rammed it down hard on the table, making a clatter. He got everyone's attention. "You two hotshots from the Sheriff's Office come in here like two spoiled peacocks showing off your feathers. Well, you're going to learn one thing in this business. You walk it like you talk it, or keep your mouths shut until you grow up and know what you're getting yourselves into before you open those flappy jaws of yours."

"Are you in or out?" Skin asked with a smile, kissing his fingertips and patting his head.

Rick turned to Ward for approval and got it. "I'm in. What's the rules?" Rick asked.

"Give me your weapon, son," Jacob smiled pleasantly. Rick handed him a gun from under his shirt. It was a four-inch Colt .357 magnum. Jacob emptied the cartridges onto the table and lay the revolver down with the cylinder open. He looked over at Cy and nodded his head, wanting his firearm. Cy leaned over and pulled his gun belt from a small duffel bag next to his chair. He also removed two pairs of clear safety glasses, handing one pair to his opponent. Jacob performed the same act with Cy's gun.

Cy stood up and strapped his belt around his waist and attached two tie-downs on each side of the holster to keep it from slipping upward when he drew his weapon. He adjusted his belt and looked at Jacob. Everyone in the room now got quiet and gathered in a big circle around Cy's table.

Jacob handed Cy's revolver to Rick. "Check it to make sure it is unloaded. If you are satisfied, give it to Cy." Rick performed the safety check and gave the Smith and Wesson over to Cy. "Cy, you holster your weapon."

Jacob handed Rick's Colt to Cy, and he checked it carefully then handed it back to Rick.

Jacob took a box of Western cartridges out of Cy's bag. He removed two .38-caliber shells and handed one to each man. "Now, look at the end of the shell. You will notice that it has wax in the end of it. There is no gunpowder in the shell, only a live primer. This is done for two reasons. One is to hear which gun is fired first. The second is to make sure the shot would have hit the target. This also satisfies the challenger who does not believe Mr. Golden here cleared his holster before firing his weapon. In other words, if the wax does not hit you in a kill zone, you win the money, if, of course, your shot hits him. Got it?" Rick nodded in agreement.

"Okay, here are the rules. Both of you two men turn and face each other. Stand four feet apart." Jacob looked around at the other people. "Please, we must have complete silence." No one was making a noise but it had to be said. Concentration was everything. Roy Orbison's "Pretty Woman" was playing on the jukebox. Someone turned the volume down to a whisper. "Unsnap your safety strap, Sergeant."

"He's a sergeant?" Rick asked Jacob.

"That's right, son, he is. You're going to try and outshoot one of the best instructors our academy has ever had," Jacob answered.

"Now, you keep your weapon on double action, hammer down, and point it at the sergeant." Rick did as he was told. "You do not pull the trigger until Cowboy attempts to draw his weapon to fire. It's his only advantage and not much at that." Jacob grinned when he called Cy "Cowboy."

Rick appeared very confident, sure he would win. Everyone in the room was quiet.

"Are you both ready?" Jacob asked carefully, observing both men.

"I'm ready," said Rick, pointing his gun steady at Cy.

"I'm ready, are you ready?" Cy asked Rick, looking at his eyes.

"I'm..." Rick started to answer.

Cy drew and pulled the trigger, shooting Rick in the stomach with the wax bullet. Rick was dumbfounded and couldn't believe what had just happened. Suddenly the room was loud with cheers. People were demanding their bets be paid immediately from their friends. Most everyone had placed a bet on the contest.

Rick stood there looking at Cy with eyes wide in disbelief. Finally, he lowered the gun. "I've never seen anything like that in my life. I just saw you flinch. I never saw you draw."

Skin walked around the table and faced Ward. The room got quiet again and all eyes were on the deputy and Skin. Ward looked at Rick in disgust.

Someone turned the jukebox up and Sammy Cook was crooning, "You Send Me."

Skin leaned over and patted the top of his head. Ward screwed up his face, grabbed hold of Skin's bald head, and planted a big kiss on his crown. Everyone laughed and Ward smiled, shaking his head. "You guys are something else. I think I've been set up."

Jacob grinned at Rick and his friend. "Are you two guys assigned to the Firestone District?"

Rick looked surprised, "Yeah, how did you know that?"

"Your sergeant, John Coleman, is my brother-in-law. He said you needed your fantails trimmed. I told him we would be most happy to oblige." Everyone laughed and the room went back to business as usual.

There are many who believe that Chemehuevi were probably the very first Paiute people to come into contact with the Europeans as they migrated into the western territories of North America. The Southern Paiute tribes and the main body of these people were located to the north and west of the Colorado River. Many of the Paiute people were on the southwest side of the Colorado and located in north-central Arizona and southern Utah.

The Paiute people shared a common language, history, and most importantly a body of traditions and cultures. The people were related to the Shoshone but more closely to the Ute tribes of Utah.

In 1598, Don Juan de Onate of Spain entered a region to the east of the Paiutes and established the colonial province of New Mexico. The Spaniards moved west, thinking the Paiute and Ute Indians they encountered were one group of people because both spoke understandable dialects and had similar traditions.

In 1680, the Spaniards were overthrown and evicted by the southwestern tribes. The Pueblo Indians, now slaves, revolted and drove out the Europeans with the help of the Hopi. Lusting for gold and other mineral riches, the Spaniards returned under the leadership of Don Diego de Vargas in 1694, and this same story of oppression repeated itself time and time again.

It is estimated that a thousand Paiute reside in Owen's Valley, which extends from north of Mono Lake to Lone Pine, California. In 1833, the Mono Paiute Indians, the Kuzedikas, saw the first trappers invade their primitive habitat. Joseph Walker led his expedition into this wild area and traded with the tribe. The Kuzedikas saw few travelers because the main routes were to the north crossing the Sierra Madres and south of Mono Lake. They also knew the immigrants crossing the Great Basin treated the Indians badly—they thought it was great sport to shoot a Paiute and leave him dead rather than have to worry about their property being stolen in the night.

The Indians did not consider it stealing to drive livestock off when they could avoid confrontation. Animals belonged to Mother Earth and not to man. All men had a right to Mother's method of providing food for their hungry families.

It was not long before gold was discovered in the gold-bearing quartz near the lake. Bodie, a few miles north of Mono Lake, was rich with it, and soon over 10,000 people made their homes there. This impacted the Paiutes who soon found themselves working for the white gold seekers, and feelings of distrust and improper treatment left a proud people bitter and destitute, never to recover. When the government tried to intercede, their gifts and grants helped ruin a people who had survived without assistance for many hundreds of years.

Deputy Raymond Tom turned the radio low, sat back in the seat of his Jimmy four-wheel patrol vehicle, and took a chicken sandwich out of his brown paper bag. He popped the cap on a pint of apple cider and looked out through the windshield toward Glass Mountain. At the south edge of Mono Lake stood Panum Crater with Crater Mountain further in the distance.

He had parked near the entrance to the Mono Lake Visitors Center which overlooked Mono Lake. He thought of his Paiute heritage and being the only Indian deputy on the Mono County Sheriff's Department. It was a fact he was the only Paiute to have ever hired on as a full deputy sheriff. The county seat was in Bridgeport, where he was born. Now he lived in Lee Vining, on Highway 395, just south of Mono Lake. He felt fortunate to be the resident deputy and to be so near his heritage and the girl he loved.

Sarah Gray had changed since she came back to the valley to live. When she was twelve, she was a budding beauty with long hair as shiny as obsidian, olive skin, and a wonderful smile. Her uncle, Benjamin Gray, allowed a Mormon family in Provo, Utah, to board and care for the girl until she graduated from high school, but Sarah had no desire to return home then, so she continued to live with her foster family. Then she was awarded an academic scholarship to attend Brigham Young University in Provo. Sarah was so different now that she had matured into a woman—especially an educated woman.

Sarah had a rare quality he had never seen duplicated in another woman. He wondered if he felt she was so lovely because she really was, or because she was a full-blooded Paiute with the fine features of a bronze goddess.

Her intelligence both scared and intimidated him. It had always been her desire to be a forester, to learn of Mother Earth and to unlock her secrets. With her bachelor's degree in botany, it was easy for her to acquire a good position with the U.S. Forest Service as a ranger specialist and work in botany. After a year of employment she was assigned to the ranger station based in Lee Vining, just below the Yosemite Mountains on Highway 120.

Raymond thought all his dreams had come true when Sarah returned to her homeland, and now he was making plans for her. His heart thumped as if electrically charged when he pictured her dark laughing eyes and her face, smooth as a baby's.

The dispatch squawking on the radio brought him back to the business at hand, his lunch. He took a bite of his sandwich and slowly chewed the food to savor the flavor. His eyes moved across the vast region and gazed in the direction of Glass Mountain—the most sacred of all mountains. How many of his ancient brothers kept the secret of their obsidian quarries from the white people or other enemy tribes? The precious volcanic glass was a much-coveted material for arrowheads and spearheads for hunting. But here was the greatest quarry of them all—not hidden in the ground but a giant mountain of glass that reached over 11,000 feet into the sky. It came from the bowels of an ancient volcano that last erupted over 900,000 years ago.

Raymond couldn't stop a smile from forming as he thought of Benjamin Gray, who owned six sections of land that provided the main access to Glass Mountain. The rest of the land was BLM, and no one would ever be able to purchase adjoining property. Ben had springs and excellent grazing for cattle. A full broad smile now spread across his face. Sarah was Ben's only living relative. If Sarah married him, someday they would both own this precious land of their heritage.

Ben, he thought sadly, was an alcoholic, and Raymond knew someday it was going to kill him. At one time Ben had a reputation as an astute businessman who specialized in raising cattle. The Donderos and Andress Paiute families had also lasted throughout the many years as native ranchers in the Great Basin.

Benjamin Gray also had a reputation for being the toughest man to ever set foot in this valley. Ben was no average Indian. His six-foot-seven frame on which hung over three hundred pounds was most uncommon.

If he didn't drink, Raymond was sure Ben would be a gentle person, enjoyable to be around. When he was drinking, it was destruction to anyone who got in his way. Raymond was always the one they called to handle him. The only problem was, if force was needed, it always took the Sheriff's and Highway Patrol personnel to assist. Tear gas was always a requisite. Only Ray, being of the Paiute tribe, could talk reason with Benjamin when he was drinking; otherwise he only wanted to fight.

Raymond looked at his watch. It was 1140 hours. Sometime around noon Sarah said she would be at the Panum Crater just a few miles to the south. She had been studying plant life in the crater and also monitored the visitors to the area. Raymond finished his sandwich and washed it down with a last swig of cider.

It was extremely painful to him that his people lost most of the valley to the whites. He was not against the whites and their technology, but he did not like the way the land was taken from his people. He looked back over to the long-reaching Mono Lake, believed to be the oldest lake on the North American continent. It was definitely a testament to man's inconsideration for nature. If the early rivers had not been diverted from this beautiful, vast body of water, it may have proved to be a world to living life instead of a dead sea. It had taken more than 700,000 years to create this body of water. No other place on earth displayed the eerie "tufa" towers, consisting of twisted formations of calcium carbonate that became exposed once the water receded.

Raymond knew who to blame. The Los Angeles Department of Water and Power was diverting the water, speeding up the recession. He hated the city of Los Angeles and anyone from there. They used his water, the water of his ancestors. It was his people, the Kuzedika, who ate the flies and larvae of the lake, and they prayed, danced, and gave thanks to Mother Earth for it. The people of Los Angeles were a selfish people. They were destroying the land of his people. The heavens would cry and bring much needed water to the valley, only to have it stolen from the sacred land.

After Raymond started his vehicle, he headed south on Highway 395. He smiled thinking of his secret pleasure in writing speeding tickets to the people of L.A. He loved it when they squawked and pleaded for leniency. He was always polite and acted as if it were not personal. His smile covered a deep and vile hatred for the white people from the "city of angels."

Raymond turned left on Highway 120 and drove east. He glanced ahead to the dramatic view of the Mono craters— twenty volcanic domes rising 2,600 feet above the surrounding plains. Glass Mountain loomed upward further to the east. These volcanic domes made up the youngest mountain range in North America. They had erupted only 600 years ago.

After going east for approximately three miles, Raymond turned left onto a dirt road. After almost a mile he came to a dirt parking lot, where the only vehicle in sight was a light green pickup with U.S. Forest Service and black numbers stenciled on the door panel. He looked up the trail that led to the top of Panum Crater's circular pumice ring. It was there he saw Sarah, standing with her back to him looking toward the north. It appeared she had some plants in her left hand and was shading her eyes with the right.

Raymond felt a strong, almost uncontrollable, urge as he viewed the beauty. No other woman held the elegant splendor Sarah possessed. She was natural raw art that only Mother Nature could have created. She belonged to him and he would soon make his feelings known to her. Raymond pressed his lips together and gave a short loud whistle.

Sarah turned and looked down at her visitor. She flashed him a smile and waved. "Hi, Ray. Come on up. I want to show you a new species that has taken hold and is growing like a weed."

Chapter 12
Mexican Justice

Los Angeles was experiencing a cold front, which was refreshing compared to the long hot summer. October, the month for the sportsmen all across the United States, meant hunting season, colors changing on the leaves, more moisture, and then the falling of the leaves, evidence the sun was distancing itself from Earth.

Juan Mores let his eyes wander over the landscape from inside the expensive upper floor of the rented estate as he spoke over the phone. Mr. Angelino was in the other room discussing business. He had given orders not to be disturbed. Juan's fingers covered the telephone receiver as if it were a miniature toy in his big hand. He made a motion with his head and said, "Yes. I'll have someone pick you up in ten minutes. Don't make the mistake of disappointing me."

Juan replaced the phone receiver in its cradle, walked over to the adjoining door and knocked once, opened it, and stepped into the room. He was the only one in the organization who held such a privilege. Three Mexican men were sitting on chairs in a semicircle in front of Mr. Angelino's desk, where he studied them with a drink in his hand.

Two other men were stationed at the back of the room, standing with their backs to the wall. They did not enter the conversation but observed everything that occurred. Their assignment was to protect their boss, Mr. Tommy Angelino.

Juan walked over to his boss, leaned over, and whispered in his ear. Mr. Angelino smiled, "Take care of it. I want to hear his jabberings. Perhaps now we can be enlightened to our present problem areas."

Juan nodded then turned and left the room. He picked up the same phone, dialed, and gave orders to Richard Padillo and Herman Duran to pick Carlos up at his apartment in Hazard.

Forty minutes later Padillo and Duran returned, the expression on their faces sober. Juan immediately became angry. "Where is he?"

Richard stepped forward. His face was moist and his eyes could not hide his fear of the big man. "Carlos is dead," he stammered shamefully.

"What! How could that be? I just talked to him," Juan screeched, grabbing Richard by the lapels and pulling him toward his ugly face.

"You're not going to believe it, Juan. I've never seen anything such as this," Richard said, visibly shaken.

Mr. Angelino came into the room. "What's all the racket about? And where's Carlos?"

"He's dead, sir," Juan said, releasing Richard.

"No! What do you mean he is dead?" Angelino spit the words from his pressed lips.

"I swear it," Richard stammered. "He was dead when we got there. Someone gored him to a wooden door with a Spanish sword. His mouth was sewed shut. Herman cut the thread and out came a huge tarantula."

"No!" Angelino screamed. He threw his glass against the wall smashing it. He stopped, thought a moment, and gave Juan a seedy grin which narrowed his dark eyes. "You know what this means, don't you?"

"The spider man has finally thrown his card into a very dangerous game. It had to be Pavlo. He wanted to shut Carlos up and send us a message in the process," Juan said, carefully watching his boss.

Mr. Angelino walked over to the window and looked out across the busy city toward Elysian Park. "He is such a fool. Greed is the devil of many men. It brings a weakness that clouds their vision and blurs their capability to be successful. He could have remained a minor in this game but his lust has preceded his good sense."

Mr. Angelino turned to Juan. "What is the name of his No. 1 runner? The one who cannot keep his hands from rearranging his little wife's teeth on a consistent basis?"

"Henry Vasquez," Juan said. "He is a pig."

"Give this pig the family treatment. A gift from Tommy Angelino. Let's air out his hostility to the streets." Angelino looked at Juan who now had an ugly smirk on his face. It gave Angelino a shiver. He would not want Juan coming after him. "Make it look like a gang elimination. No less than thirty punctures. Let us play it smart so the police will think it is a gang retaliation. Let's do it tomorrow at exactly the same time Pavlo killed Carlos. The police will not put it together but Pavlo will.

He will know he has opened a box of angry killer bees and he cannot get the lid back on before a few escape. Now he will learn a valuable lesson. The sting of the bee." Angelino left the room.

"Yes, sir," Juan nodded. "I will make the arrangements."

Scratch was assigned to break in a new man named Mark Limeman. Mark's new senior partner had called in sick. Cy and Skin had doubled up and were working swing shift in northeast Hollenbeck because of the heavy police calls coming in all day.

The weather was too cool to have the windows down. A cold front had moved the high pressure ridge to the south, changing the California weather drastically in a 24-hour period. Both men wore dark blue police jackets. They had been patrolling on the east side. Extra units were assigned to this sector. Violence had been erupting on a higher scale for the last two weeks. Cy had stopped several traffic violators, and Skin had issued three traffic citations. He was always the book man when he rode with the sergeant. The book man was responsible for all radio transmissions and paperwork. Skin didn't mind the paperwork too much, but his goal was to make sergeant; then he would have his own subordinates to wait on him. He liked the thought of giving orders—not taking them.

The radio broke the silence in the patrol unit, sending the two officers to a fight in progress in RD 448 at Soto and Lancaster. It was 1930 hours and both men had been contemplating where they would go for a coffee break. The call changed that idea. Cy turned the vehicle around and headed south on Pasadena Avenue from Broadway. The area they were headed to was heavily populated by Mexicans, and there had been numerous calls in this area the last three nights. The callous murder of a Mexican addict run through with a sword wasn't so bad. The spider thing was a different matter entirely. The Hollenbeck officers were on edge and showing signs of stress.

Cy was at the wheel. He maneuvered around traffic quickly without going code three. Using the red light and siren on dispatch calls was now only for confirmed emergencies. Skin was a little restless and his mind seemed preoccupied.

"Something wrong, Skin?" Cy glanced at him then back to the street.

"Oh, I dunno," Skin sighed, watching the road ahead. He

took his pipe out and stuffed tobacco in the bowl. "Would you mind too much if I light this thing up? I'll keep the window down. I need a smoke." He didn't wait for permission. He looked cross-eyed at the pipe bowl and put a cigarette lighter to it, sucking short breaths to get it going.

"So what's wrong?" Cy asked, making the next corner and heading east. "I thought we were buddies."

"Well, I'm not sure what's wrong," Skin shook his head. He pressed his lips together and blew smoke out the window. He enjoyed the smell of pipe tobacco. He watched the people on the street walking along the sidewalks. Every once in awhile, a person would wave and Skin returned the gesture. "I've been thinking really strong about a girl I met a few weeks ago. She's a fine-looking woman, and I have pretty strong feelings for her."

Cy showed his white teeth as he waved at a pedestrian. "I'm happy to hear it. It's about time you fell for someone."

"She's single with a young boy and I love his guts. He's a cute pup. He's got curly black hair and olive skin. I think the father is Italian or something like that."

"How old is he?"

"He's only four and he needs a daddy really bad," Skin said soberly. "His mother is really a nice lady and she's a good mother. She said her man was a bum and got involved with another woman, so she dumped him."

"Well, maybe you ought to pursue it, but don't rush into it. You don't want any bad baggage you can't handle," Cy responded hesitantly.

"That's what I'm thinking, but so far I haven't seen any. I'm no dummy, you know. I don't plan on getting myself hung up on someone that I don't think it would work out with. I will say this—she is a mighty fine person. She's warm, a good cook, and easy to look at."

"What's her name and how did you meet her?" Cy asked.

"Her name is Martha. Her son is Anthony," Skin smiled. "I met her through Susan Valin. Martha works at a woman's club that Susan belongs to. They became friends there."

Cy slowed the car down to twenty miles an hour. Up ahead a few blocks he could see a gathering of people in the street. "Sounds to me you have already taken the fall."

"I think I love her. Don't say anything about this to the guys, okay? I just want to be sure first," Skin said. "Not to change the subject, I've heard locker room talk that the academy wants you back. You wouldn't take that assignment again, would you?"

"No. I like Hollenbeck too much to go back to instructing. I just can't stand the city. I miss the country. I'm really looking forward to our fishing and hunting trip next week."

"Me too. I need a break. It'll give me time to think things out," Skin said, happy to be putting his love life on hold. He looked up the street, wondering why people were in the middle of the street as they approached Soto.

Cy was watching the next intersection. "Skin, something's not right."

Three or four men were moving their arms up and down in quick movements. "It doesn't look good," Skin replied.

"No. I'm hitting the overheads. Get us some backup!" Cy barked, stepping down on the accelerator.

The night lights at the intersection were out. Three male Mexicans suddenly turned in different directions and ran away when the car lights disclosed them. Both officers observed a bundle of clothing in the middle of the street. Cy stopped on the center line a few feet from the intersection searching in the directions the men had run. Skin was sitting on the edge of the seat with his neck stretched trying to peer over the hood of the car while he spoke into the radio microphone.

Cy opened his door, got out, and inspected the bundle of clothing in front of his patrol unit. It was a Mexican male rolled into the fetal position saturated in a bloody mess.

Skin slipped around the side of the patrol car to see what Cy was looking at. "Gees, almighty! I'll get an ambulance." He retreated to the patrol car. As he reopened the car door he looked over his shoulder and made a sweeping glance of the streets to make sure they were not in danger. He thought he saw a person about a half block away standing in the shadows. He couldn't confirm if it was male or female. He felt strongly that someone was watching them.

Cy quickly surveyed the area. It was always the same feeling he got in the pit of his stomach—whenever they found a body or a badly wounded victim, he wondered if the suspect was still in the area watching them or waiting to strike again.

Cy kneeled down trying not to get blood—which was every-where—on his pants. He knew the victim was alive because dark red blood was pumping from multiple open head and face wounds. Rivers of blood ran down the side of his cheeks and head, dripping on the asphalt. There were numerous deep contact wounds on the Mexican's hands, indicating the knife blade had many times penetrated the palms of his hands, exiting out the backs. The defense wounds meant the man didn't have his own weapon or it had been taken away from him.

Skin came back around to the prone man and kneeled partway down. He frowned at the sight before him. "Who did this to you?" he questioned the man softly.

The injured Mexican did not open his eyes. His face was covered with coagulated blood. In a raspy broken voice he asked, "Who are you?"

"This is the police," Cy said.

"Screw your mother and then your sister," the man gurgled, failing to open his eyes.

Skin leaned over where no one could hear. "Die, hombre."

Scratch and the new man, Limeman, rolled up and immediately went to work pushing the crowd back from around the incident site. Flush and Fulton pulled up with a squeal. They assisted in keeping the curious onlookers at bay while the sergeant and Skin gave first aid.

The two officers attempted to stop the more serious wounds with compresses. When the ambulance arrived, the crew took over the medical care and did the best they could to restrict the numerous wounds from bleeding freely. While the paramedics worked on the injured victim, Cy and Skin tried to get witness reports from people standing nearby. No one would come forward.

One male Mexican said, "Are you crazy, man? We know nothing. We see nothing. Get it, man? Nada."

It was typical and frustrating. The ambulance crew lifted the man onto a stretcher and moved him into the back of the ambulance. Cy went over to one of the ambulance crew and spoke softly in his ear. "It doesn't look like he's going to make it. I'm going to ride with him to see if I can get a dying declaration."

The ambulance man nodded in agreement and let the sergeant climb into the back of the vehicle. Cy looked over at Skin and ordered him to follow the ambulance to the hospital.

A few moments after the ambulance had left, a large man stepped out of the shadows. Juan Mores wrote down a police license number on his hand with a ballpoint pen. He frowned and walked away. He did not expect the police to appear so quickly. He was concerned now. Vasquez may not die.

On the way to the Los Angeles General Hospital, the man refused to answer any questions. The sirens were so loud in the back of the ambulance, Cy had to yell. The man refused to acknowledge his presence.

After the ambulance arrived at the hospital emergency room, Cy was surprised when the two ambulance attendants took the wounded man into the hallway, pushed his gurney next to the wall, and walked away, leaving him unattended. Cy took after the attendants to determine what was going on. Opening two swinging doors, he realized exactly what was happening. Emergency was packed with injured and sick people. Crying and name calling added to the frenzy. It was like another world. Obviously no one would pay any attention to him.

Cy walked back out to the Mexican and listened to him struggle for air. His lungs were laboring for oxygen through gurgling muscle spasms, the stench of blood hanging in the air. Cy asked the dying man if he would give him some names. There was no answer.

After a few moments he walked back through the double doors into the mass of confusion. People occupied every available space. There were victims of all kinds of crimes—stabbings, gunshot wounds, and fights, and people injured in traffic accidents. Blood was everywhere, and people were yelling, screaming, and crying.

Cy admired the doctors and nurses who labored through this busy commotion. He respected them for their professional care and dedication. He thought to himself that he could never be a doctor. He turned around and escaped back into the hallway to the gurgling sounds of the Mexican lying on the gurney. He understood exactly why the injured man was placed in the hall. At least he could die in peace.

A few minutes later other ambulance crews arrived, rolling in other patients and eventually filling the hallway.

Jacob Wilson crashed through the door with another officer Cy did not know. Jacob was frowning and looking concerned; when he saw Cy, he seemed to relax.

"Hey, my man, how you doing?" Jacob gave Cy a brief punch in the arm.

"It's the pits here. I hate this place. What are you doing here?" Cy asked.

"I'm here on a homicide. Remember the Mexican Tony Valin was telling us about the other night? Some guy named Carlos?"

"How could I forget. He was the one in the hospital with his throat cut and tied off with a string or something."

"That's the one. Well, he was found impaled on a wooden door like a giant insect. It appeared that his mouth had been sewn shut, but the threads had been cut. Sounds like a message about loose lips. I don't know," Jacob said, shaking his head. "Whatever it is, I don't like it happening in my jurisdiction."

"Something is going down. Skin and I witnessed a gang stabbing. No suspects yet, but I'm going to try to get this guy to talk as soon as the doctors put some life back into him."

"Where's Skin?"

"He's parking the patrol car."

"I've got to get going. I'm gonna try and get information from some of my former acquaintances on the street. Maybe the gang unit or narcs might have some ideas for me." Jacob started backing away down the hall. "You got any plans for tonight?"

"You know I haven't. Why?"

"Some of us guys are going to Jack's after work. There should be some new road deputies there that have been poaching suspects on our turf. One of them has a big mouth." Jacob's face lit up with a big smile as he backed down the hallway. "Got my drift, old buddy?"

"Yeah, I got your drift. See ya about 10:30." Cy gave a little laugh as his good friend disappeared around the corner. Cy thought a moment how much he missed being Jacob's partner.

Cy went back over to the Mexican and checked to see if he was still breathing. For a moment he thought he was dead. Blood was not dripping onto the sheets and his chest was not moving. Cy pinched the Mexican's eyelid between his thumb and forefinger and lifted it upward. With his other hand he flashed a penlight into the man's eye. The pupil contracted. Cy gave a sigh of relief.

Skin came through the entry doors with a bang and worked his away around the other patients to Cy. They spoke for a few minutes in low tones. While they were talking Skin took a long look at the Mexican lying quietly, covered in massive amounts of blood.

"That guy sure looks familiar, but I can't place him," Skin said, staring at the man.

"He doesn't look like anything I've ever seen anywhere," Cy mumbled, not looking back at the sickening sight.

"I'm thirsty. You want anything to drink?"

"No, I'm okay," Cy answered. "Jacob was here a second ago. He wants to meet after shift tonight. Can you go to Jack's?"

"Thanks, but no. I promised Martha I'd see her after work. We need to talk. Besides, she's a lot prettier than you guys," Skin chuckled.

"You lucky guy. I wish I had someone," Cy moaned, leaning against the wall.

"You will when you've perfected the special touch, Sarge. It takes a while to figure these women out." Skin turned around to search for a vending machine. "I'll be back in a minute."

While Skin was gone, the Mexican regained consciousness, almost rolling off the portable bed. His eyes rolled around in the sockets wildly, and sucking noises came from his throat and chest. Cy held him down. Finally the wounded man quieted down, but his breathing had worsened and his wounds were bleeding again.

On several occasions nurses burst through the double doors and passed Cy in a rush. Each time he told them this man was dying. Each time their response was, "Yeah, yeah. We'll get to him as soon as we can."

It became more apparent it was nothing to the hospital workers, as they jogged up and down the hallways, to have a man dying in the hallway of stab wounds. It wasn't that they didn't care. They just had more patients than they had time.

After an eternity of time had passed, the ambulance drivers returned and took the Mexican upstairs in the elevator. They wheeled him into a place that looked like an operating room. The doors burst open and five or six medical technicians rushed in, garbed in clean hospital scrubs.

Cy was literally knocked out of the way. He was pushed back to the wall as the technicians surrounded the injured man on the table. The nurses initially packed the unconscious man in large gauze pads soaked in Vaseline to contain the bleeding.

A surgeon appeared at Cy's left and stood at the injured

man's shoulder. Another doctor was on the right side of the man and another at the head. Cy realized the Vaseline gauzes were being used to plug the chest to stop the air from escaping his lungs. It appeared that his lungs were collapsing because he couldn't get his breath.

Cy watched as the Mexican turned into a big glob of red goo. It was a hideous sight. Nurses cut the man's clothing off until he was completely naked. There were more knife wounds than Cy had thought at first. The wounds other than the ones in his chest were ignored. The doctors went to work evacuating the air that had escaped from the lungs into the chest cavity. It was apparent the man was almost dead, and something had to be done quickly to plug the holes and get air back into his lungs.

Cy desperately wanted to leave the room and get some fresh air but knew he had to stay in the room in case the dying man muttered the names of the people who stabbed him. It appeared to Cy there were at least eighty stab wounds. Cy had learned since working in Hollenbeck that Mexican assassinations involved groups of three to five men. They would surround their victim and repeatedly and rapidly stab him with a three-inch blade. It would be over in less than five seconds. Some people had described it like sharks having a feeding frenzy.

As one of the doctors worked on the Mexican, he asked several times in a loud voice, "Who did this to you?" Each time the Mexican released guttural nonsense. Several times the injured man coughed and those standing around him were showered with bright bubbly spots of blood over their gowns.

The doctor made a three-inch incision into the man's chest. Cy saw the doctor give the scalpel to a nurse. In return she handed him a tool that looked like needle-nosed pliers. With it she gave him an eight-inch clear plastic tube.

Part of Cy's vision was blocked, but it looked as if the doctor held the end of the tube with the pliers and pushed it into the man's chest. Something wasn't going right and the doctor got up on the table and with both hands pushed hard with the pliers to get the tube between the ribs. The Mexican's chest was mashed inward. It was now concave as the doctor's hands and arms shook as he forcefully pressed downward.

Cy was aghast. It looked like a car was on the man's chest. Cy had difficulty getting his own breath. Skin walked in with his coffee and took one look, dropped his coffee on the floor, held his hand over his mouth, and ran out of the room across the hall to the restroom.

Cy felt his head getting light and his knees going wobbly. The Mexican screamed at the top of his lungs; then loud gasping and sucking sounds erupted from the table. Cy wasn't sure if it was machines making the slurping noises or if it was coming from the injured man. With a jerk, along with a loud popping sound, the pliers and tube slipped between the ribs.

Cy felt a cold sweat on his forehead and an encompassing fuzziness from head to toe. Suddenly there was a hissing sound as the evacuator was turned on. Cy didn't know if it was pulling the air out or pushing it in the man's body. He didn't care anymore; he only wanted out of the room. Dropping his notebook and pen, he stumbled out into the hallway.

Skin wobbled out of the men's room looking green. He glanced at Cy who looked worse than death. Skin turned and vomited on the floor of the hallway.

Jacob came around the corner. With his second step he slipped and fell flat on his back in the pile of puke. Jacob rolled over, swearing violently.

Cy opened his mouth to say something. Instead caustic bile shot upward through his esophagus. He pressed his lips together and started toward the bathroom. Both cheeks were bulging when he gave it up. The wet force hit Skin mid-chest as he frantically tried to get out of Cy's way. He tripped over Jacob, who was on his hands and knees crawling away with the dry heaves.

Cy locked himself in the bathroom. He washed his face and head in cold water. His face tightened and then the muscles in his neck and face jerked spasmodically and he began to roar.

Thirty minutes later Cy watched a nurse's aide push the Mexican out of the operating room and down the hall to where he was standing. As the patient went by, Cy saw the man's newly clean face and immediately recognized Henry Vasquez, who had beaten up his wife a few weeks ago and had been booked for drug possession.

Chapter 13
Rogue River

Midafternoon Tony Valin pulled into Eureka, off the 101 freeway in northern California. The coastal town had been their dinner stop and a trip highlight for the last two years. The four men piled out of Tony's brand-new Jeep Cherokee and stood curbside stretching.

Tony had discovered the small seafood restaurant on the corner quite by accident. It had appeared to be just another greasy spoon. It wasn't. The baked salmon and fresh bear-shaped apple fritter were beyond delectable. No other restaurant could compete with this little wayside cafe along the coast. The food was mouth watering, and it was their special place to eat. This was the last stop before Gold Beach.

"Hey, hey, hey, Bozo!" Tony yelled at Skin.

Skin turned around looking at Tony. "What's your problem, dork face?"

"Don't lean on the car, man. I don't want one scratch on this vehicle." Tony glanced around at Cy and Jacob. "You guys got that? Not one scratch. This is my first brand-new rig and I want it treated with respect." Tony was serious. The other three just looked at him.

"I'm serious, this rig is everything to me," Tony said, frowning.

"Tony, why don't you lighten up. It's us," Skin said lighting his pipe. "We don't need your crap, okay? We're tired too, and we know how you feel about your Jeep."

Jacob walked over to the restaurant. "Gees, Tony, I wish I had a new car so I could yell at my friends and boss them around." He opened the door and held it for the other three.

"Okay, we now know we can't breathe or relax around Tony's new Cherokee. Can we at least go in and eat? I'm starved to death," Cy said, after wiping off his fingerprints on the fender of the car with his sleeve.

"I'm just making myself clear," Tony said, following the others through the door. "I've been worried the whole way up here. I just want to keep it looking new. It's probably my last new car."

"Yeah, well tell someone who gives a rat's butt," Skin responded, dragging deeply. He exhaled into Tony's face when he pushed past him through the door.

Each man ordered his favorite meal and dessert. The main topic of discussion was the fishing trip, type of bait, and equipment to be used. After an hour they left the cafe and headed north.

Three hours later the lights of Gold Beach welcomed the four men as Tony drove toward the city limits. The sky to the west was only partly blue as the sun changed colors as it sank deep behind the ocean.

Gold Beach was neatly ensconced next to a harbor along the southwestern tip of Oregon, approximately fifty miles south of Coos Bay. The waters in this area were protected by a long rock dike that jutted out to sea for a distance, giving serenity to the boats in their docks.

Crabbing was a popular sport and business, along with fishing for halibut and salmon. The seagoing rainbow and steelhead enticed fishermen from all across the western states and beyond. The people who lived here loved the ocean and the beautiful view along the coast.

The Rogue River flows east to west through a beautiful wilderness area in the southern part of Oregon. The river is fed from many tributaries, including Bear Creek from Klamath Falls, and flows westward until it empties into the Pacific Ocean at Gold Beach in Curry County, Oregon. The Rogue River is famous among avid sportsmen for steelhead fishing.

Tony Valin's friend, David Bash, had retired from a northern California police department and had become chief deputy after he moved to Curry County near Gold Beach. David was good friends with Curry County Sheriff Allen Bryce. At a drug conference in Las Vegas, David introduced Sheriff Bryce to Tony. They immediately became good friends, sports fishing being their main mutual interest.

Years ago, the sheriff had purchased the only two resorts along the river—the Upper Paradise Bar and Lower Paradise Bar. He had purchased the resorts for investment purposes because there was no other competition—meaning lodging— for the three-day trip from Klamath Falls to Gold Beach. The two resorts could be reached only by helicopter or jet boat.

For groups coming from Klamath Falls, the drift guides set up camp for one night on a sandy beach and cooked Dutch oven meals. They slept in sleeping bags along the shoreline. The drift guides always contracted with the sheriff for the next two nights, allowing their parties to lodge at the Upper Paradise Bar the second night and then the Lower Paradise Bar on the third night where they could shower, have a good meal, relax, and sleep in firm beds. The river and its surroundings were well used from spring to fall, and it was believed the sheriff had made a very wise investment.

For the third consecutive year Tony, Cy, Jacob, and Skin made the long drive to Oregon for their fishing trip. They planned this year to fish for three days and then travel to Mono County, California, for the deer hunt.

After a good night's sleep at a local motel, the men went to the dock and met Sheriff Bryce. They happily packed all their gear into the jet boat, including several cases of beer to bring cheer to the evenings around the campfire. When the packing was done, the four men sat along the dock while they waited for Sheriff Bryce to warm up the engine. Cy removed three beers from the cooler and tossed one to Tony and Jacob. Skin started up his pipe and sipped on a wine cooler. Bryce went to the back of his truck and made himself busy with some equipment.

Sheriff Bryce was an ex-marine with a reputation for rigidity. He had told the men at the office he needed to get away for a couple of days to pull himself together. He was glad his old friends were there to help him escape. In an earlier phone conversation, he had told Tony, when they were planning the trip a few weeks before, that one of the men on his department had killed a suspect who had taken a hostage. Their small community was not used to shootings, and his phones had been driving him up the wall.

Bryce was in his late forties and buzzed his hair like a Marine. His personality was rough but padded with a dry humor, although he was the type of man most people would not consider joking with. He was a big guy in whom people often mistook his quietness for a bad disposition. This was not the case. He was a good man with a lot of responsibility, and he viewed his position seriously. Over the years the sheriff had established a reputation for being a strict leader who never displayed anger and who took a quiet but firm approach to his personnel. He was an impressive man who commanded respect from citizen and peer alike. The problem he had was common to most police. Most don't know who their friends are except other cops. The sheriff didn't talk a lot. When he did, he usually was direct and to the point.

Curry County had purchased two jet boats for emergency and rescue operations along the Rogue River. The jets, also called drift boats, were approximately 22 feet long with flat bottoms and only drew about three inches of water. Each boat had wide beams with rear-mounted twin jets. The boats were reinforced with steel ribbing and had two long cushioned seats to which passengers were seat belted face-to-face looking toward the center.

Drift boats were also used along other rivers such as the Eel, the Klamath, and the Trinity. The wooden drift boats were especially popular because of their ability to maneuver through rough water. The high bow and stern could be pointed up or down river by a guide, who would back paddle to allow the fishermen to cast lures downstream and reel upstream.

On the Rogue, one of the most popular lures is a wiggle lure, the 'hot shot.' Fish eggs, called roe, are also effective. They are soaked in borax to glue them together and tied up in cheesecloth.

Cy sat back and watched the sheriff work his craft. He felt secure knowing he was at the helm. He remembered his first trip up the Rogue and the eerie sensation he experienced, being restrained with a seat belt. He hadn't liked being strapped in while over water. If the craft overturned, he would not be able to escape and would drown slowly or have his head bashed against the submerged boulders by the swift-running water. Now that Cy was experienced on the river he knew he was safer strapped in. The boat could jump small waterfalls, and the jumps still gave him a thrill. In order for the boat to go up a fall, the operator had to stop the craft immediately before it at a certain angle. Somehow the boat would actually ride the rushing water; and with a boost from the engine, it would go up over a five-foot fall just like a Salmon would swim upstream. It was the damndest thing Cy had ever seen, and he would not have believed it unless he personally had seen and experienced it.

"Al, it's a work of art the way you run the river with this rig," Cy called to the sheriff over the noise of the engine and rushing water.

The sheriff gave his full attention to the river. "I believe I know every rock and danger area by now, but you never can predict the heart of this river. She has her own soul and a mind of her own," he yelled back to Cy. "One best not make her angry or he'll find out who's boss."

The sheriff approached the next waterfall skillfully. He shot off the falls, climbing to the top, and brought the craft over the ridge of white rushing water, not endangering his passengers but still providing a hair-raising thrill.

Tony and Jacob drank their beer, encouraging Skin to quench his thirst. He pulled a cold can of beer from the ice chest and enjoyed it immensely with the ride and the beautiful scenery.

The shallow river only averaged four to six feet deep, varying from 40 to 300 yards wide. One stretch of the river was isolated for approximately 18 miles from roads and public access.

The river ran through a breathtaking terrain of heavy pines and abundant wildlife. Deer watered at the river's edge or grazed on brush at the upper ledges. Ducks and geese took flight when the boat rounded a riverbend, invading their feeding ground. Cy glanced up the river and then back at the sheriff strapped in his captain's chair covered by a partial cabin to keep him from getting a soaking. Cy wished he had Al's ability to work the boat up the rough river. The jet engines roared loudly when the sheriff touched the throttle to work through the current. It wasn't long until the four men were wet with river spray. It wasn't important; they enjoyed every moment of the trip.

The flat coastal scenery suddenly changed as they headed up the Rogue River. High steep cliffs loomed upward which would make travel impassable except by boat. The color of the mountains quickly changed to a beautiful green with mossy-colored rocks and heavy pine trees.

It was a day to covet—no wind, the sky a dark blue. After hours of traveling without stopping, the drift boat finally arrived at Upper Paradise Bar. Cy could see the lodge settled about one hundred feet up a cliff above the river. He was tired and glad to be getting out of the boat and onto solid dry land.

The men unloaded their gear and headed up stairs that were cut into the side of the cliff. As Cy climbed the steep steps he wondered how the lodge and cabins were built. He had heard that they had been there since the thirties. That meant the wood for constructing the resort would have to have been brought down from Klamath Falls and shipped in by drift boats, or else the timber was cut and somehow transported downriver to this area.

The lodge was one big single pine-log building. The main room consisted of a large forty- by thirty-foot day lounge, divided by a large stone fireplace with a mounted bull elk head above the hearth and several bucks on the different walls. Two bedrooms, a kitchen, and bar made up the rest of the main lodge. Running water was piped in from a spring which serviced flush toilets, and a diesel generator provided electricity for night use. The five log cabins were supplied with oil lamps for additional light when the generators were turned off.

Cy, Jacob, and Skin stayed in a two-room cabin. The lodge workers stayed in the staff cabin. Since Tony was a friend of the sheriff and expected to be treated better than the others, he was assigned a room at the lodge. It would give Tony and Al the opportunity to visit and renew their friendship.

The clean-up crews and other workers at the bars were normally college girls who only worked one or two seasons to save money for their education. Most worked only the summer but a few stayed into the fall fishing season.

At dinnertime everyone, including some of the help, gathered around the table to eat, as was common. Tonight the evening meal was roast beef, potatoes and gravy. It was delicious and the men had second helpings. Almost everyone was companionable, sharing stories and histories.

Bertie, the cook, was the only one who did not enter into the conversations. Cy watched her discreetly as he pretended to be involved in one of Tony's anecdotes. Plain but well structured, she had the hard look of years of heavy labor and bad times. Her forty-plus years were well lined in her face, and her eyes were an icy blue. During supper, Cy noticed Bertie glancing at Tony while he ate. Tony ignored Bertie, and the others were not aware if he even recognized her presence in the room.

Tony had been married to his wife, Susan, for 12 years and had two young girls. Only his close friends knew about his weakness for other women. He was the prima donna of ladies' men. He never talked about his exploits except with his close friends. Even then he rarely spoke about them. Tony told his friends that he and his wife had a rough relationship, but he still loved her. He would never leave her and his children.

Tony was a big, good-looking guy with dark Portuguese eyes and black wavy hair that covered his ears like a mop-topped Paul McCartney. He was rarely seen on the streets without his black leather jacket, his trademark. Women were always instantly attracted to him. He felt it was his mission to be available but very discreet, not relishing a confrontation with Susan. A divorce and alimony were the last things he wanted or could afford. Many of his friends looked up to him because he was a streetwise cop, having grown up on the streets with poor and rowdy teenagers. On his left shoulder he had a gang tattoo; on his left hand, between the thumb and forefinger, a tattooed cross could be plainly seen. He enjoyed the reputation for being able to handle himself in any situation.

After dinner Cy came into the lounge area after he brushed his teeth and freshened up. He noticed the cook behind the bar and thought about her from the previous two seasons. Bertie was quick with her tongue and didn't take any smart talk from the guests. Cy had made an effort to stay out of her way, but he was always friendly toward her when that was unavoidable. She seldom spoke to the men and kept to herself in the kitchen.

Cy walked over to a large overstuffed chair and sat down. Skin's pipe dispersed a sweet aroma throughout the large room. The fireplace crackled with warmth; the ambience was simple and friendly. Skin was drinking a cup of coffee and visiting with Jacob.

Tony came through the front door with a bang. He smiled broadly to his friends who were sitting around the fire enjoying the moment. He looked over at Bertie and dropped his leather jacket on the back of a chair before he sat in it.

"Hello, Bertie, we're back." Tony smiled, wondering if Bertie even liked men or preferred the company of the college girls. He ran his fingers through his wavy hair and gave it a shake.

"Hello, yourself," she scowled, turning around and disappearing into the kitchen through the swinging batwing doors.

"Well, you certainly have a way with women in the wild, Tony," Cy laughed, snuggling down in his chair. "I figured you were the only one who could ever get close to Bertie. Now I'm having second thoughts," Cy said quietly so Bertie couldn't hear.

"Are you kidding? No one, I repeat, no one could get near that woman, and who would want to?" Tony muttered in a low tone.

"Tony doesn't have a monopoly on all the women," Skin

said, as he settled back in his seat, turning to face Cy and Tony. He wriggled around in the sofa uncomfortably then reached behind the small of his back and pulled out a Smith and Wesson .38 revolver and laid it on the table next to him. "For hell's sake. I was wondering what that lump was on my butt. I forgot I had the darn thing."

"How could you forget? I've never seen you without your weapon," Jacob said. He leaned over and punched Skin on the shoulder.

"What the heck was that?" Skin looked around as if to see something flying around. "Damn flies."

"I love isolation," Tony said relaxed. He sat next to the fireplace. "Well, have you guys checked out the women yet?"

"We have, numb nuts," nodded Jacob. "And there's no one who would look at you twice."

"Now hang on there, partner," Tony snorted. He adjusted himself on the chair and took out a cigarette and lit it up. "I have heard from good sources that the girls working this year are flower children who believe in free love. They can't say no because it is their commitment to life to give of themselves to any and everyone."

There was a shuffle at a side door leading from another room. An attractive girl of about nineteen with long straight brown hair, wearing a plaid shirt with the sleeves rolled up and tight Levis, walked into the room with a coffee pot and mugs.

"Hi, guys. I'm Sharon. Here's some more coffee to get you warmed up inside." Sharon smiled at the three men. She set the round tray on a coffee table in front of the chairs. She strolled over to Tony. "What are you?" She failed to see the others shaking their heads in disapproval.

Tony smiled, pleased at the attention he was getting in front of his peers. "I am of Latin descent, my sweet. More specifically, of the Portuguese culture, my dear." Tony stood up, holding his stomach in and expanding his chest. "I'm an avid outdoorsman who loves fishing, duck hunting, and the beauties of nature." He flashed her a big smile, allowing mock-Spanish to accent his expressions.

Sharon knew she had everyone's attention. Al had warned her beforehand about Tony. She stepped closer to him and gave him a warm smile. She reached up, placed her right hand behind his neck, and pulled his face next to hers. He knew she was going to kiss him, and he was pleased that his friends would be witnesses to his irresistible character. "You, my friend, just closed the door to opportunity. You haven't a prayer."

Sharon turned around and quickly studied the new visitors. She looked at Cy and watched his face turn red and his eyes focus on the floor. She walked over to Skin who was now puffing on his pipe. Only the slightest grin was visible on his face. "What do they call you, Mr. Clean?" The others laughed.

"Skin," he answered, pulling the pipe from his teeth.

"Cool." She gave Skin the once-over, liking his physique under his T-shirt. It was apparent he lifted weights.

"You look like a nice man who appreciates a good friendship. Am I right?"

"You're wise, little one," Skin said, taking hold of her hand.

Sharon released his hand, did an about-face, and slowly walked from the room with everyone admiring her retreating features. Her tight Levis revealed long, strong legs. When she reached the door she hesitated and looked back across the room to Skin. "Like later?"

Cy watched Skin acknowledge her remark by raising his left eyebrow and taking a long draw on his pipe. The pipe aroma smelled good, and Cy thought again how much he liked Skin—tough, reliable, and the best in a backup crisis. He was a courageous person who was not scared of anyone. Cy was glad they had remained close friends. He knew he could always rely on Skin—for anything.

"Well, Michael Fin, I guess you're the lucky man," Tony said, obviously disappointed in himself. "I surely don't know what she sees in you, a baldy with no looks to speak of, especially in my presence."

"I've got a girl, and I'm interested in no one but her," Skin offered cooly.

"Oh yeah, who's that?"

"You don't know her. She lives in Glendora and works at the Rainbow Angling Club in Azusa," Skin replied, getting up from his chair and walking toward the door.

"Oh really? What's her name, Skin?" Tony asked, his voice tight.

Skin was halfway out the door. "Her name is Martha. I'll be outside for awhile. I need some fresh air." Skin disappeared into the night.

"You don't mean Marty, do ya?" Tony called to Skin. He

was out of range.

Cy had a bad feeling. "Hold it, Tony!" he snapped. "What do you mean, Marty? Do you know her?"

"Of course I do," Tony laughed, throwing his head back. "My wife belongs to the women's auxiliary club. Marty is the host and bookkeeper there." Tony hesitated as he studied Cy. "What? So what is the big deal?"

"Not so loud, Tony," Cy whispered harshly, his stomach feeling queasy. "How well do you know her?"

"Well...I cared for her at one time, but she got too possessive," he said. "She was great to date; then she wanted me to leave my wife and marry her." He shrugged his shoulders. "But you know I ain't leaving my wife for anyone."

It was the first time Cy felt distaste for his longtime friend. Jacob only watched the two and wasn't sure what was bothering Cy. He stayed out of it by getting up and going over to the bar. He took a cold Budweiser out of the cooler, opened it, and took a drink.

"Whatever you know about Martha, or Marty, you keep your mouth shut about it," Cy rasped, getting in the man's face. "You hear, Tony? We've been friends a long time and right now I don't feel so hot about you. Skin's in love with that girl and her little boy..." Cy stopped, remembering the description Skin gave of Martha's son. Skin had told him the boy's name was Anthony. Tony is a derivative of Anthony. He had brown eyes and dark wavy hair. His mind turned on like a light switch. "Is her boy your son?"

"Hey, hey, look, this is getting too deep for me, friendo." Tony was beginning to squirm. "You said to end the conversation on Marty. Then so be it. That means you don't go asking me any personal questions that's none of your affair," Tony demanded as he stood up. His discomfort showed in his eyes.

The sheriff had been listening from the entrance of his private bedroom. Now he walked into the lounge smiling. "Anyone for pinochle? Or are you fellows smart enough to play?"

Jacob said he was too tired and walked outside. Cy excused himself and said he was going to turn in for the night. He told Al he was looking forward to the fishing tomorrow, then ignored Tony and left the room, giving him a sour look.

Cy looked inside their cabin; Skin was not there. He went out into the night and walked down by the cliff edge overlooking the Rogue River. Skin was nowhere in sight. Cy started along the cliff until he saw the shadowy figure sitting on a log.

Cy walked over to Skin and sat down. Skin did not look up and continued to gaze at the white flowing ripples of the river. Cy was trying to think of something to say. Not sure Skin heard Tony's comment, he had no desire to take the chance and reveal information to him he did not know. If Martha decided to tell Skin her story, that should be her choice and not someone else's.

The river rumbled constantly as it worked its way downstream. The night air was cool and refreshing. Cy was too tired to figure out what he should say. His heart almost stopped when he heard Skin sniff. Curious, he peered at his friend from the corner of his eye, not wanting to be obvious. Skin's shoulders were shaking. Cy felt sick and remained silent.

After a short while Skin settled down. "I'm sorry, buddy," murmured Cy. He put his hand on Skin's shoulder. Skin couldn't talk and for a long moment Cy remained quiet. Skin began to cry, and it was an awful sound. Cy had to fight to control his own emotions. It seemed life was so difficult and at other times it was so wonderful. He thought about how things in a person's life could change from good to bad so quickly.

After a long period, Skin's weak voice broke the silence. "I never dreamed Martha knew Tony. I swear, I didn't have a clue, Sarge."

"I know, I know. Don't call me 'Sarge' here. We're on vacation and you're one of my best friends," Cy answered uncomfortably.

"You're my best friend and you'll always be 'Sarge' to me. Even when you make lieutenant, you'll still be 'Sarge.'"

"I'll take that as a compliment then," Cy replied. "I know you've always called me 'Sarge.' I haven't thought that much about it, I guess." Cy hesitated a moment and went on. "I just didn't think this was the time to be distant. What you said means a great deal to me."

Skin remained silent gazing at the river.

"I've worked with a lot of people, Skin. I never thought anybody would or could replace Jacob as my partner and close friend. I was wrong. On the job, I'm your boss. Off the job you're one of my closest friends."

"Then why haven't you given me the secret code?" Skin

protested, continuing to gaze at the water.

Cy had to think back to the night he had a talk with Skin. He had said if a shootout situation were inevitable, he would not give up his weapon even if they had the drop on them. What he hadn't done was give Skin the code word which would be a warning to his partner that he was going to draw and fire his weapon.

"How did you know about that?" Cy asked.

"Jacob told me when I had your complete trust, you'd give me the code."

"I'm sorry. I was going to give it to you the other night when we were talking at Orozco's. We went back on patrol and got on another subject. I'm glad you brought it up. It won't ever happen, but if all else fails and I'm going to draw and fire, the word before I make my move will be 'onions.'" Cy studied Skin for a moment. "If we are ever under the gun and there is no way out, when you hear me say 'onions,' you immediately break away from me, go for your gun, and take out whoever you have to."

"Okay, Sarge. Thanks," Skin replied, his voice shaky with emotion.

Cy took a toothpick from his pocket and chewed on it.

"My wife, Jill, was a good woman, Sarge—a real fine woman, but we married too young. I was in the army and didn't make peanuts. She was from a good well-to-do family and was used to a lot of nice things—things that I couldn't and never would be able to give her. We were from two different worlds. When I was sent to Viet Nam, she somehow lost her feelings for me. It was painful for her and me both." Skin hesitated, cleared his husky throat, and went on. "She didn't want to hurt me, but her parents put a lot of pressure on her to go back to law school and to get on with her life. We had Tiffany, and we held things together until we both finally had to face reality. It wasn't going to work no matter what we did. It's funny. Physically we were attracted to each other like magnets. Mentally we were opposites." Skin looked over at Cy. "You see, I can't blame her for leaving me. I never cared enough for another woman until I met Martha."

"And now?" Cy tested Skin.

"And now what?"

"Is there any reason not to pursue her?" Cy asked.

"Why?"

"Did you overhear us talking in the lodge?"

"You know I did. You don't have to beat my head in with a dumb stick. As soon as he asked me her name, I knew. Why do you think I got out of there?" Skin paused for a minute, thinking of Martha and her warm personality. "It blows my mind she named her son after him, though. It's too obvious. Susan is either blind or she won't face facts."

"I think Susan is so much in love with Tony she wouldn't believe it if he was slapped in the face with a paternity suit."

"Women are hypnotized by him. He is the best-looking guy on the block. He's an outstanding officer who could stand his ground with most anyone. The very thing I like about the guy makes me hate him at the same time."

"What do ya mean?" Cy asked.

"Tony is a rough-and-tumble guy who's streetwise because he grew up on the streets. He lost his sense of right and wrong when he was a kid in the alleys, but he pulled himself out of the gutter because he was smart and he wasn't lazy. His funny personality masks who he really is. You know the old saying, "You can take the boy out of the alley, but you can't take the alley out of the boy." Well, he's a graduate from the streets. That's where his roots are, and with the exception of his tomcatting, he is one of the best men I know."

"If that's true, you can't entirely blame Martha, Skin. She may have fallen for him, but she really didn't know him. You might want to think about it and not judge her too harshly."

Skin stood up and faced his companion. "It gives me a lot to think about. I'm not making any quick judgments. I can't deny the shock and pain," he said, reaching out and taking Cy's hand to pull him to his feet. He pulled Cy to his chest and gave him a hug. "Thanks for being my friend. That's all I can say." He turned around and walked back to the cabin.

Cy couldn't answer. He hesitated a few moments, thinking of his own life and the loneliness he felt in Mary Ann's absence—not a good feeling. He looked up into the sky and at the millions of stars. He felt so small. He took his time walking back to the cabin where he, Skin, and Jacob were bunking. Skin was standing outside having a last puff on his pipe.

After a moment Skin banged the pipe on the palm of his hand. Both men walked into the dark room. Inside the second bedroom Jacob was in bed. "Is everything okay?" he asked.

"Everything is fine, Jacob. Thanks for asking," Skin said,

walking over to his bed. They both undressed in the dark and got into bed. No one could sleep, and when they each realized the other was awake, they began a serious discussion on deer hunting strategies. The last thing discussed was their expectations of catching steelhead the next morning.

Tony and the sheriff sat by the fire and talked for several hours about police work and the impact of drugs on society. Tony, who was older than his friends, was more adept at conversing with the sheriff. Al was most content visiting with such an interesting person. Finally, when both men began showing signs of fatigue, Tony excused himself and went to his room for the night. In bed in his shorts and T-shirt, he lay there enjoying the peace and quiet along with his last smoke of the night.

Much later that evening the sheriff sat in the main lounge area. The generators had been turned off and everyone was in bed. Only a small flicker of light sparked every now and then from the log embers. The peacefulness and comfort of being alone was greatly enjoyed by the ex-marine. He had slumped down in the big sofa as he faced the dying fire. He was concentrating on thoughts of retirement and of his family when he heard a footstep in the room. He scooted all the way down in his chair and braced his arms next to his sides so he couldn't be seen from the rear of the room. Ever so light was the shuffle of stockinged feet across the room to the second guest room. The guest room door opened and closed very quietly. The sheriff's face broadened into a smile when he recognized Bertie as she slipped into Tony's sleeping quarters.

Bertie was so homely and mean he never thought she would let down for a minute to allow the amorous attention of any man. He thought it was quite clever of Bertie and Tony not to let on to any attraction between them. Few things got past him, and he felt very clever to have discovered a secret that he nor anyone else would suspect in the first place.

The sheriff puffed on his pipe, concentrating on a thought, a smile of pleasure on his face.

After several hours passed, Tony's door opened and Bertie scuffled across the floor and out the front door, failing to see the sheriff still sitting in the near dark. The sheriff got up from his position, walked over to the rock fireplace, and tapped his pipe bowl softly on the mantel. After a few moments his face grew a wider smile. He turned and went to his own room for the evening.

❧

The next morning the sheriff showed his guests the upper part of the stream to the east of Paradise Bar. The boat skipped across the river for about a mile to a place called the "coffee pot." It was a spot where the water came downstream into a boiling pool formed from a small waterfall. It was also the end of the Curry County line.

Tony Valin had a reputation for being a prankster. He could keep a joke or story going for such lengths that no one ever messed with him in fear of payback. He was always pulling a prank on someone. Today was no different. The men had gotten out of the boat and were standing along the shore fishing. They were looking upriver enjoying the view of the beautiful moss-covered rocks and big pine trees when two drift boats appeared at a bend in the river coming downstream. The sheriff didn't say anything even though he recognized the first drift boat and one of the regular guides who had patronized his resorts.

The sheriff turned to Tony who was pulling a cigar from his mouth. "The guys in the first drift boat have stayed at my place for the last couple of years. They own a garbage company in Reno. I think they are connected with the Mafia."

The sheriff looked back at the drift boats as they approached "coffee pot." The two men he was referring to were both of Italian descent and appeared to be very wealthy. Each boat had two passengers and a guide.

The sheriff motioned for the boat to come to the shore so they could talk. The guide acknowledged with a wave and brought the boat over.

Suddenly Tony stood up from the rock he was sitting on. He removed his L.A.P.D. identification and badge from his pocket and flashed it briefly to the two Italians. "We're doing an inspection here. I want to know if you are carrying any liquor in those coolers."

A surprised sheriff turned to look at Tony but did not say anything, wondering where he was going with it. These were his clients and he did not want them insulted but wasn't sure how to play it.

The bigger of the two men, Molinaro, squinted at Tony and said gruffly, "Yeah, we do. So what."

"Yeah we do, so what?" Tony mimicked the stranger. "I'll tell you what. Do you know it's illegal to transport liquor by water over the county line?" Tony looked very serious and stepped closer to the boat. "Open up that cooler and let me see what's in it."

The two men were not used to taking orders from anyone, but they were not sure what to do, being out of their comfort zone. They both glared at Tony and then looked at the sheriff. He didn't afford an explanation.

Cy and Skin couldn't believe Tony would take on these two bigshots, especially without cracking a smile. Now, they weren't sure that he wasn't serious. They were unable to decipher Tony's behavior. He was too unpredictable.

"I said open it up. Now!" Tony snapped, raising his voice and stepping closer.

The sheriff felt his own anger rising. These were regular clients, and this city slicker was going to cause him trouble with his business.

The smaller of the two men, Machinano, moved over to the cooler and opened it. Only lettuce and other produce was inside. Machinano had a subtle smile because he knew the hard liquor must be in the other drift boat. He looked back up to Tony for approval.

"You are transporting produce over the county line. We are going to have to cite you for illegal transporting of produce." Tony leaned over to Machinano and stared straight into his face. "I am going to confiscate the contraband for evidence."

Both Italians were visibly angry and looked at their guide for assistance. Machinano gritted his teeth at the guide. "What the hell is going on here?"

The air was so thick everyone could hardly breathe. Suddenly Tony cracked a smile and started laughing, and after a few moments it broke the ice and everyone joined in with relief. Tony jumped in their boat and asked for a beer. He rode downstream with them. By the time they arrived at a good fishing spot they were all the best of friends.

Jacob watched the drift boat float downstream with Tony talking as fast as his lips could move. "That's the way Tony is. He may be horny and unpredictable, but he has the ability to make friends anywhere." Jacob smiled, shaking his head. "I've never known anyone like him."

The sheriff glanced around at Cy, Jacob, and Skin. A strange grin broke the corners of his mouth and then he winked at them. Under the grin he was steaming with anger.

An hour later, the sheriff pulled up on the far shore where Tony was fishing alone. The others must have dropped him off so he could get back to serious fishing. "Come on," the sheriff called. "We're headed downriver to my secret hole."

Once Tony joined the others, the sheriff drifted for approximately a quarter mile to a deep hole where small whirlpools eddied in circles, sinking into the depths of the cold water. "This is it. You guys will love this spot."

Cy jumped out of the boat and tied it off to a large boulder. The sheriff asked Skin to help him with the ice cooler. He led them over to a flat rock where they sat down and ate lunch.

While the men were eating sandwiches and sipping on soft drinks, the second drift boat that earlier had been traveling with the two men from Reno passed them by.

The sheriff stepped over to Jacob. "That guide right there," he pointed to the drifting boat, his voice angry. "His wife is divorcing him and I've got a major problem on my hands." His forehead wrinkled deeply, obviously concerned about the situation.

"Wha' da ya mean?" asked Jacob, watching the boat drift by their rock.

"My cook and he got it on." The sheriff cautiously leaned over and spoke to Jacob in a low voice. "His name is John. He told me he got the clap from my cook and he gave it to his wife. Now his wife is divorcing him." He paused a moment letting a sad expression cross his face. "I'm gonna have to get rid of her. It makes me feel bad. She's been with me for years now. She can really throw a good meal on the table."

Jacob struggled to stand so he could face the sheriff. "You can say that again. She's a wonderful cook. I guess the health inspectors would shut you down if they found out you had an employee in violation of the health code."

"That's exactly it," the sheriff grumbled, kicking a small rock into the water.

Jacob strolled a short distance with the sheriff. The others in the group ate their lunch quietly, not wanting to miss out on the conversation even though they were not invited.

The sheriff spoke in a low, confidential tone, making sure at the same time his voice carried to the others in the group. He straightened up, looked down at his boat, swore, and kicked the side panel. Venting his irritation, he swung around and walked a way off by the river edge and sat down by himself.

After lunch was over, the sheriff ordered everyone back in the drift boat and they headed downstream. His demeanor had changed. Inside, his heart was pounding with vengeance. No city boy was coming on his turf, embarrassing him, and getting away with it. Tony should never have talked to the Italians or played a joke on them, at least not before clearing it through him. Tony had made a serious mistake.

As they drifted down the river he quietly made comments to Jacob and then to his good friend, Tony. His forehead wrinkled and his eyes grew dark with hostility as he pondered his predicament. Bryce was convinced he should get an Academy Award for his superb acting performance. He had almost convinced himself that he was going to fire Bertie.

The sheriff glared at that rotten Portuguese tomcat out of the corner of his eye and noticed with a stab of joy when Tony's appearance changed from sunny to gray. The sheriff didn't say anything, but Jacob caught the stare, trying to piece this whole situation together. Jacob couldn't help but notice Tony had a peaked look on his face and was looking more somber as time elapsed.

The sheriff eventually changed the subject and began talking earnestly about the fish and hoped the weather would hold. The others in the boat loosened up with laughter and conversation. Slowly things returned to normal. Everyone except Tony was having a good time again. Conversations were centered on fishing and deer hunting. As the men caught steelhead, their spirits lifted even more.

After two hours of fishing Tony cautiously leaned toward the sheriff. "You mean the cook you have on now—Bertie?" The talking immediately stopped and the others were fixed on the sheriff.

"Yeah, the old witch." The sheriff spit in the river. "I'm dumping her."

"For sure she gave it to the guide? There's no doubt?"

"None at all. The guide said he never messed with anyone but her. There's no doubt where he got it. The sad part of it is that his wife is taking him for everything he is worth. He'll be working the next fifteen years to keep the family in the style of living that they are used to." He paused then continued, "Oh, well, let's forget about it. I'm going to fire Bertie, and once I make up my mind, that's it. We're not going to lose any sleep over it," he smiled at everyone as he finally made a proper decision. "Are we?"

Tony's face grew pale and he definitely looked ill. He stole a glance at the sheriff and hung his head. "I let her in my bed last night. This isn't good, Allen."

That was the first time Tony had ever called the sheriff by his first name. It was also obvious for the first time Tony was desperate for a close friend and he didn't care who was listening. Tony's color changed to a shade of green.

His fishing companions were shocked at the revelation. "This is really bad. This is really bad." Tony stared at the bottom of the boat.

On the way down the river back to the lodge, the sheriff spoke softly to Tony. Tony's friends were all convinced he had the clap and innocently and subconsciously moved away from him. If he was diseased, it was a serious thing. They could consider the situation better from the other side of the boat.

At the lodge Tony quickly went to his room and shut the door. The sheriff motioned for the others to step outside and explained it was a setup, that he was just getting even with Tony for embarrassing him in front of his other clients. He reviewed the story of the night before, how he sat in the dark and saw Bertie slip into Tony's room for several hours. In the spirit of cooperation Cy, Jacob, and Skin were more than anxious to participate in pulling one off on the invincible Tony Valin, the Portuguese gift to womanhood. It was especially inviting since it was the sheriff who would be taking the blame for his actions. So far, it was a wonderful day and a great vacation.

Sheriff Bryce walked over to Tony's room, knocked on the door, then opened it. When he saw Tony standing at the sink, he quickly shut the door and turned around, holding his hand over his mouth. He ran from the room out the back door bursting into hysterical screaming by the time he hit the rear porch.

When Jacob, Skin, and Cy raced through the door, they found him leaning over a wooden chair laughing out of control, something completely out of character for the sheriff. He held a towel to his mouth trying to muffle his uncontrollable screeches. His wide eyes streamed with tears coursing down his cheeks. Jacob and Cy started laughing with him, having no idea what was so humorous.

Skin grabbed the sheriff by the shoulder, "What's happening? What's so funny?"

Sheriff Bryce tried to answer but couldn't get the words out before he burst into a fit of laughter, screaming at the top of his lungs. Cy ran to the rear door, shut it, and quickly returned to the sheriff's side.

Tears had left shiny paths down Bryce's face, and when he tried to explain, only gurgling sounds came from his throat. Then he lost control and laughed harder. Bryce's whole body shook and trembled, and he finally dropped to his knees. His voiceless mouth was open and his eyes rolled to the back of his head. Finally, after gasping gulps of air, the sheriff tried desperately to share his moment with Tony's friends. On his hands and knees, he gasped, "Tony...was at the...si...sink...washing off his tal...scrubbing madly at his...tallywacker!" The sheriff continued to scream until his voice went scratchy and then only a rasping sound of air escaped from his distorted lips. He choked, "It looked like a red lobster, getting the living hell scrubbed out of it with a toilet brush. As if...as if...as if that would help anything now. Once you got the clap, you got it! He really believes it." He started laughing again and the men joined him.

Tony stayed in his quarters for an hour. Eventually he came out of his room and approached the others as they lounged around the fireplace. He walked gingerly to a chair and carefully sat down. Something was tremendously sore. Everyone knew he wanted to have a serious talk.

"Guys, I can't believe this. If I go back home and give this to Susan, she'll kill me." Tony had deep creases in his forehead. It was the first time ever that his friends had seen him worried about anything.

"What about celibacy?" Cy asked innocently.

"This isn't funny, buddy boy," Tony glared at Cy. He turned around and went back to his room, slamming the door.

The rest of the day Tony was depressed and stayed away from everyone. He felt dirty and wanted to be alone. Later in the evening they all played cards, including the guide. Tony never picked up on the unconcerned attitude of the guide nor that he did not act negatively to Bertie.

After dinner they all went fishing while Tony remained off by himself. Several times Cy felt sorry for him, but the others would not let him tell Tony the truth. Skin threatened to break his arm if he blabbed the sheriff's secret.

❧

After the third day they returned to Gold Beach. That very afternoon the Sheriff's Department was having a crab feed and the four L.A. cops were invited to stay. At the party the sheriff strolled off with Tony and scolded him for messing around with his cook. He gave him the address of a doctor friend who worked at a health clinic. He advised Tony the doctor would give him a shot to kill the virus. He told him he had to have the shot before 6:00 that evening to start the medicine working before the clap spread into his bloodstream, causing serious medical problems.

The other three thought the sheriff would tell Tony it was a joke. When he didn't, they waited until Tony was a safe distance away and then asked him what his intentions were. They were worried about it going too far. Tony's state of mind and possible feelings of retaliation were serious factors to be considered.

The sheriff angrily told them to back off. It was his hand to play, and he was going to teach Tony not to mess with him in the future. He warned them they would lose their fishing privileges if they did not cooperate, which quickly put everything into a different perspective.

The sheriff called the doctor and made an appointment for Tony. It was the first time Cy, Skin, and Jacob realized Tony had a major phobia for shots. He got sick to his stomach just thinking about it. Cy started to tell Tony, but Jacob and Skin took him aside and persuaded him to let it ride because they did not want Sheriff Allen Bryce for an enemy. It was also important not to lose their fishing contact.

After several hours of building up his courage and throwing up in the bathroom, Tony was driven down to the health clinic where he got the penicillin shot. He appeared sick when he came out of the building, and his three friends grew more and more uncomfortable with the sheriff's joke. It wasn't really that funny anymore.

Tony refused to talk to his friends and went to bed sick.

Chapter 14
Deer Hunt

The next morning Cy, Jacob, and Skin heard a commotion outside their motel when loud voices aroused them and a car door slammed shut. They looked out just in time to see Sheriff Bryce taking Tony back to the clinic for a booster shot.

"Oh boy," Skin said, looking out the window, "this ain't good. If Tony ever finds out we knew the truth, he'd never let up on us. He'll ruin our lives. He'll go crazy and destroy us in his own way."

"You white folks have got me into a peck of trouble," Jacob said, peering out the window. "That crazy man will kill us. He'd go to the ends of the earth to destroy our lives if he ever finds out we knew the truth."

"Let's make a pact," said Cy. "We promise never to tell Tony the truth, okay?" They all agreed and shook hands.

When Tony returned from the doctor, they packed up their gear and headed for Klamath Falls. From there they picked up Highway 140 to 395 and headed south toward Glass Mountain.

During the trip the three men were frightened of Tony and his crazy temper; it had become a serious concern how this ordeal was going to end. The sheriff had no idea of the fanatical zeal Tony had for revenge. They never thought the sheriff would go so far, and now they had to live with it, hoping Tony would never know the truth. When they departed from Gold Beach, the sheriff just smiled and said he would see them next year. Now they would have to live in terror of a madman for the rest of their lives.

It took all day to reach their destination. As they headed down the pass to Mono Lake on 395 they could see the majestic Glass Mountain in the distance. It reached high into the sky and was one of the most beautiful mountains in the valley. It was east of the High Sierras and approximately 15 miles as the crow flies from the Mammoths. Glass Mountain loomed out of the earth and penetrated a low bank of clouds with a magnificent sparkling beauty when the sun shone on it at the right angle.

This would be the second time all four friends would hunt in this area. One of their favorite areas had been in the Coleville range, north of Bridgeport, but it had become over-hunted. Last year the Glass Mountain area had proved to be a wild and wonderful adventure of camping, cooking, and hunting.

Cy had told them about the mountain's obsidian construction and that it produced many glass boulders bigger than a house. In ancient times Indians traveled for many miles to collect the black and brown obsidian to trade with tribes in other regions.

Tony drove his shiny four-wheel Cherokee, pulling a utility trailer, east on Highway 120 from 395 toward the town of Benton. After a number of miles he turned right on a dirt road and drove for several more to the southeast side of Glass Mountain where he located a pleasant camping area. It was partway up the mountain and had been a logging camp in the 1880s.

Cy gazed at the huge mountain and the surrounding area, and he could feel his heart thumping in his chest. He felt a strange feeling for this beautiful land. It was wild and yet accessible; small wonder he felt drawn to this region, and when he looked over at the High Sierra Mountains which bordered Yosemite, he felt a deep, private excitement. It was special to him because he had been introduced to the area by his father. This was the place he had hunted with his father and brother for the last time. With them both gone, it gave him a lonely and eerie feeling.

The four men set up camp and had a fire going within two hours. Skin, who was the designated camp cook, had a Dutch oven dinner in the makings. Cy went off for a walk while Jacob and Skin drank a beer, sitting around the fire. Tony stayed to himself and didn't talk very much. It appeared he was still worried about his predicament, and it created an uncomfortable feeling among the others. Tony was worried about what he would do if the shots didn't cure him.

When Cy returned, only Jacob and Skin were in camp. They didn't appear very happy, and Cy felt the same. None of the men had approved of what happened on the Rogue River, and it still distressed them.

"This really isn't funny anymore, guys," Cy said, sitting down.

"It's not, but what do we do about it?" Jacob replied, glancing at Cy.

"We've got a real problem, gents," Skin said, as he removed the lid to the Dutch oven to see if the food was done. "Tony's planning on getting a third shot when we get back, and he's worried to death his wife will find out. This whole thing has gone too far, and we are paying the price for it."

Jacob looked around to see if Tony was anywhere near camp. When he was sure he wasn't, he looked back at Cy and Skin. "Tony is the hungriest thing next to a randy bull when he's been away. His wife is going to figure something is wrong when he doesn't jump her bones the first three minutes home." Jacob took a drink of beer and looked over at Cy for a comment.

"You notice how his whole demeanor has changed? He's not a happy camper," Cy said flatly.

Perplexed, Skin had no answers either. One thing was most evident. Camping wasn't fun anymore. "Tony is the prankster of the group. He's always plotting and figuring who he's going to do a number on. I miss that in him, and in the same breath, I don't want him getting even with me. Hells bells, none of us would be able to sleep again. Ever!" Skin stirred the food around and put the lid back on. "It's almost done."

That night was quiet and only idle conversation passed around the camp. Tony looked like he wanted to crawl in a hole, and finally he turned in early beneath a tree. Cy, Jacob, and Skin quietly looked at each other, shrugged, and went to bed after the fire died down. Their spirits had hit rock bottom.

After breakfast the next morning the four men jumped in the Jeep and went for a ride to scout the area for hunting. Without their saying it, Cy felt everyone just wanted to go home and forget the hunt. They headed down Sawmill Road until they came to McGee Meadow. The men separated, looking the country over for deer sign.

It wasn't planned but somehow Jacob, Cy, and Skin ended up together near a spring. Above it was a plateau where Cy thought would be a great place for a cabin or homestead. As the three talked, they decided their trip was ruined and considered going home. They finally decided to tell Tony the truth. Perhaps he would take it better than they expected. Anything was better than this. Life was made for hunting and fishing, and this trip would turn out to be a disaster if they couldn't get it turned around.

Later, near the campsite, the four men were standing at the end of a large turn-around where the road ended overlooking the vast land to the south. They could see Lake Crowley in the distance and Mammoth Ski Resort to the west. Jacob went back to the Jeep for cold drinks and handed them to the others. He would rather have been in a bar fight than do what he was about to do. He was the oldest and highest ranking, and he used to be Tony's partner. Perhaps all these circumstances would be in their favor when Tony found out the truth.

"Well, what do you think, fools? Is this beautiful land or what? God knew what he was doing when he created this spectacle." Jacob took a deep breath to show the others he enjoyed the clean fresh air. He expelled the air slowly from his lungs and attempted a big smile. "We have a lot to be thankful for. Well...I do anyway." Jacob pulled a long drink on his beer. "I appreciate you goons," he hesitated a moment. "To be quite frank with you, I think a lot of you guys. You're my best friends."

"Hear, hear," replied Skin in agreement. "I love you guys and it's great to know I can depend on you when I need you. Yes, siree, you're the best a man could ask for." Skin was taken back by his own response and was pleased he could openly express his affections to his friends for the first time. Feeling comfortable with himself, he pulled out his pipe, stuffed the bowl with tobacco, and lit it.

Tony didn't say anything while he sipped his beer. He stared out into the valley far below them. Cy felt a tightness in his throat and couldn't bring himself to speak.

Jacob smiled and patted Tony on the shoulder. "You know, good buddy, life is not always what it seems. Things can and will turn out better than you think. You can depend on us to help you through bad times. We are here to stand by you, behind you, giving you the assistance and encouragement a friend should have and deserves." Jacob looked at Tony, who didn't respond. "You must realize, my good friend, things may not always be what they appear. For example this little incident with the cook..."

"I don't want to talk about it, bucko." Tony spit at the

ground not looking at the others, clearly depressed.

"Well...us three guys think a lot of you...and we have got to tell you something." Jacob looked at Tony. Tony didn't move or look at him. Cy moved back slightly and Skin was getting nervous. He felt uncomfortable next to Jacob and moved away about five feet.

"Sometimes making words from the thoughts in my head is difficult when it involves someone I care for. Because of our anxiety, I feel compelled to tell you as gently as I possibly can...this whole thing with you and the clap is a Sheriff Allen Bryce specialty joke."

All three men were staring at Tony. At first he didn't flinch or blink. His eyes were not focused and he seemed confused.

Skin stayed where he was and motioned with both hands, pleading with Tony. "Really, Tony, the sheriff set you up and it was just a joke. You got his goat when you teased those two guys from Reno. It was his way of getting back at you."

Without changing his position and staring into outer space Tony asked, "You mean I took those damn shots and have been sick for three days worrying and it was a joke?"

Cy moved further away and glanced around for an escape route in case things went bad. Jacob came forward wanting to explain. All he could say was, "Yeah." Jacob squinted his eyes and seriously nodded his head. "Yeah, it was. But it wasn't our joke."

Tony spun around, reached into the middle of his back with his right hand, and pulled out a Smith and Wesson Model 39 nine millimeter. He went to a crouch position pointing the gun at the three men, his eyes aflame with anger. "You rotten...," he swore foul and angry and pointed the gun down at their feet, firing three quick rounds into the ground.

The three men leaped into the air for fear of getting shot directly or by ricochet. This wasn't funny. Those were real bullets and Tony had lost his senses.

Tony's face had the mad glare of a man who was bent on killing. Cy ran behind the Cherokee Jeep, and Jacob and Skin jumped up on the fender screaming for Tony to stop. They did not think Tony would shoot his Jeep.

Tony was crazy with anger, but he also didn't want any dents or scuffs on his fancy Jeep with its expensive paint job.

"Get off my Jeep!" he yelled. No one responded. Nothing on earth could make them step back on the ground in the danger zone. Tony pointed the gun at Jacob and then back to Skin. "Get off my Jeep, now!"

"No way, fool!" Jacob's voice was shaky and he couldn't hide his fear. He held his hands out in front of him to block any rounds coming his way.

Tony spotted Skin's ivory pipe on the ground where it fell from his mouth after the first shot. With precision and satisfaction he pumped a round into it, shattering pieces in every direction.

"Good hell, he's going to kill us," yelled Skin.

Cy was hiding at the rear of the Jeep, standing on the bumper and hanging onto the spare tire.

Tony stood with his gun trained on Jacob and Skin. Skin's bald head was beaded with perspiration and he looked ill. The clouds in the air from the rounds kicking up the dirt gave off a dusty veil between Tony and the others.

Suddenly the look on his face changed to a smile and he slipped the gun back in the holster at the small of his back. He hesitated for a long moment and then walked over to Jacob and gave him a bear hug. "Oh lordy, you guys just took the biggest load off me I have ever had in my life." Tony gave Skin a big hug and pulled him off the Jeep. "You guys don't know how sick I was. I thought I was finished for sure."

Tony glanced around until he found Cy peeking through the rear window still stooped down on the rear bumper. Cy wasn't taking any chances in case Tony just wanted to get everyone off his Jeep before he killed them.

Tony walked over to Cy and gave him a hug. "I could see myself going through a divorce and losing my children and I couldn't handle it. Thanks for saving me. I mean it from the bottom of my heart...I really do. You have saved me." He threw up his hands and reached upward toward the sky, extremely happy with life now that the tormenting burden had been lifted from his shoulders.

"Come on, you guys, dinner is on me. I'm taking you to Mammoth and buying you all a steak dinner." Tony stepped back and looked up at the top of the mountain. "And Glass Mountain, I love you."

They all jumped into the Jeep and headed back down the dirt road, arriving 40 minutes later in Mammoth.

❦

The next morning proved to be a beautiful day. Jacob fixed breakfast while Tony and Skin took their time waking up. Cy had left camp an hour before to hike on the north face of the mountain. When he returned, he was cheerful and in a good mood. He picked up a piece of crispy bacon and tasted it. The atmosphere had cleared and everyone was in good spirits.

"Hmm, there's nothing like bacon in the mountains, is there," Cy said, grinning ear to ear. He stepped back to search over the scenery to the west of Glass Mountain.

"You got that right, buddy," Jacob said happily. He glanced at Cy and shook his head. He turned the hash brown potatoes over. "You are really in your element here, aren't you, Cowboy?"

"My heart soars in this place, Jake. I really love it here." Cy finished the bacon and studied the wide valley below them. If I didn't care about my job so much, I'd move here. I'd build me a nice cozy log cabin with a potbellied stove to keep me warm. I'd have a nice barn and corral for the horses and raise some cattle."

"I know you would. I know you would. So why don't you?" Jacob looked steadily at Cy. "These mountains are what you are all about. You have the money. Why don't you leave the city and move up here?" Jacob hesitated, "You know, my man, I like the idea of being guaranteed a good hunting spot every year. Am I right?"

"You know you would. If I didn't love being a cop, I'd do it. And you guys could come here anytime you wanted." Cy stepped over to a large boulder and looked down to the lower level of land. "The problem is, nobody would ever sell his property to an outsider. It's too beautiful. Besides, they would want to keep it in the family. That's the way they do things in the country."

The sun broke over the White Mountain Range directly east of Glass Mountain. The sky was a light blue behind the mountains with bright rays of silver streaking across the sky. Suddenly it changed to a brilliant gold as the powerful sun forced its way upward with all its intensity on the horizon. The welcomed sun brought immediate warmth to Cy's whole body as he studied the panoramic view. In the center of the far mountain range to the east stood Mount Dubois reaching 13,500 feet. Four miles north was Mount Montgomery with an elevation of 13,400 feet. South of Mount Dubois were other mountain peaks—Mount Hogue, Headley Peak, and then the most outstanding dominant mountain in the range, White Mountain Peak, with an elevation of 14,246 feet.

Cy felt a warmth within himself. It was his kind of land— the high mountains, running water, snow, pines, and then the living desert further east. He understood why the miners and the earlier traders were drawn to this heaven on earth.

After breakfast Skin placed a ballcap on his head and announced he was going to Lee Vining to make a call. No one asked who he was calling, and he assumed without the questions they knew it was Martha.

"When are you leaving?" Cy asked, putting away the last dish after drying it off.

"In a few minutes," Skin replied. "Why? You want to come along?"

"If you don't mind," Cy answered. "I need to pick up some groceries, and I want to get a few maps of the area at the U.S. Forest Service Station." Cy was already wearing his insulated Levi jacket. He walked over to the tent and took out his straw hat. It was a Bailey U-Rollit, and it showed its many years of wear.

Tony stood up and stretched. "Jacob and I are going to hike to the south side of the mountain and get a look at Lake Crowley. There should be some good deer trails over there and not as many trees on the south slopes."

Jacob walked over to his tent and picked up an orange hunter's cap and put it on his head. "We'll see you boys in a few hours." Jacob slung a small backpack filled with sandwiches and goodies over his shoulder. "I guess you know this is the best part of the hunt. Just hiking and eating munchies is what it's all about."

Skin dropped Cy off at the Lee Vining General Store and left to find a public phone. Cy stopped outside the store and studied a rack holding newspapers and real estate ads. An old Indian dressed in well-worn but clean clothes sat on a bench at the entrance. He smoked a hand-rolled cigarette and appeared thoroughly content with life.

Cy gave the old man a friendly grin. "Good morning, sir."

"Good morning, yourself," the old man answered with a distinct Indian accent.

The Indian looked up at Cy and stared at him. Cy ignored his unrelenting regard and gave him a bigger smile. "What tribe are you from, sir?"

"Why you ask?"

"Well, I was raised with Indians in southern California. Some of my best friends in school were Indians. They were a branch from the Shoshone Tribe."

"Yes. The Shoshone migrated south of Owen's Valley and the Pilot Mountains. They are our brothers," the old man said straight faced.

Cy marveled at the man's wrinkles. The sun-worn skin looked like hard shoe leather. His grey hair was thick and it matched his thick rough eyebrows. His long nose was pitted. The Indian wore a tattered long-sleeve plaid shirt. His hands were dark brown and showed many small scars. Cy imagined it was from barbed wire and many years of ranching.

"Are you Shoshone?" Cy asked, trying to be friendly.

"No, I am not Shoshone. I am Paiute," he answered proudly. "I am of the Winnemucca Paiute people." The man held out his hand to Cy. "Here, you pay dollar for so many questions."

Cy smiled and gave him two. He leaned over the paper rack and took a real estate newsletter and then entered the store.

Cy took a handbasket, went to the dairy section, and picked up two dozen eggs. He stepped around the next aisle and came to a screeching halt. A girl was standing at the breakfast foods section studying the different granola cereals.

Cy's attention was on her long hair. It was blue-black and hung in a dark wave below her slim waist. She was wearing a Levi jacket over a green shirt and green pants. Without realizing that his lips moved or his vocal cords vibrated, he blurted, "Whoa."

The Indian girl abruptly turned around. She blinked her eyes and walked away. Cy's chest caved in as he watched her retreat to the end of the aisle. He only caught a glimpse of her face. He was stunned as he watched her lithe figure cross the floor. She disappeared around the corner. He put the basket down and ran to the end of the aisle. His heart was now pounding furiously as he saw the girl going out the door and into the street.

Cy was desperate and his voice was unsure. "Miss...Miss, wait a minute."

The Indian girl stopped and turned to face him as he approached her from the entrance to the store. She stared momentarily, and when Cy only looked at her with his mouth open, she turned and started to walk to an old jeep next to Tony's Cherokee.

"Miss...please," Cy was desperate for words to control this vital moment. He couldn't let her get away from him. He might never see her again.

The jeep was an older military style without a top or doors. The girl slipped behind the wheel. Cy got to her as she was inserting the key into the ignition.

"Ma'am, please. I know I'm making a complete fool of myself," Cy stammered.

Looking into Cy's eyes, she penetrated his brain to the core. He was sure he was going to pass out. She had the blackest eyes he had ever seen; they were so black he could not distinguish her pupils. Her face was clear and smooth. He was totally consumed by her beautiful features.

There was no expression in her face as she spoke in a soft soothing voice. "No talk, tahng-wahts." Her dark eyes flashed a warning at him.

Cy stepped closer, frustrated. He felt his heart was going to leap out onto her lap. "What? I don't understand. You said, 'no talk and tang whats it'?" Cy felt his head shaking helplessly back and forth.

"Imik a tahng-wahts," she said, fumbling at the keys in the ignition.

The sight of her dumbed his speech; his mind was circling in a flurry around the inside of his head. He guessed her age to be twenty-three or twenty-four, and he was frustrated with desire to understand her, to know her.

"Miss, I'm sorry. I don't understand. Don't you speak English? Can't you wait a minute, I just want to talk."

"Cach aiyak," the girl answered, turning the key. She pressed the floor starter and the engine came to life. She backed up and drove away.

Cy stood helplessly as he watched her drive south down the street. It was a strange and desperate feeling that ran through his entire body, and it was mounting. It was a foreign feeling and a new experience.

Skin had the keys to the Cherokee; otherwise he would have raced after her. He had witnessed the most beautiful girl walk in and out of his life in a matter of moments, completely beyond his control. He let her slip between his fingers. Cy turned and saw the old Indian putting a fresh smoke in his mouth. Though his heart had been completely paralyzed by her mere presence, he was able to walk over to the old man.

"Do you know what language the girl was speaking?" Cy asked, pointing to the jeep going down the road.

"Of course I do," the old man answered matter of factly, as if insulted.

"Well, do you mind telling me what language?" Cy asked irritated.

"No, I do not mind."

When the old man didn't continue, Cy felt his frustration rising. "Well, what language was she speaking?"

"Paiute."

"Could you tell me what she said?"

"Yes," the old man answered and puffed on his smoke.

"What did she say?" Cy asked, short tempered.

"Which time?"

"Which time?" Cy had to hold his anger in check or the old man would not talk with him. "She said something like, 'tang whats it.'"

"That's poor excuse for Paiute talk, young fella." The old man gave Cy a disgusted look.

"Good grief, I've never heard this language before. What did it mean? Can't you help me out?"

"That young squaw say 'tanqwats.' Pronounce it tahng-wahts. 'Tanqwats' means 'white man.' The old man looked up at Cy, unsmiling. "She say, 'no talk white man.' Very simple. Very direct."

"What was the last thing she said when I asked her to wait and talk?"

"She say 'cach aiyak,'" the old Indian said, growing bored with Cy.

"What does 'cach aiyak' mean?"

"You must say 'cahch I-yahk.' It mean 'no thanks.'" With that the old Indian got up and limped away from the store.

Cy watched the Indian disappear around the corner. After a brief moment the old man peeked back around the edge of the building. "It was nice way for young woman to say she does not like white people, at least you. It would be wise if you not talk to her again." The Indian pulled his head back and was gone.

Cy went back in the store and bought the groceries. He

waited in the Jeep until Skin returned.

"You buy what we needed?" Skin asked, starting up the Cherokee.

"I did. Let's get back to camp."

"I thought you wanted to go to the forest office and get some maps."

"Yeah, I guess we could," Cy answered. He told Skin about the Indian girl and that he was crazy in love with her. He was exaggerating, of course, but in all his life he had never seen a woman that captivated him so completely as this Paiute girl had.

On the way to the forest office Skin told Cy he called Martha and they had a good talk. He said he thought everything could be worked out between them. He told Cy he loved her and they were going to get married. Now he could have a ready-made son.

Skin drove to the Lee Vining Park Ranger Station on the road going to Yosemite.

"Skin! There's her jeep. It's right over there. Look!" Cy said, pointing to the army jeep between two other vehicles parked near the end of the lot.

"Well, buddy, maybe you're in luck," Skin said, pulling into a parking space. "I don't know what good it's going to do you if she doesn't speak English."

"Or won't speak English," Cy said, getting out of the vehicle. He hurried into the office.

Inside he looked for the Indian girl. She was nowhere to be found. Cy was disappointed but at least he had hope. The two waited around looking at books and maps in hopes the girl would show up. She did not appear, and finally Cy bought two maps covering Mono County.

The officer working the counter handed Cy his change and said, "Thank you."

Cy pocketed his change. "Do you know who owns that army jeep in the parking lot?"

The worker looked at him quizzically, "Why do you ask?"

"Well, I'm interested in buying one. I'll need a jeep to travel the trails shown on these maps," Cy smiled back.

"Oh," the woman smiled. "It belongs to one of our range specialists. She just left and is in the field for the rest of the afternoon. If you want to leave your name and number I could have her call you."

"Could you please tell me her name?" Cy smiled innocently.

"It's Sarah...I'm sorry, I better not give you her name." The lady pushed a paper and pencil in front of Cy. "Leave your name and I'll have the owner call you."

"We're camping and can't be reached. I'll give you my name and home phone in Pasadena. I was thinking I might try again tomorrow." Cy handed the paper back to the lady. "I may not hunt tomorrow. If I don't, I'll try again to make contact." Cy turned and walked out the door. Skin was waiting outside on the grass. They got into the Jeep and drove back to Lee Vining.

"Let's have lunch before we go back," Skin said, grinning at Cy's disappointed face. "What do ya say? Are you hungry?"

"Yeah, why not."

"Good," Skin grinned. "Here, thought you might need this." Skin handed Cy a piece of paper with a California license plate number written on it.

Cy shook his head, taking the piece of paper from Skin. It was the license plate number to the army jeep. "I don't know where my head is. I can't think straight. This girl has really affected me. My brain is like mush."

Skin parked the Jeep in front of Mom's Cafe at the south end of town. They went inside and ordered a couple of burgers, fries, and two milkshakes. Without being consciously aware, they both did what all cops do without thinking—they headed for the far wall and took a table where they could sit facing the front door.

Skin and Cy sat eating their food with enthusiasm. Their conversation consisted mostly of the fishing trip and Tony's temper. Cy busily read the real estate newsletter that he had picked up earlier. An older man at the counter got up from his stool and walked over to their table.

"Gents, you're not from around here, are you?" The short heavyset man had a nice, friendly smile, the smile of a salesman.

"We're here for the hunt," Skin said. "What can we do for you?"

"My name is Matthew Morgan. I am a real estate salesman. I noticed you, sir," he pointed to Cy. "You were looking at my newsletter."

"Yours?" Cy responded coolly.

"Well, I organized the newsletter a number of years ago. Many different real estate dealers buy space." He motioned at the chair next to Cy. "Do you mind?"

"I do," Skin's tone changed to unfriendly.

"No, have a seat. My name is Cy. This is Michael Fin, but everyone calls him Skin."

"Hah, that kind of rhymes, doesn't it? Fin and Skin. Kind of catchy." The salesman took a seat laughing at himself. "I actually live in Bishop but I do a lot of sales out of the resort areas such as Mammoth and fishing sites around some of the lakes. Do you folks ski?"

"Naw, we shoot people for a living." Skin gave the man a slanted gaze.

"Good heavens, you what?"

"He's kidding, Mr. Morgan. We're both police officers out of L.A."

"Oh my, he sounded so serious." Mr. Morgan didn't try to conceal his relief.

"I was serious," Skin came back. "There's a lot of hostiles out there and the biggest majority of them don't like cops."

"That's probably true. Our biggest problem around here are drunken cowboys or a few drug dealers who service the tourists. Very little theft and things of that sort goes on."

"Mr. Morgan, is there any range land for sale around this area?" Cy asked.

"Large plots of land are a bit more difficult to purchase, Cy. Now and then when a rancher dies, we may have a possible sale if none of the family wants to run the place."

Something loud smashed into the side of the cafe. Several people jumped from the sudden intrusion. Cy went to the window and peered outside. Outside on the ground was a broken beer bottle that evidently had been thrown from a vehicle. An older yellow Chevrolet pickup truck with gray primer spots squealed around the corner and four men were laughing and whooping it up. Without being conscious of his movements, Skin jumped to one side and pulled his .38 from the middle of his back. He crouched down, looking out the window and covering the entrance to the cafe.

Matthew Morgan's eyes were showing white as he stared at Skin's gun. Cy had moved to the right but did not display a weapon.

"You guys really are cops, then. Is that right?" Mr. Morgan was excited. He couldn't take his eyes off Skin's gun.

Once he realized there was no danger, Skin put the revolver back in his belt and covered it with his shirt. He was a little embarrassed to have pulled it out. His reaction was common practice in the city. He did not think of what he was doing in this small town. "Yeah, that's right. Sorry about that, Matthew. Force of habit."

"I thought this was a quiet place around here," Cy snipped at Mr. Morgan.

"Well, I forgot about the miners. Some of them are from Tonopah and Hawthorne, Nevada." Mr. Morgan was uncomfortable. He did not want potential customers to think badly of his homeland. "They mostly come to town on the weekend to break the monotony of hard days of working underground. That would drive anyone to drink," he laughed.

Cy visited with the salesman, asking questions about the land and comparing cost per acre with costs for large parcels of land. After about twenty minutes, Skin showed definite signs of boredom. Cy knew he had to break off the conversation with Mr. Morgan.

❧

Sarah carried a bucket of dirt treated with natural fertilizer, ammonium nitrates, vitamin B, and other natural ingredients. She also had a small hand shovel to work the plants she was caring for on the south side of Panum Crater. It was early in the afternoon and she was relieved Ray Tom did not try to meet with her today. She felt awkward, not knowing how to deal with his romantic pursuits. She cared for him but was not in love with him; she was concerned about Ray's feelings and did not want to hurt him. He had been pressuring her for more of her time, but her main interest at this period in her life was her job, not romance.

Ray was a good man; however, his bitter feelings against whites had slowly built a thin wall of irritation between them. Sometimes his feelings rubbed off on her and she began to discredit people without justification. She actually loved and respected white people, especially her foster parents. Often she wished she could have both worlds.

Ray Tom seemed angry with life. He felt he had been cheated from his heritage because of the white man's progress, and his bitterness sometimes made him dishonest. Sarah would never find warmth and security in a man who distrusted life in general. She was attracted to him but those were only surface feelings. Sarah wanted and needed someone whom she could trust and love completely, someone who would give her the love, understanding, and security she craved; someone who could make her laugh and feel happy to be alive; someone who shared her deep religious beliefs; someone who would love her with devotion.

Sarah's own people called her an apple Indian and this hurt her profoundly. It meant she was red on the outside but white on the inside. She had tried desperately to be accepted among her people. Her education and her experiences of living in Utah had made her want more from life. She did not want to become a government statistic, so she was determined to provide for herself.

She knew that Ray wanted to marry a Paiute girl and that she was more than appealing to him. She was also aware of his interest in her Uncle Ben's land. She wished there were more Paiute young men for her to choose from, but her people were slowly vanishing. Sarah felt caught in a lonely trap and her future did not look good, except for her job. Working outdoors with the land was a great joy to her. It gave her space to breathe and to feel the wind in her hair and the warmth of the sun on her shoulders. She marveled how nature touched her soul. This was her life. The cry for freedom always rang in her heart and it gave her consolation and peace of mind.

Sarah's thoughts were broken when she heard the truck coming on the dirt road towards Panum Crater. It was traveling too fast for the bumpy road. Intermittently it would lose traction, causing the rear tires to spin. It would sway back and forth, and a large dust trail billowed into the sky behind it.

As the yellow truck came closer, Sarah could see four people—two sitting in the cab and two standing in the bed. She could hear them laughing and howling profanities.

Sarah became alarmed. She was isolated for miles from other people. There was no one to help her. From the noise the men were making she felt intimidated, knowing she was in a bad position. She searched the crater for an escape route. There was none, at least none she could take without being seen. She almost started to climb to the top of the crater and head down the back side toward Mono Lake. As quickly as she thought of the idea, she dismissed it. If she took off toward the lake, there would be no cover in the featureless desert. They would be able to see her easily. Sarah dropped to a sitting position behind a bush near the top of the crater, a couple of hundred feet high. It would not be difficult for them to see her if they looked in her direction. She hoped her green uniform would blend in with the ground, providing her with adequate camouflage. Whoever these people were, they made her feel vulnerable and desperately alone. Her portable radio was on the front seat of the forest service truck, but it would be impossible to get to the truck before the men arrived. In the back of her mind she wanted to believe they were just teenagers out raising a little hell, but the warning signals flashing in her mind told her it wasn't likely.

Sarah watched the truck slide around the last bend in the dirt road and enter the turnaround. She thought the driver was going to hit the forest truck, but at the last second it swerved to the left, covering it with dirt and dust. She could clearly hear their wild, crude laughter and instantly determined they were not harmless teenagers. Her stomach was knotted in fear. She scooted back, trying to shrink behind the bush. She didn't have to peer around the edge of the wild shrubbery; she could make out their images through the thin-reaching branches.

"I'm telling you guys, this is the truck I've seen that squaw driving," she heard one of the men say as he threw a beer bottle into the side panel of the forest truck.

The biggest of the four men, dark and dirty and his face covered with a short patchy black beard, opened the door on the driver's side. Paul looked inside the truck and then searched the slopes of the crater. "If she's the one I think she is, I want her bad. She's mine." Paul's voice sounded like a boot scraping over gravel.

Sarah was trembling with fright. She closed her eyes and prayed. "Oh Lord, I'm in trouble. Please bless me. Please deliver me from these men. I need thy help, dear Lord, and I need it quickly. Oh God, please protect me from these people. I am asking for thy protection..." Tears of fear filled her eyes as she heard one of the men tell the others he was going up the trail to the crater.

Ross stumbled as he ascended up the rough trail. He was intoxicated, and Sarah hoped he would not see her as he approached the top of the crater. The trail was about 15 yards from the bush where she was hiding. If he looked in her direction, he would see her immediately. She couldn't move around to the other side of the bush because the other three down below would see her.

While Ross made his way up the trail, Paul, Sam, and Joey continued to drink from their bottles. She could hear them profaning and describing what they were going to do to her. Sarah slowly reached down and picked up a piece of obsidian the size of a softball. She thought of her people having used the black glass rock for years to protect themselves and for hunting. For the first time she had a piece in hand for protection. She felt nausea in her stomach. While she maintained a vigil on the man climbing the trail in a drunken stupor, she decided she would fight until they killed her.

To her dismay two of the men started up the trail after telling the big ugly one they did not trust Ross—something about his being the youngest in the group and he would have to wait his turn. It was only a few moments before Ross would pass by her position.

Her heart thumped in pounding jolts inside her chest. She could hear the blood throbbing in her temples. Her neck pulsated as the flow of blood was restricted, trying to work its way through her jugular vein into her head.

Ross stopped for a breather not thirty feet away from Sarah. When he turned to look down the trail, he saw her hiding behind the bush. Ross gave a triumphant whoop and a holler when he had found his prey. He cupped his dirty hands around his grimy mouth and yelled down to his companions. "Hey, guess what? She's squattin' behind a bush. How about that?" Ross gave an obscene laugh; then darkness engulfed him. He never felt the sharp rock cut into the side of his head. There was no pain. Everything went black. He didn't know he was tumbling back down the side of the steep crater. His skin tore on the razor-sharp glass rocks. By the time his floppy frame came to a rest, he was bleeding from the many minor cuts over his entire body.

Sarah didn't see what had happened to the man she hit. She turned to run up the crater. She thought if she could get over the top and down the other side she could hide somewhere in one of the many cracks or holes in the terrain until they left. She was scared and knew the chances of finding just a place were slim, but at least she had to try.

Paul was waiting at the truck and could see the girl was going for the top of the ridge. If she made it over, there was no telling where she could hide on the other side. He opened the door to his truck and pulled out a 30-30 lever action Marlin rifle. He jacked a round into the chamber and leaned through the open window of his truck. He touched off a round to fire above the girl's head and it hit in front of her on the trail. He gave a short laugh when he saw the girl fall. At first he thought he had hit her, but she was up again and running.

Sam and Joey were right behind her and gaining. Paul slowed her down again with another shot, then gave a laugh of relief when he saw Joey grab the girl by the back of her shirt and pull her down. Sarah tried to break away when something slammed into her back and she went down to the ground.

Paul quickly cupped his hand around his hairy mouth. "Don't you guys mess her up. I got first grabs. Now get her down here!"

Paul put the rifle back behind the seat of the truck and shut the door. He picked up his beer and took a long pull, burping up the bubbles. He walked over to a bush to relieve the strain on his bladder. A fleeting smile crossed his face thinking of the pretty squaw.

By the time Cy and Skin finished their meal, the three men had established a friendship. Matthew Morgan was likeable enough and seemed knowledgeable on many different subjects. He was also a devoted family man. At one time he owned a lumber mill in northern California. Later, his weak heart made him change occupations. He had lived in Sacramento for many years until his wife convinced him to move to Bishop, where she was born. They built a home and real estate became his new business.

Cy decided he liked and trusted his new friend. "Matthew, why don't you give me a business card. Here's mine," Cy said, reaching inside his Levi jacket pocket. He took out a card with a police logo on it. "Someday I may be interested in buying some land to ranch or maybe for investment purposes."

"Investment in real estate is very wise," Matthew smiled

broadly, handing Cy his business card. "It's better than money in the bank. I'm serious when I say that. Land investments will make you far more money than four percent interest in the banks. Someday this land is going to shoot sky high. With the right land deal, a man could make a lot of money."

"No doubt, sir," Cy said, getting up. He dropped fifty cents on the table, and Skin matched the tip.

"Matthew, do you have any idea if there is anything for sale around Glass Mountain? Particularly on the north side?"

"Glass Mountain is mostly surrounded by BLM. The only portion that isn't is owned by an Indian who will never sell." Mr. Morgan thought a moment, then continued, "His name is Benjamin and he owns six sections. That's a lot of land. It takes up the north side of Glass Mountain and runs east."

"That is a lot of land. A section runs 640 acres—a square mile," Cy said. "Depending on the width of the parcels and the boundaries, the property could stretch a long ways. Do you think he would be interested in selling just one section?"

"Not on your life. That land is rich with springs and is great for grazing cattle. Benjamin is in financial straits because of his drinking, but he would never sell. In his day, he was quite the rancher. Now he is an alcoholic. Some think it was the Korean War that did it to him. The Indians in this area don't discuss their private lives with the white folks. They mostly keep to themselves."

"Too bad he wouldn't sell. I would like a piece of that land."

Mr. Morgan looked at the card Cy had handed him. It only had the Hollenbeck Division address and phone number printed on the front. He handed it back to Cy and asked him to write his home phone number. Cy scribbled his phone number on the back and returned it.

Matthew read the number under his breath then glanced at Cy. "Most cops don't give their home phones, do they?"

"That's right, Matthew. My giving you this number means I'm seriously thinking about land in this area. I want you to call me if a good deal comes along. I'll drive up here, and if it looks good and has an attractive price tag, maybe we can make a transaction. Okay?"

"I'll see what I can do for you, young man." Matthew Morgan grabbed Cy's hand and shook it with enthusiasm.

On the way back to camp, Cy and Skin decided they had

lost their enthusiasm for hunting. Their biggest problem was not to put a damper on their two friends back in camp. Tony lived to hunt and Jacob was a great outdoorsman. It would bother both men if half the team defaulted. Cy tried to think of a plan so he could have time to look around the country and get a feel for what land was available.

Skin drove the Jeep with Martha on his mind. He wanted to leave for home at the earliest opportunity. Hunting was the last thing he wanted now. Traveling east on 120 he talked about his new love and Cy absorbed his friend's sincere feelings. Before the road curved to the right heading toward Glass Mountain, Skin turned left on a dirt road and headed north.

"Where you going?" Cy asked, looking up the road.

"Those volcanoes fascinate me, bud. I want to take a closer look at them. Do you mind?"

"No, that's fine with me. I've been kind of curious about them myself. I don't relish seeing Tony right now. All he's going to talk about is where he wants us to go tomorrow so we can run the deer to him. He'll have it all figured out—where the deer are feeding, where they'll bed down tonight, and where they'll be tomorrow. He thinks we're so dumb when he gives out his little hunting assignments."

Skin drove almost a mile when he noticed a suspicious-looking scenario. He screwed up his eyes trying to focus on some people ahead of them at the end of the dirt road. It looked like the same yellow Chevy pickup that caused the excitement in Lee Vining. The Chevrolet was now parked at a turnaround next to a green U.S. Forest Service pickup.

Several hundred yards ahead Cy could see five people. One was backed up to the yellow pickup facing the other four. As they got closer he noticed the one person was a girl with exceptionally long dark hair who appeared to be shaking her head. When they were within a hundred yards, Cy recognized Sarah. The tall bearded man in front of her slapped her on the side of the head, knocking her to one knee. She quickly got back up.

"Step on it, Skin. The girl's in trouble," Cy choked on the words. He fumbled with the button on the glove box. When he got it open he looked inside for a revolver. There was none. He slammed it shut. "Skin, that's the girl. That's the one I've been looking for."

"She's in trouble all right. There's four of them. We

can't be nice and proper this time," Skin said, working on his plan of action.

"I want the big one that just hit her," Cy said, his anger rising to a height he had never known.

"You got it," Skin said, pulling the Jeep to a stop a few feet away from the people standing in a circle. "Follow my lead."

"Make your move fast. I'm taking that tub of guts down," Cy growled, jumping out of the vehicle before it stopped.

Skin pushed his door open and gave his biggest smile. The four men did not take kindly to being interrupted.

A hard looker with a cut on his cheek turned around facing Skin. "What are you fellas doing out here?" Ross wiped the blood running freely down the side of his face where Sarah had hit him with the glass rock.

"Not much. We're just having a beer and looking the country over." Skin could see Cy walk over to the big one on his right. The girl looked at Cy, recognizing him from their earlier encounter at the general store. She didn't speak and Cy could see the terror in her eyes—those beautiful eyes.

"That's a fine looking ranger you guys got there," Skin said. Ross relaxed slightly. He smiled, directing his eyes back to the girl. "She's..."

Skin struck the grungy man in the adam's apple with one blow, putting him out of action. Ross fell to the ground, unable to pull air through his pipes. He was on his knees until he fell onto his back in the dust.

The second man approached Skin. Before he could swing, Skin hit him across the teeth with his .38 snub-nosed revolver. One tooth landed on the ground, another stuck to his cheek, and a third caught in the man's throat. He went to all fours gasping for air and choking violently.

Cy walked up to the big one called Paul. He took off his straw hat and tossed it on the hood of the yellow pickup. "Shouldn't hit a lady, mister." Cy hit the man so fast he didn't have time to counter it. Cy struck him with combinations and then gave him a hard kick to his right kneecap. When the man bent over grabbing his knee, Cy kicked him square between the eyes with the toe of his cowboy boot, breaking his nose. The man fell backward, doubling over in excruciating pain.

Cy glanced at Skin who was off to his right. The fourth man had taken off through the sagebrush and disappeared down a ravine. Cy looked to where Sarah had been standing. She was gone. He peered over the Chevy to see her closing the door on the forest truck.

"Watch them, Skin," Cy warned. He ran around the pickup to Sarah.

"Ma'am, are you okay? Did they hurt you?" Cy's voice was so full of emotion he had trouble sucking in breath.

Kicked, slapped, and abused, this Indian girl was still the most beautiful woman he had ever seen. He felt a burning within himself. He knew it was not the time or place to make introductions. He pulled himself together and put his emotions on hold. Cy opened her door and compassionately put his arm around her shoulder. "They aren't going to hurt you," he said in a low, tender voice.

Cy could feel the girl's shoulders trembling involuntarily from sheer fear under his gentle touch. He pulled her over to him and put his cheek softly to her forehead. Promptly she began to cry. He would never forget that most wonderful and inexplicable surge of emotion. It was something he had never experienced, the nervous warmth of someone under his protection. The Indian girl's touch stunned his senses. With her forehead resting on his cheek, he could feel a restriction across his chest.

After a long moment, she pulled away from him, keeping her eyes steadily downward. She refused to allow his eyes to look into hers. She finally pushed herself back. Cy gave her freedom to move away from him.

She shut the truck door. Cy stared at her ever so lovely face. He saw tears forming in her eyes spilling over onto bronze cheeks. He thought his heart was going to stop when she reached out and lightly touched the back of his hand with her index finger. That was all she did. She touched his skin with one finger saying nothing, her eyes never meeting his. After a moment she slowly withdrew her finger and started up the truck.

Cy walked alongside of the truck as she backed up. He quickly glanced at his partner. Skin was back to doing police work. He had all three men lined up face down on the ground.

"I'm sorry for what happened here." Cy spoke easily, placing his hand on the base of the window frame. "I know this isn't a good time now, but someday I would like to talk with you." He concentrated on her face, wondering what her thoughts might be. Nothing he said seemed to register with her. "Do you understand me? Do you speak English?"

Cy thought he was going to pass out when the girl deliberately turned her head and looked directly into his eyes. The world could have ended and he would not have been aware of the changes around him. It was her long eyelashes and eyebrows that bewildered him. She was not wearing any eye makeup, yet her eyes were as beautiful as if she had been made up by an artist. She had the most beautiful eyes he had ever seen.

There was a solemn expression in her unblemished face and when she spoke her voice was like velvet. "Aiyak im nupiyum," she whispered. Then his ears came to life when she spoke in English. "My heart thanks." Tears slid from her eyes when she blinked. She said nothing more. She turned the truck around and drove away.

Cy was so taken aback he could only watch the girl drive off. He was paralyzed from his hips down. Everything else in his body was very much alive.

He was surprised and relieved when he saw a sheriff's unit appearing down the road and stopping Sarah about a quarter of a mile away. At first Cy thought the deputy would have Sarah come back to make a statement. He was relieved after a few moments when she continued on and the deputy proceeded to their position.

Cy spun around and quickly walked over to Paul who was still in the prone position.

"If you ever touch that girl again or try to get back at her, I'll castrate you on the spot." Cy leaned over, "Do you hear me?"

There was no response from the grungy man. Cy kicked him in the side and when the man doubled up, Cy kicked him again in the testicles from the back side. "I asked you a question, mister. You better answer me," he yelled. He was so furious he could have killed the man on the spot.

"Yes! Yes...I need a doctor," the man screamed in gasping pain. His voice gurgled and saliva spilled from his mouth and ran down his cheek to his ear.

Skin leaned over to Cy grinning ear to ear. "It ain't like the movies, is it, partner? Fights don't last that long and when you get kicked in the cajones, you're down for the count."

The sheriff's car pulled up and the Indian deputy came over to Skin, who was standing with his arms folded, puffing on his pipe.

Skin peered over at the man as he approached him. "Afternoon, Sheriff. We're surprised but surely welcome your company."

Cy walked over to the deputy and handed him a business card. "We are police officers and made a citizen's arrest. I guess the young lady advised you what happened."

Ray's smile briefly tightened when he read the words "Los Angeles Police Department." He may hate people of Los Angeles, but this situation was different. He did feel grateful the two officers saved his future bride from being violated.

Cy and Skin briefed the deputy on what they observed and the bits and pieces of some of the force which was required to make the felony arrests. They provided the deputy with an on-the-spot statement and signed their names and dated the document. While this was occurring, Deputy Tom placed plastic cuffs on the three prisoners and then moved them to his patrol unit. When the deputy finished his securing task, he gave the two police officers a smile after he more closely observed the prisoner's injuries.

"I'm sure you can get the information you need on the other suspect from these three," Cy said, nodding his head to the prisoners caged in the rear seat of the sheriff's unit.

The deputy went over to Skin and Cy and shook both their hands vigorously. "I appreciate you men for what you did here. I plan on sending a letter of appreciation to your chief."

"The pleasure was all ours," Skin smiled, rubbing his knuckles, feeling appreciative he hadn't killed the first subject with the chop to the throat.

Cy viewed the deputy intently. He inquired, "Deputy Tom, I noticed you talking to the victim on the way in here. Does she speak very much English?"

"Why do you ask that?" the deputy replied suspiciously.

"Well, we didn't get to talk with her. When I tried to calm her down, she said something in Paiute and spoke only a couple of words in English."

"Sarah is a very quiet person. She is especially shy around strangers." Deputy Tom didn't like the look in the stranger's eyes when he said Sarah's name.

"Gentlemen, I have to go." The deputy walked over to his patrol unit. He looked back at Cy and Skin. "Thank you again."

The deputy got into his vehicle and quickly stepped on the

accelerator when he saw Cy approaching his side of the car. He did not want to answer unnecessary questions about Sarah.

"Skin?" Cy said, standing in the dust watching the deputy pull away.

"What?"

"I'm having a hard time finding out anything about Sarah."

"I know, I know," Skin sighed. "Maybe you ought to let it go."

"I can't."

"Why not?"

"Because for the first time in my life, I'm in love." Cy smiled. "There, I said it and it's true."

"You're nuts. She hasn't even spoken to you," Skin said, rubbing his bruised knuckles.

"How can you be in love with someone you don't even know?"

"She said a couple of words. You should have heard her voice." Cy shook his head, looking at the dirt road where Sarah disappeared. "I can't explain it. I'm taken by her. Right now I love the way she looks. Now I have to fall in love with what's inside her."

Sarah stepped out of the shower and took her time drying off with a large soft towel. She slipped on a bathrobe, went over to the radio, and tuned in to a western station with the volume on low. Satisfied with the music, she walked over to a large overstuffed chair, sat down, and drew her knees up to her chin. She looked out her living room window for a long time.

Glass Mountain appeared powerful in its lonely beauty. There were no other mountains around it. It stood alone in its splendor. Her uncle was somewhere over there, hopefully taking care of his cattle. She wished she had a father and mother whom she was close to. Loneliness pained her soul. Tears formed in her eyes and her vision blurred. Today she had prayed a special prayer and it was answered by an angel. The strange white man was so charming, it took her breath away every time she was near him. She could barely allow her eyes to set on his or provoke her vocals cords to express her thoughts. She had never experienced those types of emotions.

She was angry with herself for not speaking to him. There was definitely something different about this white man. This one seemed to have sincere feelings. His aura was captivating. His brown eyes and wavy brown hair made him so handsome and manly. His straight teeth flashed without effort and his smile was like the morning sun. She even liked his unshaven face because it gave him a rugged look.

The beautiful stranger had dropped into her life twice in one day. How could she be so fortunate? She felt a kind and wonderful swelling in her chest. It turned to pain akin to homesickness, wondering if her eyes would ever see him again.

Chapter 15
Questions of the Heart

Cy sat in his patrol car in the division parking lot drinking a Coke. He sipped on the cold drink, feeling the coolness slide down his throat. He felt at a loss, pondering over the many concerns in his life and trying to determine the direction of his future.

It had been three weeks since the deer hunt. Opening morning Tony had bagged a four point and Jacob a three point. Cy and Skin did not hunt. The four broke camp the next morning and returned to Los Angeles.

Loneliness had been a constant companion to Cy from the time Tony drove across the Mono County line heading south on Highway 395 to Los Angeles. Before they left he attempted to see Sarah at the forest station. Again the employees refused to give him her full name but did advise him she had taken a medical leave and had gone to Utah to stay with her second family for awhile. Cy wondered what a second family was.

Cy was often plagued by guilt because he had released his feelings for Mary Ann to only memories of the heart. She was gone and he knew he needed to let go of the past. It was strange how he felt about his situation. He loved Mary Ann, even wanted to marry her when the time was right, but time was not important when she was alive. That was the difference. Time seemed to be everything now. He felt a burning desire to know Sarah and for her to know him. His short acquaintance with her had left him with so little knowledge of her; however, it was enough to burn in his mind, leaving him little relief. Was it her beauty? Could a man experience an infatuation for a woman because she was the most beautiful woman he had seen? Was that being in love? Or was it wishful thoughts of the heart? Or was it a fantasy he desired to materialize into reality? Why did Sarah constantly consume his thoughts? Why didn't he think more of Mary Ann? Maybe time does heal. The feelings he was experiencing with Sarah were entirely different. The passion he felt for this girl, a person who would not even speak to him, bounced around in his head like a child's ball with a toy bell inside. It never stopped ringing, and he couldn't control it nor did he desire to silence it.

There was rarely a moment Cy didn't let his reflections of her envelop his mind. He was often angry at himself for wasting his time on something that would never materialize. It was obvious Sarah had no desire to know him. Perhaps she resented white people and held them responsible for taking her family's land and inhibiting the growth of her own culture.

Cy had an idea. After shift he would stop at the city library and check out a few books on the Paiute Indians and study their civilization. The prospect of having something to occupy his time excited him, and his spirits lifted, relishing his new plan. If he could educate himself on Sarah's customs and ancestral heritage, perhaps it would open a door and allow him to explore her heart and mind. Perhaps she would come to know he was sincere and it would encourage her to talk with him.

Cy took another drink. He couldn't determine if the shivers were from the drink or his new plan. A smile tugged at the corners of his mouth. Why wait until after shift? That would be a waste of time. He would get the literature now and take it home to study later. Cy started up his patrol unit, moved out onto Soto at 1st Street, and headed straight for the library.

Sarah was seated on the floor with her head on Mary Wilson's lap. Mary sat on a sofa that faced the bay window that overlooked Utah Valley. She combed her fingers through Sarah's hair and smiled down at her, enjoying the special time with the daughter she never had. It was an important moment for Mary. She loved Sarah and was happy she came to her, especially with such pressing problems of the heart.

"Sometimes, Sarah, we feel so inadequate in not knowing the future." Mary felt she should only provide Sarah with ideas—Sarah would have to find her own answers.

"When I first met Bill, I didn't really know if our relationship would grow and mature into devoted love and companionship. Oh sure, I was very attracted to him, but I also knew that people changed after settling into a long-term relationship. I had to ask myself, "Will Bill love me forty or fifty years from now?" Then I would wonder if I would love him. I wondered if he would be a hard worker and provide for me and our children. I wondered how many children he would want.

How many did I want? Would we agree on discipline plans and standards while raising a family? You know what the answers were, Sarah?" Mary asked softly.

"There were no answers, were there?" Sarah said, not lifting her head from Mary's lap.

"There were no answers but there was something very important I could do in finding those answers. I prayed to my Heavenly Father. I prayed for guidance and the wisdom to make wise and intelligent decisions—decisions that would guide me forward and not inhibit an appropriate and wonderful love. I had a strong desire to answer my heart and enjoy a wild and joyous emotion that I knew only Bill could give me.

"The thing that has amazed me so much is...I love that man more every day. I have never been sorry that I married him, and I marvel at how much more I love him this moment than I did yesterday."

Sarah felt Mary's tears on her shoulder. The sensitivity of the moment and the gravity of its significance forced a film of moisture over her eyes. "I can't stop my attraction to this man, and I have desperately tried. I always assumed I would marry a member of my tribe. But I have not felt the passion of love and commitment for anyone. My uncle and all my tribal family assumed I would marry Raymond Tom. No one ever spoke of love.

"Mother Mary, so many times I feel ashamed the way I have hidden my desire for affection. School and work took my time. I never gave time for myself and what is deep within my heart." Sarah could not see through her tears. "My heart has such sorrow. I have never even kissed a boy."

Mary took Sarah's face in her hands and smiled through the shiny wet trails on her own cheeks. "Oh my precious child, such joy is before you. Such happiness is yet to come into your life."

Mary pulled Sarah to her breast and rocked her closely. While in Mary's embrace Sarah decided she was going to pray earnestly for guidance and carefully follow her heart. Perhaps she was an apple Indian, but she had to make her own happiness and not accept what was expected of her by her people. God loved everyone. Color and culture should not be reasons to ignore the reality of one's feelings. She would no longer hold it against the stranger for being white.

❧

Tony Valin strolled into the station. Jackie was working the counter and gave the sexy-looking cop her best crooked-tooth smile. "Hi, Tony," she beamed. "How are you doing today?"

Tony looked at Jackie thinking here was a woman who didn't know what to wear, where to wear it, and who to wear it with. She wore too much makeup and had bad breath. "Hi, toots." He gave her a quick smile and briskly walked past the front counter as if suddenly aware he was late for an important appointment. There were nasty rumors flowing through the division about her, and there was no way he would align himself with her by appearing to be her friend, especially after work hours.

Down the hall Tony looked in the lieutenant's office. Jacob was behind his desk busy at work. "Hi, bro."

"Oh, hello, Tony. I was wondering if you were going to get around to briefing me on the Fats stabbing. Chuck Fulton said there was blood up the walls on this one."

"It was a bad one," Tony said, leaning against the door-jamb. "Old Fats put up a good fight. You can get lots of blood from 350 pounds. On the reports we listed him as Charlie Moores, an inactive member of the Hell's Angels."

"I've heard he was the Hell's Angels' national president's executioner for a number of years. It's probably true."

"That's the story on him. A member never really gets out of the club. He can become inactive, but once in, he's always in. I think Fats became a middleman and was involved in running drugs. The Angels must have found out that Fats was ripping them off. A snitch friend of Fats' says two lieutenants from the Hell's Angels, who were hit men, came to his house looking for Fats. He told them Fats was next door, where he was renting a safe house. He wasn't about to lie to these guys, because they would have cut his heart out on the spot. He said the two men knew Fats was a bad act, knowing he used to be an eliminator in his day. The snitch surmised Fats knew they were coming for him. He had been on the inside long enough and was too experienced not to know what was going to happen. I guess it was something like a death wish," Tony said, leaning against the wall and chewing on a toothpick. "The snitch also says he won't testify and the information he was giving me was off the record; otherwise he wouldn't be flapping his jaws."

"Okay, so what did he see?"

"The snitch sneaked over to Fats' house and watched most of what happened through the side window. He said Fats stood his ground like a big giant with his back to the wall grinning at the two men. It probably made them nervous and that's what Fats wanted. The snitch heard him say, "I guess you got to do what you got to do." When it got too gruesome he fled the neighborhood until we routed him out of his girlfriend's pad. To make a long story short, Fats had over a hundred and fifty stab wounds all over his body. I mean everywhere," Tony said, grimacing. "It must have been horrific. It had started in the kitchen, moved into the living room and bedroom, and ended up in the bathroom. Blood was on the ceilings, walls, couches, floors, on the bed, chairs, and especially all over the bathroom. It was tight quarters in there. I don't think a mosquito could have survived it." Tony swallowed hard thinking about the crime scene.

"Good hell, so go on. Don't leave me hanging here," Jacob said, frowning.

"It appeared Fats had hidden a .25 caliber pistol on his person. Empty rounds were on the floor in different rooms. Different blood types were found throughout the house. The wounded person—I should say persons—weren't found. I doubt we will ever find out who they were. These boys are probably out of Frisco and they'll never show up here again."

"I always knew Fats wouldn't go easy," Jacob said, shaking his head. "Whoever those boys were must be licking their wounds wondering if they'll ever recover."

"You got that right. Everything, I mean everything, in the house was broken. It was not a fun episode. Everyone got injured on this hit."

"Who was the snitch?"

"Who do you think? Skin gave me the information."

"You've got to be kidding me. Marty Dominguez?" Jacob had heard rumors of Skin's and Marty's relationship but hadn't given it much credence. "He's a dead man. How can one man be so stupid as to snitch on the very gang he wants to join?"

"It takes all kinds, boss," Tony said smiling. "Changing the subject, what's this I hear about Cy? Is it true? Is he still pining over that Injun gal in Mono? I haven't talked to him for awhile."

Jacob wasn't quite sure how to respond. He respected Cy's feelings and did not want to belittle his friend's feelings for the girl. Tony had a knack of irritating people quickly and sometimes not on purpose. It was one of those times Jacob became immediately irritated with his friend.

"He's in a black hole over her," Jacob said, growing more serious. "To be honest, I'm glad he's thinking about someone, but I suggest you don't tease him about it. He may just knock your head off if you do."

"Hey, I wouldn't get Cy mad at me. He's not one to mess with when it comes to his emotions. Besides, I care for the guy. I've really been concerned about him. I'm just glad he's got his mind on something besides his horses."

"Well, the way he talks about her, she must be something. I asked Skin if she was as nice as Cy portrayed her, and he said there were no words in his vocabulary to describe her. Sounds to me like she's a rare one."

"Too bad she lives so far away. It may make the heart grow fonder, but it doesn't do much to help them get to know one another," Tony said.

"I think he plans on going to see her in a couple of weeks. He's been studying her language and customs and even sent her a couple of letters. It makes me happy to see him clawing his way back to the land of the living."

Footsteps coming down the hall caused Tony to lean his head out the door and look toward the front desk. Jackie was leading an Indian girl toward the lieutenant's office. He gasped, snapping his head around to Jacob. His eyes were wide and couldn't hold the excitement in his voice. "Jake, it's her! It's the Indian girl. She's coming down the hall. She's the most beautiful creature on the earth and she's headed our way."

"Knock it off, Tony. Don't think you are going to pull one on me," Jacob threw his head back laughing. When the girl with her long black hair stood at his door, he immediately went mute, shocked at the stunning girl standing behind Tony. Jackie had already turned around and headed back to the front desk. She didn't bother with introductions. She was disgusted with Tony and gave him the cold shoulder.

"Sarah...you must be Sarah," Jacob said embarrassed.

"Yes, sir, I am," Sarah said quietly. "You are Mr. Golden's supervisor?"

"Yes, ma'am, I am. Please come in," Jacob stood up and

pointed to a chair in front of his desk. "This is Tony Valin. He works in narcotics and C.A.P.S. or crimes against persons. He also is a friend of Cy."

"How do you do, Mr. Valin?"

Tony was so taken by Sarah he was numb. It seemed his heart was going to burst. "The pleasure is mine." He turned to the lieutenant. "I best be going."

As soon as he left the office, he stopped, turned around, and stuck his head back in the office. "Sarah, I'm really pleased to meet you." Tony forced himself to back out of the doorway and disappeared down the hallway before he made a fool of himself. He decided if things didn't work out between Cy and the girl, he was going to kill his wife and children, and that evening he would marry Sarah. He ran down the hall, turned right, jumped up the stairs, and ran to the locker room looking for Cy. A bad stench leaked from the men's room as Tony ran into Flush sneaking out of the rest room. Tony slammed into Flush, knocking him into the wall and both fell to the floor.

"Flush, you pig. You did it again and you promised not to use our toilets. I'm telling on you."

"Gees man, I couldn't hold it. Come on, man, don't tell the guys. They'll be pissed at me."

Tony held his hand over his nose. "You stinking dog. Everyone within a block will know you took a dump in there."

"Hey man, I'll have a trustee spray the place down. It'll be okay."

"You didn't flush, did you, Flush?"

"Keep your shorts on, I'm getting a trustee. He owes me one. What's your hurry anyway?" Flush said, picking himself up.

"I'm looking for Cy. Have you seen him?"

"Yeah, he and Skin are in the break room. Why? What's the big rush?"

"She's here, that's what."

"Who's she?"

"It's her, you dummy," Tony gasped anxiously. He turned and headed back downstairs toward the break room.

"Who's 'her'?"

"It's Cy's Indian maiden, you smelly butthole, that's who." Tony laughed, hopskipping away.

❧

The lieutenant was completely taken by Sarah. This soft-spoken girl was warm and humble, and he was convinced she was completely unaware of the effect she had on men. He liked her all the more for it. She was a treasure and he felt happiness for his best friend.

Of course, he was not sure why she was here, but that didn't matter. He quickly planned it out; the two young people were doomed to fall in love. Cy was convinced Sarah would have nothing to do with him. Now, suddenly, she was here in the flesh. He knew Cy was going to die when he first set eyes on her, and he wanted to watch Cy go down.

"Miss, I am most surprised to see you here," Jacob said.

"My name is Sarah. Sarah Gray. Please call me Sarah," she said softly.

"Sarah, Cy wasn't really sure if you spoke very much English."

"I'm sorry for that. I usually don't talk very much with white men."

"Well, I'm glad that rules me out." Jacob was thankful he was black. "We should be able to have a long conversation then," Jacob grinned.

Sarah flashed him a smile that almost made him gasp. Her ruby lips spread apart revealing straight white teeth. "I didn't mean that the way it sounded. I meant any stranger. Some men have made inappropriate remarks or advances to me, so I have built a natural defense for myself. By not speaking to men I do not personally know, I can usually forestall many problems."

"That is very wise, Sarah, very wise," Jacob said, studying the girl. He noticed Sarah was nervous and was trying desperately not to show it. "Are you anxious because you're in the big city or is it Cy?"

"Both. The city frightens me. Cy has my heart in the clouds."

"He's what?"

Sarah glanced at him innocently then looked at the ground. She should be ashamed for expressing her feelings so bluntly, but she liked Jacob and had dropped her guard quite unexpectedly. She knew she was going to be good friends with him someday, or at least hoped she would. "He has touched me," Sarah said, looking downward.

"He's what? I'll break his neck. I'll..." Jacob jumped up pounding his clenched fist angrily on his desk.

"No, no, no. I mean he has touched my heart."

Jacob was so moved, he could not speak. He could only stare at Sarah.

Cy took a drink of Coke from the cold aluminum can. He swallowed hard, feeling the fizzy sting of carbonation going down his throat. Skin was drinking coffee. "I have some good news to tell you, Skin."

"Oh, what's that?" Skin asked, taking another sip.

"Do you remember the real estate man we met at the Mono Cafe in Lee Vining during the deer hunt?"

"Of course I remember. You think I'm brain dead?" Skin looked disgusted.

"The man's name was Matthew Morgan. Anyway, he told me that two sections of land on the northeast side of Glass Mountain were going up for sale by the state. It seems the landowner hasn't paid his taxes for a number of years, and the guy wouldn't respond to the inquiries sent by the authorities concerning the deficit. So after numerous warnings, a public notice was made that a particular parcel of land was going to be for sale at an auction on a sealed-bid basis. Do you know what that means?"

"Sure. A person submits an undisclosed amount of money he is willing to pay, and at a particular time in a public setting the bids are opened. The highest bidder gets the property."

"That's about it," Cy said, smiling. "Well, I just bought two full sections of land, Skin."

"Whoa, whoa, here. What do you mean two sections of land? That sounds like an awful lot of ground."

"One section of land is 640 acres or one square mile. So I now own 1,280 acres of Glass Mountain on the northeast side," Cy said happily.

"No way. That's impossible," Skin said, breaking into a broad smile. He leaned forward resting his elbows on the table. "You mean where we deer hunt now belongs to us?"

"No, I mean it belongs to me."

"Well, yeah. I meant that," Skin said, letting his grin fade. "But it's like us owning it, isn't it, old buddy? We are best of friends. Right?"

"Of course," Cy said laughing.

"How much did it cost you?"

"I bid $150,000. I don't know what the nearest bid was or if I overpaid. I may have gotten it cheaper but didn't want to take a chance on losing it."

"That's a lot of money, Cy."

"Well, I've made some good investments with the ranch and insurance money," Cy said a little more solemnly. "Anyway, now we can build a cabin for real comfort on the mountain and enjoy hunting and the whole ball of wax. Right?"

"Right, my good buddy. I'm really good at carpentry. We can build it together. Jacob's pretty handy with tools, too. This is great." Skin was squirming around like a kid.

"I plan to order a log cabin kit out of Rexburg, Idaho. They have some wonderful two- and three-bedroom plans with dormers and balconies. Every log is categorized and numbered. All you have to do is have a level footing and foundation, according to the building plans, and put the logs in the proper place."

"That's going to cost a lot of money. We can help with the cost or at least the labor," Skin said with a sheepish grin.

"Money is no problem and you know it. Anyway, this is going to be a great escape from L.A. We can make it our private retreat and..." Cy stopped talking and his mouth dropped when the door opened and Sarah appeared.

She stood there not saying a word. She didn't smile. She looked at Cy with those beautiful black eyes, her hair flowing to her waist. She wore a light-blue, long-sleeved shirt and tight-fitting blue skirt, cut above her dark knees.

Cy was speechless. He jumped to his feet, his head swimming. Skin got up and moved to the pop machine for a more panoramic view of this entertaining situation.

Sarah continued to stare at Cy and finally smiled softly. "Maik," (hello). Sarah's soft voice floated across the room, filling Cy's ears.

His brain was overworking.

"Maik, Sarah. Ahkk-ahd-I-wahnee," (How are you) Cy said awkwardly.

"I-yahn," (I'm fine) Sarah smiled warmly.

Skin was so surprised he was speechless. He knew Cy was studying Paiute customs but not to this extent. Hearing his sergeant utter foreign phrases was a shock to him. "I'm out of here."

He turned to Sarah, took her hand, and gave her a warm smile. He mouthed his words carefully and spoke very slowly, knowing she probably didn't understand him. "I...must... be...going. I go," Skin said, pointing to himself and then to the doorway. It was a masterful attempt at sign language.

Sarah smiled back and raised her hand in a peace sign, feeling an urge to giggle but holding back. Skin was too cute in his efforts to communicate with her.

Skin looked around at Cy. "I'll be down the hall in Jacob's office if you need me. Don't worry, pard, everything will be okay. A-okay." He turned to Sarah and held up his hand showing her his palm, smiling. "I go. You stay," Skin said, pointing to a chair at the table.

"Yes, I stay," Sarah said quietly.

"Yes, very...good. You...stay...here," Skin said politely and humbly backed out of the room, bowing as he exited.

"So...long...Mr. Skin. You...have...a...good...day...now." Sarah locked eyes with Skin and he thought he was going to pass out. When it dawned on him that he was making a fool of himself, he spun around and ran into Jacob.

Jacob had positioned himself with his back to the wall, biting the knuckle of his index finger to keep from laughing out loud. When Skin ran into him, Jacob had to run down the hall and turn the corner or lose control within hearing distance of Cy and Sarah. He stepped into the utility closet and screamed. Skin was right behind him.

Jacob was mimicking Skin's voice. "I go...you stay," he laughed hysterically.

Cy had wondered during the deer hunt if Sarah had been hired on with the Forest Service on a government program that did not require Native Americans to speak fluent English. Now he knew she did speak English and she was here. He was anxious, wondering what was going to happen next. Her showing up at his office was totally unexpected. He was both elated and worried at the same time.

"May I sit, please?" Sarah asked, looking down at the table and avoiding Cy's eyes.

"Oh please, yes," he said. He came around the table and pulled a chair out for her. "My manners are a sorry mess right now." He got a whiff of her fragrance and nearly fainted.

He moved to the other end of the table and immediately

regretted his shortsightedness. She was too far away from him; however, he didn't want to be obvious by readjusting his position.

Sarah looked down at the table gathering her thoughts. She had worried about this moment. Now she was wondering if she had the strength to continue. She knew Cy was surprised and pleased to see her. She realized at that moment being in his presence made her feel safe from the perils of the big city.

"Mr. Golden, I wanted to thank you personally for saving me at the Panum Craters. My life would have been ruined and possibly worse if you had not intervened. From my heart I thank you." Sarah lifted her gaze and met Cy's eyes.

"Cy," he stammered. "Please, my name is Cy."

She continued, "Your kind letter touched me. I felt a tremendous need to personally express my gratitude to you. A letter would have seemed unappreciative for what I really feel."

"Sarah, you don't have to thank me. Skin and I just happened to be in the right place at the right time. That's what we do. I'm just glad we could help you."

"It would have ruined me, Cy. You were there for me." Sarah hesitated for a long moment and Cy was at a loss for words. "At the time, I was distraught. I couldn't thank you that day. When I think how rude I was to you at the General Store, my guilt has weighed heavy and I feel remorse."

"Oh, Sarah," Cy started to reach for her arm but thought better of it. He wanted to touch her skin.

"Cy, please forgive me for my impolite manner. It was not me. I was so grateful to you. The trauma of what I experienced at the hands of those men—I know they would have killed me. There was no way they could leave a witness to whatever they had planned. Many white people are prejudiced against Indians. Some think we do not feel pain and that our feelings are of little importance. In rural areas, many people feel the laws of the land do not apply as they do in the city and in other tightly controlled government areas. All types of crimes occur in the open lands because some people think they won't get caught. If you're not caught breaking the law, then you have done nothing wrong."

"It's the same everywhere," Cy said. "People who normally would not commit a crime in the city would do it if they thought they could get away it. Whether it's for financial gain or satisfying a personal need, people would always be doing something wrong if there were not laws and other people to stop them."

"Anyway, I wanted to thank you for your kindness." Sarah got up and Cy gazed at her. She was perfectly endowed with a figure slight but well rounded where it counted. Sarah held out her hand.

Cy stood up and reached for her fingers. When he felt her hand slip into his, he grasped firmly, feeling the warmth of her grip. It surprised him when she didn't immediately release her hand. "Sarah, I can't let you go this quickly. You've made a long trip here, and I want to know you better. If I can get the time off, will you have dinner with me? I'll get you a room at a motel in Pasadena. I'm off tomorrow."

Cy couldn't let go of her hand, no matter how hard he tried. His hand was paralyzed. "Please, Sarah, don't leave me yet. I need to know who you are and why I think of you constantly. I'm sorry for being so blunt, but you've been on my mind ever since the deer hunt."

"What are you thinking of?" Sarah asked.

"Hold it. Hold it right there," Jacob said, busting into the room. "Miss Sarah, you are staying with my family. There you will be honorably and properly chaperoned. Isn't that right, Sergeant Golden?"

Jacob didn't wait for a response. He pointed his finger at Cy. "Sergeant, you are to take the rest of the day off and take this lovely woman to dinner and deposit her at my home tonight. No ands, ifs, or buts about it." Jacob was very pleased with himself for solidifying this new meeting.

"Have you been standing outside the door all this time?" Cy accused Jacob, wondering if he had been eavesdropping.

"Are you questioning the actions of your lieutenant, Sergeant?"

"No sir."

"Very well then," Jacob said happily as he approached Sarah. "Will those arrangements fit in with your agenda while in our fair city, Sarah?"

"Yes sir, they will. I do accept your generous offer if Cy has no objections."

Cy stood with his mouth open in disbelief.

"That's it then. Off with you both. See you later. Cy, don't keep her out too late. I have a responsibility here."

"Yessir!"

Chapter 16
A Trip into the Past

Sarah followed Cy to his apartment in her jeep. After he changed clothes she followed him to Jacob's home in Glendora. When Cy was ready to leave, he had a difficult time dragging Sarah away from Lila, who wanted to keep talking with her. The children were on Sarah's heels following her every move.

He could see Lila and Sarah becoming fast friends. Lila and the children immediately liked Sarah. At first Elvira wasn't friendly, showing signs of jealousy, but after a few minutes when Sarah directed her conversation to Elvira, the two disappeared into Elvira's bedroom. When Sarah came out, she was holding a little black doll in one hand and Elvira with the other.

Cy was anxious to be alone with Sarah. Lila hugged Cy on the front porch as they were leaving, and whispered in his ear. "You better hang on to this one. Can't do no better."

Cy was afraid Sarah overheard her, but she did not give any sign if she did. She was bending over and hugging Elvira goodbye. Cy glanced at Sarah and slowly started down the steps.

Lila took Sarah by the hand and then pulled her into her arms. "You are a real sweetheart, honey. I love you already. I have to tell you Cy is worth it no matter what. He is worth it."

"I'm not sure what you mean," Sarah said softly.

"You will, honey. You will," Lila said, leading Sarah to the edge of the steps. "Now you two darlings go have some fun."

Without hesitating, Sarah reached up and kissed Lila on the cheek, turned around and quickly walked to Cy, who was waiting with the truck door open. Lila touched her cheek where Sarah had kissed her and whispered under her breath. "You perfect little angel."

Cy had one of the most delightful afternoons he had ever experienced. He first took Sarah to Azusa and showed her his two horses and introduced Sarah to Guy. Guy was speechless, which was not normal, but it pleased Cy immensely. He was also happy when Sarah displayed her knowledge of horses and her easiness around them. She told Cy her Uncle Benjamin kept her horse on his ranch and she rode it when time permitted.

Cy had to drag her away from the stables. The couple drove

to Newport where they had dinner on the harbor overlooking the boats coming and going from their docks. The water was like blue glass, providing easy travel for the boats leaving the bay and heading on out to the ocean. The weather was perfect, about 70 degrees, and the sky was dark blue and clear. Cy thought it was romantic sitting by the large bay window eating a good meal with the loveliest woman he'd ever known.

Sarah ate quietly, listening to Cy. She enjoyed his stories and comments. He spoke of his closest friends, especially Jacob, Skin, and Tony. He told her about his police work, and she showed an interest in his activities, which encouraged him to provide more detail about his work. She was surprised how little of the world she knew outside her homeland. It amazed her that life could be so different just a few hundred miles away in the big city.

After a long conversation, Sarah took a sip of water, put her glass down, and looked intently at Cy. "What do you know of my heritage? The letters you sent to the ranger station reached me even though you only addressed them 'Sarah.' I was touched by your sincerity in studying my culture. It made me wonder who you really are. Why do you go to so much trouble to communicate with me? I have asked myself so many times, why was this man and his friend there, when I needed him most?"

While Cy answered her questions and spoke about his learning of her culture, she studied the man sitting across the dining table from her. She wondered why he was not married or attached to someone. As she attentively listened to him, the more she found depth in her interpretation of his eyes. She surmised she was looking into his soul and found warmth and honesty. She felt herself almost too enthusiastic with his attention and glanced away, pretending to study the moving seacraft.

She was surprised when Cy revealed his knowledge of the Paiute culture. He had made an earnest attempt to read books by scholars who had studied her heritage. After he had finished telling her what he knew about her history, Sarah remained quiet looking out the window. He studied her profile and was burning inside.

After a pause in their conversation, Sarah spoke quietly in her shy manner. "Cy, I did not answer your letters because I couldn't express my thoughts and feelings on paper," she said, looking out the window afraid to look back into his eyes. Her whole body was pulsating. It worried her that Cy would detect her nervousness. She wondered if he noticed she was on the verge of going limp. She studied his expression in the reflection of the window.

Cy remained quiet, not realizing she was watching him. He thought she was enjoying the view of the boats in the harbor as she collected her thoughts. When Sarah turned and looked intently into Cy's eyes, he felt himself temporarily robbed of his senses. He became lightheaded and he feared his vision would go hazy. He felt engulfed by her spirit. At that moment he knew there was no other woman for him. How delicate would be the path into her heart?

"Are your ears with me?" Sarah asked, noticing Cy was somewhere deep in thought.

"Yes, they are," Cy said, shaking the cobwebs. "I mean of course I am. You have my complete and undivided attention." Cy said, mesmerized by her presence. "It means much more to have you come here in person, Sarah."

Sarah diverted her eyes to survey the harbor—anything but Cy's face. She felt her face flush and was embarrassed. Cy wondered why she looked away.

Cy spoke quietly. "For what reason I'm not sure, but I haven't been able to get you out of my mind. I feel guilty for these thoughts and yet I know I shouldn't."

"I do not understand. You think of me and find guilt in this?"

"I don't mean it the way it sounds. A few months ago I cared very much for a woman." Cy hesitated, gathering his thoughts. "She died of cancer." Cy felt his eyes burning but continued talking. "We had a wonderful relationship and I cared deeply for her. I thought I wanted to spend the rest of my life with her, but I had some doubts because I was unsure about my feelings."

Cy saw the confusion registered in Sarah's eyes. "I guess I'm having trouble explaining myself. I'm not sure if I understand. Mary Ann was so good and kind. We had a comfortable relationship, and I was willing to marry her because I loved her. She was fun, loving, kind, and had a wonderful outlook on life."

Sarah noticed the hurt in his eyes. She felt her heart going out to him. Who was this person who had come into her life, charging it with such force and power? She was captivated by him. He had turned her life upside down and she loved what it was doing to her.

"I didn't know until the deer hunt why I was the way I was."

"How were you?"

"I asked Mary Ann to marry me because I had a great love and respect for her, but I was not *in* love with her the way a man should be if he plans to enter a contract of marriage. By that, I mean before a man declares himself to a lifelong commitment with a woman in sickness and in health, for better or for worse, for rich or poor, and all that, a man should be head over heals in love with that woman. I had never been in love and had nothing to compare my emotions to. I felt lost in the relationship I had with Mary Ann because she was a wonderful person. I felt guilty for not wanting to be closer to her without realizing why. I didn't know why until I met you."

Cy looked at Sarah and she gave him her full attention. "I have never had a feeling like this before. From the time I first laid eyes on you, I was lost. I have very deep feelings for you, Sarah. I can't explain how something can happen on a first meeting, but it has. I care for you, Sarah. My mind is a jumbled mess, and I lie awake at night thinking about you."

Cy stopped talking when tears came to Sarah's eyes. His stomach was churning in knots. Sarah slowly reached out her hand and placed her fingers on top of Cy's hand. It was the most bold move she had ever made in her life.

Feeling the warmth of her touch, seeing this precious person before him, Cy couldn't hold back his passion. "I know who you are, Sarah. I know your heart is good and you are a warm, loving person. You are the person I have waited for my whole life."

"Oh, Cy..." tears rolled down Sarah's cheeks. She tightened her grip on his hand. "I always thought something was wrong with me. I could never have feelings for other men and I've tried so hard to have them; I wanted them, they just wouldn't come and I couldn't make it happen. I know now it was because it would have been wrong. My heart has been saved for someone special. Are you the one?"

"I want to be," he paused, spacing his thoughts. "I want to be the one who opens your heart." Cy put his other hand over the top of Sarah's. "Let me have your heart, Sarah."

"Cy, I know nothing about love. I have not even kissed a

man. I know nothing of passion and I have felt shame because I could not let my emotions loose."

Moisture collected in Cy's eyes. He didn't care if he was making a fool of himself. His feelings were too strong. "Oh, Sarah, I want to give you my heart, my life."

Sarah sat for a long moment in thought, and Cy was afraid he was scaring her away. He had thought he was on solid ground, but now maybe he was rushing the bonding of their affection. His spirits were dampened as he quietly finished his meal.

When Cy said good night to Sarah at Jacob's house, he did not kiss her. He was desperate to touch her lips with his but did not want to risk the possibility of rejection. He had established a firm standard in his mind, and that was not to give her any reason to doubt his intentions or to give her any cause to be wary of him. He was determined to impress upon her mind that he was sincere in his attraction for her character and spirit, and that it was not entirely a physical thing. Somehow he had to quench the thirst to be always hovering over her. She was of a different culture, and he knew he had to move carefully or risk offending her.

Leaving her at Jacob's door was the most difficult thing he'd done all day. His vow to treat her honorably and respectfully might bring from her the passion she had kept submerged her whole life.

Cy had breakfast with Sarah at Jacob's home. It was lighthearted and fun, but every once in a while, Jacob and Lila got hit by a flying spark. Elvira happily offered to be a passenger and ride along with Cy and Sarah to Alpine as they were leaving. Thankfully, Lila grabbed hold of her daughter's hand and held it tightly until they drove away.

Lila turned to Jacob who was watching the car disappear down the street toward the city center. "Have you ever in your life?"

"No, I have never. Never, unless it was you and me," Jacob laughed.

"It was you and me, babe, a dozen years ago," Lila sighed

and took hold of Jacob's hand. "I love you, honey."

"I love you."

Cy became confused as he drove east from North Park in San Diego. The freeway was new to him and he got lost as he entered El Cajon. He took the second off ramp and drove along the road until he found the old highway. He drove out to the Gillespie Swimming Pool, went by his old high school and the Gillespie Drive-in Theater, and reminisced about his childhood. Back on the freeway, Cy drove to Alpine, missing the road where his parents were killed. He pointed out El Capitan Mountain that stood high above the reservoir named after it. He recounted memories of everything that came to mind, and Sarah asked many questions that Cy was pleased to answer.

It surprised Cy when Sarah told him it was the Kumeyai Indians who had lived in this area hundreds of years ago. He told her that on their ranch, the Rancho Los Robles, he had found stones still lying in grinding holes on huge granite rocks.

Sarah told him it was wrong for the Indians to take the stones from the rocks because they belonged to Mother Earth and they were waiting for other tribal inhabitants to use the same places to feed their families when they traveled that way. The spirits were always protecting their own, their ground, and it should not be disturbed.

As they drove into Cy's small hometown, Sarah found herself scooting closer to him in the truck. Being nearer to him felt right. For that matter, she wanted to jump in his lap and hug him with all her might. She convinced herself it was not ladylike, and she couldn't be sure he wouldn't throw her out the window.

It had been a few years since Cy had returned to Alpine. He was astonished at the many changes in the small town. At the grocery store on Tavern Road, he bought them both an ice cream stick. Old Bill was still the owner, and it was always good to see an old friend.

After visiting with Bill and other customers about old times, Cy drove up the street to the ranch which was on the left side of the road. The owners of the ranch had turned it into a dinosaur park for the public. The rock wall with the ornate black wrought iron fencing along the top was still in place, encompassing the entrance. As Cy and Sarah walked through the gate, they noticed the huge eucalyptus trees that rose over a hundred feet into the air. There were large granite boulders and also a clear stream winding its way along the drive. Huge stucco dinosaurs of different breeds loomed out from behind the boulders and trees, taking away from the original beauty of the ranch. The house was basically the same, but the bunkhouses were all gone.

Freeway placement astonished Cy. It had cut the ranch in half. They walked past the house and looked far beyond the barn where the freeway blocked off the road to the rest of the ranch as well as the earthen and east dams that were located there. The cattle and the horses were gone. It appeared surveying was under way for a future trailer park. Deer were once plentiful and now there were none. Even the peacocks and ducks had all flown away. Cy was sick with regret. Home for so many years, this is where he and his brother had played and learned to shoot their guns and fished in the dams their father had built.

Cy and Sarah left the ranch and drove north over the freeway on Victoria Drive. The long circling road had stood as a barrier to the original ranch from the other property owners. New homes were being built on the north side of the freeway near the dams, and Cy realized the ranch would soon be crowded out by single-family homes. After searching around the new development, he located the original dirt road to the east dam.

The concrete buttress was still in place. The spring that fed the dam still ran over the spillway into the trees, trailing off into town. The trees and wild shrubbery were slowly covering the outline of the dam. In a few years it would be completely overgrown and hidden from view.

Cy led Sarah across the spillway to the other side of the dam through the brush onto a large granite rock. It was mostly flat and home to the local ground squirrels, snakes, and lizards. He walked to the end of a giant granite slab and jumped to some boulders with Sarah right behind him.

Cy was impressed by Sarah's agility as she climbed the boulders and jumped the gaps between the large slabs of rock. On top of a boulder mostly grown over by a scrub oak, Cy pointed out some Indian corn holes bored into the granite with the grinding stones still in place. If he had not pushed the tree branches to one side they could not have been seen.

"Oh, Cy, you respected the stones," Sarah said, stooping down and touching one of the smooth oval rocks in a deep round hole.

"Well, let's say my father would have kicked my butt if I had taken them out. He was pretty touchy about those kinds of things. There used to be a lot of stones in front of the main house, but now they're all gone."

Sarah grabbed one of the grinding stones and lifted it up to show Cy. "You see that the bottom of the rock is smooth with a definite rounded ridge?"

"Yes."

"The Indian women always used the same side, because once the soft or loose particles of the rock were gone or worn down, it became very smooth and easier to grind the corn or grain without leaving particles of sand in the food. That's one reason the old natives had teeth problems. They prematurely 'sanded' their teeth down to the nerve endings and were often in a bad mood after that."

"I could imagine," Cy grinned.

"Well, you've heard the saying, don't mess with a bear that has a sore tooth. The same goes for the warriors. They got sore when the white men took their land, and it was compounded by bad teeth. Poor dental health was a big problem with the people in early American history, but you never hear much about it."

Sarah felt relaxed and comfortable talking with Cy. She spoke very little with most people. She wanted to bare her soul to Cy. She wanted him to know her, to understand her.

"Cy, please, you must sit," she pointed to the boulder. "Please sit on the rock and look at me."

"Yes, ma'am," Cy said, laughing at Sarah. Today she wore her long black hair in a single braid with a red and blue colored cloth tied at the end. She also wore a blue long-sleeved shirt and Levis that fit snugly. Cy knew she had no idea how beautiful she really was.

Sarah sat in front of Cy and smiled at him. "Let's just look at each other."

"That sounds like a good idea to me."

The two people sat on the rock for several hours talking and securing their relationship. Before leaving Alpine, Cy took Sarah to the cemetery on Victoria Lane. He had told her many stories about his parents. She began to feel she knew them and loved them.

Standing by the graves overlooking eastwardly to where the ranch had existed for so many years before the freeway and the new housing development had started, Cy felt a new closeness to Sarah and his parents. It was a new era in his life. The past was gone. He looked over to where the larger earthen dam had been, remembering the summer swim parties with his brother and friends. He was wrenched by this nostalgia—not a feeling of sadness but reinforcement of his family ties. He hesitantly slipped his arm around Sarah's waist as they stood together silently.

For all he was worth, Cy wanted to take Sarah in his arms and kiss her, but he did not have the courage. Instead he said, "Vood-ahm" (let's go).

"Oh, Cy, you are full of surprises. Thank you for studying my heritage. Do you know what 'neu-nee-too-hkk-oo-veun' means?"

"No, I'm sorry, I don't. What does it mean?"

"It means 'you are my friend,' and I am so glad to know you, Cy Golden."

Cy gave her a strange look, narrowing his eyes at her. "I don't know your last name, Sarah. What is it?"

"Gray. I am Sarah Gray. I was named after Sarah Winnemucca, who was the daughter of Chief Winnemucca of the Paiute Nation in Nevada," Sarah said humbly but proudly.

"Will you tell me about your people? Your life? I need to know who you are."

Sarah walked with Cy to a tree on the edge of the cemetery overlooking Alpine Valley. They both sat down on the grass and Sarah began to converse in her quiet way.

"Our tribes spread from the Yakima to Owen's Valley and generally lived from Bishop to Lone Pine for over a thousand years. We are related to the Shoshone and the Ute Indians of Utah."

Sarah and Cy talked for several hours. After they left Alpine he took her to dinner at Anthony's in San Diego on the waterfront. An older ship, the Star of India, was docked next to the restaurant giving an exotic flavor to the tasty seafood meal.

When they left the waterfront, Cy drove north on I-5 to Oceanside, then took the beach town road at Dana Point and passed through Laguna to Crystle Cove. He drove up the two-lane road and turned left onto a dirt road and parked near the cliff of Scotsman Cove.

As they approached the cove, Sarah remained quiet, sensing Cy had something to say he was not quite ready to share. The late sky was a soft blue with waves of white strata clouds stretching across the horizon. Cy stepped out of the truck, went around to Sarah's door, and opened it. An unexpected breeze made her catch her breath, and she inhaled the tangy salt air. She marveled at the beauty of the ocean with its white foamy waves rushing to the shoreline. Below and to the left, white water slapped and crashed against the rocks. Seagulls were scattered along the sandy beach searching for food.

Cy walked slightly ahead of Sarah around to the front of his pickup. He leaned against the front fender facing the vast Pacific Ocean. Sarah followed him, stepping in front of him and pressing her back to his warm body. It was a bold move on her part and she had to force herself to do it.

He studied the back of her black hair. Its brilliant blue shine was something he had never noticed in other women's hair. Little wisps of hair curled on the back of her neck where it had pulled loose from her braid and shifted in the wind. Her shoulders were small, yet they seemed strong. Her slimness was appealing to him and he placed his hands on her shoulders.

After a moment Sarah turned and faced Cy just inches away from his face. She studied his stubbly beard, his rugged eyebrows, and penetrating clear eyes, unsure whether they were green or brown. She had never seen a man who made her heart ache so. "I think I really like you," she smiled.

Cy grinned as he carefully examined the fine features of her captivating face. How could God have created such a beautiful creature as this girl in front of him. How could he be so fortunate to be near her and have her body touching his.

He thought he was going to lose his breath when she slipped her arms around his waist and put her face to his chest. He let his lips touch her hair, and he could smell the sweetness of her scent. If he died at that instant, it would be okay with him. This was the most wonderful moment of his life.

After several moments, he reached down and cupped Sarah's face in his hands and stared into her black eyes. "You are the most beautiful girl I've ever seen. You are more lovely than any other woman in this world," Cy said, softly looking into her eyes. "You do things to me that make me want to really live for the first time. I never knew before now why I was alive. I only knew I was here. Now I know. It was for you, Sarah."

Sarah could not stop the tears coming into her eyes as she looked at Cy. Her heart stopped when his head bent downward and she felt his lips touch her cheek, a touch that brought a burning sensation to her breast. The sky, the ocean, this wonderful man in her arms. "You bring a smile to my heart, Cy."

Sarah moved her head upward separating her red lips, and pressed them carefully onto Cy's. His warmth and passion entered her soul and she felt euphoria. After a long passionate kiss, she slowly pulled back and reached up, placing her cool hands on his warm face. She felt his stiff beard and liked it. "You have my heart, Cy."

Cy rested his head on Sarah's shoulder allowing his lips to touch her neck. The radio in the truck was on. He could hear the Platters singing "At Twilight Time."

Chapter 17
Bite of the Spider

Chuck Fulton sat with Flush in the smoking section at Denny's waiting for Skin and Scratch. It was a ritual. Every Thursday the two teams got together for breakfast regardless of the time of day. Today it happened to be the mid-afternoon watch.

Skin was pulling into the parking lot with Scratch. Flush was eyeing the men's rest room wondering when the bozo who had gone in there earlier was going to clear the room and let someone else make good use of it.

"They're here. Let's order," Chuck said, getting the waitress's attention.

"I wonder what that jerk is doing in the toilet, man. Something is not right," Flush said suspiciously. "It just ain't right, man."

"No way are you going to stink up this restaurant, Flush. We made a rule and you've got to stick with it."

"Ah, you guys make me sick," Flush said, getting up. "I'll be right back."

"Where you off to? You can't leave me here. What if we get a call?"

"I'm going to use the latrine at the gas station next door. You guys give me no choice. I have no respect here." His feelings were hurt. Flush brushed past Skin and Scratch in a huff without speaking.

Scratch grabbed Flush by the shoulder, stopping him in his tracks. "Hey, amigo, where are you going? You ain't going to use the men's room here, my friend."

Flush, disgusted with his so-called buddies, pulled away. "Scratch, you have no pride; no respect for the man," he said pointing to himself. "I'll be back pronto."

"Touchy, touchy," Scratch said, smiling at Skin. He clapped his hands together and scooted around the booth behind the table. "Man, I am one hungry Jose."

"Me too," Skin said, edging in next to him.

"Is the sergeant going to show up?" Chuck asked, watching the waitress come to their booth.

"He's finishing some reports. He may, but he's not sure," Skin said. He looked up at the waitress. "Hi, Rosa. We'll take the usual, and can we have coffee now, please?"

"Coming up. I already gave the chef your order when you pulled into the lot," Rosa smiled.

"Hey, come on now. What if we decided on something different? Then what would you have done?" Skin teased.

"I'm safe on that one," Rosa said as she turned away. "You guys never change."

"How do you like that," Scratch said, taking off his hat. "I don't like being predictable."

"When it comes to food, my friend, here at Denny's it's always the same. The Senior Grand Slam fits our pocketbook; otherwise, we'd be eating somewhere else," Skin replied, jostling his rear into a comfortable position.

Chuck eyed Skin and moved back when Rosa returned with the coffee. "So what's the story nowadays with the Sarge?"

"What story? What are you talking about?"

"The girl, dimwatt. How serious is this thing with him and the Indian girl?"

"Heads over teakettle, that's for sure. I've never seen anything like it. He calls her every few days and writes letters in between calls, if you can believe that."

Chuck shook his head. "That's crazy. Writing letters is going too far. A man shouldn't have to waste time writing to a woman just to hold on to a romance." He thought a moment and added, "Come to think of it, Jeanie expects a card on special occasions. Besides, it costs too much. I don't get women."

"You got that right, pard," Flush added, sitting down next to Chuck.

"Gees almighty, you sucking dog. I can smell you, Flush," Skin said, grabbing his napkin from under the flatware and holding it over his nose.

"You lie, man. You can't smell nada. Besides, I can't help a bad stomach. I got something wrong," Flush said, feeling sorry for himself.

"Yeah, you do. You constantly smell up the place. Now it's on your clothes. You didn't wipe, did you hombre?" accused Skin.

"Hey, back off. The doctor says I have a hiatal hernia and a messed up colon, and I'm going to have to live with it."

"Maybe you do, but why should we?" Scratch asked,

frowning at his Mexican friend.

"Because the truth of the matter is, you guys have a grand amount of respect for me. I know this because my wife says you do. Otherwise you would not put up with my problem, man."

"Look, Flush, it's not flushing the toilets and destroying every bathroom you use that we can't stand," Skin said seriously.

"You fellas know I got a phobia about touching the filthy, dirty handles in bathrooms," he said defensively.

"That shouldn't include the latrines at the division, my friend," Chuck said.

"Well, so I don't go there anymore," Flush said painfully.

"Let's get back to Cy," Chuck said. "How serious is it?"

"Dead serious," Skin answered.

"Would she be willing to move out here? I can't imagine her living in the big city," Chuck said, looking at Skin for an answer.

"I can't either," answered Skin. "And I'm scared to death Cy might go to her. You know his land deal went through in Mono County. He may just up and go live on Glass Mountain, marry Sarah, and have a dozen little half-breeds running around," he said, looking down at the table. "That lucky dog. How could anybody be so lucky to get close to that gal."

"She's a fine one, all right," Scratch said. "I'd trade my woman any day for her."

"Oh man," Flush said, "she wouldn't even look at you."

Skin leaned over the table preparing to provide his lessors with the latest scuttlebutt. The men on his team relied on his knowledge when it came to concerns with the department. Since he was in tight with the lieutenant and sergeant, he often provided good information to his close working friends before the other officers in the division were properly briefed.

Chuck recognized the cheesy expression on Skin's face before he spoke. He leaned back in his seat fixing his eyes on the bald-headed officer across from him. "All right, Skin, what do you got burning in that pea brain of yours? That look on your face would put a fat cat to shame."

"Hey, bad attitude. Forget it. I wanted to share with you, but forget it."

Chuck raised his eyebrows suspiciously. "Don't give us that 'forget it' attitude. What do you know and who will it affect?"

Scratch leaned on his elbows. "Look, man, if you got info,

you best share it. It may mean a beer after work, or worse—you may lose our friendship. Think about it."

Skin was relieved. Any kind of a gratuity from his friends was payment enough. "You guys aren't going to believe this. The department is in the process of purchasing bullet-proof vests for all the officers on the street. What do you think of that?"

Chuck shook his head. "No way. Those things are too heavy. SWAT does the bad stuff, anyhow. When would we wear them?"

"All the time, dufas."

Scratch said, "No, man, it's too hot to wear a vest. Besides, it would get in your way."

Skin was pleased he had the guys encircled in his power. "You dopes don't know what you're talking about. San Diego has been trying out a new bullet-proof vest that is made out of a light material called Kevlar. You don't wear it on top of your clothes, fools, signaling the bad guys to make a head shot. You put it on under your uniform shirt. No one will know you have it on."

"Take a hike." Chuck replied. "There is no such thing. No material can stop a bullet except ceramic tiles and that stuff weighs a ton. Flak jackets don't even stop shrapnel."

"It doesn't sound good to me," Flush said. "If you had to take an emergency dump, how could you get out of the damn thing in time before the big one?"

"Obviously, you boys are not up on the latest scientific technology. Kevlar is thin and doesn't weigh much. It's stuff they use on rocket ships. They say it will stop a .22 up to a .45 caliber. It'll even stop a .40 magnum," Skin said. "Think about it, fellas. If it stops a bullet, it'll stop a knife."

"Now you're talking," Flush put in. "A blade scares me more than a bullet. A cut can slice the life out of you. Besides, we get a lot of stabbings in our area compared to the other divisions."

Chuck thought a moment as he listened to the others. "If it stops a bullet, something else must happen to you. What about the force of the bullet stopping in the material stuff?"

"Well," Skin started, "the down side of it is, wherever you take a hit, the bullet may not penetrate the flesh, but it'll feel like someone hit you with a ball bat, and that ain't good."

"You got that right," Flush sneered. "Man, that could mess your bowels up pretty bad."

"Sounds to me a direct hit would break your ribs," Chuck

added.

"You're probably right, but at least you would survive the hit," Skin said confidently.

"With five thousand officers, I can't see the whole department getting them," Scratch said skeptically.

"I don't know how or when it will happen, guys. I'm just telling you something good in the near future is going to happen to us." Skin laughed at his friends and took a sip of coffee.

The sounds of static broke the conversation. "Unit Four Adam 55, respond."

"Damn," exclaimed Skin. "I knew I'd hate these new portables." He pulled the radio from his belt and pressed the transmitter button. "Four Adam 55, go ahead."

"Four Adam 55, go to the Jack-in-the-Box on South Soto. We have a 415 group disturbance. Request ETA."

"Four Adam 55, four minutes," Skin answered. He smiled at Chuck while he spoke into the radio. "Four X-ray 68 will give back up."

"Ten-four, Four Adam 55. Four X-ray 68 for back up," the radio crackled and went on to other traffic.

Skin grabbed a drink of coffee as he stood up. Rosa was walking toward them balancing four meals with her arms. "Hey, where you guys going?" she growled.

"Sorry, Rosa. We just got a call," Skin said. He reached into his pocket, pulled out three bucks and dropped them on the table. The others did the same.

"Hey, where you guys off to?" A small skinny black man in a city maintenance uniform walked in the front door coming toward them with a big grin on his face.

"Hey, Snow Goose," Skin said, smiling at the garbage man. "We got to go. You can have all four meals on us, okay?"

"You guys are the best," Snow Goose said, sliding into the booth without hesitating. "Don't you guys worry about a thing. This chow will not be wasted. There are too many people starving to death, and I'm on a special board to see that no food is wasted."

"See you later, Goose," Skin said. They left the building.

Separating into two-man teams, the officers quickly left the parking lot heading toward Jack-in-the-Box.

❧

Tony Valin took a sip of hot coffee from the white foam cup. It was black and tasted bad, but it kept him awake. He put the binoculars to his eyes and glassed the apartment house where Herman Duran lived with his girlfriend.

Bill Engles sat next to his partner in the unmarked squad car. He didn't like spying on anyone in the Ramona Gardens housing projects, which was right in the center of RD 448. It was the nucleus of the Hazard gang territory. Talk on the street indicated a new struggle was going on between the drug lords.

If Angelino allowed people to move onto this sacred ground of the Hazards, then other territories would be in danger. The White Fence, State Street, and V&E gangs were fortifying their areas of control to avoid encroachment from outside rivals.

Bill looked over his shoulder to make sure no one had made them out. It was dark and it gave him a little comfort knowing their position was a fairly good one. It was a big problem for them to be anywhere in this area, especially after dark. One never knew when the wrong person would happen to walk by and ID them. It was a dangerous place to be. The adrenaline flowed freely in his veins.

"I see movement," Bill whispered.

"Where?" Tony asked, pulling the binoculars down and glancing at his partner.

"Up on Lancaster and Evergreen. Looks like some old verteranos talking to some young gangers."

"I know something is going down. I feel it," Tony said, glassing over the group and then back to Duran's apartment window. "Duran's out! He's walking to his car."

A moment later Duran pulled away from the curb. Bill started the unmarked police unit and moved out onto the street with the lights out. After a half block, he turned his headlights on, maintaining a two-block distance behind Duran. "You know, if Robot ever tied up with this Pavlo character, that would be a very bad team."

"No chance," Tony said, lighting up a cigarette. "Pavlo wants no competition in the ranks. Besides, Robot is too mean to have a partner. He is his own man and doesn't need guidance from an older man." Tony pointed to the car ahead of them. Duran turned left onto Soto and headed south to down-town Hollenbeck.

"Something's up," Bill said. "He's leaving the safety of Hazard. I wonder where he's going and why."

Tony turned around to search the street behind them, ensuring they were not being tailed. The street appeared clear with normal traffic. "It doesn't make sense why he is heading for downtown. Don't you lose him. I want to find out what he's up to."

Tony got on the radio and called for another tail car for backup. It met them on 4th, allowing Bill to back off. He pulled over to the side of the street and waited. Once he was sure the support unit was not being followed, he pulled back onto the street, heading in the same direction.

"Four Charley 21, this is Four Charley 33. What's your position? We lost you on Inez," Tony spoke into the radio mike.

"Four Charley 33, subject has made us. He's making various turns around the middle school. Go back to 4th and come down Mott Street and see if you can pick him up. If you do, advise and we'll back off."

"Four Charley 33 copy," Tony said, slamming the mike down on the hook. "I don't believe this! What the hell's the matter with those guys?"

Bill made a quick U-turn to head north on Soto and turned right on 4th to Mott then slowed down. Both men looked up and down the streets as they crossed the intersection. Duran had vanished.

After twenty minutes of searching the streets in the local area, Tony told Bill to head over toward the Evergreen Cemetery. Recently a few problems had been occurring on Chavez Avenue and Bernal Street between the Mexicans and Asians.

"I can't figure this bird out," Tony said. "He has no connections here, so why would he risk his neck to come down here?"

"Something's up. Otherwise he wouldn't have come to this area of town," Bill said, driving slowly along the streets.

"I'm going to have another unit watch his place. We're going to canvass this area until we turn him up."

Pavlo wiped his forehead with the back of his hand. His eye's were darting back and forth with excitement. He was so close to the power he had wanted for so long. Only a few more steps and he would control a new boundary. Within a few months he would extend his control even further until he was satisfied with his strength in the drug world. Riches would be unbelievable and he could have anything he wanted.

He looked at the tattooed cross between his thumb and index finger. Many years ago the pachuco symbol had faded along with many other tattoos on his body; however, the memories and purpose of those tattoos burned in his mind.

He was at the edge of the success he had planned and dreamed for, and nothing was going to stop him. He glanced at Herman Duran, who was bound and hanging on the stone cross in the cemetery. His arms were tied to the laterals and a leather band secured Duran's head to the top of the cross. Touching the ground to relieve some of the pressure from his shoulder joints, his feet were tightly bound at the base and his arms felt like they were being pulled from their sockets. The cemetery was deserted except for Pavlo and his two men. Duran tried to figure out what he had done to get himself into this predicament. Only greed came to his mind.

"Please," he begged. "I have no useful information for you about Angelino. Juan will kill me. Let me go, Señor, and I will return to Mexico, I swear. You can forget our drug deal."

"Cayate Pendejo" (shut up stupid), Pavlo sneered at this pathetic wretch. "You have not revealed Angelino's home to me. I want it now."

"I tell you nothing, pig. Go ahead and kill me," Duran said, knowing he would not live through the night. The important thing now was to go quickly and as painlessly as possible.

Pavlo stepped back and motioned to the man on his right. The dark man stepped in front of Duran and coolly replied, "Are you sure you do not want to talk to the patron? It would be much easier on you in the end. Either way, you are a dead man. I can make it very fast and painless."

"What is your name?" Duran asked through tight lips.

"Franco. Why do you ask?"

"I'll speak only to Pavlo, if I am to die, but only to Pavlo."

Pavlo moved closer to Duran. "Speak."

"I have my honor. Only you can hear my confession. No one else. Comprende?"

"Si, comprendo. Contesta me" (I understand. Speak to

me), Pavlo said, moving closer.

"I must whisper in your ear," Duran said quietly. It would be the last task of his life. If he angered the patron, he would most likely kill him quickly and be rid of him. At least he had nothing to lose. He was on the edge but he had been around death most of his life. That is the way life is. It comes and it goes. So be it.

Pavlo leaned closer, his ear almost touching the man's nose. "Speak."

"You smell like my dog's ass."

"What!" Pavlo pulled his head up, anger flared in his face. He stared at the man on the cross and Duran spit a gob of yellow mucus in his eye.

"Ayee!" Pavlo swore, wiping madly at his face. Pavlo pulled Franco away from Duran just as he was going to cut his throat. "No!" he said, grabbing Franco's arm. "Get me my bottle."

Franco went to the green car and returned with a quart jar hidden inside a paper bag. Duran's eyes were wide trying to look downward. It was difficult to see what was happening with his head tied so tightly, and he had limited movement. His eyes betrayed his fear when Pavlo held up the jar with a large hairy black tarantula. It's legs were in motion, attempting futilely to climb out of the glass jar.

"For the love of God. Do not do this. Just kill me. Kill me!" Sweat ran down Duran's face, and he could not hide his terror of the ugly spider.

"How do I find Angelino?"

"Kill me. I beg you. Kill me now."

"Your opportunities are diminishing. Tell me what I want to know. Last chance." Pavlo smiled, holding the glass to Duran's lips.

"Kill me!"

"Okay," Pavlo nodded to Franco and Louie. Franco had two sets of pliers. He used one on Duran's nose and the other on his lower lip, pulling his mouth open.

Louie stepped out of the way. With a pair of red hog-nose pliers he slipped a copper hog ring inside the groove for clamping it into place. He had two extra rings to complete the job of clamping Duran's mouth shut.

Duran tried to scream but his voice was gone and only gushes of gasping air blew from the cavern of his stretched mouth. He knew the poison of the spider was only minor compared to the thought of the hairy creature inside his mouth.

Pavlo reached into the glass with his bare hands and gently removed the hairy spider. His eyes glazed over and he smiled, fingering the hairy legs of the tarantula. "Now, my pet, have a nice day."

He pushed the huge spider into Duran's mouth. Louie came forward and stapled Duran's mouth together with three hog rings. Duran gurgled and tried to shake his head back and forth. Franco cut the band around Duran's head to give him more movement. He figured the suffering would be enhanced with his head swinging aimlessly, and Duran's head should be unrestricted when it would be necessary to look down.

Eyes bulging from their sockets, Duran gurgled indistinguishable words from his mouth. The staples were tearing at his lips, stretching grotesquely and causing blood to flow freely down his chin, leaving trails as the red fluid dripped onto his white shirt. He shook his head up and down frantically. Pavlo came forward with a pad and pencil.

Franco cut Duran's right arm from the cross and rebound it to the main post, giving him only enough slack to move his arm chest high. "Write down Angelino's and Juan's address now and I will end your misery."

Duran gurgled and shook his head uncontrollably from side to side as if to try and shake the spider from his mouth. A terrible sight, the flesh was tearing as he tried to force the spider out of his mouth with his tongue.

When the legs of the spider protruded from Duran's lips, Franco motioned for him to write the answers to Pavlo's questions. Groaning in terror he grabbed the pencil and wrote on the paper that Franco held in front of his grotesque face. His watery eyes made it difficult to see what he was doing. He scribbled numbers on the paper.

Somehow Pavlo believed the addresses were accurate. When Franco saw what they had come for, he slapped Duran across the mouth in disgust. With a sharp knife he sliced the main vein in Duran's neck, allowing him to quickly bleed to death.

❧

"I'm telling you I heard something somewhere," Bill said, listening carefully. He had pulled over to the curb and turned the engine off. "There it is again. Someone is in the cemetery."

"Let's go check it out," Tony said, keying the mike. He relayed the information to unit Four Charley 21 and requested assistance. Four Charley 21 acknowledged with an ETA of one minute.

Bill was parked on 1st at Rivera Street south of the cemetery. He pulled away from the curb. As they approached the entrance both men saw taillights emerge from the cemetery grounds on the north side on Ezra Street.

"Dispatch, this is Four Charley 33. Request a marked unit assigned to RD 459 to stop any vehicle that leaves the Evergreen Cemetery," Tony barked into the mike.

"Four Charley 33, that's negative. Unable to provide uniformed officers at this time. We have a disturbance at Jack-in-the-Box. All officers are on details at this time unless you have an emergency."

"That's negative, dispatch."

"Four Charley 33, this is Four Charley 21, we'll make traffic stops on vehicles leaving the area."

"Four Charley 33, roger on that. Make a traffic stop on any car pulling away from the cemetery and check it out for anything strange. We'll get back to you. We're entering the grounds from the south side at this time."

"Four Charley 21, copy, ETA 40 seconds from location."

Bill drove through the cemetery grounds looking over the lanes and around the tombstones for anything amiss. It was dark and difficult to make out most of the objects. He spotted the second unit coming into the cemetery from the opposite end of the park. Both units slowly drove around the tombstones, not sure what they were looking for.

On the radio Tony heard Skin reporting that the near riot at Jack-in-the-Box was now under control and requested a paddy wagon to transport prisoners.

Bill thought he saw something on the driver's side off in a plot of gravestones. He slowed down, squinting his eyes. He stopped the car. "Give me your binocs."

Tony handed the binoculars over to Bill. He focused in an area where tall gravestones were standing upright eerily in the night. "Oh hell, man, we got a bleeder about fifty yards back, in the Holy Cross area." Bill dropped the glasses and sped away to the place where he saw the figure hanging on the cross. He slammed on his brakes and squealed to a stop. Both officers jumped out of the car with their weapons drawn, searching the immediate area for any danger. They worked their way over to the cross and flashed their lights on the hanging man.

"Lord," Bill gasped. "This is sick," he said, watching the blood run down off the concrete slab onto the grass.

"That's a lot of blood," Tony said. "What in the hell is sticking out of his mouth?" He moved closer to inspect the hanging man. Immediately he jumped back, knocking Bill away from him. He screwed up his face when he saw the victim's lips partially stapled together with a half-chewed tarantula hanging from his torn lips and sticking to his red sticky chin.

Tony grabbed his partner by the arm and turned around, thinking they were being watched. "Let's check this area out and secure it. We may have a live one out there somewhere."

Bill crouched low, carefully moving away from Tony. He used a flashlight on the gravestones, conducting a safe search of the incident scene. Nothing came up and both men met at the car. "I don't like it here, man. This is a sick place to be. Let's get backup here now. I've got the heebie-jeebies, man, and that's not good."

Tony wiped his mouth with the back of his hand. "You're no worse off than me. Did you recognize him?"

"No. I only saw blood and that gigantic spider. Did you recognize who it was?"

"Yeah, I did. It was Herman Duran."

"That's not good, Tony," Bill said, shaking his head. "We got us a drug war going on."

"At least we know the players. Pavlo did this, and Angelino's going to go off his rocker when he finds out."

"We've got a major problem on our hands," Bill swore softly.

"Yeah, we do. We need to brief the watch commander as soon as we get relieved here. Then we've got to get a meeting going with vice and all of our informants."

"I made a real mistake and I admit it," Skin said to his sergeant back at division.

"Then why do you always think you can handle things with your muscle? You can't push those kids around. They don't push," Cy said angrily, scrutinizing Skin.

"You're right, Sarge. I saw those two officers not backing down to those kids, and there were about fifty of them. I thought by being tough with them, I could de-escalate the situation. It used to be if you take out the loudmouth or the leaders, the rest would back down. I thought I could take out the ringleader and the others would disperse."

"You were wrong, man. You almost got me killed again," Scratch said, looking at his partner.

Skin didn't like Scratch butting in and gave him a sour look. He waited a second and looked back to his sergeant. "That's the first time I've ever had my butt saved by football players. If the team hadn't stepped in and intimidated the other students, they would have turned our car over and set it on fire," Skin said.

Cy asked, "Is the one student you arrested the main one who started the whole thing?"

"Yeah, he is. The jerk should be castrated. Instead, the juvenile courts will give him a gold star for innovation," Skin said disgustedly.

Cy looked at both men. "So what did you learn today?"

"To back off when the time is right," Scratch cut in before Skin could respond.

"What we learned was you can't bully kids around like you can adults. Adults know there are repercussions. Kids don't care and they have this pride thing," Skin said, sitting down on the edge of his sergeant's desk. "The courts won't do anything, and they know they have the power. If it wasn't for a few outstanding jocks that came to our aid, we would have been in serious trouble."

"Hey," Tony yelled from the front desk down the hall. He slid to a stop in front of Cy's office.

It surprised Cy when he looked up into the ashen expression on Tony's face. Tony was a hardened cop. Normally, he was not one to be rattled easily.

"You guys won't believe this one. Come on into the lieutenant's office. Have I got a story to tell."

Chapter 18
Onion

November 22, 1971

"Are you love struck or what?" Cy asked, looking questionably at Skin. "Ever since the deer hunt, you've had your head up your butt. What's your problem?"

Skin sat on the chair in front of his sergeant. The more he thought about it, things hadn't been going that well on the job lately. He lived for his work and wouldn't want to do anything else, so it didn't make sense why things were going the way they were. He decided he better make some corrective career changes.

He belonged to the best. Hollenbeck was the top division in L.A. as far as he was concerned. He had the best sergeant. Actually, Cy was his best friend, and he didn't like putting him in a bad situation as his supervisor. The mistakes he had been making at work were really not that serious; however, an accumulation of on-the-job errors would not go well on his evaluation report. He also knew with any more mistakes, it would be a difficult task for Cy to do his job and feel good about himself and their relationship.

"Sarge, this is the truth, so help me," Skin said, raising his hand to swear.

"Yeah, I'd like to hear this one," Cy said, sitting back in his chair.

"Well, boss, last Thursday I went home sick, remember?"

"What does that have to do with your filling out reports and failing to make a comprehensive response in them? I also was told you don't even remember who you arrested. So yeah, let's have it, Officer Fin."

"Now, Sarge, don't get mad. I know it doesn't look good, but hear me out."

"I'm waiting," Cy said, disgusted with his friend. He thought it hurt him worse than it did Skin for being on the receiving end of his criticism.

"Okay," Skin said, taking a deep breath to collect himself. "Okay, here it is. When I went home that night, I was really sick with a cold and a bit of the flu." Skin pointed to his nose. "See? Can you hear? I'm still congested," Skin said, sniffing his nose.

"What does that have to do with bad reports?"

"Okay, okay. I'm getting to that. My throat was burning like a bonfire, so I took a couple of swigs of Nyquil. Just how many swallows I don't remember because my throat kept burning, and I was trying to dampen the fire.

"I really don't remember being called back to work or even going into the station and getting my helmet and riot baton. I don't remember getting into the van or being shuttled to the parking lot where the riot was taking place at the convention center.

"I kind of remember a bunch of people acting unruly, but I don't remember arresting anyone. I do remember putting some people in the paddy wagon and that's it." Skin held up his hands indicating his honesty.

"So explain your actions the next day," Cy demanded, looking at Skin and shaking his head.

"Well, Sarge, after the shift I must have gone home and gone to bed sick. I woke up the next morning to gunfire. I grabbed my weapon and dove for the floor; then I got on the phone and called dispatch and asked if a gunfight was going on and if police were present. Dispatch told me it was some kind of a foreign celebration, something like the Fourth of July. Everyone was going nuts with fireworks. I don't know whether it was Chinese or Middle Eastern. So I crashed. I put a pillow over my head and didn't wake up until the next day. When I came to work the following day the guys were laughing, telling me how I went nuts at the convention, knocking people out with my baton. They said I got into the middle of the fighting and was even kicking people and that I conducted more arrests than anyone else.

"I don't remember it, Sarge. I took commands and did my job kicking ass and taking names. We cleared the riot out but I don't remember a thing. I never even got one scratch, whereas a number of the guys got hurt. I noticed Chuck and Flush both got bruised up. But me, I don't know."

"That's the damndest story I ever heard, Skin. I saw you and you were like a wild man. In fact, some of the time we were back to back, fighting off the crowd. It's a crazy explanation."

"I know, but it's the truth."

"Write it up so I have it on file."

Skin stood up and looked down at his sergeant. "I gag on that Nyquil crap. I don't even remember tasting it. Is that a bummer or what?"

"Get out of my office."

In Cy's voice was a sound of forgiveness and it lifted Skin's spirit. He knew when to quit. He spun around and went down the hall to the report room.

The phone rang three times before Sarah could get it. She grabbed the receiver, expecting to hear Cy's voice. Her smile quickly faded when she heard Ray on the other end of the line.

"Sarah, it's your uncle again. He got drunk and beat up a couple of guys at the Buckhorn Bar in town last night. We had to arrest him. He's in a holding cell at Mammoth. Do you want to bail him out?"

"Not necessarily, Ray. Did he hurt anyone badly?"

"It wasn't so bad this time. There were two of them and they left town without pressing charges. There's something to his fighting this time, Sarah."

"What do you mean?"

"Ben said some outsider has pulled his land right out from under him. He says he's destroyed and disgraced."

"What are you talking about?"

"Ben told me he lost half his ground to a foreigner—to some white man in Los Angeles by the name of Golden. That name sounds familiar but I can't place it."

"No! That's not true," Sarah gasped into the phone. "Cy Golden?"

"Yeah, that's the name. How did you know it? Ben says he'll kill the man if he ever comes to this valley. That's Indian ground, Sarah. It's the last of our sacred land. How did you know the name? What's going on?"

Cy smiled to himself thinking about Skin's explanation of his work activity. Skin was one of his most dependable officers, and he wanted him to continue in that vein. He thought if Skin married Martha and raised her son as his own, it would bring strength and stability into Skin's life. The phone rang and he picked it up.

"Golden here."

"This is Sarah," the voice sounded strange, almost lost.

"Sarah, it's so good to hear your voice but something sounds wrong."

"Did you buy a large parcel of land in Mono County?"

"Yes, I did."

"Was it on the plateau on the north side of Glass Mountain?"

"Yeah, that's right. How did you know that? I was keeping it a secret."

"I'm sure you were. Did you think I wouldn't find out? Or didn't it matter to you," Sarah's voice was trembling. "I trusted you, Cy. How could you take that land away?"

"Hey, whoa, wait a second here. What are you talking about? I purchased that land legally, and I am really excited to have it."

Sarah held the phone tightly to her ear, on the verge of breaking down. Hearing Cy's confession, she felt her world crashing down like an avalanche. All her hopes and dreams were vanishing as she listened to Cy's voice. "You used me somehow. Ben told me how you used me to do what you have done. How could you be so cheap? How could you do this to me?"

"Sarah, what are you talking about? I bought that land before I ever knew you. I plan to put a nice log cabin on the place someday and use it for a hunting lodge. Who is Ben?"

"So you and your white friends can come and kill the deer and trespass on..."

"Stop it, Sarah. You don't know what you're talking about. That land is mine fair and legal. It's a place I've wanted for a long time."

"Oh, so you've been planning this for a long time. Was I in on the deal? You used me for this. How could you? How could you, Cy? I thought you were a man of principle, and I trusted you."

"It has nothing to do with trust. I wanted that land and I bought it. Simple as that. What did I do wrong? It was up for grabs."

"Up for grabs? Oh, you are so very cold. You have icicles in your veins. Don't call or write me again," Sarah cried into the phone.

"What?"

"You heard me. Don't contact me again." She was hurt and Cy's explanations did not make sense. "I never want to see you again."

"Sarah, you're upset over nothing," Cy was saying when Sarah tuned him out. How could the man of her dreams cut her heart out so viciously? How could he take the land of her heritage and so coldly make it into a hunting lodge for strangers to desecrate? How could he be so cold to say it was nothing? Nothing?

"If you bother me, my husband will deal with your arrogance. Goodbye."

"Husband? What are you talking about?"

"It's always been expected of me to marry my own kind. Raymond Tom has asked me to share his life, and I will, since my life is of no consequence to you." Sarah slammed the phone down and began to cry.

Cy was stunned. He held on to the receiver studying it as if it held the answers to a sudden mass of questions. He was devastated, ruined. He thought Sarah loved him. How could she be engaged to another person? Was that Indian culture? No, that was insane. What could be the logical reason for her reaction?

He went to the break room and was relieved it was empty. He poured a cup of coffee and took two aspirins for his terrible headache. He wanted to cry. He wanted to think things out but his mind couldn't focus on any one subject. Sarah had said so many confusing things. Why was she marrying someone else when she said she loved him? Why didn't she tell him she was in love with another person? How could she love two people at the same time? Why wasn't she loyal to the other man in her life? Why hadn't she been loyal to him? How could she have visited him and taken his heart and given of herself if she cared for another man? His head was a spiral of pain. It was happening again. He had lost another person dear to him. His whole being was engulfed with despair.

"Cy, can you come into my office for a second?" Jacob's voice broke his thoughts.

"Huh?"

"What's the matter? Is something wrong?"

"Nothing I can't handle," he replied sourly. "Yeah, I'll be right in."

"You don't sound very convincing," Jacob said. "You know

how Skin is always talking about a blue night, a bad cop's night. Well, tonight may be a blue night. See you in my office." He disappeared into his office. Cy took another drink of coffee. Nothing in his life made sense.

"Juan, take Padillo with you to the alleyway behind Pavlo's office. I am going to assist on this one, but I want Jose with me," Angelino said, checking the cylinder of his handgun.

"We better have two shotguns," Juan said.

"No. That would show too much force, as if Pavlo is a person to be feared. Pistols will be sufficient and the four of us will be enough. This worm will scream before he dies very slowly. I want a bullet in each kneecap and elbow before the final one to the head."

"Sounds good to me, boss," Juan smiled. "No use of the knife then?"

"No, I want this one swift and clean, right in the open, right in front of the world. I want this killing on the streets to be a message to anyone who thinks of challenging our territorial rights."

"1st and State Street is pretty open. Are you not worried about detection? That's only a few blocks from the police station."

"The doorway and wall behind his office will give us plenty of cover, and I will use a silencer on my gun to keep the noise down. For the last few weeks, there has been no other person in that area at night, according to your reports. And if there is a witness, which I doubt, the incident will not be spoken of," Angelino smiled grimly.

"It must be accomplished quickly then."

"Of course."

Cy pulled his patrol car into the parking lot behind the White Memorial Medical Center off Brooklyn Avenue. Already waiting were four patrol units. Chuck and Flush were standing outside their unit talking with Skin and Scratch along with four other officers. Drained, Cy felt he was working in a thick fog. Sarah had become his life, his hope, his dreams. He tried to force her from his thoughts. He looked at his men, confident he was disguising the pain and weakness in his heart.

"The lieutenant has been briefed by Tony Valin in the narcotics division," Cy said. "It appears this may be a high-incident night. He says the word on the street is that something is going down in RD 453 or 452. What is going down, no one knows. So I want a heads up.

"At no time are you to be away from your radios. Shotguns are lock and load, not in the electra-locks. Whatever it is, it will be necessary to respond quickly and effectively to curtail all situations. We have two other units who will be patrolling RD 455, 463, 451, and 462. That should be plenty of coverage. Skin, you and Scratch are to take RD 452. Chuck, you and Flush take 453. Tom, you have 463 and 451. Brad, you take 462 and overlap with Tom in 451. The lieutenant will be out and around plus we have alerted Central Division for additional units if needed."

"I had a feeling about this being a blue night. I haven't felt good all day. What are we looking for, Sarge?" Skin asked, leaning back against his police unit. He had his thumbs hooked in his Sam Brown, looking serious.

"I haven't a clue. It may be nothing. Tony believes there may be a retaliation to the homicide at the cemetery. He can't confirm his suspicions but there is talk. That's what it is right now, talk. There are no gang activities to speak of and the streets are quiet."

"That's the problem, Sarge," Skin cut in. "It's too quiet. There doesn't seem to be the normal hustle and bustle on the streets. It ain't normal."

"I know, that's what bothers me, too. It's like the calm before the storm. Anyway," Cy said, looking over his men, "I want good preventive patrol techniques and close backup when traffic stops are made."

"What rotation do you want us to use to roll as backup, Sarge?" Chuck asked.

"I'll be the first responder," Cy said, pointing to himself. "I'll be in RD 453 and 452 most of the shift. That puts me in the middle of everything. When I hear radio traffic indicating a stop, at that point I'll provide first backup.

"Chuck or Skin, your crew will respond next, depending on who's making the stops and your location from the stop. First responder will be the unit adjacent to the stop. I'll roll on all stops unless it gets too busy."

"Are we to take it that you don't mean normal traffic stops?" Skin asked.

"You take it right. I only want suspicious suspects stopped and questioned. Forget traffic violations unless it's important or life threatening."

"What about breaks?" Flush asked sheepishly.

"No breaks until the lieutenant gives me an all clear signal. That reminds me," Cy said. "We'll have three undercover units out tonight. So keep an eye out for them. Make sure you don't stop any of them. We don't want to blow anyone's cover."

"Well, Sarge, my stomach's acting up. If we have no break later, I got to go now, man." Flush expressed himself by crossing his legs and bobbing up and down. "Okay?" Flush grimaced.

"Chuck, you better get him to the park and let him take a dump or you'll be needing a gas mask before the night's over," Cy replied, in answer to Flush's request.

"Roger that. Come on Flush, you miserable walking commode," Chuck said, hitting Flush on the shoulder as they walked toward their patrol car.

After the other four officers left, Scratch went over to his unit and waited for his partner. Skin walked with Cy back to his car. "Sarge, I want you to know something. I've been thinking about what you said and especially what you didn't say. I'm going to do a better job. This work is my life. Also, I called Martha and after shift tonight we're going to have a long talk about our future. I want you to know I really care for her, and if she'll have me, I'm going to marry her."

"Skin, that's wonderful," Cy said, grabbing Skin by the arm. "I'm really happy for you."

"Sarge, is there something wrong? You're looking a little strange."

"No, I'm okay. I've just got to work some things out with Sarah that I don't understand."

Skin was taken by surprise. "You've got to be joking. You haven't had a dumb attack, have you?"

"It's not me. It's her. I don't know what's bothering her and I'm not sure how to handle it," Cy said, slapping Skin on the shoulder. "Come on, let's get to work. Don't forget, the lieutenant will be out and about tonight, so heads up."

"Ten-four, back door, gotcha covered," Skin laughed, heading for his car.

2130 hours. At State Street near 1st, Angelino waited in the car for Juan's signal. All indications were that Pavlo had no idea of the events they had planned for him. He was busy working in his office. Pavlo's bookkeeper was a valuable man to Angelino. He would be well rewarded.

Angelino smiled, thinking how he was going to be rid of an annoying parasite. The telephone sounded; Angelino picked up the receiver. After a moment he replaced it in the holder and told Jose to proceed to the alley off of State Street between 1st and 2nd.

The alley was dark. Angelino ordered the driver to park on the right behind a closed office. Jose pulled into the alley and turned into the first parking slot. The wall of another office blocked the view from the rear entrance to Pavlo's office halfway down the alley and to the left side. Pavlo's business faced 1st Street between State and Brittania streets.

Angelino sat in the back seat; Jose was stationed behind the car watching for activity up and down State Street. Juan had parked his car at the other end of the alley and moved to the rear office door with Padillo. Pavlo would be coming out any time. His bodyguards had stepped out twice to check out the alley through the rear entrance but did not give it a careful inspection. They would have been eliminated if they had stepped directly into the alley. If this were to happen, Pavlo's execution would take place inside the office. Time slowly ticked by. Angelino was getting nervous. He rechecked his watch. It was 9:30 P.M. Pavlo should be closing shop.

2130 hours. Cy pulled over at Pennsylvania and State, Jacob having already arrived. Cy got out of his car and walked over to his lieutenant. Jacob opened his car door and got out.

"Yeah, boss, what is it?" Cy said in a small panic.

"What's up, Cy? I know you too well. What's going on?"

Cy hesitated, took a deep breath, and told Jacob about the phone call from Sarah.

Jacob looked surprised. He wrinkled his forehead while shaking his head. "This doesn't make sense, my man. You're going to call her back, aren't you? You've got to get this thing straightened out."

"I can't handle losing another person in my life, Jacob. This has done me in. I don't care if I ever see or hear from her again. Besides, why would she even talk to me if she is marrying someone else? I find it strange that she has always planned on a marriage to someone else. I wonder where I fit into her plans."

"No, there's a rat in the woodpile, Cy. Something's not right. Let me call her. I'm not emotionally involved and I'll get to the bottom of it."

"Absolutely not. This is my affair and I'll deal with it," Cy said vehemently, then guiltily reached his hand out to Jacob. "You're my friend, Jacob, and I appreciate your concern. I'll work it out."

"Well, do it right away. I'm not saying anything to Lila. She was really taken by that girl. I don't want anything to spoil it if you can work it out, okay?"

"Thanks, Jacob."

"Well, you get back to patrolling. It doesn't look like anything is going to happen. For a Thursday night it has been quiet. We'll break it off at 2230 hours, okay?"

"Yeah, okay. I'm going to make a big circle and head back to the office," Cy said, turning.

"Do you want to meet at Jack's Piss Hole after work? I'll buy you a beer."

"Why not. I feel like getting drunk."

"See you after watch change."

"Okay, I'll find Skin and Scratch and see if they want to go with us."

2131 hours. Unit Four Adam 55 turned onto State from 3rd Street and headed toward 1st. Scratch was behind the wheel. He slowed the patrol car as it approached 2nd Street. "Did you see that up ahead?"

"See what?" Skin asked, searching the street ahead of them.

"It looked like someone just stuck their head out of the

alley behind the corner drugstore, but I'm not sure," Scratch said, studying the street.

"It's probably nothing. It's been a dead night and I'm tired."

"Yeah, me too. Maybe we ought to get a cool one after work. Wha' da ya say?"

Skin looked at Scratch out of the corner of his eye. "Sounds good to me. It'll have to be a short one. I've got other plans tonight. A cool one will calm me down. I've had the jitters all night."

Scratch stopped in the middle of the street and then pulled over a few feet from 2nd Street. He turned out the lights. "Man, I must be going nuts. I swear I saw a head peeking around the corner from the alley."

"I didn't see it. Let's sit here a second and watch," Skin said, settling back comfortably in the car seat.

2132 hours. Juan heard the handle on the rear door to Pavlo's office turn. He stepped further back into the shadows and gave the other man a signal. Padillo was standing at the end of the building next to the alley. He turned and signaled to Angelino, who was now standing at the front of his car. Jose was acting as rear guard, positioned behind the Lincoln close to the sidewalk and watching State Street.

The door to the building emitted a grinding squeak. Two Mexicans stepped into the small parking area behind the office. Juan barely moved as he peered around the dirty brick wall in time to see a third man exit the office. It was Pavlo. He hesitated, then turned around to lock the door.

The first man out of the building strolled to the end of the parking spaces toward the alley, lighting a cigarette. The second man, Franco, went to the parked car and unlocked the door. He opened the car door and reached inside to unlock the rear door for his boss.

"Nice night, boss," the man said, holding the door open.

"What's nice about it?"

"Nothing, I guess."

Pavlo hesitated as he started to get into the car. "Start the car. I have to go back inside a moment."

Franco climbed in behind the wheel, put the key into the ignition, and turned it.

Pavlo's man at the alley was blinded by the match as he lit his smoke. He heard a rustle to his right but saw nothing. A hand wrapped around his forehead and he felt a hot searing pain across his throat. A gush of bubbly air escaped through the red gap in his neck and his voice was gone. Darkness. Then all went black.

❦

2132 hours. Skin hit Scratch on the shoulder with the back of his hand. "There, I saw him. Somebody just looked around the corner from the alley."

"I didn't see him this time. We better check it out," Scratch said, grabbing his baton.

Skin decided to call the sergeant. He took the mike from the police radio and pressed the transmit button. "Four Lincoln 22, this is Four Adam 55. We are going to be out of the car checking the alley out on State between 1st and 2nd. We spotted a guy looking up and down the street and then disappearing. It may be nothing but we'll check it out."

Cy grabbed his mike. "Four Lincoln 22, copy. I'm on Pennsylvania crossing State now. I'll come down Brittania and come in on foot from the other end of the alley."

"Roger that, Four Lincoln 22; we'll be on foot on the State Street side." Skin replaced the mike, took his nightstick, and quietly opened his door. Scratch followed suit.

The sergeant turned right at the next intersection and went south. After he crossed 1st Street, he pulled over to the right curb and parked approximately three car lengths from the alley opening.

The two officers walked briskly north on State toward the alley. "It may be nothing," whispered Skin, "but let's keep it quiet in case we have a sale going down."

"Quit talking then," Scratch answered, switching his flashlight to his left hand to free up his gun hand. Both men crept stealthily along the sidewalk. When they approached the alley, Skin stopped, took a breath, and sneaked a quick peek around the corner. He saw a black Lincoln parked a few feet away facing down the alley.

He relayed the information to his partner and scanned the alley for a second time. Approximately forty feet away he saw a man walk around the corner of the building.

Skin bent his head toward Scratch. "We have one man in the alley to the left, one building down. The car appears empty," he whispered. He took another quick look and saw a police officer at the other end of the alley step into the shadows on the north side moving toward him. Relieved, he knew it was Cy.

"The sergeant's coming down the alley on foot. He's on the left side in the shadows. Go back to the car and get Chuck and Flush for backup just in case."

"You stay here until I get back, okay?"

"No problem, but hurry. This may be a sale going down, and we could make a felony here," Skin whispered to Scratch.

"I'll be right back. Wait for me, man."

Skin couldn't figure out why he was so nervous. As yet there was no reason to feel edgy. He glanced around the corner and thought he saw the sergeant almost halfway down the alley. "Damn," he said to himself. Cy had made his way further down the alley than he had expected. He looked over his shoulder for his partner. Scratch was approaching the patrol car. He glanced back down the long dark alley and then decided to enter it.

Skin crept over to the black Lincoln. He looked inside. It was empty and unlocked. He put his hand on the hood. It was warm.

2136 hours. Jacob was in his office going over reports when Tony and Bill rushed through the door. "Lieutenant!"

Jacob's head jolted up. Tony Valin's face was painted with excitement. "What's your big hurry. We're off in twenty-five minutes."

"Forget that. What are Skin and Cy doing at 1st and State? I just heard them on the radio as we were pulling into the office."

"I didn't know they were there. Cy told me a few minutes ago he would be heading into the station after he talked to Skin. Why?"

"There's a Mexican exports store in the middle of the block on 1st. The owner is a prime suspect in the cemetery homicide. His street name is Spider. For sure we know he has been involved in disputes concerning territory violations in Hazard and other places."

"The hell you say!" Jacob said jumping up. "I didn't know nothing about that place and neither did my men. Come on, let's get over there." Jacob grabbed his duty hat and ran down the hall with Tony and Bill on his heels.

At the front desk the desk sergeant spun around in his chair when he heard the lieutenant running. "What's up?"

"Have dispatch radio for backup to all the special patrol units. Advise there is a suspicious occurrence at 1st and State Street. Send a unit in from the south and west side. Tony's crew and I will go in from the east and north side."

"Got it, Lieutenant," the sergeant said, picking up the hot phone.

"Tony, you and Bill hit the pavement."

"On our way," Tony yelled over his shoulder, making a mad dash for his car.

2136 hours. Skin was hugging the alley wall in the shadows slowly advancing toward Cy. Cy was taking his time making his way toward him. There was no one in the alley, and he thought perhaps it had been a drunk or someone relieving himself, a common enough occurrence in a dark, deserted place.

Neither officer had his weapon drawn because there was no reason to think they'd be needed. Skin walked past the open space behind Pavlo's office. All was quiet and the man he had initially seen had disappeared. Nothing seemed out of the ordinary. He walked over to his sergeant.

Cy rolled his shoulders back and forth, trying to work the tiredness out of them. "There doesn't seem to be any problem here. What did you see?"

"I'm not sure. It could have been a derelict," Skin said, looking around the alley.

"Did you check the Lincoln?"

"Yeah," Skin said quietly. "It was empty, but the hood was warm. It could have been a business owner or someone who has a legit reason to be here. It certainly is quiet enough."

Cy pointed to the car parked next to the building on his right. "You said a man was looking out of the alley. That bothers me. While we're here let's check this car and see if anyone is in the store."

"I think it's an import store," Skin said, as he flashed his light inside the car. The beam of the light caught a man lying on his back, his throat slashed. It startled Skin. He jumped back involuntarily. "Holy...hell." A second body lay in the front.

A voice spoke from the shadows. "Don't move, either of you. You'll die on the spot if you do not do as you are told," Juan said, stepping out from behind the blind wall to Cy's right. Skin and Cy both did as they were told. A second Mexican came out from behind the same hiding place with a revolver in his hand, pointing it at the two officers.

Angelino came out of the store when he heard Juan's voice. He quickly surveyed their situation. "This is getting too messy," he hissed at Juan. He spun around to Jose. "Bring Pavlo here now. Juan, you keep them covered," Angelino snapped.

Pavlo was on his hands and knees when he was brought to light under the small naked bulb hanging from the hall ceiling. Jose gave him a hard kick to the buttocks while keeping his gun trained on the man's back. When the old man, crawling, reached the pavement outside the building, Jose grabbed him by the collar of his jacket and pulled him backward to a kneeling position. Pavlo held his head down, assuming a submissive posture. Angelino wanted him to beg for leniency and slobber like a baby. Pavlo's demeanor angered him.

Cy tried to step back enough to keep partially in the shadows, away from the glare of the light inside the hallway. He could not understand why the Mexicans had not disarmed Skin and him. It gave him a small measure of relief. He decided that the Mexicans felt safe because their guns were holstered and he and Skin were carefully guarded. Cy had hooked his thumb on his gun belt next to the handle of his .357. He gave no indication he was going to be any kind of a threat.

Cy gave Skin a side glance. Skin was carefully surveying their situation and appeared to be holding it together. In reality, Skin was sick to his stomach. He could not figure out how the two Mexicans could have concealed themselves so well. He knew Scratch would be coming and was convinced he was their only hope. Timing was everything.

He glanced at Cy and knew his sergeant was calculating their chances, which by now had probably risen to zero. He also noticed Cy had moved slightly away from him and to his right. It was a stance they had practiced many times. Skin knew if the shooting started he had to take the two men in front of him and to his left. His first target would be the well dressed man who was giving the orders. His next responsibility would be the second man guarding the old man. He gathered himself, mentally preparing various possible scenarios. He was fearful but knew he would do what had to be done.

Skin was uneasy, wondering if Cy would go for his gun if and when the time was right. He didn't want Cy to worry about his safety. Practice is one thing. This was real. He realized he would have to trust Cy to take out the ugly Mexican and the other man on his right. He hoped Cy would make his move and concentrate on the Mexicans.

The realization of the situation hit Skin hard. This was it. This was the end. Even if he survived the shooting, he knew he would take a hit.

The four men had guns in their hands, and he wondered if a person felt a bullet entering his body. It was his under-standing that if it didn't hit bone, it wasn't too painful unless you took a belly shot. That hurt like hell, especially if the bullet blew your guts out. He shuddered.

Angelino stepped over to Pavlo. "You stupid fool." Angelino butted Pavlo across the back of his head with his revolver. "Greed has filled your brain. Fortunately for you, time is of the essence now." Angelino walked around to the front of Pavlo and casually shot him in the left knee, followed by a second round to his stomach. The silencer kept the noise muffled and would not be heard a hundred yards away.

Cy knew once Angelino finished off the old man he and Skin were next. Fear engulfed Cy. He thought he was probably going to die. He winced as he listened to the old man's suffering. He glanced at Skin from the corner of his eye without moving his head. To his surprise, Skin gave him a weak smile. He could rely on Skin. It gave him what he needed—a tremendous boost of courage.

Cy shuddered when Angelino reached down, put the gun barrel to Pavlo's head, and squeezed the trigger. The report was muffled. Pavlo's body fell forward, slamming hard into the ground.

Skin looked at Angelino and said coolly, "You haven't any hair on your balls and your breath smells like rotten onions."

To Cy, everything was happening in slow motion, but his draw was so fast no one could counteract his lightning speed. He fired one quick shot at the big Mexican with the scarred face, striking him in the upper chest, right of center, at point-blank range.

Cy's second discharge sent a round into the other Mexican standing off to his left. The projectile struck the man dead center, putting a neat hole in his sternum and blowing him backward. He was dead before he hit the ground.

Something pulled at Cy's right side and he felt himself falling backward. He let off two more rounds at the direction of the muzzled blast. Instantly, he felt another tug on his left shoulder, spinning him in the other direction.

Cy fell to a sitting position on the ground but was able to get off two more shots at the third Mexican who had been holding Pavlo. The bullets hit the man in the hip and neck, dropping him where he stood. Angelino was lying over the old man whose stomach streamed blood. That meant Skin had taken out the boss man.

Cy looked for Skin while he reached for his speed loader on his Sam Brown. He knew his gun was empty and needed to reload. When he tried to reach for his speed loader his left arm did not seem to respond. A terrible pain spread across his left shoulder into his back. He felt himself falling over backward and the world became unfocused. Lying on his back, he attempted to come up into a sitting position.

He was fumbling for the speed loader with his right hand when he focused on the big Mexican standing above him. The man's shirt was covered in blood, a bright red foam still pumping from the man's chest. He raised his gun to Cy's face. The gun barrel expelled a blinding flash and deafening sound. Then there was no further sound, nothing.

Juan stood for a moment looking down at the police sergeant he had just shot. The bullet entered Cy's forehead above his right eye and appeared to have blown off the back of his head. Juan could see the officer's scalp in pieces where they lay.

He glanced around to determine he was the only one alive. Blood coursed down his chest. His other two wounds, one in the thigh and another in his left arm, were minor. He was still in shock that the officer shot him so many times before he could react. The whole shooting episode had not lasted more than five seconds. It seemed impossible that so many people could die in such a short period of time.

Juan limped down the alley to his car. It was parked near the east entrance. Once inside he started the car and pulled out into the street. In his rearview mirror he saw another police officer enter the alley on the run with a long gun in his hands. He heard police sirens in the distance. He stepped on the accelerator; halfway down the next block he turned left into another alley. At the end he turned right onto the street, entering the next alley and finally disappearing into the night.

When Scratch approached the corner of the building, he could already smell the fresh stench of blood and death, no other smell like it. He slowed his movement and rounded the corner with his shotgun leading his sight range, prepared to discharge. To his horror, bodies were scattered everywhere.

Sergeant Golden, lying on his back, looked dead with a contact wound to the head. He also had sustained wounds to his chest and side.

Skin was lying on his side, his knees pulled up to his chest, in a fetal position. Scratch had seen this phenomenon before but never from another police officer. He cautiously moved forward; the Remington 12-gauge was fixed tightly in both hands. His eyes were wide open, taking in every aspect of the scene. His breathing was slow and deep.

Once he was sure the Mexicans were dead, he went over to his partner.

"Skin! It's me, Scratch." He reached down and touched the badly wounded man on the arm and shoulder. Two puncture wounds were exposed to the front with one exit wound in his back. The pavement was sticky with blood. Skin blinked slowly, staring into space. "Oh buddy, it's me. Scratch."

A groan coming from his right made Scratch jump and twirl around with his gun at the ready. His eyes were wide with disbelief. His sergeant was in a sitting position, half of his rear scalp dangling to his shoulder emitting blood and mucus.

"Sarge! You're alive!" Scratch could see the bullet hole in Cy's forehead. How could he be alive? He had heard of people being clinically dead but continuing to shoot or walk because the blood hadn't stopped in the brain. How could the sergeant possibly be in this condition and still be alive? He quickly moved to the sergeant and kneeled on the asphalt next to him.

"You look good, Sarge. You look real good," Scratch's voice faltered. He was in shock, having been completely sure his sergeant was dead. "Don't move, Sergeant, we've got help on the way." Scratch could hear sirens coming from all directions.

Cy couldn't hear anything. It was a silent, bloody, worthless dark world. His head throbbed tremendously, and he felt hot liquid on his neck and back. His left arm would not work, and his body was burning up with pain. His eyes searched the bodies around him until he saw Skin lying on his side a few feet to his left. When he tried to crawl to him, something tried to restrain him. Somehow he found the strength in his right arm to free himself. He crawled through the blood and gore to Skin.

He couldn't understand why the scene was so quiet and fuzzy. A fog must have rolled in off the ocean. He gritted his teeth pulling Skin onto his lap. With his right arm he cradled Skin's head to his bloody chest.

Skin's eyes were open but didn't appear to register images. They didn't blink. "Don't do this to me, buddy. Don't you leave me. For God's sake, don't you leave me! Do you hear me, Skin? That's an order."

Scratch stood back as Jacob and Tony came running up. Other officers secured the area, rushing into the store and checking it for other hostiles.

Jacob was so stunned when he saw Cy's critical condition and cradling Skin in his lap that he froze in position. "An ambulance is on its way," he said quietly to Scratch. His heart was pumping in his throat and he wanted to cry. Tony clamped both hands over his mouth to keep from moaning, his eyes streaming and his shoulders shaking as he wept freely.

Cy pulled Skin's face to his and he kissed him for a long time on the forehead. "I love you, buddy." Cy was terribly confused, but he could still recognize the presence of death. "I'm sorry, my friend. Sorry." Suddenly Skin's body went rigid. His mouth opened, sucking in a large gulp of air and then he expelled a single breath.

After a long moment, Jacob bent over Cy and wrapped his arms around him from behind. Cy had a tight grip on Skin. At first he refused to release him. "Cy, you have to let him go." Jacob pressed his cheek next to Cy's as he tried unsuccessfully to pull Cy's hand free from Skin's shirt. "Let him go, Cy. He's gone."

Tony stepped around to the front of Cy, bawling openly. He bent over Skin. He took hold of Cy's hands and pried them loose.

"Oh, Lord," Cy whispered. He closed his eyes and blackness overcame him.

Chapter 19
Return to Glass Mountain

Jacob was sitting in a chair next to Cy's bed when the attending physician came into the room. The hospital staff was aware of the existing danger for the police officer because he was the only witness to the killings in Boyle Heights.

A uniformed officer was always either in the room or stationed at the door. The policemen were from the Hollenbeck Division. No one could keep them away from Cy's room. Sergeant Golden was a fallen officer who had almost died, and they would give their life for him in a heart beat. He was a hero to his peers, one who had survived the impossible.

It was the third day after the shooting. Jacob held Cy's hand. He had been thinking to himself how dark his hands were compared to Cy's, except for the palms. He didn't know if this gesture comforted Cy. It didn't matter. It made him feel as if he were contributing something to the recovery process.

It pained him greatly to gaze upon his old partner, wondering what was in his future. He studied Cy's face. Both eyes were completely swollen shut, red and purple discolorations streaking across the soft skin tissue from the top of his head to his chin. It was a ghastly sight.

When the nurse entered the room and changed Cy's dressing on his head for the doctor's inspection, Jacob caught his breath. The bullet wound in the forehead reminded him of a miniature volcano. From the swollen entry wound made by the .22-caliber, hollow-point bullet, a red angry line ran from the front of Cy's shaved head to the rear where it had blown out the back of his scalp. The bullet had entered the thick layer of skin at an angle and ricocheted off the bone, skipping around on the inside of the skin to the back of the skull. The exit wound looked like someone had taken a sharp hatchet and chopped at the back of his head like a block of ice. An inflamed red line ran in a crooked path leading away from where the bullet exploded out the rear of his scalp. Black threads of nylon crisscrossed the red swollen tissue, holding the folds of skin together. It reminded Jacob of railroad tracks spiraling away from a train station.

The lieutenant was discouraged because Cy was not improving as quickly as he should, at least according to the attending physician. Cy would not speak after Skin's death had been confirmed. It had been seventy-two hours since the shooting incident.

Dr. Rogers had made several comments the previous day to Jacob concerning Cy's condition. He said Cy was not mentally trying to recover, and he felt this threatened the normal healing rate—his health was in jeopardy.

Jacob wasn't sure if the doctor's concern was about Cy's physical or his mental health. He told Jacob it was a miracle that Cy was alive. He said he had read and heard of other patients who had received head shot wounds similar to Cy's. In very rare cases, it was recorded that gunshot victims had survived point-blank gunshots to the head. Instead of the projectile breaking through the cranium, it ricocheted off the skull, skipping along a path of least resistance. Thus, the bullet might run along the inside of the scalp next to the bone and come to rest somewhere along the scalp lining, or exit, as it did with Cy.

Everyone agreed it was the only reason his friend was alive or not severely brain damaged. If the shooter had realized the bullet didn't enter the brain, he would have shot him again.

The doctor took Jacob aside, speaking softly. "Lieutenant Wilson, my nurse left a note for me. She said you had questions concerning Mr. Golden. What can I do for you?"

"Could you tell me what's going on with my officer? His face looks like hell, and you have all these tubes sticking in him. What are the extent of his injuries and what do you think about his recovery? I've known this officer ever since he joined the department. I need to know his prognosis, if you'll help me out here," Jacob said, fighting back his emotions.

Dr. Rogers studied the black lieutenant's face for a moment. He patted him briefly on the shoulder. "Let's step outside."

In the hallway Jacob leaned against the wall near Cy's door.

The doctor spoke calmly, and Jacob could feel the physician's genuine concern for his patient. "Let's begin with the lesser injuries and then on to the more serious, okay?"

"Okay, Doc."

"Mr. Golden received a non-threatening flesh wound in his right side. The bullet entered approximately one inch from the side and above the hip bone. It entered here," the doctor pointed to his right hip area with his forefinger, "and exited out the side without damaging vital organs. A little deeper toward the center and the projectile would have torn into the intestines. That would have been a major concern. Disinfecting a stomach area when the bowels are torn up is not a pleasure and the recovery time is greatly extended. At any rate, that particular wound was not serious and only requires suturing and good doses of antibiotics."

"That's good," Jacob said, nodding his head.

"The head wound looks pretty bad, but in reality, it's not as bad as it looks. Most patients swell up, making them appear worse than they are. Sergeant Golden was extremely fortunate with this injury. The bullet was not a large caliber, as you know. The .22 is often used in assassinations, and lucky for your officer, the projectile entered the front of his head at an angle and slipped under the skin, zipping around to the back of his skull and out.

"The tearing of the scalp is conducive to exit wounds; and once the skin grows together and the swelling is down, the hair will grow back. No one will be able to see the scars unless they were to lift his hair revealing his scalp lining. Of course, that's not likely.

"This injury is one of concern mostly because the patient received a minor skull fracture or brain concussion. With plenty of rest he should recover without permanent damage. I expect he will experience major headaches for a short time."

"I guess he was really lucky with the head shot," Jacob said.

"He most definitely was," Dr. Rogers smiled, assuring the lieutenant. "Now, the more serious injury was his chest injury. We term it a 'sucking chest wound.' The bullet entered well below his clavicle and luckily between the ribs. It punctured the top of his lung and lodged under the medial border of the scapula or the shoulder blade in the back.

"Now, when a bullet punctures a lung, it collapses. Sergeant Golden suffered what we call a tension pneumothorax. That means blood enters the lung, taking up air space, allowing air to expel into the chest cavity. The air between the lung and chest cavity is a danger to the heart until the lung is repaired.

"The main danger is putting pressure on the heart, and that is why we have inserted a tube into the chest cavity. As the patient inhales, the tube sucks air from the cavity which creates a vacuum, inflating the damaged lung. The tube is made airtight with petroleum jelly and gauze."

"I'm having a hard time understanding what you're saying," Jacob said, frowning.

"Okay, visualize it this way. Think of the lung as an inner tube inside of a tire. When the tube goes flat, air enters the cavity between the tube and the wall of the tire. That air must be removed in order to inflate the tube again. Are you following me?"

"Yeah, I understand that, but what happens next?"

"This type of injury causes a great amount of distress on the patient because he cannot breathe normally and must take short breaths, as you heard Sergeant Golden laboring in his room."

"Yeah."

"This is termed pulmonary compromise, which means oxygen is not getting into the bloodstream. By using a chest tube inside the chest cavity, we are able to pull the unwanted air out, allowing the lung, like an inner tube, to fill up inside the tire cavity."

"Okay, that makes sense, but how long will it take him to recover from that type of injury? I mean he looks like death warmed over in there," Jacob said, nodding his head towards Cy's room.

"Normally, in about three to five days we should be able to remove the tube and in four days the patient can begin walking. In three weeks he should be able to participate in light activities." The doctor hesitated a moment and went on.

"The one thing I didn't mention is that I removed the bullet that caused all the damage. After viewing the x-rays, I determined the location of the bullet to be resting against and under the wing of the shoulder blade. The .22-caliber bullet loses velocity quickly when it enters the flesh. That is why it did not cause damage to the rear caliper. I was able to make a small incision in the back, pulling the medial side of the wing up, and using a Kelly clamp, I extracted the bullet. In fact, I gave it to your detectives who are analyzing the evidence in this case."

"What is a Kelly clamp? I thought you always used forceps."

"Sometimes forceps are used for extractions. It depends on the size and the placement of the object to be removed. That is what dictates to the doctor what tool is best to use. The Kelly clamp has blunt tips with ridges in the jaws for a better grip on certain objects. When you probe with this type of tool, it is easier to find a small object than with the small ends of the forceps."

"That makes sense. So there won't be any permanent damage, and my man will be back to normal?"

"In time, yes. However, it's Golden's mental attitude that has me concerned. Considering the types of wounds Mr. Golden received, he should experience steady and aggressive improvement. When a patient's psychological demeanor is poor, it may and probably will interfere with the normal healing process. It appears to me that this patient does not desire to improve or to live, for that matter."

"Doctor, he lost a good friend. A girlfriend died a few months ago. His parents and only brother have died in the last five years. He is having a bad time of it. He had a new girlfriend but she left him just before the shooting incident."

"What you just described indicates to me he is going to need a very close friend to pull him through this. Are you that friend?" Dr. Rogers asked Jacob, looking him squarely in the eyes.

Jacob felt the impact of the doctor's question. It rested heavily on him. His voice wavered slightly. "Yes, doctor, he is my very best friend. I'll see him through this."

"I'm sure you will, Lieutenant, and believe me, he is going to need you." The doctor gave Jacob a healthy slap on the arm. "Now give me a moment with my patient." The doctor stepped back into the room, went to the end of the bed, and picked up a clipboard to study the entries on Cy's health chart.

It had been five days since the shooting incident and Jacob visited Cy daily. Jacob made an effort to contact Sarah on several occasions. Her work station advised she was not taking any outside calls. That angered Jacob, and he decided not to make further attempts to advise her of Cy's injuries.

On the sixth day, Cy spoke only when it was necessary to medical staff and very little to Jacob. He mostly ignored anyone who came to see him. He pretended to be asleep or too weak to talk to visitors.

On the eighth day, Cy had made some decisions concerning his future. Even though he was cool to Jacob, he needed him to do certain things for him. He decided to leave police work. He told Jacob in short and labored breaths that he was quitting the department.

Cy pressured Jacob into promising his assistance with a few important business details. Jacob was reluctant but felt compelled to help his friend. It was his life and his decision.

Cy asked Jacob to get some log cabin building plans from his apartment and send an order for a log cabin kit to the company in Rexburg, Idaho. He signed a check and showed Jacob the particular log cabin kit that he had circled in an advertisement.

Two weeks after the shooting, Cy moved in with Jacob and Lila to convalesce until he was well enough to care for himself. Cy's attitude slowly improved with his recovery. It was the new plan of moving to Mono County and starting a cattle ranch that lifted his spirits. It gave him something to occupy his mind. He wanted to become a recluse and isolate himself from other people.

He decided he didn't need or want anyone in his life. His preference now was to be left alone and to get on with his solitary life. He was determined to forget Sarah.

He tried desperately to blame himself for Skin's death, but in the end, he knew it was not his fault. He did feel it was his responsibility to have somehow gotten Skin out of that situation or at least taken the fatal bullet himself. After all the arguments between himself and Jacob, he accepted the fact he had done what he could.

That did not satisfy the emotional trauma of losing another person in his life, which contributed to his depression. Had it not been for Jacob and his family, he wouldn't have cared whether he lived or died.

Four months later, Cy packed up his belongings, loaded up his horses, and moved to the Mammoth Ski Resort village. After he arrived in the small community, he rented a small apartment for temporary housing.

A few days after he settled in and decided on a game plan, his spirits began to lift. He sent a check to Jacob's bank and anonymously paid off his and Lila's mortgage. He smiled as he slipped the check in the mail. Jacob always wanted to have his home paid for, so he could spend more time with his kids. It would be a shock to his friend when the deed arrived in the mail, thinking it was a mistake. Now he would be able to do the things he wanted. He decided it was good therapy to do nice things for deserving people. He had cheered up a little and looked forward to getting started with his new life as a civilian. The spring weather was good and he would start work tomorrow.

Cy's injuries were healing faster than he had expected. The pain in his chest and shoulder was almost gone entirely, although certain movements of his left arm still brought discomfort. His hair grew back, covering the deep scars on the back of his head.

He had grown a mustache and decided to let his hair grow a little longer than usual. At this juncture in his life there were no rules for him to follow, no one to order him around, and no one to answer to. He was his own boss and he liked the feeling. He was financially solvent and it gave him freedom to move in new directions.

Cy was surprised he was able to quit law enforcement so easily because it was something he had loved and was good at. Now he had no desire to be in confrontational situations. All he wanted now was his cattle ranch, and he had selected the perfect location on his new property. When everything was done, he would invite Jacob and Tony to come visit him. It would be good to have his home finished and friends with him. That's all he needed in life. Perhaps a dog would fit into his plans eventually.

Cy looked up Matthew Morgan in Bishop. At first, the real estate man was nervous when Cy walked into his office. But it was obvious to Matthew that Cy had not yet had a run-in with Benjamin Gray. He decided things would probably work out. Ben had been on a drinking spree for the last three months. Perhaps he had become disabled by booze. The more he thought about it, it was not his problem. He was a businessman. It was also unethical to frighten away potential clients when a good deal was in the making.

Matthew was happy to assist Cy with certain requests. He recommended a local contractor who would provide excavation work to prepare the ground for the footings and foundation. Cy also needed road graders and concrete workers he could depend on. Matthew gave him a list of reliable men who were electricians and plumbers and carpenters if he needed them.

Cy went to a local sports store in Mammoth and immediately became friends with the store owner. He purchased a 10 by 12 feet canvas wall tent with a wood-burning stove for cooking and warming the tent on cool nights. He also purchased a gas stove for cooking and as a second heat source along with a large ice chest and a complete outfit for long-term camping.

He went to the local hardware store and picked up a large Honda generator and electrical tools. He also stocked up on ammunition for his rifle, shotgun, and revolver. He already had most of the other essential items to make his life as comfortable as possible until he could occupy his new cabin. He felt relieved to be moving out of his apartment.

Cy loaded all the equipment into his horse trailer. He had boarded both horses with a man named Jim Reese on the east side of town. Reese had acted a little strange when Cy told the man where he was going to ranch. The man stared quizzically at him for a moment and then wished him luck. Cy wasn't quite sure how to read the man and shrugged it off.

It was the first of April and the weather was warming up to a beautiful day. Cy was anxious to set up camp and to stake a building spot. He had no time to waste if he was going to have the ground ready by the time the trucks arrived with the logs for his cabin.

Cy was having trouble getting a contractor to work for him. They all shied away from him as soon as they found out who he was and where he planned to build. No one told him why. They only made excuses that they were too busy or that his building site was too far away.

At noon he talked to Tom Payton, a rough-looking contractor who lived a hard life of working and drinking. When Cy told him where he was putting his cabin, he smiled broadly at him. "You're sure you know what you're doing?"

"I don't get it. I don't understand why people in this bloody town back off as soon as I mention where my land is located. Are they really afraid to travel a few miles out of town?" Cy asked, showing his disgust. "I'll pay my way. What's the problem?"

Tom studied the man and liked what he saw. "You got the guts to build there, I've got the guts to help you. You say your name is Cy Golden?"

"That's right," wondering what he meant by 'guts.'

"Well, I'm Tom Payton, and I'll see you through. When do you want to start? I'm presently working on some condos, but I can juggle my schedule around."

"Give me five days, Tom. I need to go up on the land and make sure I made a good decision where I want to put my cabin. I need to check out a couple of springs and determine the best access from the main road."

"Works for me," Tom smiled, cautiously. "Give me a call when you're ready."

"I'll do that," Cy said, moving away.

Tom opened the door to his office and let Cy pass by. He watched the man walk away, wondering if he would hold out. "Watch out for the Indian," he called after Cy.

"Say what?" Cy answered as he stopped and turned around.

"You heard me. Keep your eyes on your back side."

"I always do that. See you in a few days."

Cy drove north on 395 from Mammoth and turned right onto Highway 120 south of Lee Vining. After two and a half miles, he glanced to his left and saw Panum Crater. Instantly his face got hot and his eyes stung, remembering when Skin knocked down one of the men who had attacked Sarah. His breathing was labored and his chest wound began to bother him.

He missed Skin and his funny personality. He was a special friend and loyal fellow officer. A man could rely on him. He proved that with his life. Skin had killed Angelino; if he hadn't, the man surely would have killed him.

Cy longed for things to be different, but they weren't; he couldn't go back and change anything that had happened. Sarah flooded his thoughts. A different kind of sadness took hold. He thought of her beautiful soft features. Good thoughts changed to bitterness. Why had she abandoned him for no apparent reason? It hurt him to the very core.

That empty pain now gave him emotional relief. Not having Sarah in his life meant not losing her. He would not be responsible for anything that happened to her. If she was not involved in his life, then he couldn't lose her, except that he already had. Besides, she was probably married now and out of his life. So be it.

He enjoyed driving along, looking over the cedars and sagebrush. A white four-wheel police unit came up on him from the rear, red lights rotating. Cy checked his speedometer. He was only going 50. He pulled over to the side of the road, thinking the officer was going to pass him, headed to an accident or other police business.

The patrol car pulled over to the side behind him. Cy killed his engine and got out of his vehicle. He felt relief when he recognized Deputy Tom, who had arrested the four men who had assaulted Sarah. He was glad to see the county deputy, whom he thought had recognized him and was welcoming him to the valley. The frown on the deputy's face changed that idea.

"Deputy Tom, hi, it's good to see you," Cy said easily, smiling at the man.

"Let me see your driver's license and registration," the deputy snapped.

"Sure, but what for? I haven't broken any laws, have I?" Cy said, surprised at the deputy's attitude.

"Just give me the paper work," Deputy Tom growled, stepping closer to Cy.

"Hang on a minute there, deputy. Don't go getting excited," Cy tried smiling. "What's the problem?"

"Don't give me any trouble, mister. You do as I tell you, now!"

"You don't need to address me in that tone or manner, Deputy Tom. You know who I am and I know who you are," Cy said, carefully. "You have initiated an arrest by using your patrol unit to pull me over and restrain my freedom to conduct my business. You have asked me to identify myself. That's fine, and I will, but first you are going to have to advise me what laws I have broken and what I am under arrest for, okay?"

The deputy started to sputter, showing anger in his dark eyes. "You do as I tell you or you're going to jail."

"I don't think so," Cy said, shaking his head with a twinge of anger. He walked to the front of his vehicle where he was out of line of any on-coming traffic. The deputy was right on his heels.

"You hold it right there, mister. You do as I tell you," the deputy scowled, color mounting in his cheeks. He put his hand on the butt of his holstered gun.

"You're making a fool out of yourself...Raymond," Cy replied, reading the man's name tag over his right dress pocket. "There's no need to talk to me this way. If I've done something wrong, advise me of the violation. I'll show you my identification and registration as you have requested."

Tom cursed through clenched teeth. "You don't tell me what to do. I'm the law here; now take out your wallet and let's see your license if you've got one."

Cy protested. "You're not seeing anything until you conduct yourself in the proper manner."

The deputy was visibly shaken, having lost control of the traffic stop. People never spoke to him this way. He had the authority, not the stranger. "You'll do as I tell you or I'll hand-cuff you and take you in."

"Not really," Cy said, quietly. "You're not going to put cuffs on me without proper procedure."

"What? Who do you think you are? You'll do as I tell you."

"I don't think so. You're out of line, deputy. You've got a big black bug up your butt for whatever reason, I don't know. Whatever your problem is, it's not mine. You used your red lights to pull me over. That constitutes an arrest. You've arrested me without properly disclosing the reason for my arrest and the specific charges. As far as I'm concerned, you have violated the California Penal Code by violating my rights and not following proper procedure. Now, you can stand there all day spitting and slobbering all over yourself. I've got work to do." Cy moved to the side of the deputy to go around him and get into his truck.

The deputy grabbed his arm and Cy pulled away, reaching for the handle of his door. From the corner of his eye he saw the deputy start to reach for his gun. He stopped, turned around, and faced the man. "Don't draw your weapon, mister."

"You don't tell me what to do." The deputy drew his weapon and started to point it toward Cy. Cy quickly stepped closer to him, hit the back of the deputy's wrist with the palm of his left hand, and grabbed the barrel of the revolver with his right, twisting it out of his grip.

"You can't do that!" Deputy Tom yelled.

"No, you can't do that," Cy said, uncomfortably. He didn't like doing what he just did.

"Give me back the gun."

"Don't you find that a little embarrassing, to have to ask for your weapon back?" Cy was furious. "You're out of control and you've overstepped your authority. What's this all about, Ray? What's really going on here? I didn't break any laws, which means you made a false arrest under the color of the law. That puts your sheriff and department at risk of a class action lawsuit. You committed a felony by drawing your weapon and pointing it unlawfully at a person without justifiable cause. That person, being me, has the right to protect myself against an unlawful arrest and assault by anyone, including a law enforcement officer. You've gotten yourself in a bit of trouble here, and I don't believe your sheriff, who is an elected official, would condone this action. Am I right, deputy?"

Raymond Tom glared at Cy with such hatred it set him back. Cy knew no reason why this man should be hostile. If anything, he should have been friendly and given him a warm welcome into Mono County. Ray glared at Cy, as he held out his hand for the revolver. Cy pushed the side release, opened the cylinder, and emptied the six bullets into the palm of his hand.

"Give me the gun," Ray snapped angrily.

"You answer my questions or I'm placing you under arrest for an unlawful arrest and excessive force. I'll be taking you in, you got that, fella? You know I can do it, and I will unless you start making sense of what you've done here."

"You couldn't, you wouldn't," Ray sneered.

"I feel like knocking you on your ass and kicking some sense into you. If you don't start answering my questions, that's what I am going to do." Cy put the deputy's gun inside his belt at the small of his back and took a step forward.

Ray couldn't misread the look in Cy's eyes. He had badly misjudged this man and realized he had made a serious mistake. He didn't know if he had a way out of it. He decided Cy was streetwise, and he probably couldn't take him in a fight. If he did fight him, it would probably mean his job as a deputy sheriff. He didn't want to take the risk. Being fired with cause would ruin him in the valley.

"You stay away from Sarah," Raymond sneered.

"Sarah? What does Sarah have to do with you and me? I..." Cy suddenly recalled the name Sarah had mentioned in anger on the phone. She was going to marry Ray. It had to be Raymond Tom. He had not put the names together nor had he remembered the deputy's first name from their first meeting on the deer hunt.

"You heard me. You stay away from her or I'll kill you."

"You are badly mistaken here if you think I want to see Sarah or start something up with her. Besides, she's your wife, and I don't want anything to do with her. I'm here to make my home. That's all."

Ray wondered what Cy was talking about. "You're lying. All you white people lie."

"Now you're being a racist, Deputy Tom. Let's not add to all your other legal problems."

"I'll get you for this, and if I catch you bothering Sarah, I'll kill you." Ray held out his hand for the revolver.

"I care nothing for Sarah. Like I said, I don't ever want to see her again. I don't ever want to see you again. You two have a happy life. Start your own little tribe and stay the hell out of my life. I want to be left alone to work my land."

"Your land? The land you stole? You make me sick. First you fooled Sarah; then you stole the land. You are a person without honor."

"My place is paid for and I'm building it into a ranch. There is nothing you or anyone else can do about it. I just want to be left alone, and I'll mind my own business."

Cy took the empty gun out of his belt and tossed it to the deputy. "Here, take this damn thing and stay away from me. I won't say a word about what happened here today as long as you don't cross me again. I'm not looking for trouble, but by hell I'm not walking away from it, either."

"You walked into trouble when you took Benjamin's land."

"I didn't take nothing. I made a bid for it and got it. End of story. Now get your sorry ass out of my sight." Cy turned around, got in his truck, and drove off while the deputy picked up the six bullets off the road.

Ray angrily returned the shells to their cylinders. He knew how people were. It was only a matter of time before the newcomer would tell someone how he disarmed the Indian deputy and he would be shamed. He could be fired from his job. If he was, he would have to leave the valley.

For a brief moment he thought about going after Cy and killing him on the spot. The more he thought about it, the more he doubted he could kill the interloper. He decided Benjamin Gray would eventually kill the squatter, and he would stay away from the whole thing. Benjamin was the answer to his problems.

Twenty-three miles down the road, Cy turned right onto the dirt road that led to the back of Glass Mountain and Sawmill Meadow. The eleven-mile stretch was the same road he used for the deer hunt.

Cy's confrontation with the Indian deputy convinced him he did not care what other people thought of him. It reconfirmed his decision to be a loner. He was determined not to allow his spirit to be dampened by his poor reception from the local law. One deputy did not represent the department as a whole. He would put the episode behind him and find enjoyment in planning and building a home and ranch.

Traveling south on the dirt road he passed the left fork in the road that led to Black Canyon. The road became bumpy as he traveled on. One of the first things he would do would be to have it widened and graded flat to smooth it out. He stopped several times, checking the soil on the road, and was pleased to discover there was substantial gravel and road base that would maintain a firmness during the wet months. The shoulder of the road was sandy which he knew would absorb a great amount of moisture.

At 5 1/2 miles the road forked again. The left went to the old sawmill site and the right to McGee Canyon. Cy took out a topographical map and the legal description of his property. The map was now crinkled from the many hours he spent studying it while he was convalescing at Jacob's home. After a surveying crew shot the land designating his boundaries, a copy was sent to Cy.

Checking the yellow marks on the map, he turned the engine off and got out of his truck. After studying the terrain and checking several gullies, he walked up a hill toward McGee's Meadow. The ground leveled out and he observed some trees near a damp riverbed.

It was beautiful country with sufficient growth for range cattle. By leveling certain sloping benches that pleasantly rolled into valleys lined with springs, he could plant alfalfa, grain, and pasture grass. He would have ample land for ranching cattle and growing winter hay and grain. To maintain good water planning and conservation, he would build reservoirs and irrigation ditches, turning the mountain benches and valleys into a green paradise.

About three hundred yards above the meadow he found a small clear stream that ran through some rocks and disappeared into a floor of large stones and obsidian. Cy was elated to find the water—he had known about it from earlier hunts and was relieved that it still existed.

If water existed year after year maintaining a constant flow during each season, there would be a good chance he could tap the headspring to supply his personal needs for his home site. When the cabin and other buildings were completed, he would make plans for a deep-water well. This would guarantee water twelve months a year, every year.

Cy pulled a small glass bottle from his pocket and took a water sample. Tomorrow he would have it tested for culinary use. He felt confident he would not have to dig a well the first year. He also knew of other springs on the land that would be sufficient for livestock.

He unloaded his trailer and set up camp.

After three days Cy had placed all the stakes for the cabin site, barn, and several sheds. He called Tom Payton from Lee Vining to start the digging as soon as possible. He also ordered concrete and rebar for building a water storage tank and headgate which he planned to place at the mouth of the spring above his cabin.

The water sample had passed inspection for human consumption. Now he would have to protect it from the animals to keep it purified. He decided a three-hundred gallon holding tank with a three-hundred-foot long two-inch water line would be sufficient for the water pressure he would need for his cabin.

Tom Payton arrived the next day with a DC 8 and a backhoe. Both men studied the blueprints, and Tom advised him it was a simple plan and easy to do. While the DC 8 was used to grade a level cabin site, the backhoe was used for the spring and for burying the power lines to the main power station for all the building structures. Footings were dug. In two days the steel was in place and the cement was poured for the headgate, holding tank, and footings for the cabin and barn.

Cy studied his log cabin plans while Tom's crew started the cleanup. The assembly plans displayed a specific tag on each log with a letter and number to assist the builder in the proper placement of the logs, according to the plans of the blueprint. The procedure allowed amateurs like Cy to put the cabin together without professional assistance. The kit contained all the instructions and equipment necessary for completing a 2,000-square-foot cabin.

Tom's men loaded up their equipment on a flatbed trailer. Cy stood with the contractor, admiring the work they had completed. "You're going to have one of the most beautiful places in the valley, Cy. I've got to hand it to you, son."

"What do you mean?" Cy said, wiping the sweat and grime from his forehead with the back of his sleeve.

"You had a dream and went for it. No one else around here would do it. Plenty of people wanted this place, but not one was brave enough to bid on it. Did you know you were the only person who put in a closed bid at the land auction?"

"No, I didn't. That doesn't make sense. If other people wanted this land, why didn't they bid on it?" Cy said, mystified.

"Benjamin, that's why," Tom said, spitting tobacco juice on the ground, then wiping his lips with the back of his sweaty hand.

"So, who's Benjamin? I've heard some talk about him. But I've never seen him. You mentioned him the first time we talked."

"He's the previous owner."

"It seems to me if he wanted to keep his land, he should have paid the taxes on it. Besides, I understand the owner still owns four sections."

"That's true, Cy, but this land had been in his family for a long time. You, being a newcomer, won't settle well with him. You took some of the prime land with the best water."

Cy nodded his head in agreement. "I do have good water. I also wouldn't mind sharing any extra I might have with other ranchers. I guess I better look this Benjamin up and have a talk with him."

Tom spit again and shook his head. "No, no, don't do that. He'll be looking you up." Tom had been looking out over the panoramic view to the north as the two stood on the graded site. Mono Lake was to the northeast and Black Lake was to the northwest at the base of Antelope Mountain. "You'll meet him soon enough. Don't you go looking for trouble."

"I don't want trouble, but I'm not afraid to face the man who owned this land before me. It was his responsibility to maintain ownership. I'd rather be the person to buy it than someone else."

"There is no question in my mind, fella, that you can handle yourself. I personally wouldn't want to tangle with you, but you don't know Ben. He's big and he's ugly. He's drunk most of the time and he's ashamed of himself."

"What do you mean he's ashamed of himself?"

"Benjamin's family owned this land for how long, no one knows. At one time he was a successful cattleman. He had great potential. Then he served in the army during the Korean War. While stationed stateside, his wife and children were with him; then he received his orders for combat duty in Korea. His brother ran the ranch and did a good job while waiting for Ben to complete his tour of duty. Finally, when Benjamin showed up, he was alone with no family. No one knows what happened to his wife and kids. Anyway, Ben and his brother got in an awful fight over how the ranch should be run.

"To make a long story short, the brother turned up missing and no one knows what happened to him. Some think Benjamin either killed him on purpose or by accident. Either way, the brother disappeared."

Cy was taken aback by Tom's account. He wondered what kind of mess he had gotten into. "Were the authorities notified to conduct an investigation?"

"Oh, sure. Some blood was found but no body. Ben told the Sheriff that he had a fight with his brother and he won, so his brother left."

"That doesn't sound right," Cy said.

"Well, whatever happened, we'll never know unless Benjamin wants you to know. The Indians don't talk about their own. We are the outsiders. Whatever happened is probably known by other Paiutes in the valley, but they'll never talk about it." Tom took a long breath and looked at Cy.

"If you've got some cactus in your blood and can stick it out, you can have your dreams come true. It won't be easy, but you do have the law on your side. In time, things may slow down and bad feelings can get buried. Then you can make a life here. I hope you do, Cy. I like you and I want you to make it. No one else had the nerve to bid on this place, and there were plenty of ranchers who wanted it."

"I plan on making it work. I don't want any trouble," Cy

said, grinning at Tom. "After I get things going here, I'll look Benjamin up and have a friendly talk with him. I'll see if we can be good neighbors. I certainly want to get along with him, and everyone else for that matter."

"You don't get it, do you, Cy? I'm trying to tell you, you don't have to go out of your way to meet Ben. He'll show up some day and you'll have to grab your butt with both hands and run before he takes a bite out of it."

"I see. Well, maybe I'll wait till he comes to visit me, then. I'll talk him to death," Cy laughed. "Thanks for the work, Tom. The trucks with my logs are coming tomorrow. I've got a lot of work to do and little time for socializing. I'll give you a ring when I need you again."

"Okay. I'll bill you and send it to your post office box in Lee Vining. How come you didn't use the post office in Benton Hot Springs? It's a lot closer," Tom asked, walking toward his truck.

"I would have, but there are no stores for my needs. When I make a trip to town, I want to conduct a lot of business at one time so I don't have to make too many trips."

"Makes sense. Luck to you," Tom waved, and drove off in his truck, leaving a trail of dust behind him.

Cy stood on his building site watching Tom's truck tires whip up the dirt. So, the previous owner was a Paiute. He wondered if there was any connection with Sarah. After a moment of concentration he shook his head, deciding it didn't matter to him about Sarah. He wasn't going to think about her. She was married and her business and her life were none of his concern. He grew angry thinking how the woman of his dreams had deceived him.

Chapter 20
Slam Dunk Lee Vining

Benjamin's anger grew with every blow of the hammer echoing across the canyon. The hammer might as well have struck him time and time again in the heart. His eyes flinched with each sound of the new white man raising a cabin on his land. The rage within him overwhelmed his reason. Resentment festered deep into his soul.

Benjamin slammed the binoculars down on the ground and spit to the side. The saliva didn't clear his chin and hung in the air, swinging back and forth like a pendulum until it stretched from his chin to his dirty shirt. It took every ounce of strength in his large body to refrain from screaming. In a violent outburst of anger he wanted to feel the trespasser in the grip of his hands.

His long thick, straggly black hair was filthy with blades of dried yellow grass and dirt clinging to it, giving him the appearance of a wild mountain man. His shirt was shot through with holes in the back and elbows.

He rested his giant frame against a large rough boulder. Again, the government had taken land from him and his people. He shouldn't have to pay taxes on land owned by his family for generations. It was his birthright. Years ago, before he was born, the government declared the land was taxable because it was not on reservation land and it was privately owned and productive. The government had no business in his private affairs. He cursed his ancestors for giving up their rights to this land. He cursed them for not fighting when they outnumbered the land grabbers when they first appeared in the valley. He cursed them for selling their heritage and taking small land parcels in trade. He cursed himself for letting his taxes go unpaid.

He hated himself for being what he was—a drunk and a failure. At one time in his life, he and his brother could have owned most of the valley. His wife and sons were gone now. His brother was gone. The only good thing in his life was Sarah.

Sarah and Benjamin were the last of the Grays. Sarah and his ranch were his only reasons for existence. His spittle-covered lips almost spread into a smile thinking of Sarah. She was a beautiful child and his shining star. She lit the last of the dimming light inside his vengeful heart.

The sound of a falling board across the draw brought him back to the stranger—the sneaking white cheat who stole his land. He wondered how the man knew he was behind in his debts. He wondered if the land grabber had been studying him for a time and who the insiders were who tipped him off to the sale.

He didn't know whether the stranger had friends in Mono County or not. Regardless of the consequences, he had to get rid of him. The man somehow used Sarah to get information without her realizing it. It was time for him to pay for what he had done.

Obviously, if he killed the man outright, an investigation would lead to him because he would be the most likely suspect. Even Raymond Tom couldn't help him out of something so serious. He thought for a long moment, took a swig from his whisky bottle, gargled it, and swallowed.

He picked up the binoculars and located his subject carrying boards into the new cabin. Anger flared again. There was only one way to be rid of this varmint in his midst; he would kill him in a fight. It wouldn't be much of a task, but the stranger must be a willing participant. Ray told him once that if two men were openly and willingly engaged in a hand-to-hand altercation, neither one could be charged with assault.

Benjamin's jumbled thoughts took him on a circuitous route back to his youth.... He sat with his grandfather under a tree to keep cool in the hot summer heat near the site of the new cabin. The old man had told him killing a white man was not murder to an Indian. It was a form of warfare, to kill the enemy on your own terms. The white people had better equipment and were many in number. To an Indian not bound by white men's laws, it was a positive action if one could engage and kill the enemy in the night without taking the chance of being outgunned, wounded, or killed.

Benjamin struggled with his blurred thoughts for a long moment. He decided the next time the stranger went to town, he would approach him and somehow engage the man in a fight. He would beat him to a pulp each time he found him in town. The stranger would be embarrassed by his public beatings and leave the valley a defeated and broken man. It would also send a definite message to anyone who had designs on his property in the future.

Benjamin was now pleased with his decision. It was a wise and intelligent one. Tracks of whiskey left running trails down the corners of his mouth. If this plan didn't work, he would have one last fight and simply kill the man in self-defense. Nothing to it. It would be an unforeseen occurrence, one that was entirely innocent. Everyone knew the two men did not like each other. The newcomer, a land grabber and greedy outsider, challenged the old drunk Indian to a fight and pitifully but accidentally died of his injuries.

The more he dwelled on his new plan, the more he relished in it. The broken-down Indian, a drunk and discouraged old man, was provoked into a confrontation. It would be an unpleasant and unintended situation. Yes, it would be an unfortunate mishap when he killed the stranger—nothing but an accident.

There could be no forethought or planning of such a situation. It just had to happen naturally—both men showing up in the same place at the same time. It was bound to happen sooner or later. It would be terrible that the stranger died, of course, because everyone knows Benjamin Silver Gray never killed anyone. Except in the Korean War. Yes, he was a decorated veteran. He had fought and killed in Korea. He even had a purple heart and was the local hero.

Benjamin regrettably let his mind go into a slump. He thought back to the awful day as he did almost every day of his life. He and his wife had a terrible fight. She threatened to take the children and leave him if he did not stop drinking and wasting money. He was going to show her. No woman was going to back talk him like that. His wife knew he loved her and the children. They were his whole life. What he didn't like was her constant nagging and hounding. He told her if she wanted to leave, he would drive her to the bus station. Yes, sir, he would call her cheap bluff.

What he didn't plan on was the car accident. He squeezed his eyes tightly shut, remembering his wife's face and his beautiful children. The movie in his head played the scene again and again. He was drunk, driving down the road to town when he turned to face his wife because of her sharp remarks. The crash happened so quickly, he never felt a thing. There was no screaming or crying, just darkness.

He lost his whole family in the flicker of an eyelash. His survival of the crash was his shame. He knew he did not deserve to live. Whiskey was his only relief, whiskey and his plan to leave his land to Sarah.

By birthright, Sarah should have the ranch. Sarah and Raymond Tom could work the ranch together and have a good life. It was Paiute land, not the white man's.

Perhaps by ridding himself of this new affliction, things would get better. He hated the stranger with a passion. A smile of distaste crossed his lips as he contemplated the painful death the man would experience. He pressed the rim of the bottle to his lips and took a long pull. It tasted good and it gave him courage.

It was the first week in May when Cy decided he would be able to move out of his tent and into the log cabin. It was only partially completed but he was tired of the cramped quarters in the kitchen tent. With the roof now completed on the cabin, he could move his personal belongings inside and use the tent for other storage items. He did not want to have anything in the cabin that didn't need to be there while he was working on the finished carpentry.

His septic tank was in place and hooked up to the toilet system. Water had been piped in from the spring holding tank, and the bathroom sink was connected and thankfully didn't show signs of leaking. It was a miracle because Cy knew little about plumbing. He had purchased several how-to books on the basics in building, and the articles on carpentry, electrical work, and plumbing saved him from making many mistakes. For certain technical projects he would hire professionals to complete the work. Even though he could well afford to employ others, he enjoyed doing most of the work himself. As far as he was concerned, this was his last home, and he wanted it to be a creation from his personal vision and efforts.

His mind seemed to clear as he worked with his hands. It was a time of continued healing. His palms were now calloused and his muscles were hard again. Keeping busy was his road to stabilizing the emotional strain he experienced in losing Skin and separating himself from the rest of his friends at Hollenbeck.

It was also a time to recover from losing a girl who had

completely captured his heart, then broken it. Many times at night his eyes burned from trying not to think of Sarah. Cy knew he was bad luck for anyone close to him. He came to realize it was better that things had worked out the way they did. Even if Sarah left Ray, he would stay away from her. She was too pure and good to be mixed up with him. Given time he knew he would be able to erase her from his mind.

He enjoyed the isolation of living alone and giving all his time and talents to his ranch. He tried to concentrate totally on building; however, in moments of quiet solitude his thoughts often drifted to Skin. He hadn't realized how much Michael Fin had meant to him until he died. He was glad Jacob was in southern California and away from him. He cared too much for his friend to lose him, too.

He knew in time he would be stronger by spending all of his time working hard and enjoying his life—building sheds, putting up fences, raising animals, and establishing a working ranch.

Cy planned a trip to Bishop to pick up a stainless steel double sink he had ordered for the kitchen, a full-length tub, fiberglass shower, gas stove, and refrigerator. The most important items were the refrigerator and the sink. He dearly missed ice cold drinks. He had quit drinking beer but had become addicted to Mountain Dew. Next to water, it had become his beverage of choice.

His finish carpenter, Buzzy Long, promised the windows today. The doors, which were hung yesterday, included an electric double door for the garage.

The two greatest expenses in the building project were getting the electric power to his cabin and improving the road. He hired a crew to bring hundreds of yards of road base and gravel. A road grader leveled the road so that it had a slight crown in the middle to allow good drainage to both sides. In several areas culverts had to be placed in low spots under the road to maintain the natural drainage from different draws and slopes.

In the evenings, after the workmen left, Cy would take a towel and bar of soap and go to the spring for a spit bath from the holding tank. The water was so cold it was painful to wash his entire body. So that he wouldn't contaminate his tank, he washed and rinsed from the overflow pipe jutting from the holding tank at the top. A three-inch flow pipe allowed a continual run of icy clear water into the rocky waterbed, and it meandered downstream and eventually disappeared into the earth. Tomorrow he would be able to take a hot shower, and his life would be greatly improved.

Cy picked up his supplies in Bishop and had lunch at a Mexican restaurant in Mammoth. He decided to pick up some groceries in Lee Vining before returning to the ranch. It was a beautiful day, and he was enjoying the break from the grueling work on the ranch. He decided he would get a dog but wasn't sure what breed he wanted. On his father's ranch they always had Blue Heelers. He wanted a dog that didn't shed and could take the cold of winter. Most of all, he wanted a companion.

It was mid-afternoon when Cy drove into Lee Vining. He pulled his truck up to the Lee Vining General Store at the south edge of town. The same old Indian was sitting on the bench outside the store. For some reason, Cy was glad to see him.

The old man had not changed in any way since the deer hunt. He had an unlit hand-rolled cigarette between his lips and appeared to be asleep. Cy was sure he wore the same frayed shirt. Cy turned the engine off, walked over to the bench, and sat down next to the old man.

"Maik (hello)," Cy said, leaning back against the store wall.

"Maik yourself," the old man said with his eyes closed.

"Ahkk-ahd-I-wahnee (How are you)? I haven't seen you for a long time."

"Seen better days. No complaints from my lips." The old man maintained a sleepy posture. Underneath the exterior of his expression, he was very much alive. At that particular moment he was smiling to himself, pleased that Cy had said a few words to him in Paiute.

He remembered this young lad well. It brought him pleasure as he recollected the time when this young man's heart jumped from his chest the first time he laid eyes on Sarah Gray.

Cy sat for a moment inspecting the street and stores. Finally, he gave the old man a sidelong glance. If the Indian had not just spoken, he would have thought the old man was asleep or, for that matter, dead. "Niyaani (my name is) Cy, and I'm happy to see you again."

"Why you happy to see me?" the old man asked with his eyes closed.

"Oh, there's something about you I like. I'm not sure what it is, though."

"Cy, you seem like a nice person." The old man opened his eyes and looked at Cy. "I know you have heavy heart. I know of you. Sarah is good girl. Very good girl. You very nice boy. You work hard every day. You have big hopes. You should go to Mammoth and stay out of Lee Vining. It's not good for you here."

Cy was surprised by the old man's comments. "Why do you speak of Sarah?"

"All Paiute know each other."

"But you spoke as if you had knowledge of Sarah and me."

"I know you have a heavy heart, Cy Golden."

Cy was taken by surprise. He sat erect on the bench and examined the old man. "How did you know my last name was Golden?"

"I know many things. Because I am old and tired does not mean my brain is dead."

"It's the specifics I'm talking about. How do you know my last name?"

"I sit and I soak in knowledge from many people," the old man spoke quietly in his Indian accent. His words were slightly slurred and his lips gave a clicking sound when his lips parted in speech. "I also know Sarah. I have known Sarah all her life. I know her feelings."

"Her feelings are not my business," Cy said flatly. "She's a married woman and is not my concern."

"Married?"

"She either told me she was getting married or that she was already married, I'm not sure which. It doesn't matter either way," Cy said, disgusted, getting up.

"Why does it not matter?" the old man asked, looking up at Cy. He wondered what was going through this young lad's heart.

"I'm bad luck for anyone I get close to." Cy adjusted the western-cut straw hat on his head. "I have my ranch and that's all that matters to me. What's your name, if you don't mind me asking?"

"Why you ask?"

"Can we be friends?"

"If you want. I don't dislike you." The old man's face was

grim, but his eyes had a glimmer of warmth to them. "Joseph. Not Joe, not Joey. Joseph Dondero. The Donderos have been here since before the town was born."

"I'm pleased to know you, Joseph. I hope we can be friends."

"We can," the man said carefully. "We can, as long as you do not hurt little Sarah. She has attached herself to my heart and is like family to me. I have a little advice for you. Stay away from Benjamin Gray. He is bad. Very bad. He sometimes is plagued with boils. When he is infected, he is worse than bad. You are not welcome on the mountain, but I have no quarrel with you." The old man leaned back and closed his eyes, appearing to fall asleep.

Cy turned and entered the store. He purchased enough food supplies for a week. He went to the post office and stopped at a service station across from the general store. Joseph was still sitting on the bench. He filled up his truck and paid the attendant, who looked nervous when he took the money.

"You better get out of here, mister," he said under his breath.

"What?" Cy wasn't sure if he understood the man.

"Get out of here before you get hurt. Don't look, but there's a big, mean Paiute leaning against the restaurant behind you. Rumor has it he's laying for you."

Cy took a quick glance and saw the huge Indian. The giant was leaning against a strangely shaped diner next to the service station. The diner had a slanted roof that peaked high in the back and ran downward almost to eye level in the front. The building was rectangular in shape and appeared as if the end of the structure had been cut off short at the south end where a back street ran alongside it.

Cy glanced across the street to the general store. Joseph was sitting up now and looking across at him. He thought he saw the slightest movement of the old man's head, nodding to him and motioning for him to leave. He started to turn for his truck when he recognized Sarah's jeep in front of the store. His chest tightened as he moved toward his vehicle. He did not want to see her. He cursed himself for coming into Lee Vining. His heart was pounding hard and his breaths grew short knowing she was so close to him.

He stopped at the door of his truck and reached into his pocket for the keys. A shadow loomed from his right. He looked up into the meanest eyes of the biggest man he had ever seen.

The Indian stood at least 6'7" and weighed no less than 300 pounds. The man was like a mountain next to him, and the angry look in his eyes was frightening. When Cy opened the door to his truck, the giant reached out and slammed it shut.

Cy knew who the man was without introductions. "So you're Benjamin?"

"You smart-mouth little dog turd."

"Does this mean you don't like me?" Cy said easily, sizing the man up. If he couldn't talk his way out of this, at least he was on open ground and could move around. Well, hopefully he could. He wondered if he dare run.

"Turn-around. Is that what they call you?"

"I don't know, whiskey breath. Is that what they call you?"

Benjamin was so aghast at this young spit of a man in front of him, he did not know what to say. Most men backed away from him. Why didn't this one?

"Hello, up there. I believe I asked you a question. Please respond or I'm going to think our moment of bonding is a failure." Cy was smiling cynically and Benjamin was fuming.

Cy didn't notice the people from the diner and other businesses gathering in closer. Everyone but the tourists knew something downright nasty was going to occur, and no one wanted to miss it. Willis, the service station attendant, shook his head at his boss. "Can you believe it? The way that guy is talking to Ben?"

"Ben will kill him. No one has ever talked to him like that. This guy must be nuts. No one can talk that way to Ben and walk away." Rick, the boss, spit tobacco juice on the ground. "No one."

"You've got to give the new guy credit for speaking his piece," Willis said.

"I heard the newcomer is an ex-L.A. cop. He must be a tough one, but there is no way he can hold his ground with Ben Gray."

Benjamin growled, giving Cy his best junkyard dog look. "Turn-around, get your skinny white ass out of Lee Vining and this county."

"Turn-around. And just what does that mean?"

"Turn-around is what a man is when he can't take the pressure and leaves with his tail between his legs."

"Mister, if you lost your land, that's your fault, whatever the reason. I purchased it fairly. Now that I have it, I'm keeping it," Cy said, moving sideways away from his truck. He wanted the sun to his back if things went bad.

Cy continued. "I don't want any trouble with you, but if you're thinking of rearranging my teeth, you're going to find yourself on your hands and knees, shaking your head and wondering how you got there."

Benjamin's bloodshot eyes flared, showing red ridges around his eyelids. His mouth was sour and his temples pounded with anger. He decided to kill the man on the spot. He reached out to grab the young pup and smash his head in.

"Hold it!" Cy ordered, holding up his hand, palm facing Benjamin.

Benjamin stopped but only for a second. He realized his mistake too late. He saw the blur of a foot shooting upward into his testicles. A searing pain engulfed his whole body, causing his eyes to snap shut. Two quick blows to his temples and a hammer punch to the neck between ear and shoulder blade dropped him to the ground. It was merciful that he was knocked out cold. Otherwise, the pain in his groin would have caused him immeasurable embarrassment as he screamed in agony in front of the townspeople. Cy knew striking the man in the carotid artery would close off the blood to the brain and render him unconscious for only a few seconds. The pain would return, but he would not be able to get on his feet for a long time.

"Good Lord Almighty!" Willis gasped. "I never would have believed it if I hadn't seen it."

"I don't believe it and I just saw it," Rick sighed. "The new guy is a dead man now. There is nothing on this earth that will save him from a horrible death when Ben comes to."

"I'm putting my money on the cop, or ex-cop," Willis said. "That's the fastest precision move I've ever seen."

Rick smiled, shaking his head in disbelief. "I'm afraid Ben's down for the count." He walked over to the stranger and took him by the arm. "You must be Cy Golden."

"Seems everyone knows me," he said quietly, catching his breath.

"Mr. Golden, you may have done an awful thing here putting Ben down like that. He'll come looking for you."

"I know he will. I didn't come looking for trouble. I don't want trouble with anyone. I just want to be left alone."

"Well, you got trouble now. Ben will never live down what

you've done to him. Vengeance runs in his blood. I'm afraid you are a dead man and don't know it."

"I know I mind my own business, and if you don't want my business, I'll go somewhere else."

"No, no, no. Don't misread me here. You are plenty welcome. I'm just warning you to watch your rear from this point on. Ben will be there when you least expect it."

"I'll be watching," Cy said, walking to his truck, "and I'm not letting him keep me from Lee Vining. I like this town and I'll come back whenever I need to, for supplies or for whatever or maybe for no reason at all."

"Okay," Rick said loudly to Cy. Under his breath, "Good Lord in heaven, help us all around here. We have a newcomer in the valley that ain't backing down."

"Tell me," Willis smiled. "Holy tomollies, did you see how he dropped Ben like a sack of potatoes?"

"Yeah, I did. Now we've got to worry about what's going to happen when he comes to. He might decide to tear the place up. We have a problem on our hands here," Rick said, turning to the station office. "I better call Deputy Tom to come over and work this thing out so we don't all take it in the shorts."

"Gees Almighty, you're right. Hurry before he wakes up. This could be a catastrophe," Willis said, wondering if Benjamin would take it out on them for what happened here.

Joseph was building a smoke, deep in thought. He was completely taken by surprise by the quick and deadly movements of Cy Golden. He never thought he would see the day another man could put Benjamin Gray on the ground in a fair fight—fair fight meaning anything goes with the bare hands. He wondered if there was a nerve or something in the neck that would make a man go down like Ben did when it was punched.

Sarah walked out the door and looked across the street to see Cy pulling away in his truck. She quickly sat down on the bench next to Joseph, her knees trembling. She glanced back across the street at the crowd standing in a circle. It appeared someone was lying on the ground, but she couldn't be sure.

"What happened, Joseph?"

"Oh, not much."

"What do you mean, not much? Is there someone hurt over there?"

"I think so," the old man mumbled, lighting a new smoke.

"You think so. Joseph, what's going on? What happened over at the station?"

"Do you remember Cy Golden, that stranger from Los Angeles? You know, the one who you said stole your heart. Well...."

"Stop it," Sarah interrupted him. "Who's over there?"

"Benjamin."

"Uncle Ben?" Sarah's head turned from the old man to gaze across the street. "Did Uncle Ben hurt Cy?" Sarah moved rapidly to take the old man by the arm. "Talk to me. What happened?"

"Well, Benjamin made a big mistake, little one." Joseph took a long draw on his smoke, inhaled to the back of his lungs, and slowly exhaled. "He made a big mistake."

Sarah released his arm, grabbed a handful of shirt and wadded it in her fist, and pulled the old man to her face. "You talk to me, Joe, or I'll knock you into the next room."

"Sweet mother of earth. You still love him, don't you?"

"I didn't say that. And never mind my romantic status. What happened?"

"Well, Benjamin bit off more than he could chew, little one. He ran up against a man who doesn't backstep too well."

"What happened, Joe? I'm going to start swearing if you keep this up."

"Ben walked over to the young man and started a fight with him. Before Ben could ever lay a hand on him, he got his balls kicked up between his shoulder blades and got hit about three or four times. He went out like a light," the old man said excitedly. "You wouldn't believe it unless you saw it, Sarah. It was a work, I tell you. I've seen tough men before, and fast ones, but never have I seen anything like that."

"I have," Sarah smiled. "I saw him and his best friend the day those four men attacked me. I never would have thought two men could protect me from those awful bullies."

"Do you still love him?"

Sarah glanced away from Joseph. "Why do you ask that? You know I'm going to marry Ray."

"Sarah, I'm a very old man," Joseph said tenderly. He reached over, putting his arm around the girl, remembering how often he had wished she was his daughter. "I know the difference between the 'look.' I know, Sarah. I know."

Sarah could not bring herself to look at his piercing eyes.

"What are you talking about?"

"You have the 'look'." It's like a young woman with child. A certain light shines in a mother's soul and it lightens her eyes. She cannot hide it. It's just there. I know the look in your eye. You cannot marry a man who does not have your heart. Ray is a fine person, but he is not for you. He has not captured your heart. The new one has, and there is nothing you can do about it. Follow your heart, little one. If you marry Raymond only because of our traditions, you make big mistake. Follow your heart." He pulled Sarah over to him and kissed her on the forehead.

"Oh, Joseph, what do I do? Uncle Ben and Ray told me Cy somehow tricked me and stole my uncle's land. It's not like Cy, but he did not explain himself when I called him on the phone."

"Did you have your ears open to your heart or your brain or to nowhere when you talked with him? I do not believe this young man is dishonest. I see a great sadness in his eyes and he is heavy in heart. You know old Indian proverb, 'there are two paths to every story.'"

Joseph laughed quietly at his humor. "You must talk to him again. Let him speak of himself to you. Does he seek you out? No. Does he think you belong to Raymond Tom? Yes. Does he have honor? I believe so. He would not shame you, little one. Give much thought to this thing."

Across the street people started to drift off at the same time the large figure wobbled to a standing position. Sarah could hear the roar of her uncle's angry voice. "Where's the turn-around?" No one responded. Only slight murmurs could be heard.

Sarah ignored the happenings at the service station. "I've been so confused, Joseph. I have experienced so much pain and turmoil over my emotions for Cy. My intuition tells me he is good and speaks only truth and wisdom. On the other hand, my only living relative, the brother to my father, tells me this man has used me and cheated him out of his land."

Joseph asked, "Has Benjamin explained to you how Cy Golden tricked you or him out of his land?"

"No, and that bothers me greatly. After I called Cy in California, I asked Uncle Ben and Ray to explain what Cy had done. I showed my loyalty by cutting Cy from my life; I expected a reasonable explanation from both men and they have not satisfied my concerns. They only give me excuses, like it's a 'man' thing and I would not understand the details. Now

I have doubts as to their honesty, but they are family. I have lost face with Cy and cannot seek him out to question him concerning these matters. It would make me look like a fool."

"A fool is a person who does not open one's self to understanding."

"Joseph, I cannot go to him. I lose too much face. I am so ashamed of myself. I am so lost in my misery. Just seeing him drive away in his truck made me tremble. He is the only man who has touched my heart, but that feeling of warmth and joy I once had has changed. Joseph, what must I do?"

Chapter 21
Hostile Environment

The next five days, Cy kept busy at work installing his kitchen appliances, the bathroom, and the finishing touches on the cabin. Next, he would put the fences up and send in an order for a starter herd of cattle. His father had always purchased breeding cows in Collbran, Colorado, from a man named Bill Charlesworth at the Rocks Springs Cattle Ranch near the Plateau River south of town. Cy decided to buy two bulls and some young heifers from the same place. Before the cows arrived, Cy had to set up water troughs for the grazing cattle and store up winter hay before fall set in. The following year he would have enough level ground seeded and harvested to meet his needs.

Thursday evening after the sun went down, Cy placed two pistols in separate metal boxes, and sealed them watertight before burying them on the ranch away from the cabin. It was a precaution he didn't like taking, but he had spotted the glare from binoculars or a rifle scope in the distance. He knew he was being watched, and he knew there were two men of his acquaintance who wanted him dead. Obviously, there was Benjamin. The second was the ugly Mexican who shot him in the head. Once the man discovered Cy had lived, he would try and hunt him down because he was the only witness who could identify him as the cop killer and assassin.

Cy thought it over many times and did not think the Mexican would be able to find him. He was eager to meet the killer again, but only on his terms. He knew the man was extremely dangerous, but he also wanted to avenge Skin's death.

Only Jacob Wilson and Tony Valin knew he lived in Mono County. They would never give away that information. So, it was unlikely the man with the binoculars was the Mexican. It had to be the Indian. That was bad enough. After the incident in Lee Vining, Cy knew he had to be careful to avoid another altercation at all costs.

In some ways, he felt sorry for the man who had lost part of his ranch. In other ways, Cy felt the man had not worked the ranch to make it a productive and useful venture. If Cy hadn't purchased it, eventually someone else would have taken it.

Cy knew he had taken the man by surprise at their first altercation. He would not be that lucky again. He decided he would keep a gun on or near him at all times. He would try to avoid town as much as possible. He would only go in for food and gas at the beginning of the week, never on the same day, and always at different hours. He also would alternate his shopping with Mammoth, about 24 miles south of Lee Vining.

When Cy wasn't working around the cabin, he took long rides on Cole. Riding his horse on his own land gave him many quiet hours to plan his ranch, not to mention peace and comfort. He loved the mountains and the beautiful scenery, and he felt exhilarated to own so much land. He planned the sites for windmills for watering the stock. He surveyed the benches and determined which areas he would dry farm with grain in the spring and which areas he would irrigate by sprinkler for winter alfalfa and pasture grass. There were hundreds of acres of wild range with native grass for grazing the cattle. He knew his first year it would be critical not to overgraze and cause damage to the existing flora. It was also in his mind to protect the plant life to entice the deer and elk to continue their habitat range in this area.

To make a profit was not the full purpose of his ranch. He was financially healthy, but he wanted the ranch to prosper in order to maintain his stock holdings and bank assets. Careful ranching and hard work would give him the opportunity to be successful.

Cy estimated it would take him three years to complete his goals and sustain a working cattle ranch the way he wanted. By the end of that period, he should be able to break even in ranching costs and start making a profit once his hay and grain fields were established and the cattle bred and re-bred, building his herd. He was raised on a cattle ranch, and now he would be able to create his own business and use the skills his father had taught him.

Even with all his plans and many projects, Cy couldn't control his thoughts of Sarah. He was consumed by his memories of her—her beauty and warmth—almost to the point of distraction. He tried not to think about her, but he could not forget the satisfaction and comfort he experienced holding her in his arms, touching his lips to hers. He lacked the power to erase her from his mind. Sometimes he didn't want to.

Cy realized he was a failure when it came to Sarah. With her married, even if she didn't love him, he was lost in despair. He struggled to recall every detail of their three days in California. He remembered the feeling he experienced just seeing her jeep at the general store in town. He thought about her beautiful dark eyes and shiny blue-black hair that caught the sunlight; the thought of her smooth soft bronze skin and her lithe but mature figure made him ache with desire.

He wondered if he would ever get over her. He wasn't sure if he wanted to, in reality. Thinking of her was such a pleasure. He visualized her standing on the rock with the grinding stones in Alpine, folding her arms talking to him in soft shy tones about the Indian people. If this was love, why did it have to be so painful?

He had almost made up his mind to seek her out and talk to her. He had to forcibly remind himself that she was married and made a promise to let it go. As he analyzed his recollections of Sarah, he first experienced great joy. Now, it was growing into a painful memory.

Work was the answer. He made up his mind to exert all his energy and talents in building his own private paradise on the mountain where he wished to die someday.

He hired a trucking firm out of San Diego to ship the farming equipment he was now glad he hadn't auctioned off when he sold his father's ranch. He sent for his combine, baler, driller, and tractor with accessories. Other equipment he would buy at farm auctions or from dealers in Bishop.

Juan closed the door of the automobile and stepped over to the sidewalk leading to the four-plex in the projects in north Hollenbeck. He watched a woman park her car and pick up her groceries from the trunk. When she came up the walk he moved into the light of the street lamp so he would not frighten her.

Joan Sausedo stopped when she saw the dark figure. She knew who it was by the size of the man and immediately she felt nausea.

"Un momento, Señora. I need to have a word with you," Juan said, keeping his voice low.

"Are you loco? Not out here." Joan shocked herself by

speaking so rudely to the man. "Come inside, please, before someone sees you." Joan unlocked her door and Juan followed her inside.

She put the groceries on the kitchen counter, turned the living room light on, and closed the front curtains. "What has Armando done now? Is he in trouble again?" Her eyes displayed the horrible thoughts going through her mind.

"No, no, nothing like that. He is doing fine. I am here for another reason."

"What could you possibly want from me? I have nothing you would want."

"I need an address from you. Nothing else."

"No! You get out of my place now. I have nothing. I know nothing. I give nothing," Joan cried. "Please leave me and my son alone. Please!"

"Señora, be quiet. You are getting excited over nothing." Juan stepped closer to the Mexican woman. He had known her for years. She was a hard-working, productive woman, and he didn't like invading her life this way, but he had no choice. She was his only hope.

"What do you expect from me? My son is lost to your drug world. My life is ruined because of you and your business. Please, just leave."

"Señora Sausedo, do not get excited. You must keep your voice down or I will become upset." He stepped forward, grabbed the scared woman by the back of her hair, and slammed her head face first against the countertop. "You must not anger me, Señora. You do that, terrible things may happen—to you, to your son, to your mother, bless her heart."

"Oh, no, please leave us alone," Joan cried. The pain from her head hitting the countertop was pulsating up and down her face. She felt a large welt swelling on her forehead. Blood from the corner of her left eye dripped onto the counter.

Juan continued to press the woman's head against the Formica slab. He leaned down to her ear. As he spoke, specks of saliva entered her ear and sprayed her face. It was obvious the man was crazy, and if she did not cooperate, he might kill her son and her. It would not be an easy death, she knew. "What do you want?"

"That's better. I need you to get me the address of an ex-cop who left the department last November. You see, it is not a conflict with you. It is a man who has nothing to do with your precious department anymore. All I want is to know where he is living now. That's all. Nothing more, and I will not bother you again."

"Swear you will never bother me or my son again. You release him from your debt. Swear it, now!"

"I swear it. Give me the address and you will never hear from me again."

"Swear it on your mother."

"On my mother. I swear it, you old hag. Now listen to me." He ground her head with great force on the countertop. She cried in pain and he pushed harder. "You get me the address of Cy Golden. He is the officer who was wounded in a shootout. He quit the Hollenbeck Station eight months ago. Get it for me and we are through. You will never hear from me again. Understand?"

"I work in payroll, not benefits. That information is in another office."

"I know where you work. I also know you can walk into that office during your lunch break and act like you're doing your business. So don't give me any of that nonsense. You have a choice, woman. I kill you fast and your son slowly if you do not provide me the information I want. You do what I ask, you will never see me again."

"Okay, okay, stop squashing my head. I'm going to faint," Joan gasped, and fell backward when Juan released her.

"Joe Molino and my associates will know nothing of this. It is between you and me only. You get me that address and your son's slate is washed clean."

"How do I get to you?"

"Don't worry about it. I will come to you," Juan growled, annoyed with her. "If you tell anyone, I will kill you. Comprende?"

"You think I am crazy? I will say nothing to no one. I swear," Joan said, wiping her face and smearing blood across it.

Juan turned and left her apartment, closing the door behind him. Joan walked over to a large soft armchair in front of the television and lowered herself into it. She cried for almost fifteen minutes. When she finished, she went into the bathroom and washed her face in cold water and dried off with a bath towel.

She picked up a small personal phone directory, looked up a number, and dialed. On the other end a male voice answered. "Hello?"

"Jacob Wilson?"

"Yes. Who is this?"

"Jake, it's Joan. Joan Sausedo. You were right. It has finally happened. I have been contacted for Cy Golden's address. It was Juan Mores. He will kill me if I don't give it to him."

"Okay, Joan. Tomorrow I will meet you at the administration building. I'll talk with you and your supervisor in a safe room," Jacob said calmly. His forehead was getting hot and he felt uncomfortable, but his voice was reassuring. "Everything is okay. You did fine. I'll talk to you tomorrow when it is safe. God bless you, Joan."

"I'll need it when you realize who you're dealing with." Joan put the phone back on the holder and stared at it for a long time. She decided she would have to move from Hazard. This was her home and her people, but things were different now; she had to get out. She took a deep breath, rubbed her eyes and slowly let it go. Tomorrow was another day. She hoped she had made the right decision. It may be one that would send her to the grave.

Two weeks passed without further incident with Benjamin. Cy's farming equipment arrived. He graded level pastures and set up two windmills to pump water into holding tanks besides placing two other water troughs below near two hidden springs. It was too late in the season to plant grass. He would wait until fall when the weather cooled.

The cabin was complete with a spare bedroom upstairs. It had a small balcony with a view of the mountains to the north. Behind the cabin was powerful, mythical Glass Mountain, and Cy decided he was going to climb to the top of it someday. He had never been to the top, and he always wondered what the view was like from so high up.

At noon he drove to Lee Vining and went to the general store for supplies. He needed milk, eggs, bread, and butter, along with other incidentals. When he pulled up to the store, he was glad to see Joseph Dondero sitting on the bench. He got out of his truck, walked over to the Indian, and sat down next to him.

"Well, it looks like you have had a rough day, sir. How are you?" Cy laughed.

"It has been a hard day now that you mention it," the old

Indian said quietly. "I started early this morning when most people were asleep. You see, I rise before the rooster crows at first light. I water my horse, gather a few eggs, kick the dog, and do my daily honey-do's for the boss woman."

"I didn't know you were married. That really surprises me, Joseph. I assumed you lived alone."

"Well, I don't live alone and I'm not married, so there," Joseph snapped.

"Okay. That's okay with me. I could care less."

"You could care less about what?"

"I could care less about you living in sin with some old woman," Cy teased.

"Why you say it is in sin? You a preacher or something?"

"No, I..."

"No, nothing. Who I live with is my business. However, since you brought it up, she really isn't that old. She only forty-five years," Joseph said proudly.

"Now, that's something to brag about, at your age," Cy said.

"How old you think I am, young man?" Joseph looked sideways at Cy.

"Well, you have ten thousand wrinkles. I suspect you are at least eighty-five."

"Hah! That shows you are a poor judge of age, besides character."

"How so?"

"I am eighty-four and the woman is my daughter. So there. You misjudge me badly. I have sore eyes for you. You think through something other than your head."

Cy laughed and slapped the old man on the leg. "You are sly like a fox, Joseph."

"Now you have judged me correctly, young man."

Cy reached inside his Levi jacket and pulled out some zigzag papers and two bags of Bull Durham. "Here, this is for you."

"What is this?"

"We'll say it is a peace offering. I like you and I wanted to give you a small gift." Cy got up and started for the store entrance.

Joseph grinned mischievously. "When one gives a peace offering to a Paiute, he must in turn, do something nice to the giver. So I will share with you some Indian humor. Is that agreeable?"

"Sounds good to me. Let's hear it."

"The youngest of three tribal brothers went to his father one day to ask him a very important question. His father was chief. He was a very big and strong, but silent, warrior who did not talk to his sons except when he was in the camp after the hunting was finished. The young boy stepped up to his big father and said, 'Old wise chief, why you name oldest son Screaming Eagle?'" Joseph said, sounding like a young boy.

"The father looked annoyed at his little son. He folded his large arms across his chest and answered in a deep voice. 'One day when squaw give birth to oldest son, she go out of tepee down by river. Just as No. 1 son come into the new world, a glorious eagle flew across the sky screaming a song of the hunt. So squaw named No. 1 son Screaming Eagle.'"

Cy felt a warmth for the old man as he waved his arm mimicking a flying eagle.

"'Father? Father, why was No. 2 son named Running Bear?' Joseph said in a high-pitched voice.

"'Mother and I on trail for the fall hunt,'" the old man said in a deep voice, folding his arms Indian-style across his chest. "'When baby come, she stepped out of lean-to and go by the river to bring son into this world. Just as No. 2 son come into this world, a black bear ran across the river and into the trees. So she name the boy Running Bear.'"

Looking at Cy as if he were the young boy, Joseph asked in the chief's voice, "'Why you ask many questions, Pooping Dog?'" The old man laughed so hard, he almost fell off the bench.

Cy threw his head back laughing. He slapped the old man on the shoulder. "I can see you are going to be receiving many gifts from me if you have more jokes like that one." He turned and went through the front door.

After a few minutes he reappeared with a sack of groceries. "You have a good day, Joseph."

"My good friends call me Joe. Indian Joe."

"Does that mean we're friends?"

"What else would it mean?"

Cy laughed. "Thank you, Joe. That means a lot to me."

"I knew it would," the old man said, as he put his head back and closed his eyes.

"See you in a week or so," Cy said, walking toward his truck.

With his eyes closed the old man moved his lips. "What you think of Sarah is wrong. Sarah good girl."

Cy stopped and spun on his heels. "I have no doubt she is a good woman. I hope she is happy with Ray."

"Ray not good for Sarah. Maybe you be good for Sarah," Joseph said, not opening his eyes.

"I have no say in that matter. Too late, old man. It's too late. She made her choice. I wasn't part of it." With that, Cy got in his truck and drove south on 395. After he turned left on Highway 120 and headed east toward Glass Mountain, he pondered on what the old Indian said. It didn't make sense. Sarah said she was either marrying or was married to Ray Tom. That was almost eight months ago. If she wasn't married then, she surely would be now. His stomach got tight thinking about her and he again felt lonely.

By the third week in June all the small detail work was finished on the cabin. The water tanks were filled and functioning. Cy ordered double-strain barbwire and six-foot steel poles. He hired two Mexican migrant workers to put them in. Jesus and Louie were good workers and well worth the money he paid them. Both men liked working for Cy, and they were especially happy when Cy cooked for them on occasion. One evening he took the two men to dinner in Mammoth to a Mexican restaurant. Neither man could believe their boss would personally take them into a public restaurant and have a meal with them. It was unheard of, but they were grateful for his kindness.

It was Saturday morning and Cy went back into Lee Vining to stock up and to purchase a third pole pounder to help the Mexicans install the steel poles. He had paced his trips into Lee Vining, not wanting to make frequent appearances in town. He took a chance, deciding his supplies were more important.

Cy told his two men to take some time off until the rest of the fencing came in. He promised to call them when it did. He picked up the things he needed at the hardware store but was disappointed not to find Joseph sitting in front of the general store. He filled his truck up with gas and drove across the street to the store. He decided to buy some tobacco for Joseph. He would stop at the Donderos' place and give it to him on his way home.

When he left the store, he saw Benjamin leaning against his truck with a sour smirk on his face. Cy was going to ignore him and leave. "Stop right there, Turn-around. Today is my lucky day. That means your lucky day, it is not," Benjamin laughed.

Ginny, the store clerk, saw what was happening in front of the store. She got on the phone and rang the Sheriff's Office in Bridgeport. "Hello, this is Ginny Wickem calling from the Lee Vining General Store. Benjamin Gray is out front. He looks drunk and mean, and he is getting ready to beat up a much smaller man. Can you send someone right away? I believe Deputy Raymond Tom is on duty. I saw him not ten minutes ago going north on 395." After she received confirmation that a deputy would be sent, she hung up the phone and looked out the front store window.

The last thing Cy wanted was to tangle with the Indian. If anything, he wanted to be friends with the man, especially since they were going to be neighbors, and also because the man once owned his land. It did not make sense to continue to be hostile to each other. He wondered what the man had said to Sarah to turn her against him. Perhaps it was Deputy Tom's doing.

As much as he didn't care for the deputy he wished the man was there to intercede for them. He didn't want a fight and he especially didn't want to get hurt. The more he thought about it, Benjamin was a frightful man.

If Cy couldn't talk his way out of a confrontation, he knew he would have to use every dirty tactic he knew from his years of teaching at the police academy and working the streets.

"You're a scary guy, Benjamin. I didn't want to mix it with you last time and I don't want to today. Can't we just be friends? If not, how about being good neighbors."

"You toad head. Who do you think you're talking to? Good neighbors? You land grabber. You stole my land out from underneath me. Just how, I don't know. You used Sarah somehow," Benjamin growled.

"What does Sarah have to do with you and me? I never spoke to her concerning my plans to buy the place. For that matter, I didn't even know who the land belonged to. I made a sealed bid on land that someone had not paid their taxes on for a number of years. Good hell, if I had known it was yours, I probably wouldn't have bought it, but I did and I'm staying," Cy said angrily. He was losing his temper. He didn't want that to happen. He had a terrible temper and if he lost it, he would walk right into the middle of a bad fight.

"You piss and vinegar little pimple on my ass. You split tongue lying sack of crap. I'm going to split your head. You don't speak my niece's name to me. Your mouth is raw with filth and lies," Benjamin yelled, walking around Cy, sizing him up.

Cy moved back, keeping his distance from Benjamin. The man was half-crazy with anger.

If he was going down, it would not be without a fight. He was mad now. So Sarah was his niece. And Sarah had accused him of using her to buy the parcel of land. She didn't give him the chance to explain what really happened. His anger and frustration doubled.

"You fat blubbering drunk. That's why you lost part of the ranch. You obviously need someone to blame for your short-comings."

"You!" Benjamin screamed like a gut-shot panther. "I'm going to tear you apart like a dog on a deer hide!"

Cy backed up, stepping into the street to have more room. Benjamin might have had a lot to drink, but he was not intoxicated. Cy carefully scrutinized the man, anticipating his angle of approach. He was trying to make the decision whether to be on the defense and attack on the reflex or be on the offense when he noticed the Sheriff's patrol unit coming down the street from the north. He felt a moment of relief until the patrol car turned off the main drag and disappeared.

Cy thought to himself, proper action in hand-to-hand altercations required three things: to remain alert, to be decisive, and to have a planned practiced response in mind. If he was in his right mind, he would turn and run like hell. That was exactly what he wanted to do. He would have disappeared like a rabbit, but there would always be another time and another place. This was the time and the place. There were no other options.

Cy circled Benjamin to get to a relatively good defense position. If he could get to his side, he would have the advantage.

Cy trusted his instincts and decided to anger the Indian to the point that he would not be thinking clearly on good defensive moves; instead, he would want to tear Cy apart, without thinking of his own danger areas.

"You talk like the wind, Benjamin. It just blows on and disappears in the distance. Sarah told me she was called an apple Indian by her people because they thought she was red on the outside and white on the inside. You, I call cotton candy. You look to me like you could be anything you wanted to be, but you're like cotton candy—take a bite of you and there's no substance."

Benjamin yelped as he jumped for Cy, who sidestepped and kicked Benjamin in the knee as hard as he could, giving a smashing blow to the patella. It surprised him when the big man did not go down. Most people would have been incapacitated after receiving a strike to such a vulnerable area.

The man roared in anger, intensifying Cy's terror. He knew, now, if Benjamin got his hands on him, he would kill him for sure. Cy quickly stepped to the man's left side and kicked him hard in the other knee. This time the Indian fell back against the wall of the store but still did not go down.

Cy could not believe his blows had failed to disable the giant. He knew he was in serious trouble. Kicking was not his usual tactic at the beginning of a fight. Now, he had to pull every trick he knew to survive. The Indian did not respond to pain as most people would—his pain tolerance was too high. Cy would have to initiate other tactics.

"Little squaws fight like you, pissant. You use your feet like a child. It is of no consequence to me," Benjamin rasped, looking at his knees and then glaring at Cy.

Benjamin swung with a right roundhouse. Cy ducked and hit him with two quick, powerful blows to the ribs and stepped away bouncing on his feet to keep his balance, preparing to move in again. He wondered where the damn deputy had disappeared to. He figured it was Ray, and Ray wanted Benjamin to hurt him bad.

Benjamin was blinded with anger. Saliva dripped down the corners of his lips and dangled in midair. He knew there was only one outcome. He would kill this bloodsucking leech. He moved in and swung a left, clipping Cy on the forehead. It spun him around and almost knocked him off his feet.

People were gathering around the store. Joseph Dondero appeared, wondering what was going on. When he recognized Benjamin, he was worried, knowing Cy didn't stand a chance. He looked up the street and saw Ray Tom's vehicle behind Sally's Restaurant north of Rick's Service Station. He was sitting behind the wheel watching through a pair of binoculars. Joseph motioned to him but the deputy ignored him.

Cy shook the cobwebs from his head and saw Benjamin

coming in for a second round of punches. Cy feinted with a left jab, swung for all he was worth with his right, and connected on the left cheekbone. Cy jumped back in disbelief. Everything he had was not enough. His blow did not even slow the man down. He moved back to the side, careful not to get pinned next to the wall. He would be finished if Benjamin could pin his arms.

Benjamin was more angry than he could ever remember. This spit of a man would not hold still, and his sharp blows were taking their toll on his ribs. He was having trouble breathing as he gulped in air. He got Cy after two tries with a right hook to the side of the head. Cy went down and rolled over. When Benjamin reached down to grab him, Cy kicked him in the knee twice, sending him stumbling backward.

His head buzzing and his stomach knotting with fear, Cy did not know how much longer he could last. Benjamin's blows were like hits from an ax handle. He was in trouble and no one was going to intercede and help him. He would die on this street if he couldn't counter the big man's attack.

Cy rolled away from Benjamin. Cy's thoughts raced, recalling the three C's of street survival: concentration, cohesion, commitment. He decided he was going to live, and he would kill this giant if necessary. His mind went to the very things he did not learn in the academy. He would go to the extreme. Jacob had showed him moves that were not taught in any school but only learned on the streets. He had only one hope if he couldn't reach his opponent's testicles, and that was not likely. Benjamin was carefully protecting himself, as he had not forgotten his last altercation with the white man.

Cy slowly came to his feet and kicked Benjamin again in the left knee; with the sole of his boot, he raked his shin downward to the top of his foot. Cy then stomped on the top of his foot with three quick blows using the heel of his boot, causing Benjamin excruciating pain. Cy raked the shin again and moved to Benjamin's left, punching him with two hard blows to his rib cage just below the breast. Benjamin backhanded Cy across the side of his face, knocking him backward.

Benjamin backed off to get away from the crazy white man. He did not like the way this altercation was going. He would have to work in close to get his arms around Cy and squeeze the life from him.

❧

Sarah drove into town after leaving work. Today she staffed the front counter at the Lee Vining Ranger Station. She was tired and depressed. Her life was not going well. She even considered quitting her job or asking for another station away from Mono County.

On her way home she was going to stop at the general store, but first she needed gas. She drove into Rick's Service Station. Ray was sitting in his car at the stop sign facing 395 next to Sally's Restaurant. She got out of her jeep and walked over to Ray. He was busy looking through his binoculars and did not notice Sarah approaching him from his left.

"Hey, Ray," Sarah laughed. "What are you doing? Got nothing to do but look at the girls?"

Ray jumped, almost hitting his head on the head liner. "Gees! You gave me a start there," Ray said sheepishly.

Sarah was suspicious of his expression and tone. "What's going on, Ray? What are you looking at?"

"Oh, nothing much. I was just trying to make out what was going on over by the general store."

Sarah looked over and saw people standing in a circle to the south of the store in a vacant lot. Joseph Dondero was limping across the street with a rock in his hand. When he got close enough he threw it at Ray's vehicle and hit the windshield, cracking it.

"Hey, what the hell's the matter with you? Why did you go and do that?" Ray yelled.

"You...you're a disgrace to our nation. You miserable excuse for a man, a Paiute, and lawman," Joseph said angrily with tears in his eyes.

Sarah frantically looked back to the deputy. "Ray, what is it? What's going on?"

❧

Cy took two smashing blows to his midsection and the air was knocked out of his diaphragm. He went crashing to the ground facedown. He worked his way up to his hands and knees gasping for air.

Benjamin leaned over and grabbed Cy by the hair with his left hand. He saw the small round strawberry scar on Cy's forehead and used it as a target. He landed a hard right blow to Cy's head, almost hitting him between the eyes, knocking him back to the ground and causing him to fight consciousness. Coming to, he tried to focus and adjust his vision but found that he could not.

Benjamin reached down and picked Cy up like a sack of potatoes. He had him now. Before Cy had a chance to get air into his lungs, Benjamin maneuvered Cy into a face-to-face bear hug, lifting him high in the air, where he hung limp. People groaned when they saw the life being forced from the young man's body.

One man came up behind Benjamin and hit him in the back with his fist. It had no effect. He yelled for someone to get a board to hit Benjamin with; there wasn't one and people stood in awe at the two men before them. Another man picked up a garbage can and hit the big Indian in the back with it. It had no effect. Benjamin tightened his arms like a boa constrictor. It was a death grip that no one could stop.

Cy's face turned blue from the lack of oxygen. His vision was blurred and his strength was going. He swung a hard blow to the Indian's throat, striking the man's trachea in an attempt to crush his esophagus. Again, no effect. Cy was losing consciousness. The noise ceased and his vision was full of black spots and fading. He was dying and he knew it. Skin always said go for the eyes. It was a sure thing. It was time to pull the last trick out of the bag.

Feeling victorious, Benjamin gritted his teeth, feeling bones breaking under his crushing grip. He felt Cy's thumb slip into the corner of his wet mouth. It was of no matter. He had him now. He felt the thumb withdraw from his lips and he looked up to see Cy's wet thumb disappear into the corner of his left eye.

Cy thrust in his thumb, burying it to the hilt in Benjamin's eye. He bent his thumb at a right angle and pulled outwards. Benjamin roared in pain. His left eye lay on his cheek. He dropped Cy and fell to the ground. Cy fell to his side and passed out. Benjamin screamed, grabbing the left side of his face and trying to determine what was lying on his cheek.

Someone grabbed Benjamin by the shoulder and pulled him over on his back. "Holy hell," Deputy Raymond Tom muttered in shock. "Ginny," he called over his shoulder to the store clerk, "call an ambulance. Quick!"

"Who's the ambulance for, Ray? Ben or the tahng-wahts

(white man)?" Dondero asked angrily.

"Nu nung-wants nah-nah-poots (I am an Indian, old man); I have honor," Ray muttered, disgusted with the situation and himself. This had gone too far.

"Eem cahch eem (you no good Indian)," Joseph said sourly.

"Inik-a num-pi-cant (you are crazy)," Ray hissed.

"Ee-mee spood-ae oee-yoom, Raymond Tom (your heart is cold). Who you call ambulance for?"

Ray hesitated and finally spoke. "Both."

"You better use two different hospitals. When they come to, they'll kill each other for sure."

Rick, who had been watching the fight, stepped forward and looked carefully at Cy. Cy was moving his head and blinking his eyes. It took a while but Cy finally focused in on Rick, who was frowning at him. "Rick," Cy choked. "Get me...to my...truck."

"No, man, you got to go to the hospital."

"Help...to my...truck, Rick." Cy passionately gasped. "For God's sake...help me. Help...me!"

"Okay son, okay," Rick said, patting Cy on the shoulder. He turned to one of his employees. "Willis, start his truck and move it here quick." People moved away as Willis went for Cy's pickup. He started it and drove it around to the side of the store.

Both men helped Cy behind the wheel. He was in terrible shape and he cried in pain with every step. Cy knew he had broken ribs, but he was not spitting up blood, which was a good sign. He couldn't take a deep breath, and his whole body was in excruciating pain. Willis stepped around to the other side and put a sack of potatoes next to Cy to hold him up behind the wheel.

"Hey, Cy, let us drive you home. You're in no shape to make it alone."

"I...don't...need your...I don't need anyone," Cy gasped.

"Yes, you do, you're really hurt bad. Let us help you," Rick said, sick to his stomach.

"Where were...you when...I needed you. Where...was one... who would help...me. Not...one. You can...go to...hell!" Cy cried, choking. His left eye was now swollen shut and he could barely see out of the other. He was an awful sight and the people did not like looking at him. Cy pulled away and slowly drove down the road, headed for his cabin.

Chapter 22
Mending Hearts

Sarah drove east on Highway 120, worried she would not know which dirt road to turn on. She hadn't been there for years. Joseph told her it was the old Sawmill Road that would take her to Cy's ranch.

She passed the Mono Mills historical site on her left and later almost turned right on the historic River Wagon Road. She saw Glass Mountain ahead and to the south. She continued on until she recognized the Sawmill turnoff.

The dirt road was now improved. It was graded with a hard road base and it was wider. The chuckholes and washboard bumps were gone. She was relieved because now she knew the improved road would lead her directly to the ranch.

In a state of turmoil and apprehension, Sarah could feel her heart thumping like a bass drum in her chest. She was filled with anxiety as she wondered about Cy's condition. She wished she had not waited for two days.

She was thankful that Joseph demanded she check on Cy. It was what she needed to help her make up her mind. It wasn't a matter of pride anymore. She had none. She didn't know what was truth or what were lies or exaggerations concerning Cy. She didn't trust her uncle and now she had no respect for Ray.

A weak feeling gripped Sarah when the cabin came into view. How could she have ever doubted Cy? He had been so kind and tender with her. He made no improper advances and treated her with respect. It was inconceivable that she could have dishonored him by not trusting him.

That morning, after she talked with Joseph, she called Jacob Wilson's home and talked to his wife, Lila. She told Lila about the fight with her uncle, but didn't know Cy's condition. Lila told her the story of Skin's death and the part Cy had played in it. She explained to Sarah how Cy blamed himself for Skin's death and how he was feeling about losing everyone in his life who was dear to him. Lila told Sarah that Cy did not want to be near anyone close to him.

After talking with Lila, it took Sarah only a second to grab the keys to her jeep and head to Glass Mountain.

Tears formed in Sarah's eyes and ran down her cheeks. She blamed herself for not giving Cy the opportunity to explain away her false claims against him. She should have known better than to trust her alcoholic uncle. Ray had no excuse. He was an educated and intelligent man who let his pride cloud his vision.

At first, she marveled at the cabin's natural setting. It was built between huge fir trees on a small knoll overlooking the valley. She was startled when she saw the horses in the corral running back and forth in a terrible temper. She rushed over to them. Cole was running up to the rails and bumping them in the heat of desperate hunger. Sarah threw hay over the top rail and immediately went to the cabin.

She walked up the three steps to the front door. To her surprise, it was partly open. As she stepped closer, she could hear her heart pound in her chest. She wanted to cry out for fear Cy would not forgive her. She loved him so desperately. Those thoughts halted when a terrible odor wafted through the door, stinging her nostrils.

Inside, Cy was on the floor in the living room, flies flying and crawling all over him. The smell was atrocious. Sarah ran to Cy and kneeled next to him. He was unconscious and the sight of his condition made her gasp in horror. Both eyes were swollen shut and crusted over. Flies had landed on his face and body as if he were their last meal. She thought for a moment he was dead. She hesitated then reached out to feel his body temperature. He was warm; a small sound came from his encrusted lips.

He had defecated and urinated in his pants. The smell made her gag, and she ran over to the sink and washed her face in cold water. She turned on the hot water and searched for some towels. When she found them in the bathroom, she returned to the kitchen, filled a large pan with soapy water, and carried it over to Cy. She tenderly washed his face, disturbing the angry flies.

A brownish-yellow crust sealed his eyes shut. The warm water softened the crust and eventually she cleared his eyes. She carefully rolled Cy from his side onto his back. He groaned in pain. She wiped the rest of his face clean, went to the bathroom, and found eye drops in the medicine cabinet. She spread the swollen tissue around his red eyes and placed moisture drops in them. Then she got a glass of cold water and gently poured drops of water onto his lips that dribbled into his mouth.

Sarah gagged again from the stench. She rushed to the front door, sucking in fresh air in heaving gulps. Tears came to her eyes. She knew now she was never going to leave this man if he would take her back. She loved him more than life itself, and she hated herself for having ever doubted him.

During all those months of torturing herself, wondering why Cy did not come to her and explain her charges against him, she had no idea that he had experienced the emotional ordeal in the shooting death of his friend. She was in disbelief that he had come so close to death himself, for she had no knowledge of his condition.

She remembered Joseph's words that morning when she explained the phone call to Jacob's home and his wife's explanation. Joseph told her Cy was like Glass Mountain. The mountain in and of itself stood tall and powerful; but the basis for its structure was obsidian, and one earthquake could bring it down to a heap of broken rubble. He said Cy had the earth pulled from him time after time, as people vanished from him. He told her Cy was a family man without family. He had no one he could be close to, in fear of another one being taken away. Cy was like Glass Mountain. He was strong and powerful, but his heart was like glass, easily shattered.

Sarah took a deep breath of fresh air, wiped her eyes, and walked back inside to Cy. She unbuttoned his bloody shirt and pulled it off. She unbuckled his belt and unbuttoned his Levis. She moved down to his feet and pulled off his cowboy boots. She removed his socks and then pulled his pants off. The smell was terrible and she had to work with her teeth clenched to keep from throwing up.

She was thankful he was unconscious; otherwise, she did not believe he could have taken the pain of moving with broken ribs and the embarrassment of having released his bowels on himself.

She found paper towels in the kitchen and wiped his body down, then she washed him clean with hot soapy water. She then wiped him down with rubbing alcohol.

Sarah went to his bedroom on the main floor and pulled his mattress into the large living room, placing it on the floor next to Cy. She struggled until she had Cy on it comfortably, then covered him with a blanket.

In the kitchen she found a cotton dishtowel. She carried it to the mattress and laid it down, folding it into a large diaper. She removed the blanket and scooted it under Cy and pinned it up through his legs and around his stomach.

When she finished, she bawled until her throat was swollen and she couldn't cry anymore. Finally, she went to the phone and called Dr. George Krain of the Family Health Centre in Mammoth. She explained why she couldn't bring him to Mammoth, so he agreed to come out to the ranch.

After she hung up, she went back to Cy and placed her hand on his cheek and felt his fevered face. She put a cool damp washcloth over his face and went back to the phone. After staring at it for a number of minutes, she picked it up and dialed Lila in Glendora.

When Lila's voice came over the receiver, Sarah couldn't talk and began to cry. It took her a long time before she could tell her story. Lila said they would be there that night and to stay with Cy. She said she would call Jacob at work and leave for Mono County as soon as he got home.

Lila held the phone to her ear with tears in her eyes. "Sarah, hon, I love you, dear. Now don't you worry about a thing. We'll be there for you. We'll be there before dark, I promise."

"Thank you, Lila. Thank you, and I love you, too." Sarah cried as she hung up the phone.

She sat for a long moment looking out the window, wondering to herself how she could have misjudged or failed to trust a man she loved so deeply. Cy had not shown one weakness in character to her, and yet she did not give him the opportunity to defend himself when she made false accusations against him. She thought about his strengths and his needs—the loneliness he must have felt. She especially felt shame for her failure to have faith in Cy.

Dr. Krain finally arrived in the afternoon. He wanted to have Cy taken to the hospital where he could perform a better physical examination. Sarah would not allow it. She was afraid for Cy's life if her uncle found out he was in town. She suddenly realized she did not know the condition of her uncle, and it surprised her that she wasn't worried about him.

The doctor told Sarah that Cy had some broken ribs, but it did not appear the lung was pierced. He also suffered a concussion, besides other cuts and bruises, as well as a high fever. He told her Cy would be much better once the fever was down so the mending process could begin. He prescribed antibiotics and painkillers and said he would have them delivered to the ranch. It would cost a considerable amount to have them delivered so far in the country but there was no other choice.

He asked Sarah not to leave Cy alone and to get warm broth and liquids into his stomach until he was well enough to eat solids. He said he would send some hydrogen peroxide to bathe the cuts and instructed her on how to keep him clean. Dr. Krain wrapped Cy's ribs, gave him a shot, and left the mountain cabin.

Sarah sat down next to Cy and lifted his head onto her lap. She leaned against Cy's couch for support while she patted his head with a cool damp cloth. She felt a strong urge to be close to him. She leaned over and kissed the round mark on his forehead and then pressed his head to her warm breast. It felt good having him so close. She almost felt like a mother caring for a child, a nurturing love that enveloped her whole being. Pent-up feelings had been hidden too long. Now she could give her love to Cy. If he would have her, she wanted to share her life with him.

When the prescription came, Sarah paid for the drugs and walked back to the kitchen. She had difficulty in getting Cy to swallow the pill. She finally crushed the pill in a soup spoon and dissolved it in warm water. With an eye dropper, she forced the antibiotic down his throat a drop at a time until it was gone; then she gave him the painkiller. She knew in time he would rest and start to feel better.

Jacob and Lila arrived at dusk. Both came running to the cabin. Sarah met them at the door, giving them a brief description of the doctor's prognosis. Jacob didn't wait to hear all the explanation and went over to Cy, who was asleep on the floor. He took one look at his friend, sat down next to him, and began to cry. He couldn't hold it, and he didn't care who was in the room with him. This was his best friend and old partner. Cy had gone through so much over the years. He thought of Cy's dreams of living here when they went deer hunting and all the campfire discussions they had to solve the world problems.

After a while Lila and Sarah got up from the sofa and sat down next to Jacob on the floor. He had Cy's head in his lap, rubbing his hands gently through his hair. Looking at Sarah he said, "It's about time you know who Cy Golden is. He was the best partner and the best cop I have ever known. If he had stayed on the department, he had great promise. Cy was loved by everyone, and I want you to know his story. I promised Cy I would not call you or tell you about him. But I want you to know how fortunate you are to know him. I want you to know the truth behind his buying this ranch."

Three days after the fight, Benjamin lay in his bed with a splitting headache. His left eye was swollen shut and he was sure he had been hit by a Mack truck, not some puny city slicker. The doctor had placed double-wrapped gauze under a black eye patch to brace his eye. He tried to get out of bed to relieve himself. It was almost too painful. Pains shot down his side. The doctor confirmed he had four cracked ribs. The damn doctor lied; he knew they were broken. The index finger on his right hand was busted and in a splint. Both knees were the size of cantaloupes and he could not get them to bend. He grabbed a jar setting by the bed and peed into it. Mostly in it. He missed part of the time but he couldn't help it and didn't care. He was hurting far beyond anything he had ever experienced.

Ben swore to himself, it was not worth it. He would not cross Cy Golden again. The pain wasn't worth it. He never wanted to see the man again.

He lay back in his bed wishing he had a whiskey to take the edge off the morning misery. He'd just have to think about it. He knew he couldn't move that far. If Cy showed up on his doorstep this moment, this day, he'd ask the man to shoot him in the head.

Lying there with his thoughts, Benjamin knew it was his fault he lost a big share of the ranch. He knew he had the taxes to pay and refused to answer the government inquiries. Sometimes he was so stupid, so full of ridiculous pride.

After another hour he tried to get up and again his ribs and knees hurt too much. This time he wet the bed. He wanted to die. If it weren't for Sarah, he'd call it quits.

"What do you mean she's moved?" Juan shouted, slamming his fist down on his desk.

"She's gone. That's all. Someone has moved her from the projects. It looks like she has been transferred to work somewhere else."

"Check out her son, Armando. He'll know where his mother is. Cut him with a knife until he tells us what we want to know."

"Can't do it, boss. Armando is gone, too."

"What?" Juan jumped up from his chair and came around the desk to face Reuben.

Reuben did not like being the bearer of bad news. "Armando can be found nowhere. He has vanished. No one knows where."

"You stay on it and find him. Check on some other contacts and spread the word. I want Joan and Armando Sausedo. Also, talk to the traffickers who travel in and out of the state and tell them to keep an ear open for information. I'll pay them well."

"Yes, boss, consider it done."

Sarah slept on the mattress next to Cy. She gave him liquids during the night and changed him once. The swelling in his eyes had gone down only a little, but there was no more crust, and the redness was subsiding.

Cy's head felt like a drum that someone was hammering on. It seemed to vibrate when he wanted to move, but when he tried to move, he couldn't. The pain in his ribs shot through to his chest, and he caught his breath. He couldn't open his eyes. They felt hot and heavy. He struggled for awhile and finally got both hands up to his face and pulled his puffy eyelids apart.

What he was looking at was not real. A dream was sleeping next to him, Sarah, in all her splendor. Her long black hair lay over her shoulders and across her breast. He couldn't believe the length of her long black eyelashes. Her nose was perfectly molded to her smooth face and her black eyebrows were thick, accenting her eyes. He knew she was a dream, and he fell back to sleep.

Jacob took his time descending the stairway to the large open living room. For a moment he stood on the main floor looking at Sarah resting quietly. Cy didn't appear to have improved, except his color was better. He felt the two sleepy people were destined for each other. He hoped Cy would accept Sarah back into his life. It would be insane to allow this woman to escape because of his crazy idea that he was bad luck to anyone who got close to him.

He glanced at Sarah. She was so beautiful. Her slim figure made her appear taller than she actually was, and her skin was a healthy looking bronze. He was glad he was happily married; otherwise he would have to kill Cy for the young beauty.

Jacob smiled at himself and went outside. He fed the horses and walked around the cabin and up to the spring that supplied the culinary water. It was a beautiful morning. He looked up through the pine trees at Glass Mountain to the south and over to the giant White Mountain Range to the east. A magpie flew out of a tree and screeched at another magpie not far away. He walked around for about an hour and returned to the cabin.

Sarah was fixing breakfast and talking with Lila when Jacob walked through the front door. The two talked like they had known each other since childhood. It pleased Jacob to see them get along so well. The smell of death in the cabin was almost gone and the flies had disappeared. Jacob walked over to a free-standing steel stove sitting on a brick hearth. He turned the metal handle to the stove and checked inside. The stove had not been used, and sitting on the fire brick was a .357 magnum in a holster. Jacob smiled and closed the door.

The smell of bacon was making his mouth water, and he looked forward to eating a good meal with Lila and Sarah. Something about being in the mountains always made him hungry. He didn't know if it was just his imagination, but just being out in the open country always made him ready to eat.

After breakfast was finished and the dishes were done, Jacob took Lila for a ride in Cy's truck to show her where their old deer camp was located not far from the ranch house. He told Sarah they would be back shortly. Besides, Cy was still asleep and Jacob wanted to get some fresh air.

The sensation that ran from his toes to the top of his head was not pleasurable. Every muscle ached and his nerves were tuned to the frequency of the pain source. His forehead felt cool and he realized an ice pack had been placed across his forehead. Cy slowly reached up to pull it off so he could open his eyes and check his surroundings. A warm hand touched his arm and long fingers wrapped around his wrist, pushing his arm back. He felt a warmth next to him, and he wasn't sure what it was until he heard her voice.

"Lie still, my darling. You mustn't move." Sarah's voice was distinct and her lips touched his ear as she whispered gently to him. Her breath was warm and reassuring. "I'm taking care of you, Cy, and you're going to be fine in a few days."

"Sarah?"

"Yes," she answered.

"Why? I don't understand," Cy whispered weakly.

"I know you don't, but I do. Cy, I am not married like I led you to believe. I also accepted things that were not true without giving you the chance to explain. You don't have to, now. I know everything."

"You do?"

"Everything."

"Who have you been talking to?"

"Jacob and Lila are here, Cy. I've been talking to them," she whispered, kissing his ear. "And I have to tell you, there is nothing on this earth that could tear me away from you. You're stuck with me whether you want me or not."

"I am?"

"You are."

"Good Lord, I must me dreaming," Cy mumbled, and went back to sleep.

Five days later Jacob and Lila returned home. Cy was awake most of the time, and Sarah reduced the pain pills to one at night so he could sleep. She fed the horses and fixed his meals. When he had to go to the bathroom, she put his arm over her shoulder and walked him there. Twice a day she washed him while he lay in bed. Nursing Cy back to health was much more enjoyable now that he was able to take care of his private bodily functions on his own.

As time went on, Sarah became more at ease. She tickled his feet when washing them, and she had to stop because it hurt his ribs to laugh. Cy could not cough, laugh, or take deep breaths without excruciating pain. He had to be very careful not to catch the food in his throat when eating. If he coughed he would die for sure. He couldn't even blow his nose.

Cy was sure of only one thing. His love for Sarah had returned. He once tried to convince himself he wanted her out of his life but he could not do it. She worked her way right in under his skin and he fell in love with her all over again. He relished the way she took care of his needs. She kept the cabin spotless and her cooking was superb. He loved watching her move around the cabin, picking up this shirt or dusting that table. She had the most desirable figure, and his mind was running wild because he wanted to run his hands over her so badly.

Sarah caught herself subtly teasing him. Sometimes she would put Cy's head in her lap and would absentmindedly let her breast brush his head. It wasn't exactly planned, but she didn't try to avoid it either. She loved the touch of his body next to her, and she never wanted to be away from him again. How many times had she heard it? If she died this moment, this day, she would be satisfied with her life.

She still loved Cy the way she had the first day she found him unconscious on the cabin floor. The flower in her heart bloomed. She knew she was a desirable woman. Her petals were in full array, showing the world her colors were for Cy and no one else. There was one small problem she had yet to deal with, but that would come later. Religion was not an issue she wanted to face at this time. Her church was her life and her commitment to her God was strong within her, but she did not want to take the chance of damaging this mortal dream. At least not today. Perhaps tomorrow. Or the next day. Not now. She needed the time to nurture her love for this man in her life, and she wanted him to develop those same feelings for her.

By the tenth day, Cy was moving around without assistance. He was still in pain but he was more mobile and could more or less take care of himself. Sarah went back to work during the day and returned to Cy in the evenings. She fixed him a different meal every night. In the mornings she made him eat hot cereals and grains to get his strength back.

The more Cy was around Sarah, the more she grew on him. He loved to look at her. After supper, Cy sat on the front steps with Sarah. The sun had already dipped behind the High Sierras.

"Nu-nung kwa-achung wa eem (I am hot you)," Cy said, smiling.

"Say what?" Sarah giggled. "So you've been studying again,

have you."

"Well, yeah. Did you understand what I said?"

"Of course I understood what you said. But what you said is not what you wanted to say," Sarah grinned at him, rolling her eyes to look at him from her peripheral vision. "You said you were hot and then said 'you.' What you wanted to say, if I'm reading you right, is that you have the hots for me." She giggled, holding her fingertips to her mouth. Cy's heart turned over.

Sally Dondero was not in a good mood when she walked up to Benjamin's cabin. It was a long drive and she did not have a driver's license. She would not be here if her father, Joseph, had not insisted she check on Ben. For years she wondered why the large man never looked at her. She was forty-five and getting older. Her bones were tired and her youth was gone. For ten years she watched Benjamin from a distance, wondering about him. He never saw her with his eyes.

She banged on the door until she finally thought she heard a sound. It didn't matter what kind of a sound; she took it as a welcome into the household. When she stepped inside, her anger increased.

The cabin was a large one-room building with the kitchen on one half and the living room on the other. The bathroom and single closet were off to the left corner of the room. The place was a mess and smelled awful. She wasn't the cleanest person herself, but this was disgusting.

"Mike (hello) Benjamin," Sally said, frowning.

"Mike Sal," Benjamin growled from his rumpled bed. He was lying on his back and did not look good.

Sally walked over to him. A solid woman who had experienced a difficult life, she had served many people with calloused hands. She felt her temper rise as she looked at Benjamin Gray, the man who once ran the most cattle in the valley.

"Ahkk-ahd-I-wahnee? (how are you?)" she glared at him without pity.

"Nu-ni yu-um pa-kang-oi (my leg is hurt)," he answered. "Ahkk-ahd-I-wahnee?"

"I-yahn (I'm fine)," she said, looking at the filth around her.

"Neu ahn-eeen-tooee-ahk ee-vee-ee (I want a drink)."

Sally went to the sink, found an empty whiskey bottle, and

poured water into it. She walked back to Benjamin and held it to his mouth.

He took a long pull and spit it out. "Inik-a num-pi-cant (You are crazy)!" he scowled, throwing his head back on the bed and grimacing in pain. His left eye was swollen and still bulged out slightly from its socket. He looked awful, and Sally wondered what she had ever seen in him.

"Hey, you want me to leave? You don't talk to me like that. I am only here because of my father. He was worried about you. He said the tahng-wahts (white man) cut you a new halter. He was afraid you might die of starvation or drink yourself to death."

"What business is it of yours what I do, woman? You are not my woman."

"What woman would want a mess like you?" Sally spun around and walked over to the refrigerator to see what food was available.

"You don't talk to me like that. I ought to knock your head through that window."

Sally came back to the bed and grabbed Benjamin by the shirt and yanked him forward. "You miserable nothing, I'll smack the daylights out of you if you talk to me like that," she screamed, raising her right fist threatening him.

Benjamin was afraid of Sally, all right. He thought for sure he was dead. If she even touched him lightly anywhere above the neck, his eye would pop back out of his head. Thinking of what would happen to him if she followed through with her threat made him queasy. He almost threw up and decided this woman was not to be toyed with. "Oh, mother of earth, don't hit me. You'll empty my eye socket. My eye muscles are all stretched and strained. You'll blind me for sure."

"Then hold your wagging tongue, Chief," Sally said, releasing his shirt. "I'm here and that's that. You keep quiet and I'm in charge. Any questions?"

"Oh, hell no. I have nothing to say. Just stay the hell away from me."

"What?" Sally spit, coming closer to him. Both her eyes were wide open in direct confrontation.

"Sweet mother of earth, I mean nothing. Do what you want. I can't take anymore. Don't touch me. It hurts just to have you look at me."

Sally stood over him with her hands on her round hips.

"You'll do what I say and not until I say otherwise. You got that?"

"Yes."

"Yes, what?" Sally yelled at him in a husky voice.

"Yes, ma'am? Is that what you want?"

"'Yes, Miss Sally' will do just fine. Now you lie there and let me do my work."

"Yes, Miss Sally." He decided if he recovered from his blinding injuries, he would kill Joseph for sending this crazy squaw to pester him.

Chapter 23
To Kill or Not to Kill

After five weeks' recovery, Cy drove to Grand Junction, Colorado, the first week in September. Driving across the warm Utah desert on I-70 made him drowsy. When he passed Green River, Cy made a big decision. He was going to kill Benjamin. He now knew Benjamin was Sarah's uncle, but it didn't matter. In fact he did not give it a second thought. He knew as long as Benjamin was alive, the man would someday corner him when he least suspected it and beat him to death.

He had heard about the injuries Benjamin received in the fight, but it was only talk. Cy knew the pain and suffering he himself had experienced was almost unbearable. He never wanted to even come close to that again. Benjamin was the strongest and meanest man he had ever crossed. The only way to ensure his safety was to kill him and bury his body where it wouldn't be found. No one would suspect an ex-cop from L.A. He was a gentleman and an honest, hard-working man. Without facts and the direct evidence of a corpse, it would only be circumstantial evidence, even if he was a suspect.

Once he arrived at Grand Junction, he headed north then east. He crossed the Colorado River and drove north approximately fifteen miles, turning right on Highway 65. It was a two-lane road that ran along the Plateau River, which ran westward and emptied into the Colorado.

It was a magnificent drive, going through the cut between the high cliffs that twisted in giant semicircles, working their way to open ground near the Grand Mesa turnoff. Grand Mesa was the largest flat-top mountain in the United States. Cy remembered when his father took him and his brother, Richard, up to the top, past the Powderhorn Ski Resort. It brought back fond memories of their trips together.

He remembered, before starting the high climb to Grand Mesa and just before the turnoff on Highway 330 to Collbran, that the road made a sharp curve to the right where it crossed the Plateau River. On the left side of the curve was a large boulder with Indian petroglyphs depicting stories of ancient travelers. As a young boy he was fascinated by this native art.

As Cy approached the very same curve he glanced to his left and saw the same boulder with the white-stained travelers. He drove several hundred yards further and turned left for Collbran. He passed the Longs' dairy on the right. It had closed down, and the big barn was deteriorating. A tall slender woman was standing under a large tree in the front yard, petting her dog. He wondered if it was Gladys Long and if she would remember him from his previous trips. He would have stopped to visit but he was anxious to look at cattle.

A few miles further, he turned left onto a dirt driveway and approached a beautiful old two-story home. In the old days it was the Pitts' sheep ranch, and now it was the centerpiece of the cattle ranch belonging to Bill Charlesworth.

Cy eased slowly up the drive looking at all the clear springs running over the land. If he had that much water on his ranch he would be a rich man. He parked his truck alongside the fence next to the house. Bill was inside the large open shed to the left of the house, talking to a man leaning over the engine of his John Deere tractor. Bill looked up momentarily and continued talking until Cy came up to them.

"Mr. Charlesworth, I'm Cy Golden. I haven't seen you for a long time. I'm not sure if you remember me or not," Cy said, holding out his hand.

Bill took it and squeezed it hard. "Sure, I remember you but you've changed. You're taller, you have longer hair and a mustache, and you've filled out some. I remember you, Cy. You were hell on wheels back then. You look like you may have cut your own path since then."

Cy gave him a big smile. "I have, Mr. Charlesworth."

"Call me Bill." The cattleman turned to his mechanic. "Cy, this man here is Frank Anselm. He's the best damn mechanic in these here parts. What he can't buy to fix something, he makes."

Frank stood up from working on the engine. He was a tall slender man in his sixties and his hair was gray and receding. "Howdy, boy," he said, in a high-pitched voice, holding out his hand. "Where ya from?"

"California ways. I'm only here for the night. I'm picking up a few head of cattle and shipping them back to my ranch near Lee Vining."

"Lee Vining? Never heard of it," Frank said. "Where you staying tonight?"

"I'm not sure yet," Cy replied. "I thought I'd get a room at the old hotel in town."

"Can't do that," Frank said, shaking his head.

"Why not?"

"I'm the owner."

"You mean you won't rent me a room for one night?"

"No, I mean it closed down for good. It's too old and the county made me shut her down," Frank said sadly.

"Well, I'll go back to town and get me a room at the Junction," Cy said.

"Not really," Frank said seriously.

"Why not?"

"Because you'll stay with the missus and me at my place. Nadine is the best cook in the valley. Besides, I have an old log cabin next to my place and you can stay in it for nothing."

"You mean it?"

"I said it, didn't I?"

"Why are you doing this anyway?" Cy grinned at the older man, liking him immediately.

"Because you look like a hunter, and I want to hear a few of your stories. I have a ton of them to tell and everyone around here has heard them all. So, tonight, you're the lucky one, son."

"It wouldn't be polite to turn down an offer like that, now would it," Cy replied.

"Good grief, man, you don't know what you're getting into," Bill frowned, shaking his head.

"Cy, you don't know this, but me and my best friend, Old Doc Zegal, killed five bears in one day. I'll have to tell you about it."

Bill stepped closer to Cy and took him by the arm. "Come on, Cy. Let's go to the house. You get Frank here talking about hunting and he won't get my tractor fixed."

Cy promised Frank he would come to his home in Collbran later that evening. He followed Bill to the house. Mrs. Charlesworth met them at the door and gave Cy a friendly smile and hug. "Good heavens, boy, you have really grown. I would have never thought it. You're even as good looking as your daddy was, bless his heart."

"Well, thank you, ma'am. You're as pretty as ever yourself."

"That did it. I've got a hot apple pie in the kitchen. While you and Bill discuss your cattle business, I'll cut you both a piece. How's that?"

"Suits me fine," Cy said, giving the woman a warm hug. He followed Bill into the grand living room and sat down in a large sofa across from a huge fireplace.

"You're looking good, Bill. How you feeling nowadays?"

"Better since I quit smoking and drinking. I miss the damn stuff, but it don't do my insides no good." Bill picked up a notebook and looked through it. "I think I have just what you need. You said you are ranching about seven thousand feet and some of the terrain is steep and rocky. That right?" he glanced at Cy over his reading glasses.

"You've got it right. I need cattle that will have good footing on steep slopes and are willing to scratch for grass when necessary. When I bring them out of the upper benches, I'll have pasture for the winter feed."

"Sounds good. I have a breed you need. Brangus is a cross between Angus and Brahma. They're black and have small ears. I've crossbred them for high mountain grazing. They fare well at high altitudes and work for feed, and they are easy to round up and don't scatter like some straight breeds. They like water but can go for long periods without it, if it's not too hot."

"I have plenty of water, so that won't be a problem," Cy said. "My biggest dilemma is purchasing these cows so late in the season. That's the reason I am only getting a small starter herd for now. My first winter will be the most expensive, considering the cost of hay. I figure next year I'll mix some more cattle and build the herd from there by breeding the cows with my new bulls."

Mrs. Charlesworth came into the room and handed each man a plate of pie and a fork. There was a knock at the rear door and Frank entered the room. "Say, I smelled some fresh pie and thought I'd better check it out. What da ya think, ma'am?"

"Oh, go sit down, Frank, and talk your head off," the woman laughed and went back into the kitchen.

Bill looked over at Frank and then to Cy, cocking his head to one side. "You're in for one heck of a night." He paused and then went on. "After pie, we'll go check the stock. They're in the holding corral next to the barn. If everything looks good, we'll seal the deal in the morning and you can be on your way."

"Sounds good to me. I have two cattle trucks on the way here. They'll be at the loading ramp at six in the morning."

"Good enough, let's eat."

❦

The next morning the two trucks were loaded with the cattle and Cy gave a check to Bill. He left ahead of the truck drivers, after giving them the directions to his ranch. He had a long drive ahead of him, and he wanted to be ready for the new stock when they arrived.

For most of the trip back home, Cy could not keep his mind off Sarah. He wondered why a girl so beautiful would even look at him. She could have any man and yet she cared for him. There was nothing he would rather look at than her. He had visions of her face with those beautiful dark eyes and her full lips. He was anxious to see more of her and get to know her better.

He wanted to have quality time with her. He visualized them sightseeing, going to dinner, horseback riding, and walking the hillsides together. He could see himself holding her hand and holding her warmly in his arms. Her womanhood stirred him. He knew his emotions were going to struggle with his desire for her. Sarah seemed both untouchable and accessible at the same time, and it sent goose bumps up his neck, fantasizing about her.

Cy was much healthier now, his body almost back to normal. All the pain was gone and he was ready to take the next step. He had two big problems. One obviously had to be dealt with soon. He thought of the many different ways to kill Benjamin. He decided to keep his distance and shoot him somewhere on Benjamin's own ranch. He would take his body and bury him where no one would ever look, deep in the ground, and pour lye over his remains. The body would decay rapidly and disappear into the ground forever, and his life would be free of persecution.

The second problem was the scar-face Mexican who killed Skin. Jacob had called Cy and told him they felt they had a good lead on a man who had worked for Joe Molino and Tommy Angelino. He had put pressure on a female employee who worked at the L.A. administration complex. There was no question from Cy's description that it was the deadly killer, and the police were making every effort to find the man. The difficulty came in communicating with the local Hispanics in the Hollenbeck area. The Mexican families were so tight-lipped, it was almost impossible to get information from them. Jacob told him it was only a matter of time. He promised Cy it was his personal goal to find the man who killed Skin.

The next two weeks kept Cy constantly busy working the new cattle. The fences had to be rechecked and the water tanks had to be tested to make sure they were working. Cy had to buy chopped corn silage as a supplement for winter feeding. With a front loader he cut a rectangular pit in the side of a low hill next to the feed yard to store the silage. After sprinkling preservatives over the corn, he covered it with a black plastic tarp and weighed it down with used tires to keep it moist and to prevent spoilage.

Sarah continued to come out to the ranch after work. They often rode horses around the ranch, watching the stock to monitor their behavior in their new environment. They spent many hours talking.

Cy knew he loved Sarah for her beauty. Now he wanted to love her for what was in her heart. He had a thirst to know her thoughts. On some subjects he felt she was leaving something out but he wasn't sure what. He did know he was consumed by her mere presence, and he wondered if she would marry him if he asked her.

One major obstacle stood in their way. Benjamin would try to stop the marriage or he would attempt to kill him. Cy could never kill anyone without just cause; this was the exception. There was no question in Cy's mind—Benjamin Gray would kill him at his first chance. Several times he had noticed the big Indian on the outskirts of his ranch, spying on him.

After several weeks Cy, having done his own homework, decided today was the day he planned to act. Every Friday like clockwork, Benjamin climbed the hill to the south of the cabin and spied on him. The property belonged to Cy, and it irritated him that the Indian was trespassing. His property line extended up to the base of Glass Mountain. He knew the Indian was planning to make a move soon.

Cy knew he had to act first and the time was now. He saddled Cole and holstered his 30-30 Winchester in the front scabbard. He also carried a four-inch Smith and Wesson .357 on the inside of his belt. He guided Cole up to the south side of the ranch as he normally would until he spotted Benjamin lying under a tree. That bothered him. Why would Benjamin be lying down in plain sight? Perhaps the Indian was dead drunk or maybe he was trying to sucker him out into the open for a clear shot. That wasn't going to happen.

Cy ignored the area where Benjamin was located, pretending he was not aware of being watched. Finally, when he entered a draw, he dismounted and climbed up the slope to get up behind Benjamin. It took him ten minutes and he had to stop several times to get his breath.

As Cy moved toward the Indian, hate gripped him. He had to kill Benjamin before Benjamin killed him. He was almost blinded by pure determination to do something that went against his value system.

Only God would know, and surely he would understand. It had to be done. He could never live a normal life until he knew the man was no longer a threat. There was no talking and negotiating with the man. Benjamin's mind was scrambled by alcohol, and he had lost his ability to think intelligently. He was incapable of understanding right and wrong.

The anger built inside Cy's head. The more he thought of Benjamin, the more he looked forward to squeezing the trigger that would discharge a powerful round to blow apart Benjamin's brain, splattering in the rocks around him. His temples began to pound. He cringed at the thought of going to town and having his body broken up by the crazy Indian again.

Sweat rolled down his forehead and neck. The next ridge would reveal his prey. He would look over the top, take careful aim, and shoot the fool in the head. It was easy, it was wonderful. He smiled, preparing for his move.

Cy slowly stepped up to the top of the ridge with the revolver in his right hand and peeked over the top. Benjamin was lying on his stomach only a few feet away. His big head was facedown on the ground. Water dripped off his face, making little mudballs in the soft dirt. Cy determined the man was drunk again and passed out. He aimed at Benjamin's forehead, started to squeeze the trigger, and then stopped. This was too easy.

With gun in hand, he climbed over the ridge and walked over to the Indian. The man's back was wet with sweat. It looked like he had urinated in his pants—there was a large wet spot on the seat of his pants. "Wake up, you puke face. I want you to see it coming."

Cy held the gun in front of him, pointing the sights at Benjamin's head. The Indian groaned and lifted his head. When he saw Cy holding the gun on him, he smiled. "You pitiful thing."

Cy's face turned red and he decided to kill him on the spot. Benjamin started laughing and attempted to roll over. Instead, he yelled in pain. When the misery subsided, he groaned, pulled his knees under him, and slowly staggered to his feet. "You ain't no turn-around, but you are a coward to sneak up on a man like this. Now shoot me, you little piss ant," Benjamin cursed, "Shoot me!"

Cy tried but couldn't bring himself to pull the trigger. He desperately wanted to, but he couldn't. All his police training and education and moral fiber wouldn't allow it.

"You yellow-gutted mutt. Can't you touch off one round? Or are you afraid if you shoot, I'll get mad and take that damn little toy out of your hands and pistol whip you with it?" Benjamin laughed and his eyes looked sick.

Benjamin fell backward. He screamed out and tried to roll over onto his stomach in a sandy spot. It was too painful. Cy couldn't figure out what was causing the problem.

Cy walked over to him and kicked dirt in his face. "Get up, you miserable snake, so I can shoot you standing up."

After a moment of hard breathing, Benjamin got to his feet. "You ain't going to shoot me or anyone else, numb nuts. You haven't got it in you, you squirmy little dog turd." Benjamin turned around and stumbled down the hillside toward Cy's horse.

"Hold it right there or I'll shoot you in the back of the head."

"Oh, please do. Please do, sonny boy."

Cy couldn't believe what was happening. He had complete control of the situation and then lost it. Benjamin was taking charge. He had to kill the man. He had no choice. Cy discharged a round at Benjamin's feet, kicking up dirt on his pant legs. The big man jumped and groaned in pain. He kept walking down the hill, stumbled once, got up and continued downward. "Shoot me, piss ant. Oh, that's right, no gonads. I forgot."

Ben reached the bottom of the draw and stumbled along a dry ravine. Cy decided to shoot the man here and bury him on the spot when he noticed the back of Benjamin's pants were wetter and moisture was trailing down his leg. Ben turned around and took a bottle of Old Crow from his pocket. "Here." He held the bottle up toward Cy. "I drink to my death." He took a long drink and belched, looking back at Cy. "Can you do it?"

Benjamin started to turn but his right leg would not function. His legs wobbled under him and he fell to the ground. Cy thought at first the man was trying to sucker him in close so the Indian could grab him. If Ben got him in a bear hug here, he would crush his ribs and kill him for sure.

For a long moment, Cy carefully maintained a safe distance from the downed man. Benjamin tried to get up but couldn't, then he passed out. Cy didn't know if it was from whiskey or from an injury or illness.

Cy stepped close enough to kick Benjamin hard in the stomach. Benjamin only groaned. Now Cy knew something was definitely wrong. He went over to his horse and pulled some orange baling twine from his saddlebags. He leaned over Benjamin and tied his hands and feet to some small cedars in a spread eagle position. Satisfied he was safe from the Indian, Cy took a canteen from his saddle horn and poured water on Benjamin's face.

Benjamin shook his head and blinked his eyes. "You gutless dog turd. Why did you not shoot me?" Saliva and water mixed erupted from Ben's mouth in his anger.

"You wanted to die too much. Why?"

"Not your business, land grabber. I hate your white ass. A man would shoot me, not tie me up like a dog in heat."

"Well, that's life, you fat-ass Indian."

Benjamin struggled so hard Cy thought the twine would not hold. He started to jump up when the big man relaxed in resignation. Cy wiped the sweat from his forehead, thankful the knots held. Benjamin was crazy with rage. "I curse you, you ball-less sack of cat crap. I curse you that your blood turns to water and your bones to chalk. I have the power. It is an old ancient Indian medicine that never fails. When you are weak, a stray dog will come upon you and eat your liver while you watch in weakness."

"Good grief, spare me," Cy said, throwing a small pebble at the back of Benjamin's head.

That made the Indian mad again, but the twine held. "May you swell from the inside and spit your stomach out."

"Oh come, Benny Boy. Where have I heard these sayings before, huh?" Cy reached forward and pulled the Old Crow from Benjamin's pocket.

"Take anything but that. That is mine and only mine."

"Anything?" Cy asked, stepping closer. Cy removed a buck

knife from Ben's leather scabbard and opened the largest blade. He reached down and cut out the back of Benjamin's pants until he exposed his large buttocks. Cy smiled when he discovered what was causing the wetness on Benjamin's pants. Two of the biggest boils Cy had ever seen were raised in the middle of his left cheek. They were red mountains of swollen tissue that came to a round yellow pus-infested point. The lower one had broken and was leaking, but the core of the boil was still imbedded deeply in his sick flesh.

Cy cut the rest of Benjamin's pants off, humiliating him further. He sat down on the ground next to Benjamin and began to laugh as Benjamin raged. He cursed Cy with every invective he could call up—English and Paiute. Nothing had any effect on Cy. Cy lost control and was lying backwards in the dirt almost passing out because of lack of oxygen.

When Cy's laughter subsided and it had been quiet for a few minutes, he crawled on his hands and knees to Benjamin. "I'm not going to kill you with a gun, Mr. Gray. I'm going to kill you with kindness. I'm going to administer first aid and pop those damn volcanoes of pus and save your sorry ass so you can enjoy life. These damn things on your fat ugly butt are so infected you're dying of poison. So," Cy started laughing again. This time he almost could not get his breath. "So, now we disinfect."

Cy opened the Old Crow and poured whiskey on the two boils. Benjamin screamed awful oaths and Cy laughed harder. He poured more whiskey on his stained hands and wiped the excess off on his dirty shirt. Then he spit on his fingertips. "Okay?" he laughed. "Okay? Are you ready for a little field surgery? I'm going to talk you through this procedure." Cy sucked air into his lungs. "Okay, now we take our disinfected hands and smash the little dickens until they snap, crackle, and pop!" Cy cried with exhilaration. With his thumbs and fingers he grabbed a large piece of flabby swollen flesh and squeezed with all his strength.

The first boil emitted a muffled pop, then squirted blood and pus into the air, some hitting Cy on the shoulder. The smell was horrible and the sight almost made him sick. Benjamin screamed and begged Cy to release him. The pleas for mercy made Cy happy. He grabbed the second boil and squeezed the flesh until it popped the core. It landed on the side of Benjamin's head. Pus and blood ran freely.

"Well now, big chief, how does it feel, you slimy red snake? Huh? How does it feel?" Cy squeezed again and again until there was nothing but the red flow of blood. He watched Benjamin's body shudder as he howled in protest. It was music to his ears. "You broke my ribs. You nearly killed me. Now, you hear this. I'm going to marry your niece. You got that? How does that make you feel? Huh?"

"Ayee!...No! Let go of me, you white-eyed..." Benjamin yelled again when Cy applied pressure to his tender buttocks. "Kill me, but don't marry Sarah. She is too good for you. You can't mix our blood. Oh, you cursed dog. Kill me here and now!"

"I can't, Benjamin...I mean Uncle Ben. I can't kill my future uncle, the great-uncle of my children, now can I?"

"Don't do this thing. Don't take it out on Sarah. She is the milk of goodness. Let your brains match your guts and let her go. She is the angel of this earth. You cannot marry her."

"Think about it, Uncle Ben. My children will inherit the whole ranch when we all die. Get it? It all goes back to the Indians when you and I are gone."

Benjamin stopped resisting, raised his head, and looked at Cy. "Say that again."

"Sure, good buddy." Cy started laughing again, realizing himself what he was saying. "If Sarah marries me, our children will inherit all six sections when you and I are gone." Cy fell backward, laughing at his summation. "And you'll be my uncle. Ha, ha."

Benjamin let the words register in his mind for a long moment. Then he started laughing. After a short while, Cy cut him loose and they both laid back and howled together. Benjamin lost his head and gave Cy a quick hug. "You be good to my Sarah or I will give you a bear hug that'll pop your brains out. Understand me, white eyes who is no turn-around?"

"I understand you, bulging eye." Cy returned Benjamin's hug. He never felt an emotion so strange. That morning, he was determined to kill this man; now suddenly he felt great affection for him.

When all was done, Cy rewashed the two ugly holes on Benjamin's backside, wiping them with his handkerchief, and they slowly walked back to the cabin talking about the fight in Lee Vining. At the ranch house, Cy turned to Benjamin. "Ben, do you mind me calling you Ben?"

"Whatever the hell you want," he answered. "By the way, the pain is subsiding now that the poison is gone. I walk better now."

"Good. I've got to know something. How did you know I was not going to shoot you?"

The big Indian looked at him a moment before answering. "You did not have the stare of death. You know what I mean?" Ben asked.

"Yeah, I know, but I fully intended on shooting you. I'm surprised you knew I wouldn't."

"It's strange. I wanted to die this morning. Nothing was going right. Dondero's daughter wants to be my woman, and I am smothered by her. I lost part of my ranch. You nearly blinded me. I don't know if my eye will ever stop hurting. You stretched all six muscles holding my eye in the socket. You crippled me for weeks. You beat the hell out of me in town in front of everyone, and this morning two boils were poisoning me to a slow miserable death." Benjamin shook his head, ashamed. "I see you doing things with this ranch that I should have been doing. I felt like hell and wanted to return to Mother Earth."

"That's it?"

"That's it, you dog fighter. I wanted you to shoot me because in the end I would win. You would pay the price and go to prison for life or maybe they would hang you. I figured some good Indian buck would seek Sarah out. They would have the ranch and all would be well."

"Sarah is not just any woman, Ben. She is really special. I don't think you realize how special she is. I would die for her. I want to give my life to her and build a home with love and children."

"Can't ask for more than that. I'm glad I did not kill you," Benjamin said. "I had planned to kill you, you know."

"I thought so after our first meeting; I was positive at the second. I really planned on killing you today, but when it came down to it, it wasn't in my genes."

"That's good, Cy Golden. It shows you have some kindness in you. Before today, I thought you were the meanest junkyard dog who walked the earth." Benjamin thought a moment and said, "Besides me, of course."

"Of course."

"Maybe there is hope for you yet."

"Maybe."

Chapter 24
Coming Clean

Reuben Ortega and Albert Alvarez closed the door behind them and approached Juan Mores. He was busy writing at his desk.

"I think we have your cop, boss," Reuben said proudly.

Juan dropped the pen and looked up. "Well, out with it. Don't play with me."

Albert answered, not liking Juan's expression. It had the cold look of death and it always caused shivers to run down his spine. "I spoke with two of our traffickers that do business in Carson City and Reno. They stopped in a little nothing town by some dead lake on the California-Nevada border. One of the men overheard a conversation about a big fight between a local Indian and some newcomer who was white and an ex-cop from Los Angeles."

"And what makes you think it is who I am looking for?" Juan frowned.

"The people talking said the man's name was Say or Cy. It has to be him," Albert said, proudly.

"This is too good to be true, hey?" Juan rubbed his big hands together, smiling and frowning at the same time. "I want you two to go to this dead lake and check it out. What is the name of the town?"

"Lee Vining. It is north of Bishop," Reuben answered.

"Check it out and lay low. Speak to the local Mexicans without raising suspicion." Juan got up from his desk and walked to the window. "I am sick and tired of hiding all the time. With Golden dead, I am a free man." He faced Reuben and Albert, a broad smile displayed on his ugly face. It was something they were not accustomed to. "Get going and report back to me as soon as you find him, but don't approach him. He is a deadly man and I want him for myself."

"What about Joan Sausedo and her son?" Reuben questioned.

"For the present, forget about them. Maybe the heat will fade off me if we stay away from her. I have a feeling the man in Lee Vining is Golden. If it is, he is a dead man."

❧

"So where are you taking me, Miss Sarah?" Cy asked happily, looking at the woman he loved. Sarah did not have the top on her jeep. The air was chilly but they had on warm jackets. Her hair was blowing in the wind. It was a cool but pleasant day, and they had just passed the Lee Vining Ranger Station as they headed west up a long grade on Highway 120. Cy had never been on the road or seen Yosemite National Park.

Sarah had fixed a picnic and brought a blanket. The high cliff scenery and the vision of loveliness next to Cy was almost overwhelming. He reached over and grasped her thigh, then released his hold. It was the first time he had touched her leg, and he thought he might lose his breath. Sarah wore Wrangler jeans and hiking boots and a plaid shirt under her insulated Storm Rider Lee jacket. A red bandanna was tied around her neck.

She smiled at him. "What cha' got goin' there, fella?"

"Me? What do you mean?"

"What are you thinking, Mr. Golden?"

"Miss Sarah, I'm thinking how lovely you are with your hair blowing in your face and over your shoulders."

"You know what I'm thinking?"

"I have no idea. What?"

"I'm thinking I'm the luckiest girl in the world."

"Why?

"Because you are sitting next to me."

"Serious?"

"Of course I'm serious. Indian girls don't joke around," Sarah laughed, and then made a funny face. "Well, maybe once in a while. You have my eye, you know. Looking at you makes my heart pound hard like the heart of a wild mare being chased by a stallion." Sarah put one hand over her heart. "I think you are the most beautiful thing in this world, and I love looking at you." She hesitated and went on. "It's not just because of your looks, Mr. Stallion. It's because of who you are and the goodness inside your heart."

"I was thinking that about you. Are you really serious?"

"No joke." Sarah pointed to the right of the road as the jeep labored up the steep grade. She had to gear down and drive slower. "There, you see that?" Sarah pointed to the jagged cut walls of a giant cliff next to the road rising several hundred feet. Hundreds of small springs dripped down the cliffs over the rocky shale, veils of water washing the rocks and glistening in the sun.

Cy looked up the steep cliff. "Yes, yes I do. And?"

"Mother Earth is still crying."

"What do you mean?"

"When the white settlers or miners cut this road, it hurt Mother Earth deep in her heart. This was virgin territory known only to natives who migrated back and forth to the valleys, depending on the season. You see, it is too cold to winter up this high." Sarah shivered. "It freezes me out just thinking about my ancestors dealing with the snow and cold without electricity or gas heat. I am not tough like they were."

"None of us are," Cy smiled. "I don't understand why Mother Earth did not cry when the Indians passed through here on the trails they made."

"Well, silly, they walked over the ground. They did not cut and tear into it with heavy machinery and explosives."

Cy looked back along the cliffs with moss and water cascading down the sides. It was more splendid at second glance. He never once thought about why the water was there. Indians had a wonderful way of thinking. They understood the natural things in life—the things with deep and spiritual meaning.

Sarah stopped the jeep at the Tioga Pass entrance. A ranger came to the window, and Sarah introduced her to Cy. They entered the park without paying because Sarah was an employee. Cy liked the idea of getting in without being charged.

The world suddenly changed to some of the most enchanting scenery Cy had ever seen. The old jeep passed between rough mountain peaks and lush green meadows with clear streams crisscrossing the grass, giving it a glossy life. The weather grew even cooler at the higher elevation.

"This place is called Tuolumne Meadow," Sarah said, pointing to each side of the road. "And that is Tuolumne Peak on the right."

"This country is something else." Cy stole a glance at Sarah's profile and looked out across the green meadows disappearing into the distant firs. "I'm in heaven. That's all there is to it. I'm the luckiest guy in the world."

"Hummm, perhaps." A few minutes later a lake, guarded by high mountain cliffs and lined with evergreen firs along grassy banks, appeared on the left. "On the right is Polly Dome. Pretty intimidating, huh?"

"I've never seen so much granite. I can't believe the power of this place."

"Look. Over there is Mount Hoffman. Why it has an English name, I don't know. Everything else is named after the Indians, of course."

"What's the name of this place? It's beautiful." Cy pointed to their left.

Sarah smiled, displaying her white teeth. "Teneya Lake. It's my lake, Cy. It used to be a special place for the Indian maidens to come for peace from the rest of the world. When I have a heavy heart or difficult problems to deal with, I come here. It is my lake; my little place in the world."

Sarah drove to the west end of the lake and parked the jeep along the side of the road. Cy grabbed the blanket and lunch basket, and Sarah sang Paiute songs as she led Cy through the trees and tall grass. The wind was still and the lake reflected the large mountains that rose up, reaching into the sky on the east side. Granite, water, evergreens, and blue skies dominated the scenery.

Sarah stopped in a grassy meadow and turned around to face Cy. "Close your eyes."

"Why?"

"Just do it," she demanded. Her eyes were sparkling and he reluctantly closed his eyes. "Now keep them closed, okay?"

"Okay."

"Promise?"

"I promise," Cy laughed.

Sarah moved up to Cy. Her voice was soft. "Take a deep breath and tell me what you feel."

Cy took a long deep breath. Sarah waited patiently, studying Cy's facial features. She could feel hot blood mounting. It was much easier to study his features when his eyes were closed. She was pleased she was getting over her shyness. Today was the day she had to talk, but for now this moment had to be special.

"What do you feel, Cy?"

"I feel...I feel free here. I smell clean air. The sound of the birds in the background is the sound of life. I hear water and a fish jumping. I feel something much more, though."

"What, Cy? What do you feel?"

"I feel the aura of a real woman. I feel the passion of a girl who has waited for the right person to come into her life. It's all around her. She shines like gold and glows with love and goodness."

Sarah moved closer and touched his lips with hers. Cy felt

her body heat and he dropped the picnic basket and blanket. His arms pressed her to his body and he felt his heart pound when her breast touched his chest and smothered him with her warmth. He wanted to consume her with his lips.

Slowly they separated. He opened his eyes and looked into hers. "Sarah, Sarah, I love you more than anything else on this earth."

"Me, too, Cy Golden. There is no one else for me but you. I've always known there was someone out there for me. It just took you so long to find me. It was Glass Mountain. I know it was. It is a sacred mountain of the Kuzedika, and I am of the Kuzedika people. Oh Cy, I am so sorry I did not trust you— that I did not believe in you. When my uncle and Ray told me you purchased the range on the north side of Glass Mountain, they were so convincing that you were using me to avoid opposition with Uncle Ben." Tears came to her eyes and she put her arms around his waist.

"That part of our lives is over, Sarah." Cy combed the back of her hair with the palm of his hand. Then he gazed directly into her eyes. "I was never one to believe in love at first sight; but I have to tell you, I was smitten when I first saw you at the store when I came up here during the deer hunt. I thought if your heart was as beautiful as your face, I would do anything for you."

"I feel the same, Cy. You were too good to be true. My second mother always told me as a child not to judge a person by only their appearance. I always believed that. In fact, I often found that people who are exceptionally appealing on the outside were often cold and hard on the inside. Pride can sometimes do horrible things to a person."

"I'm glad that you never let your looks harden your heart, Sarah."

"Me? My looks are nothing. Besides, I take smart pills. No way will I become stiffed-necked."

"What do you mean you take smart pills?"

"Long story," Sarah laughed, pushing herself away from Cy. She folded her arms and bowed her head, collecting her thoughts. After a moment she raised her head and looked into space.

"Oh, no," he said smiling, watching Sarah change her expression in preparation of going into one of her Indian acts.

"Please be silent, little one; open your ears." In her deepest voice with her chin to her chest, Sarah began to speak. "Indian brave wandered around camp in despair working up courage. Finally, he approached Chief Eagle Eye. The humble brave looked up to the chief and say, 'Chief Eagle Eye, I not too smart. I make many bad decisions. I need many horses to buy young maiden from her father. I can no think of way to do this thing. Can't you help me, old wise one?'

"The chief looked distastefully at the young buck. 'Perhaps. What have you to give in trade for my knowledge? My spirit must soar for the answer to your question. Have you a gift for your chief to help his mind seek wisdom?'

"The young brave pulled a well-made knife from his loin strap. 'Will this do?'

"The chief quickly took the knife and hid it on his person. Then from under his leather thong he took out a doeskin pouch. Loosening the leather straps he pulled it open and took out one small round pill. 'Here, young brave. This is a smart pill. It will help you gain knowledge. Take it and chew on it slowly.'

"The young brave looked at the pill and put it to his mouth. He took a small taste and looked bitterly at his chief.

"'Again,' the chief said. 'Taste it again.'

"This time the young brave chewed the pill and swallowed it. He wiped his mouth and frowned at his chief. 'Oh, Great Chief, this pill taste like rabbit dropping.'

"'Ahah! You see, dimwit one? You already getting smarter.'"

Cy laughed and pulled Sarah into his arms. "You have a wonderful sense of humor. I hope you never change." He gave her a hug and kissed her cheek. Cy looked at Sarah and asked, "Who is your second mother? You have never spoken of your parents."

Sarah thought for a long moment, searching the lake and the tree-lined mountains. Cy saw the change in her eyes. He pulled her back into his arms, gave her a tight hug, and released her. He picked up the basket and blanket and followed Sarah to the edge of the water. She jumped from the water's edge onto a large flat granite boulder, approximately twenty feet square, with a smaller boulder, some grass, and a lone pine tree on it. It was a little granite island, but it was their island. It was now their world.

Sarah took the basket while Cy spread the blanket on the ground. They were surrounded by the clear smooth lake. Bluejays screeched in a nearby tree. The two people barely noticed the tourist fishing further north on the lake. Their part of the lake was abandoned. It was as if they were the only ones left in the world.

Sarah sat down on the Indian blanket. She did not open the basket. Cy saw the worried look in her expression and smiled warmly at her. "It can't be that bad, can it?"

"I hope not." A look of long-suppressed sorrow came to her eyes as she watched him. "Cy, there is one part of my life we have not talked about. It is something so very important. I didn't discuss it before now because I did not want to take the chance of losing you."

Cy started to speak but Sarah quickly touched his lips with her fingertips. "Please don't say anything. Just listen to me." She hesitated a long moment as she searched her mind and wiped her tears away with the back of her hand.

"Cy, when I was a baby, my family was killed in an automobile accident. I was sent to live with a Paiute family in Bridgeport. When I was ten years old, I went to live with a family in Utah. Their names are Bill and Mary Wilson. They had four boys and no girls. I was able to participate in this arrangement because of a church-organized educational opportunity for Indian children called the Indian Placement Program. The purpose of the program was to give underprivileged native children a better education and acclimate them to the modern world. It was a labor of love from a very special people."

Sarah stared at him and her eyes began to burn. "Cy, I believe I come from an ancient people who migrated across the continent many hundreds of years ago. I presently have not committed to a religion; however, I feel very strongly about Christianity." Sarah searched Cy's face for his reaction. She thought she saw a calmness but she wasn't sure. At least he didn't throw her into the lake.

"It is important to me that the man I marry believes in God and Jesus Christ. Someday I want to join a church and be baptized." Sarah now saw the concerned look in Cy's expression as he pondered over her words.

"Sarah, this is starting to scare me a little. Are you expecting me to join some religion if we were to marry? I love you. I want to marry you, not some church."

"Whoever I give my life to, whoever I enter into marriage with, must believe in God."

"I believe in God, but what are you saying?"

"I've been thinking very strongly about a particular church.

Their beliefs are so good and my heart is filled with love for them." Sarah hesitated, looking down at the blanket then up to Cy. "I guess I'm saying someday I may want to be baptized. It is important that I would have support from my husband. How would you feel if I was baptized?"

"I think a person has to follow his heart, and as long as you take your time and choose carefully, I would have no complaint."

"Oh, Cy. You really mean it?"

"Of course I do," he smiled, relieved. Cy was worried at first that Sarah would want him to join some Indian cult religion. "My parents were pretty strong Baptists, and I have an opinion on religion, myself. As long as you believe in God, Christ, the Holy Ghost and the ten commandments, I have no problem."

Sarah sat up looking at Cy. "Now, I have a confession, sir."

"Oh, no. Are you going to drop something heavy on me?"

Sarah's face grew somber. "Yes. Are you listening?"

"Sarah, you don't have to tell me about your past. I love you for who you are. I don't need to know what happened in your life before me, okay?"

Sarah's eyes narrowed slightly. "This concerns you. Can I go on?"

"Well, yeah, if it concerns me. That's different."

Sarah swallowed hard. "I desire your nearness."

Cy smiled. "My nearness? Does that mean you have a desire to be close to me? Physically?"

Sarah looked down at her lap and tears fell on her twisting hands. "Yes. I want you so much I can't sleep at night. I have awful...I mean explicit dreams about you. I'm having trouble controlling my thoughts and desires."

"Thank the Lord for that." he laughed softly. "I thought there was something wrong with me."

Sarah thought he was serious and looked up into his eyes. "Oh, Cy...you are so beautiful. I have never seen a man like you. I love your blue eyes. They are like the evening sky. I love your wavy hair and your silly smile when you question things. I love your muscles and I feel so safe in your presence. I know you could protect me from anything and I cherish that feeling. I love your inner strength. You are a good man, and I have eyes for no one else but you.

"I know it's not fashionable now-a-days, but I hold true to my convictions. I decided when I was a young girl that my husband would be the only person who would know my nearness."

"I find nothing wrong with that. I love you for who you are, Sarah. I also respect your beliefs. I would never dishonor you."

"I know this to be true, because you really do love me." Sarah put her palm over Cy's cheek, caressing him. After a moment she removed her hand and went on. "Cy, nature can get along without man, but man cannot survive or get along without nature. Have you ever thought about that?"

"That's a deep thought. I think you're saying the world could do without man's influence, but the power of nature can greatly affect man. Is that what you're saying?"

"Basically. Nature has powers beyond man's reach. Winds and rain can destroy human-kind in an instant. Volcanoes have great power deep inside the earth. One eruption could be more powerful than all the bombs and explosions put together in all the history of mankind. We have no control over nature, but nature does control us."

"What does this have to do with our feelings for each other?"

"When we were separated, I felt as if life was nothing. I lost all hope and I was in despair. When I nursed you back to health, I went through a period of purification of the heart. While I sat with you, when you were sick and not aware of my presence, I experienced a healing in my heart. It was my time for healing and getting my head on straight. I realized how little my life was without the person I loved. I also realized how wrong I was not to fully have an understanding of you and you're feelings. I should never have hung the phone up on you. I never gave you the chance to explain yourself."

"I have to agree. It was a very bad time in my life. I never wanted to see you again. The problem was, no matter how hard I tried, I couldn't erase you from my mind."

"Cy, I think we have a pure love for each other. In fact, I know this to be true. Pure love is a spiritual love. Nothing is so important as loyalty to each other and friendship and belief in God. It all comes together, and we all need each other to survive."

"So with everything you're saying, does this mean you want to spend the rest of your life with me?"

"I just asked you to marry me, Cy. Wasn't I clear?" Sarah smiled.

"You think I would be good to you? Good for you? Giving you the space you need to feel free and yet captured at the same time?"

"I trust you with all my heart, Cy. I see your goodness in your eyes. Through your eyes, I look into your heart."

Cy stared at Sarah for a long moment. He glanced away from her and looked across the lake. He looked up to the top of the mountains and he looked back into her eyes. Sarah was shocked to see tears in his eyes.

"Sarah, that is the only reason I haven't been aggressive, because I really do love you. I have been fighting a war inside my heart not to give in to my desires. I was always taught to respect a woman, but I want you like no man has ever wanted a woman."

Sarah reached out and pulled him into her arms. "You have given me the happiness I have always wanted. Oh, Cy, I love you so much I cannot describe my feelings."

Off in the distance, two men appeared from out of the pine trees and walked towards the couple. Cy rechecked his revolver in the small of his back under his Levi jacket. Finally he relaxed when he recognized Jesus and Louie. Both men were quiet as they approached the couple. Cy was somber as he carefully observed the two men. Usually they were smiling and jovial in general. Not today. Now they were serious and appeared to be stressed.

Jesus stopped in front of Cy. He removed his hat and wadded it up in his hands nervously as he held his gaze at Cy's feet.

"What is it, Jesus? What's wrong?" Cy asked.

"Señor Cy, we have bad news. Louie and I have been approached by two very bad men. These men are very dangerous. Louie and I acted dumb, as if we know nothing, but I do not think we fooled them."

"What men?"

"Two very bad Mexicans from Los Angeles," Louie responded. "They ask questions about you. We told them nothing, but they ask many questions from other farm workers and a cousin of mine. I'm sorry Señor, but my cousin told them where you live on the mountain," Louie apologized, looking sick and twisting his hat unmercifully. "You are in very bad danger. Jesus and I must leave this area, and you must be very careful, Señor Cy. They will return to kill you. I know it. They are mafiosos."

"You are right," Cy said, stepping forward and grabbing Louie's hand. "You both better leave town for a little while, and don't mention our conversation to anyone. Thank you." The two Mexicans walked away.

"Who are they?" she gasped, shaking. "Why would anybody want to kill you?"

Cy answered, watching the trees to make sure there was no one else. "My past is catching up to me. The man who shot me in the head and killed Skin has found me."

❦

Benjamin sat at the kitchen table. His heavy brows came together, indicating his troubled mood. His forehead was furrowed in concentration. He racked his mind over and over thinking about what he should do.

"I think Sarah should leave this place and not come back until it's over," Benjamin said.

"I agree. Where can she go where it will be safe?" Cy asked, looking at Benjamin.

"We have Paiute families who will take her, or she has a second family in Utah."

"No!" Sarah replied firmly. "I am not leaving. I don't care what happens to me. If Cy gets hurt, I have to be here. If our lives are endangered and Cy is killed, then I will die with him." Sarah pronounced her words distinctly.

"That's heavy talk, little girl," Benjamin grumbled.

"Don't make fun of me, Uncle Ben. My life is with Cy. This is my home. If I go with him, then I die in peace."

"Sarah, it would be much safer and wiser if you were out of the state. If they got their hands on you, they would use you as a wedge to get to me. I can't let anything happen to you," Cy said, hoping he could change her mind.

"That is all," she raised her voice. "There is no choice here. This is my home. You are my man and I am not leaving you. Besides, I have a hard time believing anyone could take you two in a fight."

"One on one they would have a difficult time," Benjamin sighed, glancing at Cy for confirmation. "But bullets and knives leave a permanent impression on the body. They will have to figure out how to get up close or use long-range rifles."

"They have this pride thing," Cy said, looking at Benjamin. "They are afraid of no one. I mean no one. They usually do their work up close and they are very dangerous."

Sarah came around the table and stood behind Cy, putting

her hands on his shoulders. "Do you think they will come here or wait until you go to town?"

"They will come here when they think we will least expect it. It may not be right away. It may take hours or days for them to make their move. They will make a plan and execute it at a time to their advantage. They will not think the two workers warned me. That's to our advantage."

"I think it will be soon," Sarah said. "They do not know how close you were to Jesus and Louie."

"That's true. They could be coming anytime now," Cy replied, standing up and walking to the kitchen window to look down the road.

"Where are your two Mexican workers now?" Benjamin asked.

"They've left town."

"Why would they not stay? What do they have to fear?" Benjamin asked, shaking his big head in a quandary.

"They left because if the Mexicans returned and found them, they might be tortured for more information. They had to leave town until this is over."

Sarah leaned over Cy, applying pressure to his shoulder muscles. "Don't you think we should call the Mono County Sheriff?"

"I've been thinking on it. I'm not sure what is the best action to take when it comes to the local authorities. The proper thing to do is to call the Sheriff's Office. The only reason I haven't is because of Ray. If he is the resident deputy and takes the call, I don't want him shooting me in the back—by accident, of course," Cy said snidely.

Benjamin chuckled. "He will not bother you, Cy. In fact, I think he feels pretty bad about himself. He will not be against us. He is stubborn, but he is a good man—at least where the Kuzedika are concerned."

"And he is a good deputy," Sarah said. "He was thinking with his heart, not his brains. Now that he knows I have made my choice he will side with us. There is no doubt of this."

"I'm glad to hear that." Cy's tone changed, and he looked around the cabin. He had placed a rifle at the window in the upstairs bedroom. On the main floor he had a double-barrel 12-gauge shotgun at the front door and a Remington 12-gauge pump at the rear. Earlier that morning he had installed two-by-fours into holding brackets across each door. The entries were secure so they could not be kicked in. They also could not be taken by surprise. "The Mexican Mafia have many connections. I have no idea how many will come, but enough to get the job done, I suspect."

"That could be any number," Benjamin replied.

"I'm thinking we're in big trouble, and I'm sorry to get you two involved in my personal problems." Cy's voice was as grim as his face. Concern stood out in his eyes.

The hum of an engine drew their attention to the front window. Cy jumped from the chair and crossed the room and pulled back the curtain. After a long moment he looked back and gave Benjamin and Sarah a big smile.

Cy walked over to the door and opened it wide. Two weary travelers walked inside. Jacob Wilson and Tony Valin came through the door, threw down their war bags, and gave Cy slapping hugs.

Cy was so shocked his vocal cords tightened up and the words stuck in his throat. Jacob gave Cy a second hug. "You didn't think your friends would abandon you at a time like this, did ya?"

"But how did you know?" Cy asked, surprised.

"Sarah called." Jacob gave a reassuring smile to Sarah. "She called yesterday and told us what happened."

Cy looked at Sarah. He couldn't make up his mind if he should be angry or pleased. Looking at his two friends, he couldn't be mad at Sarah for calling without his permission.

"Holy tamales," Tony said, taking a good look at Benjamin getting up from the kitchen chair. "Is this the mountain you took on?"

"This is Benjamin Gray. He is Sarah's uncle and my good friend," Cy said warmly.

"I'm glad of that," Tony laughed. "I sure as hell would hate to tangle with you." Tony went over to Benjamin and grabbed his hand and pumped it. "Friends, Ke-mo-sabe."

Benjamin pulled his hand out of Tony's grip. "Damned white folk," he grumbled, then gave a little smirk of pleasure.

Jacob looked at the giant and shook his head. "I saw how you almost killed Cy."

"I don't know if that's true. I spent too long recovering myself. I never got to see what damage I inflicted on him. I do know I was so sick I thought I was going to die and afraid I wasn't."

Jacob took hold of Benjamin's hand and then gave Sarah a hug and kissed her on the cheek. "I hope that fool white-eyed boy appreciates you, Sarah."

"He better, Jacob. I'm going to have his children."

"What?" Benjamin jumped out of his chair with fire in his eyes.

"Say what?" Jacob jerked around wide-eyed at Cy.

"Hey, whoa, whoa," Cy laughed. "She means I asked her to marry me and she's accepted."

"Is that true, my little bird?" Benjamin asked Sarah with relief.

"No, it is not true. I asked him and he accepted."

Benjamin was overcome and pulled Sarah to him with one arm, giving her a hug. Tony laughed. "I never thought you had it in you, Cy. I figured you for a confirmed bachelor."

Jacob grabbed Sarah from Benjamin, pulling her into his arms. "Let me give you your last hug from a real man. Cy is inexperienced; however, when time permits, I'll have a long talk with him on the proper way to treat a lady."

Jacob glanced around the room, spotting the guns at each entrance to the cabin. He eyed Cy soberly. "Joan Sausedo, a police benefits clerk, was contacted by the man who killed Skin and shot you. We issued an APB and almost had him. Our undercover men had him located and were on surveillance when they lost him leaving Los Angeles late last night. Word is, he either was going to fade out or he found you. Tony tried to call you early this morning but your phone was out of order."

"My phone is working." Cy walked over and picked it up. He listened to the receiver and set it back. "It's not."

"It could be a coincidence and then again, it may not," Tony offered, leaning against the wall. He pulled out a .357 from the middle of his back, checked the cylinder, and put it back. "Juan was lost near the Devore cutoff which means he could have been headed toward 395."

Cy moved back a step. "What's his name?"

"His name is Juan Mores. He's dangerous and he's slippery as an eel," Jacob said to Cy. "Have you ever heard of him?"

"No, but I'd never forget his face. He's a big ugly man with a scar across his face."

"That's him," chimed in Tony. "He's one bad dude. We

figure him for a number of killings. In fact, we now think he is attempting to move in on Joe Molino and take over the drug trafficking in Boyle Heights. The problem is, we are always one step behind him. The Hispanics hate him but they are also afraid of retaliation."

Jacob pulled up a chair to the kitchen table. "Come on, guys, we need to talk here. We've got a lot of work to do and I need a layout of the ranch. We need to plan our strategy. Tony brought some explosives; we may want to set up some home-made charges."

Tony pulled up a chair, turned it around backwards and sat in it. "We stopped in Lee Vining and called the Sheriff's Department. They're going to send a deputy out here to talk with us. What's the local law like around here? If this goes down, we're going to need help and a lot of it."

"It's a small department, but they work together with the CHP and they seem pretty territorial. I don't think they're going to like outsiders coming here with intent to commit murder," Cy said, looking at Benjamin for confirmation.

"He's right. The problem is, how many cops can they get out here? Not many. I think we are more or less on our own," Benjamin said, wishing he had a cold drink.

Jacob sat back in his chair. "So, it's a small department and the availability of manpower is not definite. I think we better get into town and call some of the boys at Hollenbeck. We can depend on at least three more on this short of notice. What do you think, Tony?"

"It seems to me if the sheriff knew how serious this is, he could round up people in his county to assist. Small agencies compensate all the time by deputizing local law enforcement agencies to help each other."

Cy stood up and got a drink of water from the kitchen faucet. "I better make a trip to town. I'll check with the sheriff and buy some groceries."

"Can I come with you?" Sarah asked, getting up from her chair.

"No. It's too dangerous. You would be more of a liability. I can't take the risk of you getting hurt."

Jacob walked over to Sarah and put his hands on her shoulders. "He's right, you know. We don't know what we're up against. Until we can identify the danger area and determine a plan of action, it's best if you stay here where it's relatively safe."

Chapter 25
Deadly Encounters

It was late in the afternoon when Ray was dispatched to the Golden Ranch on Sawmill Road. When the dispatcher described the location given to them by the caller, Ray advised he knew the location of the ranch. The call was to check out a possible assault situation involving Mexicans from East Los Angeles and an ex-police officer. Ray told dispatch he would check it out and would call if other assistance was required.

Two California Highway Patrol troopers came on the air and advised Ray they copied the transmission. One trooper would gravitate to Lee Vining from Mammoth and the other was south of Benton on Highway 6. They both would be in the area if they were summoned for assistance. It gave Ray a measure of comfort knowing he had backup if needed. There were no other deputies on duty in the south end of Mono County.

Before leaving Lee Vining he drove around town checking out the people to observe strangers in town or who would appear to be troublemakers. He did not notice any Mexicans or anything that would cause concern.

He left town and drove east on Highway 120. Ashamed of his jealous actions against Cy Golden, Ray knew he had been wrong and hoped Cy would accept his apology. Benjamin had accepted the stranger as well as everyone else in the valley. There was no reason for him not to be decent about it. Sarah had made her choice, and he cared enough for her not to make any further attempts to change her mind. He also wanted her to be happy. He felt in time it would all work out.

It was a long drive out to the Glass Mountain turnoff. He watched the side roads for traffic but did not see anything out of the ordinary.

Juan stepped out of the Lincoln at Indian Meadows. It was a small flat of dry grass just past the turn from 120 to Benton and five miles before the dirt road that lead to Cy's ranch. He and his men were located about a half mile south of the main highway on a dirt road that was locally called the Owen's River Wagon Road.

Juan was out of his element. He did not like being out of the big city and couldn't understand why anyone would want to live out in this God-forsaken open country where everything was sparse and dead. He missed the buildings and busy streets. He wanted to get this over with and return to Los Angeles where the action was. With Golden dead, there would be no witnesses to the Hollenbeck killing. Sausedo and her son would be found and eliminated in time. She was not a problem.

Golden's phone lines had been severed late last night. With his communications down he would be cut off from the world. Now he was a sitting duck.

After a short while, a dark green four-door jeep appeared in the distance, coming off the main highway and leaving a dust trail that slowly dissipated in the breeze. Juan lit a cigarette and motioned for Reuben Ortega to hand him a cold beer. Albert Alvarez was standing about a hundred feet up the road on a large rock with binoculars, watching the vehicle as it approached them. Finally he turned and gave a nod to Juan, climbed down off the rock, and walked over to the car and waited.

It infuriated Juan when the car did not slow down as it approached them. When it came to a stop, a large cloud of dust followed, covering Juan and his two men. Juan threw his beer down and stomped over to the car, opened the door, and pulled the driver out by his lapels. He slapped him alongside the head. "You stupido. Where are your brains, huh?" He slapped him again. Roberto looked fearfully back at Juan and apologized. He hated Juan but Juan was the boss.

Rosco got out of the car and hurried over to Juan. "Boss, it does not look as good as we had hoped for. Golden is still in the cabin. He may not know the lines are cut and he hasn't been out of the cabin. The girl is in there with him. A man with a long braid, could be an Indian, went into the cabin about an hour ago."

"So what is the problem?" Juan snapped, wiping the dust off his clothes. The other men had gathered around them, except for Albert. He opened the door on one of the cars and stood on the floorboard watching the road with binoculars.

Rosco stepped closer to Juan and pointed towards Cy's ranch. "A vehicle pulled into the place and two men got out. I don't know who they are, but one is black."

"What do you make of it?"

"I can't be sure. Maybe these guys are looking for work. They did not look bad to me," Rosco swallowed hard, watching Juan's expression.

"Well, that's too bad for them. We'll kill them all if we have to." Juan rubbed his chin and patted his hair with his hand. "I don't like it with the other two men; perhaps they will leave shortly. With Martin watching the road with two other men, we have nine. The odds aren't good enough. We'll give it some time. The visitors may leave. If the Indian stays at the ranch, we will kill him also. We can leave no witnesses."

"Hey, boss, a sheriff's car just went down the road toward the cop's place," Albert said excitedly. He put the glasses down and turned to Juan. "We better put a car on him and see where he is going. If he goes to the ranch, Martin will spot him then and we'll see what they are up to."

"Get on it," Juan said to Rosco. "You, Roberto. Drive and don't make no dust if you get off the road again."

"No problem, boss." Roberto went to the jeep, wondering how one drives on a dirt road without making dust.

Cy spent the afternoon showing Jacob and Tony the inner perimeter of the ranch and cementing a plan of action. It was frustrating at times because it was not known how many would come and where and when they would make their stand. Today, tomorrow, a week from now? Sarah fixed a meal and tried to act calmly.

Cy decided to go to town with Benjamin. He would check with the Mono County Sheriff's Department and contact the phone company to have his lines checked while Benjamin bought supplies. Jacob and Tony would stay at the ranch and look it over, setting up observation points and grape-shots at locations where a rear entry was undetectable behind the cabin. Tony explained to Benjamin and Sarah that grape-shots were explosives set in the bottom of a number ten coffee can. Approximately two pounds of nuts and bolts would be placed on top of the concave-shaped charge to give it a forward thrust when detonated, and set off by a trip line and a number eight blasting cap. The grape-shot was comparable to a lightweight claymore mine and would kill or maim anyone who was within twenty feet of it.

Cy briefed Tony and Jacob on three good locations for

setting the charges, keeping in mind the livestock and where they themselves would be walking. They were only concerned with avenues of entry in the event someone tried sneaking up behind the ranch buildings. After all was done, three explosive charges were set on pathways leading to the cabin.

Cy was slipping into his Levi jacket when he heard a vehicle approaching. Everyone remained quiet as the noise caught everyone's attention. Jacob went to the front window and Benjamin to the rear door. It surprised Cy when he peeked out and recognized the sheriff's car pulling up.

Jacob and Tony stood at opposite windows looking around the car. "It looks okay to me, Cy," Jacob said, scanning the outside area. The light in the sky was growing dim; it would be dark in an hour.

Tony maintained his position at the window without letting his gaze leave the interior of the vehicle. "It's clear inside unless someone is hiding in the back seat. Have the deputy come inside. I'll keep watching his rig from here."

Ray was relieved when Cy opened the door and invited him in. Jacob and Tony went out to the patrol unit to confirm he was alone, then both did a walkabout around the immediate ranch structures looking for anything suspicious.

"How serious is this?" Ray asked, surprised at the tension in the room.

"Serious enough," Cy retorted coolly, not knowing if he could trust Ray. "I've got some people who want me dead. This all has to do with a Mexican Mafia shooting that occurred in Los Angeles before I left the department. A number of people were killed. I'm the only witness."

"How did they find you?"

Sarah edged closer to Ray. "They have their ways, Ray, and we're scared."

"Well, I haven't noticed any strangers in town, especially Mexicans. I checked the dirt roads for any strangers or anything out of the usual. I didn't see anyone that would make me suspicious. It doesn't seem very smart for people to come out here in the open country and on unfamiliar ground with intent to murder someone."

Jacob leaned forward. "What you don't understand, my man, is that these guys are professionals and they are not afraid of anybody or anything."

"You're probably right. I've never dealt with big or organized crime figures. The few homicides we've had in our jurisdiction have always been local people, and it usually involved a family member or a lover's quarrel."

It took Cy ten minutes to tell Ray the whole story. It convinced the deputy he needed to take steps to ensure Cy and Sarah's protection until the suspects surfaced. It was agreed it would be safer for Sarah to ride back to Lee Vining in the sheriff's car and Benjamin would go with them. Cy would now stay at the cabin and discuss further plans with Jacob and Tony. After a brief argument, Cy and Jacob convinced Sarah she would only be a liability if she stayed at the ranch. She finally agreed to stay with Joseph and Sally Dondero for twenty-four hours. After that she was coming back whether they agreed to it or not.

Cy looked at Sarah admiringly. "I love you for this. You have taken a big load off my mind. With you gone, I can concentrate on what I have to do here."

"I know you're right; it's just hard leaving you." Sarah floated into Cy's arms and held him tight. "I love you with all my heart, Cy. You mean everything to me."

Cy felt the blood pressing against his temples. "I love you too, darling." He kissed her lightly on the lips and pushed her back. "Okay, now get going, before I change my mind." Cy turned to Ray. "You take good care of her."

"I'll guard her with my life, Cy. You know that." Ray put out his hand and both men grasped each other in a gentleman's shake. Ray faced Benjamin. "You ready to go, Ben? The sooner the better."

"Let's stop jawing and do something then," Benjamin broke off and stared at Ray. "I'm riding shotgun."

Ray smiled, "Glad to have you." He stood up. "Let's get going. I have a lot to do."

Cy felt a hard pull on his heart, watching the car disappear down the road. He was sure he had made the right decision by sending Sarah to the Donderos.

A few hundred yards before reaching the main highway, Ray spotted an AMI telephone repair van stopped at the side of the dirt road. A man at the back of the van was looking through a tool box. A second workman was climbing down from the telephone pole. It was the last pole before the power lines leading to Cy's cabin were buried.

"That's a relief," Sarah said, speaking over Benjamin's shoulder from the back seat. "At least Cy will have phone service."

Ray's spirits were lifted by seeing the phone men working. He pulled in behind the van. "Well, maybe this thing isn't as serious as we thought. Let's hope so." He stopped and got out.

Benjamin leaned forward, staring at the van. "Ray, maybe we should keep going. This isn't a good idea."

Ray waved him off. "I'll only be a second. I want to check with the phone men and see if they've got the line fixed and if they've noticed anything strange." Ray left his door open and walked over to the van over Benjamin's protest. Benjamin felt uneasy and tried to get the shotgun out of the electra-lock. He couldn't find the release button. "Sarah, do you know where the damn release is?"

Sarah's expression registered concern at her uncle's uneasiness. She leaned over the seat searching the front panel. She was frightened by her uncle's sudden nervousness. "There it is, Ben, on the left side of the steering column by the ignition key," she pointed with her finger. "It's the silver toggle switch on the lower part of the dash."

Ray approached the back of the van. "Evening. Have you guys found the problem with the phone? Mr. Golden reported to me it's been down several hours now."

The man looked up with a crooked grin. "We're working on it, mister."

Ray felt as if he had been smashed in the face with a sledge hammer. The Mexican wore a company shirt at least two sizes too small for him. The three top buttons were missing and the lapels were pulled apart at the neck. Ray stepped back and reached for his revolver.

Benjamin leaned over the seat and reached for the release switch. He barely glimpsed feet appearing at the open door, and at the same time, Sarah yelled a warning from the back seat. The barrel of a gun came down on his head. It knocked him dizzy but not unconscious.

He heard Sarah cry and fought desperately not to fade out. He heard two shots come from the direction of the van and glanced up in time to see the gun barrel coming down again.

He reached up, blocking the downswing of the man's arm. He pulled hard and the man fell inside on top of him.

Benjamin gave a quick jab to the man's face, knocking him backward out of the patrol car. Benjamin was still in a fog and his ears were ringing, but he managed to spring out of the front seat, letting his weight hit the man with full impact, knocking the air out of him. He came fully upright and turned to the van. A blow from a hard object struck him on the left cheekbone. He swung back with his left elbow, catching the second man on the side of the head, sending him sprawling.

Sarah screamed, causing Benjamin to panic. He swung with a left and right to the man's face, knocking him to the ground. Benjamin could feel his left eye swelling. He knew he had little time; he would have a big disadvantage with only one eye.

Glancing at the first man who was now on his hands and knees, he planted his foot in the man's rib cage. The man rolled over and came up with a revolver in his right hand. Benjamin was on top of him before he could raise the weapon. He grabbed the man's chin and head in a powerful grip and snapped his neck with a loud pop.

Benjamin snatched the second man by the lapels and threw him to one side. He looked around frantically for Sarah. It was difficult to see in the twilight. His left eye was closing. Out of his right eye he could see a dark-colored car parked to the rear of the patrol vehicle. He wondered how it ever got there without his noticing it. Perhaps it appeared during the fight.

A big Mexican was holding Sarah with his forearm in a choke hold. The man had a smile on his face as he stared at Benjamin. Ben could see the terror in Sarah's eyes as she squirmed helplessly in the man's grip.

"I have no fight with your kind, Señor," Juan said carefully. "We do not want to hurt this maiden; however, she is a drawing card for our purpose."

"And what is your purpose?" Benjamin gasped heavily, catching his breath.

"We need to eliminate Mr. Golden."

"Why?"

"It is not your concern. It is not my purpose to kill anyone unnecessarily, especially not my brother, the Native American."

"Brother?"

"Native Americans and Mexicans have interbred for

hundreds of years now. We have a common cause," Juan answered, trying to gain position with the man.

"What is the cause?" Benjamin sneered.

"To survive the white man's trespass on our land."

"You sucking pig!" Benjamin screamed. "The Indians were here long before Spain and everyone else. You made slaves of my people long before any damn white man. You are on Indian ground now. You are holding an Indian hostage now." Benjamin looked over his shoulder at Ray who was lying face-down on the ground. "Is he dead?"

"Unfortunately, yes. It was not planned this way. We did not want to kill an Indian, let alone a deputy sheriff. We don't need any more enemies. I need your cooperation. Tell Mr. Golden I have his woman. If he wants her, he must meet me on open ground. This is between him and me," Juan said. He knew he would have to eliminate all the witnesses once Golden was out of the way as well.

"Where can I meet him alone? I will not harm this one if he comes to me," Juan said, tightening his hold on Sarah, who was wincing.

"There is only one place you can meet him alone. It is an abandoned mill site up the dirt road a couple of miles."

"Up this road past the cabin? What, you think I am stupid?"

"To meet Cy Golden one on one, I would say yes, you are stupid."

Juan slipped his big hand around Sarah's neck, choking her. "How do I get to this mill?"

"There are two roads to it. One goes past the cabin. The other is up the road a short distance. It turns right off the highway and intersects this road to the mill. It is a dead end road." Benjamin slowly moved closer to Juan as he spoke. He wondered where the other men were. He saw the driver behind the wheel and another man on the other side of the car. He didn't know the condition of the second man he had put down but figured he was dead.

"You tell Golden I will meet him at the mill in one hour. He must come alone, or I will kill the girl after I have pleasured her." Juan moved his big hand from Sarah's waist over her breast to her neck. "If anyone comes with him, I will cut her eyes out."

Benjamin surprised Juan with his quick speed and his voracious hunger to break the man into pieces. He yanked Juan's hand away from Sarah's throat, tossing her aside like a rag.

Benjamin struck Juan in the chest with his shoulder, knocking him backward. He dove on top of Juan and they rolled over and over in the dirt with surprising ease and with the power of two great bulls. Sarah was pulled away by another man to the rear of the car. Juan came to his feet. "Very stupid move," he yelled hoarsely.

Juan grabbed Benjamin by the hair and one arm, catapulting him into the side of the car with a sickening impact. A terrible rage lashed hot and powerful through Benjamin's brain as he struck the car door and hit the ground. He did not expect the powerful strength of the Mexican and knew this could be a fight to the death. Benjamin saw the flicker of steel in Juan's right hand swinging toward him. He parried with his left arm, throwing Juan off balance. He hit Juan twice in the stomach and once in the face. Most men would have been finished with the punishing blows, but Juan was strong as a horse and took the hits with only moderate effect. He glared at Benjamin sharply. He wanted to finish this fight one on one but he knew he needed his strength for Golden. "Reuben," cried Juan hoarsely.

A club to the back of the head knocked the big Indian to his knees. Reuben couldn't believe the man was not out cold. Benjamin tried desperately to get back on his feet, his head swimming. He barely caught the glimpse of the flickering object as it smashed into his left thigh. The searing blow was so painful Benjamin screamed out but refused to relinquish his position. His vision was spinning, and he felt as if he had been shot. Nausea rumbled through his stomach.

Juan came forward, took a handful of Benjamin's hair, and pulled the Indian's head up. He watched the injured man's good eye roll back. "The mill! Remember the mill. One hour, savvy?" With that, Juan kneed Benjamin in the face, sending him to the ground with a loud thud.

Sally Dondero left Benjamin lying against a boulder in the sagebrush only a few feet from where she had found him limping along the dirt road. She was sick with worry but thankful she had checked the road where she had seen the lights from the other two cars pulling away. His face was badly smashed and swelling. A boot knife was stuck in his leg and she was frustrated because she was not strong enough to pull it out.

She knew of the danger to Sarah if she did not do as she was told. Ben made her promise to tell her father what had happened and then Joseph was to deliver the message to Cy. When Sally asked Benjamin what she should do about him, he told her it was none of her concern, and swore at her until she reluctantly left.

Sally drove as fast as her father's old truck would go down the road, across the highway, and up another dirt road to Benjamin's cabin. She pulled to a skidding stop, causing billows of dust. She jumped from the truck and ran toward the cabin to call her father, but to her surprise and relief, he was already standing on the front porch. After a brief explanation, Joseph told his daughter to make three calls, giving specific instructions for each. After telling her he was headed to Cy's ranch, he instructed her to go back to Benjamin and help him back to his place. Joseph doubted Sally would find Benjamin but it was necessary to make the attempt.

"Daughter, you know what to do. Yes?"

"Yes, father. I know what to do."

"I must make a call before I go to Cy's ranch," Joseph said. He walked over to the phone and picked it up, dialed Jessie Durrant, and waited for an answer.

Jessie was the oldest Paiute Indian in the valley and stemmed from a long line of Kuzedika. The old man slowly got up from his wooden chair and went to the ringing phone. His long gray hair hung over his shoulders, and his face was old and wrinkled. His eyes were as clear as his mind. "Brother Dondero, you have a worried sound. What is it, my old friend?"

"Elder Durrant, we must talk."

Benjamin tried twice to pull the knife from his leg and failed. The pain was now going into the hip joint. After analyzing the situation, he knew he couldn't wait any longer. This time he meant business—no matter what it required. He grasped the knife with both hands. With all his strength, gritting his teeth, he pulled harder and harder until his big arms shook as he desperately strained. A dull pop preceded an eruption of pain bursting deep from within his large thigh. Again he experienced nausea as the knife pulled free.

After Benjamin managed to remove the knife from his leg, he lay there a few moments longer, feeling somewhat victorious, but mostly needing to get strength back into his body. He closed his eyes, feeling dizzy, knowing it wouldn't be long before he could deal with this problem. He needed a little more time to recuperate before going to Glass Mountain. A tremendous mental pressure had engulfed the giant. Benjamin's mind put in overtime working through the cobwebs of confusion.

Chapter 26
Mexican Standoff—A Time to Die

Joseph Dondero sat down on a kitchen chair after giving Benjamin's message to Cy. They discussed several options on what they could try in order to get Sarah back safely. Cy was becoming more and more nervous as the time passed, and he finally told the others he was going to the old mill alone, as Juan had demanded.

Tony looked outside and shook his head. "I don't like this, you guys. The wind has picked up and the edge of a front is on its way here. It's starting to snow lightly."

Jacob didn't like the plan but he had no say. Cy had made up his mind and there was nothing he could do about it. "We work better as a team, Cy. Let me come with you," Jacob pleaded.

"It's too dangerous. If Juan sees you, he may think it's a trap and hurt Sarah." Cy checked the revolver to make sure it was loaded. "I can't take the chance of doing anything that would endanger her." He set his equipment bag on the kitchen table, pulled out his Second Chance vest, and put it on under his shirt. "We agreed on this. You and Tony will cover the two roads out of the old mill. If Juan shows up with Sarah, then you know I failed and you have to stop him. There is no further conversation on this. You can use Ray's police radio to call for the highway patrol backup once I have left."

"I'm calling for assistance as soon as we get to the patrol car," countered Jacob.

"Good idea." Cy pulled on his deerskin gloves.

"No chance of changing your mind on this one?" Tony asked, discouraged. He didn't have a better plan, and he didn't know what to suggest.

Cy put a knife in his boot and a second gun in the middle of his back. "My life is finished if anything happens to Sarah. Everyone in my life dies. It can't happen this time. I've got to get her out of this."

"Stop talking like that," Jacob demanded, folding his arms. "You stop this damn talk about it being your fault. You didn't make any of this happen. It's them, not you."

"Jacob, I'm like that damn mountain!"

Jacob screwed up his forehead. "What are you talking about?"

"That mountain," he pointed towards Glass Mountain, his voice quivering. "Me and that mountain have poor footings, Jacob. My whole system is made of glass right now, and I don't have much confidence in myself. I do know I am not afraid to die. My fear is for Sarah. Can't you imagine what is going through her mind? She is so sweet and innocent of any of this. I have to try and save her on Juan's terms. I don't know if he has any honor or not. He said he would not kill her if I came alone. He knows he is a wanted man and that is because of me, and me only. I was the one who cornered him and he wants revenge."

Cy walked over to the back door and picked up his Winchester double-barrel shotgun and rechecked the barrel chambers for loads. "I don't expect to make it off of that mountain, but I'm sure going to give it everything I have. If she doesn't make it, I don't make it. I have to do this my way."

Cy turned with the shotgun in his left hand. "Sarah's uncle is probably dead by now or he'd be here. No matter how badly he is hurt, if he was alive, he would be here. It means everything to me that you guys came to help me. Now, I ask both of you, don't let Juan off this mountain alive. If he has Sarah with him, he'll never let her go. She'll need your help, okay?"

"Okay, Cy, okay," Jacob said huskily then turned to Tony. "We'll promise you Juan does not leave this mountain alive."

Tony walked around the table closer to Cy. He stared at him a moment, put his arm around him, and then pushed him gently to arm's length. "You know the back game trail to the mill site. That's the best way to go. You've gotta stay off the road. They'll be waiting for you."

"That's the way I was going in. I'm taking my horse in most of the way to conserve my energy. Once I cut the trail on the north slope, I'll release Cole and he'll come back down to the corral. I can follow the trail all the way into our old camp undercover and without making any noise. My big worry now is if the snow starts collecting and covers everything. It's pretty easy to get turned around if the weather gets bad. It's to my advantage that we're meeting at our old camp—thanks to Benjamin, wherever he is."

"I'm going to check on him at his ranch house. It'll only take me a couple of minutes once I hit the main highway." Jacob said soberly. "If he's alive, I'll get a doctor for him."

"I have already called an ambulance," Joseph said. "I sent Sally to go back to him and bring him to his cabin. She said he was hurt pretty bad." Dondero looked admiringly at Cy. "You must go now if you want to make it on time. The storm will not hit in full strength for several hours. These are only broken clouds. You will have good vision in the moonlight when it clears from time to time. You must ride to Sawmill Canyon cutoff and then work your way to a game trail from there. After you begin climbing the mountain, your night vision will come back and you will be able to see very well along the way to the mill. If not you, your horse will."

Cy could hardly believe what was happening to him. His life, his love, his friends. It was too much to comprehend. He looked at the others unhappily. "You guys mean a lot to me. Take care." Cy pulled up the collar of his Levi jacket, put on his brown hat, and stepped outside, closing the door behind him with Jacob on his heels.

Jacob looked equally unhappy as he watched Cy saddle his horse and holster his shotgun in the rifle sheath. Finally he took hold of his arm. "Once you're there, take your time and let them throw the hat out."

"That's my plan if all goes well." Cy nodded to him, stepping up into the stirrup. He turned Cole south and rode up the dirt trail, skirting the lower bench of Glass Mountain.

Five minutes after Cy left, Joseph stepped out onto the porch and rolled a cigarette. He took a deep draw and slowly exhaled. Tony came outside and had a smoke with him.

Joseph's face was sober. "The outsiders have sadly underestimated us."

Tony looked at him sideways, taking a puff on his smoke. "What do you mean, Mr. Dondero?"

"They should have never killed a Kuzedika. Not many of us left, and what there are of us, we hold very sacred. They make big mistake. This is hallowed ground. It was not a fair fight with my Indian brothers. Ray Tom was a good man and we were very proud of him for his work with the sheriff. To take a woman is very bad. To steal a Paiute maiden is lower then a maggot eating dog droppings." The old man changed his gaze from Glass Mountain and looked at Tony with deep conviction. "They have broken Kuzedika law."

"I'm not sure what you mean."

"Maybe no one come off the mountain."

Tony didn't know how to respond and was worried of offending the old man. "Well, Cy is special, too. I've never met anyone like him, and those dope runners are going to think they fell into a sackful of rattlesnakes when he finds them."

"Yes, I think you are right. I hope you are right." Joseph sat on the front step puffing on a smoke. A few moments later he watched Jacob and Tony drive down the road to block off the escape routes in case things went bad for Cy on the mountain.

Joseph finished his cigarette and field stripped it out of habit. An Indian was dead and another one may be dying. Glass Mountain had been cursed and it was necessary to draw more blood to wash away the curse, if life was to go back to normal.

Cy led Cole off the wide dirt road and up into the sagebrush. He was a little worried about the noise made by Cole's hooves clicking on the rocks and obsidian. He finally convinced himself he was a long way from being heard. He took a long look at the height of the mountain, well over eleven thousand feet. He was glad he did not have to climb to the top; he only had to hike up a thousand feet to hit the main trail that led to the mill site.

Cy took a quick look back at his ranch. The cabin lights gave a warm glow in the distance. It didn't matter if he survived this night, so long as he could free Sarah. She was the only important thing. She was everything. If he was wounded or even died, it was acceptable, just so she was safe from Juan. Juan had to die and Cy committed himself to killing him.

The clouds were broken. The moon intermittently sent its rays of light onto the mountain. Cy could see clearly when the moon was able to get through. Off and on light snow fluttered to the ground. His eyes had adjusted to the darkness, and he climbed his way up the steep mountain without difficulty. Though it was cold, the climb and nervousness caused him to perspire under his heavy clothing.

The cedar trees grew sparse with the pine trees now dotting the landscape. Large boulders of obsidian sparkled in the moonlight. When the gap in the clouds closed, blocking the moon, he could still see the trail. It was a hard climb and Cy was thankful he and his horse were in good physical condition. He hoped because of his health and youth he could outlast Juan. He knew Juan was stronger than he was, but Cy knew that he could move faster, and his coordination should be superior to the big Mexican's.

Cy took a break to give Cole a breather and checked his bearings. He looked down the mountain. In the far distance he could see the lights at his ranch. Further to the north across the highway he could barely make out a light in Benjamin's cabin. He gave a short prayer for Benjamin. Cy thought it was ironic. At one time he hated and feared the Indian and he wanted him dead. Now he prayed for his life.

He thought of his father and mother. He wondered if they could see him on the mountain. He pictured his brother lying in a jungle dying. He wondered how much pain Richard suffered before he died. He wondered if people saw each other after death. He was ready to die and did not fear it. It surprised him how easily he accepted his fate.

He let his mind work on all the possible scenarios for when he reached the sawmill. According to Joseph, Benjamin told Sally there were at least six men and perhaps more. If that was true, Juan would have his men placed in strategic locations waiting for his arrival. He laughed to himself. They were not used to cold weather and they would be freezing even with the light snowfall. He visualized Juan's men hunkered down, peering down the road and watching for him to make an appearance.

Because of the cold and snow, Juan's men would not be very alert, and this would give him an advantage. Accepting his own possible death made him very dangerous, whereas Juan's men might be careless. At least he hoped they would be.

The mountain was getting steeper. Cy had to remind himself to keep his horse at a slow steady pace. Cole was eager to climb, maintaining a good stride. Time was important, and he wanted to get to the mill site faster than the Mexicans would think possible without a vehicle. He needed to get there and study the area before making his entry.

When Cy reached the main game trail leading to the mill, he got down off his horse and turned him down the trail. Cole did not hesitate heading down the trail towards home. Cy turned and climbed along the trail at a fast rate.

Cy never knew what happiness could be until he met Sarah. She entered his heart like an arrow. It hit him with full impact. He understood now why Mary Ann was discouraged with him for not making a commitment to her emotionally. He loved her as a close friend. He cared for her greatly, but he had no idea what a strong and enormous motivation love was until he looked into Sarah's dark eyes.

Cy's attention snapped to the present when he thought he heard someone walking. He stopped, pulling the shotgun out, gripping it in a port position. He relaxed when he realized it was his heart thumping loudly in his chest, pulsation echoing in his ears. He stopped again to catch his breath.

He wondered if he was really bad luck or if life was a test of adventures. Perhaps people were tested with adversity to make them better people or perhaps more compassionate. Perhaps life was a path of trials to determine who were the strong, who were the weak, and who were the survivors.

Cy's father was a good one for keeping his personal commitments. He was a hard-working man who could not rest until the chores were finished. He loved the earth and treated it with care. He irrigated and fertilized the ground, providing the nutrients that it required, and in return he received the fruits of a profitable yield. Frank never let his animals suffer. He always fed the ranch animals before he satisfied himself at the supper table.

He was thinking of his mother's cooking—her homemade breads and biscuits, her pies, and most of all, mashed potatoes and rich brown gravy. Life was bountiful when he was home. He wished he had shown his gratefulness to his parents when he had the opportunity.

A cold breeze brought him back to the misery of the mountain. He climbed over fallen trees and worked his way upward along the rough trail. If he had not known the game trails, the climb would have been impassable in the night. He knew Juan would think he would use the road, and at least two of his men would be posted as sentries guarding the entrance to the mill. He wondered where Sarah would be hidden and whether she was hurt and cold.

He couldn't think about Juan, or one of his men, abusing Sarah. She was so innocent and tender to the hard times of life. She did not deserve this treatment. He had to free her.

After twenty minutes of continuous climbing, Cy's body was hot. His legs were rubbery and his shoulders ached. His forehead was crisscrossed with rivulets of sweat. He caught his breath when he saw a large familiar pine tree with a crooked trunk growing out and away from the mountain instead of vertically into the sky. He was only a hundred yards from the mill. He stopped to catch his breath and gather his wits; he had to be extremely quiet from this point on. He pulled a leather wine pouch from his waistband and took a long drink of cold water. He could feel it all the way to his stomach and it chilled everything it touched on the way down.

From his rear pocket Cy withdrew a blue handkerchief and wiped his face and forehead. The time had come. Sarah was close. He was now going to face people he did not know and try to kill them. How strange life could be; destroying a person's life was not easy at any time. He wondered how loyal Juan's men were. Would they stand and fight to the finish?

Cy circled in search of any dangers that lurked in the cold night. Once, Cy thought he heard movement above him and to the right. He stooped down and listened for a long moment. When the night remained silent, he moved on, his eyes panning back and forth.

Jacob shivered in the cold. He buttoned up his jacket when he stepped away from Benjamin's cabin. Sally told him Benjamin was gone when she went to find him. She had no idea where he was, unless he had gone to the sawmill. If he passed out along the road, he would freeze to death.

Nervous and worried, Jacob got back into Sarah's jeep and drove to the main highway and waited at Sawmill Road.

Down the road to the west two sets of headlights approached Jacob. As they drew closer police overheads lit up the night. Two highway patrol troopers stopped their cars, blocking the dirt road.

The second trooper called for additional backup and gave their position when he spotted the black stranger with an exposed weapon strapped to his side. The first trooper opened his car door and spoke into his mike. "I am Trooper Gentry Pace from the California Highway Patrol. Drop your weapon and step away from the vehicle now."

Jacob was relieved. He gave the troopers a big grin and carefully laid his revolver on the pavement. He stepped away from the gun and slowly pulled his wallet from his coat pocket. "Hold on there, boys. I'm Lieutenant Jacob Wilson from the Los Angeles Police Department." He flashed his ID as the two troopers slowly walked toward him with their weapons trained on him. "Easy guys, I'm not the enemy here."

The tall blonde-headed trooper came closer to Jacob. He didn't look friendly and Jacob hoped he would not overreact. "Where is Deputy Tom?" Trooper Pace demanded gruffly. "He gave dispatch this location and now no one can raise him."

"He's dead," Jacob responded solemnly. "He was killed by drug traffickers out of L.A. They came here to kill one of our ex-officers, Cy Golden. Ray Tom got in their way and they eliminated him."

"What's your part in this, mister?"

"You need to set up a road block and you need more backup. My partner is on that mountain and he needs our help. Tony and I are supposed to stay here and we can't do that. So here's the story. I can't tell you twice and don't ask questions; we're in a hurry."

Juan's voice was as grim as his face. "It is going to be my pleasure to crush the last breath of life from you after I kill your friend, little squaw."

Sarah's hands were tied in front of her and the rope extended to the bumper of the car. The parking lights were on so Cy could see her when he arrived—if he arrived. Sarah gave Juan a cold glance and looked towards the road. "Why don't you leave here? It doesn't make sense. If you kill Cy or me, everyone in the county will be looking for you. You have nothing to gain."

"I have my reasons. That is what matters," Juan said, backhanding Sarah across her mouth.

Blood appeared at the corner of her lip. She looked straight at Juan. Sarah was surprised with her inner strength. She did not let her feelings register on her face. "You were very foolish leaving the safety of your city. The code is different here."

"Code? What code? What are you babbling about?" Juan said, breathing heavily.

"You are going to find out any moment now," Sarah murmured quietly. "Cy has told me of your people in Boyle Heights. You have a code and people must respect each other or you lose face. This is Paiute country. You are out of your element. No one knows of our secret order, but you are about to find out. Then all will be rectified. And you, Mr. Juan, will be gone. Not to Mexico. Not to Los Angeles. You," she smiled defiantly, "will be disposed of like a fat bug under the heel of a boot."

Juan eyed her coolly. "Who do you think you're talking to? Huh? You know nothing."

"A blood tick."

"A what?"

"You are a tick that sucks the life from everyone you touch," Sarah said, raising her gaze to meet his. "You have trespassed on our land. The ghosts sleep in the day and work at night. Tonight you will feel the bite of death. Tomorrow my people will feed your liver to the dogs."

Juan looked at the Indian girl in amazement. She had been quiet up to this point. Now he couldn't shut her up. The things she said were pretty brazen for someone whose life was being threatened. Why was she not begging for mercy instead of taunting him? None of this made sense, and it confused him.

Reuben Ortega searched intently at the edge of the large turn-around where the old mill had once stood. He did not like what he was hearing from the Indian girl. He also felt they should not be here and wanted to go home. He was cold and worried.

"Señor Juan, why do we not leave? Those men at the ranch house know who you are, who we all are. Why do we not go? It serves no purpose now."

"We are not finished here, that is why."

"But what if it starts to snow so much that we can't get out of here? I have never been in the snow. I hear it is very dangerous."

"Be quiet," Juan cursed. "You do your job and watch for Golden. He should have been here by now."

Sarah smiled the best she could. "This is the home of the dead. You have broken a Paiute law."

Juan wanted to strike the girl again. He remembered she started all her talking when he hit her the first time. Instead of hitting her again, he walked over to Reuben and slapped him alongside his head. "Check on the men. Make sure they are alert and in position. If Golden comes in alone, I will kill him with my bare hands, and then we will leave."

"What about the girl?"

"We'll decide that later. Now get going." Juan pushed the man toward the dirt road that led into the camp. He looked back at Sarah and smiled, thinking of the pleasure he would receive in killing her. He wanted to watch the light fade in her eyes as she unwillingly accepted death.

Cy stopped when he saw the glow of a cigarette under a pine tree about fifty feet ahead of him. He took out the small binoculars that hung around his neck from inside his jacket. The man was facing toward the road and had not noticed Cy behind him.

The Mexican was leaning forward, searching for any movement down the dirt road, when everything went black. The gun barrel crushed his head, splattering blood on the skiff of snow on the ground around him. Albert Alvarez was laid out unconscious.

Cy backed up and took his time moving around the open perimeter of the mill. He could see a dark car parked in the middle but no people. He knew men would be stationed in the tree line. He began circling through the trees searching them out.

He saw the shadowy outline of a man to his right approximately 100 feet away stationed between some huge pine trees. A rustle, not very far behind Cy, signaled him to hit the ground rolling. He scanned the terrain and bushes. He knew there was something there but could not make it out. He waited a few more moments. When nothing else alerted him, he moved slowly on his hands and knees toward the man in the trees.

Cy stopped short when he heard Sarah talking softly from somewhere ahead of him, near where he saw the car. He moved noiselessly to the edge of the trees as fast as he could. On the other side of the car, Sarah was sitting on the ground with a guard next to her. She appeared unharmed and he felt relief. He decided to continue with his plan.

It seemed like a long time before Cy saw the second man again. He heard Rosco shivering before he spotted him. The Mexican was squatted down, holding his arms around his stomach, shaking. He appeared to be in total discomfort. Cy was relieved to see the man distracted by the cold temperature and not attentive to his post.

Cy crouched low to the ground catlike and carefully moved toward the man. He made no noise but the man's sense of danger made him turn around. Cy was only a few feet away and was ready to move in. Rosco pulled a revolver from inside his jacket. Without bringing the shotgun up waist high, Cy shot the man in the chest. Falling immediately backward in a slump, Rosco squirmed back and forth but couldn't get his eyes to focus or his arms and legs to move under him. Nothing seemed to work.

Cy jumped to the side and rolled two times for cover in the trees. It was the only thing that saved his life as bullets pounded the ground where he had previously been, ricocheting into the night. Rosco took two hits by the gunfire, and they finished him off.

Yelling could be heard from down the road and from other locations around the open area. Cy cursed himself for having to discharge the shotgun, alerting the other men on guard. He started to fade back deeper into the trees when a large Mexican exited the back seat of the car next to Sarah.

"Mr. Golden," Juan called from the car. He did not appear disturbed that one of his men had been shot. Cy wondered how the other men felt about their boss's indifference to their deaths and injuries.

"Mr. Golden, I have a proposition for you." Juan stepped over to Sarah. He grabbed a handful of her hair and pulled her to her feet. "You fight me one on one without weapons. You win, the girl is yours unharmed. You lose, you die and the girl will be taken care of in the most appropriate manner in one of my houses," Juan smiled, looking at Sarah. "She is a very fine piece of meat and will bring a good price on the market. Your choices, I'm afraid, are limited." Juan pulled Sarah in front of him as a shield. "But, it is your choice. There is a chance you could take some of my men, but not all of them. They will kill you, and I will have your woman for my pleasure. Can you endure that?" Juan hesitated, searching the area where he heard the shotgun blast. "We can talk this..."

The man who had been guarding Sarah at the car suddenly felt his feet being yanked out from under him. He hit the ground hard, knocking the wind from his lungs. Cy was on him in an instant plunging a knife through his heart. In the same movement, Cy side kicked Juan just above the hip, knocking him off balance. Sarah pushed away from Juan.

"Cy! On your left!" Sarah cried. Cy turned, hitting the man full in the face with a straight left. He followed through with a right hook with revolver in hand, catching the man along his jawbone.

Cy knew Juan would be on him and rolled to his right, bringing up his feet and kicking Juan in the midsection as he leaned over to Cy. The kick shoved him backward.

Cy rolled over and got up, looking for Juan's henchmen. He hadn't planned on confronting Juan out in the open and knew his time was extremely short; too short before the other men would overtake him.

Reuben appeared from out of the dark and wrapped his arm around Sarah's waist and yelled at Cy to stop. He held a knife to her throat, threatening to slice her jugular vein. Without hesitation, Cy drew his .357 and shot him through the right eye, blowing out the back side of his head. He was dead before he hit the ground in a heap. Juan was on top of Cy in a flash, knocking the gun out of his hands. Cy struck Juan with his fist, but his blow glanced off his hard chin without effect.

Juan hit Cy twice in the face with jolting effects. He encircled Cy's neck in a hard grip with his left hand and was preparing to land a crushing blow with his right, when Cy reached up between his arms, grabbed his larynx, and twisted. The air shut off to Juan's windpipe, making him release his grip. When Cy pulled his hand backward, twisting his grip on Juan's throat, it should have rendered the man helpless, but all it did was give Cy a second opportunity to pull away from Juan, who was gasping for air.

Cy grabbed his gun as he got to his feet, untied Sarah, and they turned to head for the game trail, but their path was blocked by Roberto, gun in hand. Cy was about to shoot when Juan hit him with a heavy blow to the back of the neck, dropping him to the ground. Martin and another Mexican took hold of Cy, pulling him to his feet and throwing him against the car. Both men pinioned his arms.

Juan walked over and pulled Cy's face close to his. "You little piece of nothing. You have caused me a lot of trouble. I have lost good men because of you. Now, you will die the death of horror," Juan screamed, his face contorted with pain and anger.

Flecks of spittle dotted Cy's face. He refused to show the fear that Juan craved and expected. "Death by you? Or do you need help?"

"My men will have the pleasure of sticking you," Juan's eyes glared. "You remember the man you found on Soto Street? Henry Vasquez, the wife beater? That will be your fate."

"So, that was your doing?"

"Of course. He was a vacuum of dishonor—sucking in his lies and deception into our business. It was necessary for the proper example to be set for our family members." He paused. "And now you." Juan's face darkened with anger. "You have caused me a great amount of discomfort and have interrupted our business."

Cy displayed his best stone face, stalling for time. He knew the longer he talked, the sooner the other men would start to relax. They had not searched him, and he still had a second knife in his boot. "So, that was you in the doorway the night of the stabbing. My partner, the one you killed, said he thought he saw someone watching us."

"Yes, it was me. You see, you have been a thorn in my side for some time, whether you knew it or not. Your woman, here," Juan motioned to Sarah, "must now go also. You know this, of course."

Cy knew they would kill Sarah after they had their way with her. He had to get to her before they did. His death was not important. He could not let her die by their hands. He must do it himself and do it swiftly. His temples pounded like a wild thunderstorm. He knew he would have only one quick movement. He must get the knife and plunge it into Sarah's heart for a quick and painless death. It would be the last accomplishment of his life—killing the only woman he had ever loved and wanted. His mind raced to consider alternatives, of which there were few.

"You're a sorry wet ass punk," Cy smiled sardonically. Sarah glanced at Cy, terrified. "Your men do not respect you because you expect them to do the work you cannot accomplish yourself. They know you are nothing without them."

Juan's voice was sour. "What are you saying?"

Cy's face was fused with fury. "You are a coward and a disgrace to your race. You haven't the courage to meet me one on one like our agreement. I came because that is what you wanted. Now you command your men to kill me because you know you cannot do it alone. Even me without a weapon and you with whatever you have at your disposal cannot take me without help of your people. It is a sad day for them to see their boss exposed as the degraded coward that you are."

Cy glanced around at the three other Mexicans. He thought he saw something in Roberto's eyes and had to take the chance of playing it out. "Your so-called Mr. Juan Mores, here, is a fake and sniveler. He scares you because of his ugly looks. That scar on his face did not come from a fight with another man. It was done by a woman when he was running from her."

Juan grabbed Cy by his jacket and looked into his eyes with disgust before responding. His face was lined in fury. "Roberto, give him the circle of death."

Roberto studied Juan for a moment, not moving. He looked questionably at his boss. "Perhaps, boss, perhaps it would be better if we stand back and let this man face you as you requested in the beginning." Roberto's face was stern as he tried to conceal the tremor in his hands.

"What? You question me?" Juan whispered, shaken.

"Oh, no, Señor, I do not question you," Roberto replied hastily. "It was your desire to meet this hombre one on one. You said you would kill him with your bare hands. We have been looking forward to this. Besides, we have come here with nine men. Now, I only see five. This man," Roberto pointed to Cy, "has killed three of your men tonight. It is only right that you dispose of him as the Patron. Do you not agree?"

Juan was stunned and it registered in his eyes. He turned to his most loyal man. "Martin, shoot the man in the stomach and then in the head."

"Señor?" Martin echoed doubtfully.

Juan swallowed his surprise.

"Losing ground, Patron?" Cy questioned.

"Martin! Now. Do it!" Juan cursed between his clenched teeth.

"Si, Señor, si." Martin stepped forward and put his hand on the handle of the .38 Colt in his belt. The silent night was broken by a swish that ended with a loud slamming thud.

Cy flinched, looking at Martin. A long arrow was protruding through his neck. Dark gray feathers from the arrow were embedded halfway, while the remainder of the shaft was out the other side of his neck, painted in a crimson red. The light in his eyes said his brain could not register what had taken place. Martin looked questioningly at Juan. He reached up to his throat and felt the shaft of the arrow. As the warm stickiness touched his fingers and ran down his neck, his knees buckled and he fell to the ground.

Sarah looked at the dead man in fear but understood what was happening. She and Cy looked at each other in surprise.

From the perimeter of the trees a dozen Indians walked forward with rifles; one had his bow notched with a second arrow. In the middle of the approaching men, a giant Indian stood above the rest. It was Benjamin, limping badly with one eye swollen shut.

Cy caught his breath as Joseph Dondero stepped from the shadows, dressed in leather and a single feather hanging in his hair. He led the Indians into the open with Benjamin limping at his side. As they drew closer, Benjamin followed the old man toward Juan while the others remained a short distance away. Juan was speechless as he watched the two men approaching him.

Joseph stopped a few feet away. In his slow and easy speech, he stared at Juan Mores, ignoring the other Mexicans. "You," he pointed to Juan, "not a man of your word."

"What is this?" Juan questioned the men with a short laugh. "We negotiated here. Why are you interfering, and who are you?"

"I am Joseph Dondero, second elder of our tribe. You, Juan Mores, you are wad of dog spit. You have no honor. You embarrass your men," Joseph said, stepping closer, fearless of the weapon in Juan's hand.

"Who are you? How did you know my name?"

Dondero ignored his questions. "Europeans came over the ocean to this land for religious freedom. The Native Americans lost their land, lost their religion. The Indian people understood survival and the land, what it gave in food and herbs for sickness. The tahng-wahts, white man, had educational ways that taught a new knowledge that wasn't grasped by my people. The whites' communication was superior. In other words, Mr. Dog Spit, the whites learned from the Indian but we did not learn from them."

"What in the hell are you babbling about? This makes no sense," Juan sputtered between his teeth.

"Silence or I'll cut out your tongue," Joseph hissed. As if emphasizing his point, another arrow flew through the air and sank into the side of the Lincoln.

"For your information, Tommy Fasthorse, here," Joseph

pointed over his shoulder without taking his eyes off of Juan, "would have gone to the Olympics if it were not for the cost. His next arrow will cut a hole in your stomach. I suggest you listen to me. It is your choice, of course."

Juan remained quiet, studying the old man. Joseph pointed to the other Indians. "To my people, murder is a form of warfare. There is no distinguishing between the two. You have an objective and you do it. Long ago it was our custom that when an Indian killed another Indian from a different village, to prevent a war the family of the killer went to the victim's chief and offered goods as payment—beads, rope, deer hides, baskets, etc. If it was not enough, relatives and friends would join together and help pay the debt. This would happen even if the death was accidental."

"My great-grandmother is buried near this very spot, as are some of our other family members from ancient years, here and there," Benjamin pointed in different directions.

The Mexicans looked uneasy, although Juan remained completely calm.

Snowflakes were intermittent and the air was cold. The falling snow left a trace on the ground, and it would have been a beautiful night under other circumstances.

Joseph continued, "We have always thought the tahng-wahts were too obsessive with their earthly possessions. We believe everything belongs to the earth, not to man. Nothing belongs to man individually. Everything belongs to everyone. That is, until we, the Kuzedika, a tribe of the Paiute, have nothing left to enjoy as our fathers once enjoyed. So we have changed, Mr. Dog Spit. Now we hold onto everything with self-ishness in our hearts. If we do not do this, it will all be gone.

"A mountain lion marks its claim up to 150 miles. The cougar is the spirit of the mountains protecting her hunting area for survival." Dondero's voice grew low and scratchy. "Mr. Golden is a stranger here but has lawful claim on part of this land. His wife-to-be will reclaim this land through her sons and daughters. He is one of us now. We will die for him when his life is threatened.

"You," Dondero pointed to Juan, "you are pond scum. You want to suck the life from what is ours, and this cannot be done. Are you justified in coming here to kill our own?" Dondero asked seriously.

"I have my reasons," Juan said, slowly trying to think of a reasonable explanation. He wondered if the old man could read his mind. He glanced at his men. Their looks did not give him satisfying support.

"Your earthly possessions are drugs...women of the night. You are not an honorable representative of the Mexican people who are a good hard-working people and part-brothers of our heritage. You have dishonored the same as a brush tick on a deer. You suck the blood from all society until it falls sick."

Dondero studied Juan for a long moment. His voice softened and was barely audible. "You have asked for a duel mano a mano. It was your proposal, your idea. Because it was your special request, it is granted. If you win, you will have to return to Mexico because there are many witnesses here."

Preparing to fight Juan, Cy was stunned at Joseph's remarkable eloquence. He only knew the old man as a person who sat at the general store rolling smokes. There was something about the man that had initially invited his friendship, though he had no idea what it was he had liked about the man except his calm and friendly smile the first day they had met. He had no idea the man held such importance in the Indian community.

Juan licked his lips, knowing that even though surrounded by a dozen or more Indians and one loco blanco, he still had a way out of this. He would kill Golden and be on his way. "I agree," he said sternly.

"Very well." Dondero glanced around to the other men. "The rest of you," he spoke to Juan's men, "throw your weapons to the ground and step back. It you do not, at this moment you will take your last breath." Without thought, each man dropped his weapon like hot irons and moved away from Juan.

Joseph Dondero stepped over to Sarah. He cut her bound hands and smiled warmly at her. He put his arms affectionately around her shaking shoulders and led her back a safe distance. "Upon your agreement, we let the test begin." Dondero looked at Cy. "You, my friend, come put your arms around your woman and keep her warm."

Openly surprised, Cy had no desire to argue. His first thought was to move Sarah back into a safer area in case things went bad. At this point and time, her safety was his main concern. He walked over to Sarah and slipped his arms around her and turned to Dondero.

"Sarah, I have a great revelation for you, my dear. Benjamin is going to take the place of your loved one here." He pointed to Cy. His voice became very gentle. "Your father has made the bid to battle the scar face."

"What?" Sarah responded in disbelief. She thought she misunderstood Joseph. "Who did you say?"

"Your father, little one. Benjamin has had a heavy burden upon his shoulders for many years. His heart has been heavy with guilt and shame. He was not strong enough to remove the millstone of guilt from his heart. Now, you need to know the truth."

Joseph looked over at Benjamin and went on. "Your father had a terrible car accident when he was in the military. Your mother and two brothers were killed. Benjamin was badly injured; you were only a baby and were not hurt. When he recovered he went to honor his country in the Korean War. During that war you were raised by a Paiute family and then when you were older, your father, Ben, gave permission for you to be cared for by a Mormon family in Utah, who greatly wanted a daughter. He knew the family that raised you would provide you with a good education and high values. Our tribal people promised not to speak the truth until your father's death. His shame was more than he could endure.

"All our people have known that Benjamin was your earth father, but we honor our word and could not reveal your parentage. This night Benjamin has given me permission to tell you of these things, but only if I gave him permission to stand for Cy Golden in this fight with the ugly one." Joseph pointed sternly at Juan.

Sarah looked at Benjamin in disbelief. "You are my father? Then who was my uncle?"

"Benjamin traded places with your uncle when he disappeared many years ago. But so much history is for another time." Joseph looked at Juan. "Your weapons will be your brains and your endurance. The Indian rules are, *there are no rules.* Only one will walk away from this battle. May Mother Earth bless the righteous one to survive." Dondero gave Juan a look of despair. He studied the man and said, "Farewell, scar face."

Juan didn't hesitate diving at Benjamin's feet. He did not expect the injured man to be so agile and thought he would have the Indian on his back. Benjamin sidestepped Juan and slammed his fist into the man's nose, breaking it. Juan rolled to the side and came up swinging, catching Benjamin again and again in the rib cage and sternum.

The blows were powerful swings of destruction. Benjamin coughed and took a deep breath, feeling his insides caving in. After a few moments of battle, he knew it would be difficult to outlast the Mexican in a long battle. He had to be quick in ending this thing if he was to survive.

Juan came in swinging his left and then his right. "I'll tear you apart," Juan said, breathing heavily. Benjamin stepped backward, feinting off the harmless blows. Benjamin caught Juan on the side of the jaw, knocking him down on all fours. He jumped forward and struck Juan in the side with three hard fast blows, knocking the air from his lungs.

Juan rolled over on his back and kicked Benjamin in his wounded leg, knocking him to the ground with a loud crash. Benjamin's rage knew no bounds. "You will not leave this mountain alive," he roared, standing up and spreading his legs.

Juan remained unmoved, glancing at the people standing around him. "You can all go to hell." He swung his big head around to Benjamin, a knife in hand. "I'll gut you here and now."

Roberto spit on the ground, disgusted with Juan. "You kill him, big one, or I will myself."

Juan made two fast jabs with the knife. On the third thrust, Benjamin grabbed the hand with the knife and pulled Juan forward into an armlock. He applied enough pressure that Juan dropped the knife. Facing Juan with the look of a lion, Benjamin pushed Juan backward.

Juan lunged forward and slugged it out toe to toe with the big Indian. The sounds were piercing to the ears. It was frightening to hear the wrenching sounds of bones smashing into the flesh. Juan proved to be a very tough fighter, and Cy didn't believe he could have taken him. Benjamin was giving ground fast, and it appeared he was losing the battle. He knew the Indians would not interfere if Juan won the fight. Benjamin had to win or they would live their lives in fear, knowing that someday Juan would return when they least expected it.

Benjamin was badly hurt. Besides the leg wound, his lower lip was cut to his chin and the blood flowed freely onto his chest. His right eye was swelling shut and soon he would be temporarily blinded. It wasn't good. He did not fear for his life, but he did want Juan's. He came forward with an uppercut that caught Juan squarely on the chin, sending him flying backward.

Juan shook his dizzy head. Cobwebs clogged his vision and everything spun around him. He staggered to his feet and fell to the side. Benjamin came in and landed two left hooks, rocking Juan on his heels until he fell flat on his back.

Benjamin stood his ground, swaying back and forth. There was not one place on his body that did not hurt. He knew he had to end it here. As he stepped closer to the man on the ground, Juan kicked him in the thigh directly over the knife wound. Benjamin was felled like a large tree and lay there without moving. Once he tried to get up but fell back with a dull thud.

Juan slowly got to his knees and crawled to the big Indian. He put his knee in the middle of Benjamin's chest, holding him down while he struck him with two powerful blows. Benjamin blacked out. Somewhere he heard a girl's voice intoning, "Kahdoo'kee nuni muang" (get up, my father).

Like a bee-stung bear Benjamin roared, rolling onto his knees. With a smashing blow he struck Juan in the lower side, cracking his ribs with a loud popping sound. For good measure he used his elbow and swung backward, crushing Juan's diaphragm. Benjamin slid around Juan from behind, pulling his body to a kneeling position. With one powerful move, he grabbed Juan by the top of the head and the lower chin and snapped the man's neck with a loud crack. Juan fell limply to the ground. Benjamin fell on top of him and passed out again.

No one moved for a long moment, looking with disbelief at what they had just witnessed. Finally Roberto approached Joseph Dondero, apologized, and said his people would never return. The three remaining Mexicans left without looking back.

Sarah ran to her father and threw her arms around his bloody frame. She cried as Cy knelt next to her and placed his hands on her shoulders. After a moment Cy looked around and noted with astonishment the Indians had disappeared. They were gone, vanished!

Cy pulled the jackets off the dead men and placed them carefully over Benjamin who was still lying on top of Juan like two dead bears in a heap.

It wasn't long before headlights topped the turn in the road and stopped next to the three people. Jacob and Tony got out of the car and ran to them.

After a quick survey of the area, Tony kneeled next to Cy

and Sarah. "Good Lord, Almighty," Tony exclaimed dumbfounded. "I missed the fight of all fights."

"No," came a gurgled moan from deep in the throat of Benjamin. Both eyes were swollen shut, and blood was streaked all over his face. His torn lip exposed his lower broken teeth. "No, you missed what Cy did to me in Lee Vining."

Sarah hugged her father and then turned to Cy. "It's over, Cy. Now I have you for the rest of my life, and I am never letting you go."

"God bless this mountain," Cy spoke softly. "I didn't cave in. I was afraid my soul was made of glass like this mountain."

He took Sarah in his arms and kissed her softly on the lips. "You are my life, Sarah."

About the Author

Jerry C. Scott is a 29-year-veteran law enforcement officer. After four years in the U. S. Air Force as an air traffic controller during the beginning years of the Viet Nam conflict, stationed in Okinawa, he began his work as a city police officer in the state of Washington, in 1966. He spent a year as a motorcycle cop, walked the beat in the downtown tavern district, worked radar, and performed patrol duties.

After five years he moved to Provo, Utah, in 1971 and took up his profession with the Utah County Sheriff's Department. He moved through the ranks as a patrol deputy, patrol sergeant, lieutenant division commander, and finally operations bureau chief, holding the rank of captain before his retirement in 1995. His many police experiences include being a co-captain and assisting in the organization of the first department SWAT team in 1974. The team members joined the #19th Airborne Special Forces Group with the Utah State National Guard, and they held the distinction of being the only jump-qualified SWAT team in the United States. Jerry's assignment was sniper and bomb technician. He was a graduate of the Redstone Bomb School in Alabama, and was a member of the International Association of Bomb Technicians and Investigations (IABTI). He was also an explosive instructor for a number of years at the Utah State Police Academy and Weber State College. As a jail commander during the 80's, he rewrote the Utah State Jail Standards and served on the Utah State Jail Inspection team.

During all the years of his law enforcement career, nothing was more rewarding and enjoyable than his patrol duty assignments. The excitement of conducting arrests of drug suspects and burglars, and the assistance to the public in general, are experiences he holds sacred.